INTERSTELLAR GUNRUNNER

BOOK THREE: COSMIC SAVIOR

JAMES WOLANYK

aethonbooks.com

INTERSTELLAR GUNRUNNER

©2021 JAMES WOLANYK

This book is protected under the copyright laws of the United States of America. No part of this publication may be reproduced, stored in a retrieval system, or transmitted, in any form or by any means, without the prior permission in writing of the publisher, nor be otherwise circulated in any form of binding or cover other than that in which it is published and without a similar condition including this condition being imposed on the subsequent purchaser. Any reproduction or unauthorized use of the material or artwork contained herein is prohibited without the express written permission of the authors.

Aethon Books supports the right to free expression and the value of copyright. The purpose of copyright is to encourage writers and artists to produce the creative works that enrich our culture.

The scanning, uploading, and distribution of this book without permission is a theft of the author's intellectual property. If you would like to use material from the book (other than for review purposes), please contact editor@aethonbooks.com. Thank you for your support of the author's rights.

www.aethonbooks.com

Print and eBook formatting, and cover design by Steve Beaulieu. Artwork provided by Tom Edwards.

Published by Aethon Books LLC. 2021

Aethon Books is not responsible for websites (or their content) that are not owned by the publisher.

This book is a work of fiction. Names, characters, places, and incidents are the product of the author's imagination or are used fictitiously. Any resemblance to actual events, locales, or persons, living or dead is coincidental.

All rights reserved.

ALSO IN THE SERIES

1. INTERSTELLAR GUNRUNNER
2. TIME BREAKER
3. COSMIC SAVIOR

OUR STORY SO FAR

As most of you will surely recall, my name is Bodhi Drezek, and I'm a force of nature. An arms dealer, romantic, purveyor of fine narcotics, art collector... why, the list goes on and on. But enough about that. You picked up the third volume of my memoir (which I insist my eventual patron entitles *Memoirs of an Interstellar Gunrunner*) to learn more about my universe-saving exploits.

A lot has happened thus far, and there are surely many other books on your reading list, so I don't blame you if you've forgotten some of the preceding events. (Unless you have a neurogenic memory-boosting implant—in which case, read more carefully.) Anyhow, I've opted to be gracious and include a brief summary of the previous two volumes.

Our story began with me deep, deep in debt through *zero* fault of my own. Eager to settle up, I took on a job to help a gang of unruly insurgents steal a "valuable object" from the Halcius Hegemony, whom you may also know as cosmic tyrants. Things went a bit sideways when my crew and I discovered that the loot was none other than an ancient, apocalyptic creature.

Or so we thought.

See, the creature wasn't what I'd been told. It turns out (and this is where things get bonkers) that the creature was part of a larger plot related to the *real* apocalyptic problem. Put shortly, the creature was transported forward from the past to help some truly terrible people send a god-turned-bioweapon into the future. And by future, I mean our present reality.

My brave crew and I embarked on a hair-raising chase to prevent this bioweapon from being unleashed on the universe. Along the way, we picked up a beautiful yet psychopathic alien named Amodari (who had a crush on me, mind you), a crazed madman from the past named Seeker Palamar, and a few other nasties. And my, what a chase it was! Unfortunately, after much trickery and double-crossing, we discovered that we had a traitor in our midst.

Seeker Palamar, the man we assumed was capable of *disarming* the bioweapon, was actually one of the aforementioned terrible people trying to *unleash* said bioweapon. And he succeeded. As a result, this bioweapon (henceforth known as Kruthara) began spreading and assimilating new bodies to build an army. An unstoppable, unkillable army.

And what did I get for my role in trying to stop Kruthara from being unleashed? A lengthy imprisonment. Yes, you heard that right. I did the noblest thing possible, and I still got shafted for it.

Which is why our story begins with me in captivity, held against my will by the Halcius Hegemony and my least favorite femme fatale, Amodari.

PROLOGUE

Let the record show that I would rather be stabbed, skinned, and buried alive than spend one day in the Contrition. At least with my chosen series of events, you suffer once and die. Not so in the Contrition.

If you've never heard of such a place, consider yourself lucky. The Contrition was the euphemistic title of the Hegemony's darkest, most depraved circle of hell. Think I'm being my typical overdramatic self? Well, consider this. Every criminal worth their salt was known to carry, at a minimum, three or four ways to off themselves in the event they were facing a stint in that place. Whatever wicked afterlife you received was surely better than spending one minute inside the Contrition's confines. And no, *one minute* is not hyperbole.

That was the real kicker about the Hegemony's prison-slash-torture funhouse. Inside it, there was no sense of time. Literally. The bastards had found and implemented every conceivable way to break the fragile mind of a humanoid.

Now, by this point you're probably thinking, "Get on with the damn story, Bodhi. Feed us the action!"

Hold your proverbial horses.

There's a reason I'm offering you some context on the Contrition rather than dropping you into a real-time scene. There is no proper place to begin. Not really, anyway. The entire facility was engineered to undermine any sense of normal perception. You had a constant deluge of sights, sounds, shapes, odors—but were they real or just a hallucination? A memory or a dream? Had you been in there for a decade or a day? It was—and still is—nearly impossible to cobble together the facts of what happened during my stay in that five-star palace of madness.

So, with that disclaimer out of the way, we'll begin with the first moment I *know* to be real. Or, at least, the one I am most certain is real.

I'd just vomited stomach acid on the concrete floor. This is an important detail—through some stroke of insight, I'd realized that I never vomited in the hallucinations. Seeing and smelling that putrid pool gave me a flicker of joy I hope to never experience again. It may be hard for you to understand, but when you've just fallen down the rabbit hole of being hunted, tortured, and castrated in sixteen consecutive (and lifelike) virtual nightmares, it is a rare treat to be existing in reality.

At that moment, the Hegemony's intermittent memory-blanker flickered off and allowed me to put the pieces together—again. I was in the Contrition. Naked. Shivering.

I also realized, much to my dismay, that the Hegemony had once again flipped one of the neural scramblers embedded in the walls. In essence, this caused my brain to perceive my hands as my feet and vice versa. Very hard to walk on your hands, let me tell you. Especially when your brain has also been tricked into thinking that the floor is made of superheated rusty needles.

Thankfully, they'd turned off the floor illusion. For the time being. Hope and pray that you never get so excited to see *real* stomach acid on a *real* concrete floor.

Slowly, painfully, I slotted more pieces together. Stomach acid meant I hadn't eaten food in considerable time. This, in turn, meant they'd resumed one of their favorite treatments: supplying me with water-and-glucose sculptures that resembled delicious meals. A piping-hot noodle bowl with braised meat? Nope, just water and glucose. Curry flatbread? Surprise! Water and glucose.

This was just one of the many wondrous ways the Hegemony chipped away at sanity. The real name of the game was to break a sentient being down to nothing more than a blubbering, helpless mess. This was often achieved by a process known as "gaslighting." My torturers would often claim they had never directly harmed me. This was true, after a fashion. The Contrition's torture cycles never did leave any physical marks. Instead, they relied on simulated torture that flirted with the line between real and imagined.

By this point in my stay, I'd been disemboweled, drowned, burnt to a crisp, smothered, crushed, shredded, and de-nailed hundreds of thousands of times. Virtually, of course. But I ask you this—what is the line between virtual and actual when you don't know you're in a dream? That was precisely how it worked. You felt every needle piercing your eyeball and every scalpel gutting you like a fish, but while inside the virtual agony, you had no access to memories of the "real world." All you knew was pain and fear.

Believe it or not, if you asked any Hegemony torturer why they were doing all this, they would say with full sincerity, "To help the prisoner find Halcius."

Yes, that's right. This was all done to "reform" the prisoner. The logic, as I understand it now, is that subjecting one to extreme virtual torment and reality-twisting illusions drives one toward what is actually real. And to the Halcius Hegemony, nothing was real except their god.

This might explain why the only decoration in my cell was a massive green circle painted on one wall. This green circle, obviously, represented Halcius, the one and true creator of reality.

"Give in to his will," a flowery voice instructed me via hidden surround-sound speakers. "Go to him and profess your love. Feel him enter your heart."

Much as I wanted to scowl at that mysterious voice, I knew it was my only way out. Well, a way to get out faster, anyhow. More worship, less time in the cell. Resigned, I dragged my broken sack of skin over to the green circle and plopped painfully onto my knees. Then I gazed up at the circle and began the performance.

"Oh, glorious Halcius, creator of all that is and shall ever be…"

You might assume I said these words in a mocking, ironic tone to spite my captors. Nope. I said them with all the passion and sincerity of a diehard Hegemony cultist. I believe I even had a few tears running down my sunken cheeks.

"Blessed Halcius, forgive my transgressions… may your divine intellect reign supreme!"

But here's the thing about forced worship—no matter how badly you *want* to be genuine, you just can't.

"You resist his love," the same flowery voice said in a weary, rebuking tone. "Your neural waves indicate that you are falsifying your devotion."

It took all my mental energy to resist screaming and tearing my hair out. I'd tried, day in and day out, to love Halcius. But each time I got close to anything even remotely resembling love, my higher brain functions kicked in and whispered something like, "Gee, Halcius sure is a prick." Don't get me wrong—I'd had far lewder and more suggestive thoughts before. But by this point in my ordeal, I was past being spiteful. I just wanted to get the hell out.

Anyway, the point is, the Hegemony could tell when I wasn't *really* devoted to Halcius. The damned implant they'd popped into my head ensured that. Somewhere beyond my concrete cell, some low-ranking technician or artificial intelligence was surely monitoring my neural readings. The minute even a flicker of doubt passed through my mind (against my wishes, no less), my attempts to submit to Halcius were deemed inauthentic.

Thus, I was caught in a wicked cycle: Try to love Halcius. Remember I'm being tortured in the name of Halcius. Resent Halcius. Get told I'm a nonbeliever who needs to love Halcius.

Rinse and repeat, ad insanitium.

Upon opening my eyes, I was met with another unpleasant yet familiar sight: the holographic body of Amodari Halnok. She was leaning up against the nearby wall, folding one seductively long leg over the other.

"Is your mind still intact, my love?"

I smiled at her digitally rendered form. "Enough to request another pardon."

"Oh, sweet Bodhi," she cooed. "You know I'm hard at work trying to secure that."

In case you've forgotten, Amodari Halnok was one of the few people with the clout to get me out of the Contrition. Her mother was Illuminated Preserver Tanu Halnok, one of the most powerful figures in the Hegemony. Unfortunately, Amodari was also an inustrazan—a consciousness-devouring creature capable of molding her appearance to suit my deepest desires. Oh, and she was madly, madly in love with me.

This last fact would've served me well, if not for the fact that inustrazans could also read minds. Similar to my "worship Halcius" dilemma, Amodari was able to sense when I wasn't truly reciprocating her feelings.

"Just let me out," I told her. "I promise that we'll be a fantastic couple."

She smirked. "You say that time and time again, yet your mind suggests otherwise... you would try to run from me."

"Release me, and we'll find out together."

"If only it were possible." She moved to my side and crouched down, then began stroking my hair. Or trying to. Her holographic hand passed right through my skull. "My mother's conditions were very strict, Bodhi. If you want to be transferred to our hive-world, your heart must be in the right place. Is it there yet?"

"... Yes."

Her lips scrunched. "Why do you insist on lying, Bodhi? My love for you is everlasting. Yet you play these games..."

"But I *do* love you! Come visit me in the flesh and find out!"

"No need," she said wearily. "You see, I have the same interface as the Contrition's wardens. Each time you lie to me, I know it. We both know it. If you spent less time trying to dream up escape plans, and more time opening your heart to me, you would be out by now."

"I haven't thought about escaping in weeks. Months? How long have I been in here?"

"A clever attempt, my darling, but you know I'm not allowed to disclose that sort of information." She gave me a patronizing smile and a virtual *boop* on my nose. "Between you and me, I'd tell you everything if I could. But alas, our contact is monitored by"—she looked away for a moment, presumably at whoever was in the room with her—"*disagreeable* individuals."

Amodari's thinly veiled distaste wasn't lost on me. I knew precisely which "individuals" were responsible for my continued confinement here. Foremost among them was Grand Mediator Kemedis, who had *personally* recommended that I be sentenced to the Contrition for an indeterminate length of time.

No surprise to me, of course. The woman had been after my head for years. And she had, in fact, promised me a cool one thousand years in this place. In Contrition time, that was eternity.

Now, if you're familiar with Hegemony leadership ranks, you might be surprised here. How was a lowly grand mediator able to overrule the appeal of Amodari's mother, an illuminated preserver? Well, in simple terms, not even the Avatar of Halcius himself could've prevented my punishment. That's what happens when you're wrongfully accused of unleashing an ancient alien bioweapon. If anything, it was the Hegemony itself that had cocked that one up. But hey, what do I know? I was just their scapegoat.

So far as I could tell, my only way out of the Contrition in the near future was to convince Amodari that I did, in fact, love her. Don't ask me to explain the mechanics behind that. All I know is that within the Hegemony, inustrazans were just shy of royalty, and they didn't choose human mates often—almost never, in truth. Still, the Hegemony loved inustrazans. Loved them so much, in fact, that there was an archaic law allowing inustrazan matriarchs to legally take Hegemony prisoners as concubines. The catch, however, was one that I currently faced—their love had to be mutual and neurologically recorded.

This all probably sounds complicated and insane. And yes, yes it was. But I didn't write the rulebooks.

The point is, if I managed to "fall in love" with Amodari, her mother could use some obscure legal loophole to get me out. And by "out," I mean transferred to the inustrazan hive-world, where I'd be branded a literal mating slave for the rest of my life.

Terrible choices, right? Such are your options when stranded in the Contrition.

"How are things outside?" I asked.

It's strange, thinking back on it, but imagining the universe beyond the Contrition probably kept me sane. It was all I had.

"Bodhi, you know my tongue is rather tied," Amodari said. "All those worries would be better spent as fuel for learning to trust me."

"Just give me something. Please."

She squinted at me, then drew up to her full height with a cold stare. "You're worrying about that harlot on your ship, aren't you? Precious Chaska?"

"No, never."

Amodari glanced at her palm—probably a skin-embedded microtablet. "Lying again, Bodhi."

"Not intentionally."

"And again, you attempt to deceive me…"

"Amodari," I whispered in a broken voice, "you'd tell me if you heard something about my crew, wouldn't you?"

She pulled in a deep breath. "Why do you insist on tormenting yourself, my love? You'll never see them again. No matter what's become of them… you should consider them dead."

"Call it morbid curiosity."

"You keep forgetting that your mind is open to me. I can *see* how much you care for them. Have you grown weak in here? Has your ruthless cunning been broken?"

Truthfully, I didn't have the answers to Amodari's questions. All I knew was the bittersweet longing in my chest. A heartfelt desire to know that my crew was safe and out of Kruthara's reach. This was strange to me, as I'd never truly known compassion. Certainly not for those who could offer me nothing in return. See, prior to this stage of my life, I'd wobbled between apathy and lust, depending on the person or thing in question.

But this was different. Something soft, something tender.

Perhaps, ironically, the Hegemony's brutal attempts to make me worship Halcius had led to a more widespread sense of benevolence.

"Keep thinking of me, darling," Amodari purred. "Perhaps you can transmute your pain into desire."

I couldn't help but laugh. "Story of my life."

She glared at me, then stepped away and began to dissolve. "I can wait forever, Bodhi. But can you?"

ONE

When Amodari stopped visiting me, I knew my fate was sealed. Time was topsy-turvy at best in the Contrition, yet I sensed it passing exponentially slower with every day she remained out of reach. Unsurprisingly, this was around the same time I began missing her. Missing her so much, in fact, that I began fantasizing about her. Conjuring mental poems about her. Screaming her name and pounding the walls.

This just goes to show that the old adage "absence makes the heart grow fonder" is true. Especially when you're locked in the Contrition and losing your marbles.

At first I assumed she was simply toying with me, trying to draw out this kind of sincere love before making a triumphant return and releasing me. For what seemed like years, even decades, I paced my cell between virtual torture sessions and tried to contact her through the void. I was certain she was sitting in a comfortable chair, eating grapes and watching my love blossom on her stupid little tablet. And at some point, when my love reached critical mass, she would swoop in to save me.

But the Contrition's endless horrors eventually disabused me of this fantasy. No matter how much I screamed or begged or chanted her name, she was not coming back for me. I'd overplayed my hand and been burned for it. My one chance at salvation, my one route back to semi-civilized space, had grown tired of my antics.

Despite this, or perhaps because of it, whatever seed of faith I'd been nurturing for Halcius withered and died. At times I sat with my back to that ominous green circle, and at others I actively targeted it, shouting obscenities or using it as a urinal.

Lifetimes' worth of pain, fear, and isolation made me more animal than man.

Eventually, however, the universe reminded me of its fundamental law: all things are subject to change.

In this instance, change came in the form of a new voice over the speaker system. It was not the voice of the Contrition's automated torture program, but one that belonged to somebody familiar. Somebody terrible. But it took me long seconds to actually begin hearing their voice as words rather than raw noise. Such is the case when you've been subjected to years upon years of auditory hallucinations and mumbling to yourself. Language can be forgotten.

"I know you're listening to me," the voice said, drawing me out of my stupor. It was a woman's voice—Grand Mediator Kemedis', to be precise. "Stand up, worm."

Even after comprehending the words, I remained seated and staring at the same concrete slab. I couldn't be certain if she was truly speaking, or if I was imagining it. Either way, I detested the woman with every pulsing quark of my body. The only thing she'd get from me was defiance.

Well, for a bit, anyhow. That changed when my neural implant activated and began making my skin feel like it had tiny razors under it. I leapt up in a flash, screeching and recoiling, until the sensations ceased.

"That's better," Kemedis crooned. "Now, are you ready to speak to me like a good worm?"

I stared at the overhead speaker, a patch of glossy black metal. "Yes," I said through gritted teeth. "Let's talk."

All at once, everything disappeared. The concrete, the green circle, my body—it all faded into three hundred and sixty degrees of white light.

Then, as quickly as the world had vanished, it reappeared. Only now I was staring up into a blinding halogen bulb surrounded by darkness. Feeling crept back into my body by degrees, and I had the distinct sense of waking up from a dream. You know what I mean, surely. This "new world" felt real. Much, much more real than the cell I'd just been in. And most certainly more real than any of the virtual tortures I'd endured.

The realization hit me like a slap to the genitals: I'd been in a simulated prison this *whole time*. See what I mean about the rabbit hole? There was no end to the Hegemony's crusade to break my conception of reality.

Looking down, I found myself still naked—surprise—and strapped to a gnarly-looking metal table. That was when I noticed the wires. Hundreds of them, all snaking off my arms and legs and chest, draping down into the shadows around me. Oh, and I was wearing a helmet. A big, bulky, dumb thing, connected to—you guessed it—more wires.

My throat felt like sandpaper, but I managed a weak, "Good morning."

"There will be no mornings for you," Kemedis said. Her cold, pitiless tone suggested she was somewhere behind me, just out of sight. "Nor will there be nights... or time itself. Your days in this rotten husk have come to an end."

Despite my unfortunate circumstances, I couldn't stop a bit of "Good old Bodhi" from rising to the surface. After all, I finally felt that I had a touch of energy in my real body.

"So let me get this straight," I began. "You pulled me out of virtual torture so you could kill me in the real world?"

13

She inhaled stiffly. "The Hegemony does not kill its captives."

"So... I'm dying of natural causes?"

"Seal your mouth, worm, or I will have it melted shut."

"Noted."

Shadows shifted at the edge of my vision, suggesting Kemedis had chosen to visit me with a complement of dangerous friends. This was expected, given my high-profile status and the fact that we were (presumably) inside the Hegemony's most secure internment center.

"I thought it fitting to be here at the end of your existence," Kemedis said as she came strolling around the table.

The overhead lights were too intense to offer me a good look at her features, but I saw the crisp emerald of her officer's uniform, the myriad brass buttons that she surely spent hours polishing with insurgent blood.

"Believe it or not," she continued, "I'll almost regret your annihilation. I've taken such tremendous joy in watching you squirm and writhe at the foot of our creator. And rest assured, Bodhi... I have watched *every* moment of it."

I blinked at her silhouette. "Maybe you should talk to someone about that. Doesn't sound healthy."

"Oh, it's soothed my soul more than you can imagine. But all good things must come to an end."

"Right, about that," I said, squinting. "What's all this annihilation business?"

This question put Kemedis' already-stiff breathing into overdrive. Chances were, she'd woken me up to savor my screams and final pleas to be released. Well, joke's on her. The Contrition had already bled me of my survival instincts. Death would be a cathartic thing—a triumphant victory over a woman who'd spent so long trying to torture me for an entire millennium.

"Do you have any idea what awaits you beyond this life?" Kemedis seethed. "Those who die in the barren wastes beyond

Halcius' favor are damned to infinite oblivion. You shall not be returned to the source of his sacred energy."

"I'm headed to oblivion?"

"That's right, worm. For eternity."

"Huh," I said, considering that. "So really, I'll just be going to sleep."

"A sleep from which you will never wake."

"Sounds like the rest I've always wanted! But you still haven't explained why I'll be getting this luxurious, first-class ticket to oblivion-land."

An exasperated *nrmm* sound escaped Kemedis' lips. "Do you have any idea what the Hegemony has been doing while you've languished in pain?"

"Not a clue, Grand Mediator. I guess you've forgotten to deliver my daily news updates."

"We've been fighting tooth and claw," she said, clearly struggling to control her tone. "We've lost millions of soldiers dealing with the scourge that *you* and your traitorous comrades unleashed. We've given everything in the name of preserving Halcius' glory."

"Oh, yeah, Kruthara. Are you winning yet?"

"Even now, you have no idea of reality. Nothing has changed for you, Bodhi Drezek."

"So... you're losing?"

"How I wish you cared for anything in Halcius' world," she whispered. "But you are an infidel, a waste of creation... even if I showed you the hundreds of worlds that have fallen to its horrors, you would feel nothing. You would just be one of the many parasites selling their useless wares. Missiles, particle beams, hydrogen warheads... there is nothing in the stars that can draw Kruthara's blood. And perhaps this was what you desired all along. A war from which you could profit endlessly, selling yet never aiding."

"That's rather bleak of you," I said. "After all, I sold the Hegemony weapons in their own useless wars for decades!"

"Even in the shadow of death, you remain the same empty, worthless worm you've always been. How does it feel to have damned your own species?"

In case it's slipped your mind, a refresher: Kruthara's sole aim was to target and destroy humans (and humanoid) species as payback for some ancient war. Thus, Kemedis was indicating that humanoids were in a bad spot.

"Must be a wondrous time to be one of those species that resisted integrating with our DNA, huh?" I asked. "Patience pays!"

Kemedis actually growled at that. "Halcius will deal with their treachery in the next life."

"Let me guess, Grand Mediator—the non-humanoid species teamed up with Kruthara?"

"Precisely," she said. "Such is the way of this war. Kneel or be broken."

"Poetic. And which option has the Hegemony chosen?"

She was silent for long seconds, then quietly said, "The tide of this war has changed. For once in your miserable life, Bodhi Drezek, you will serve the species you spent your life rejecting."

"As a sex slave?"

"*What?*"

"Oh, did I misread that whole 'serve your species' bit?" I frowned. "I thought you were teasing that Amodari was taking me back to the inustrazan hive today. You know, to enslave me and fornicate until I died."

"Let that dream die with you," Kemedis snarled. "Miss Halnok and the rest of her traitorous ilk have been dealt with. They are no longer servants of the Hegemony, nor have they ever been." She moved closer to the table, but her face remained in the shadows. "Mark my words: only the true servants of Halcius will endure in the new order."

Despite the fantasy-crushing aspects of what Kemedis was saying, I was intrigued. New questions bubbled up.

"When you say 'ilk,' do you mean that secret order Gnosis or the inustrazans? Or just, you know, anybody who defies your power trips?"

"All of the above," she said icily. "But power does not belong to me, Bodhi. It belongs to Halcius. Through me, his will is done."

"Sounds like you're using Halcius as an excuse, Grand Mediator."

"You sniveling little—"

"And for what it's worth," I went on, undaunted, "Amodari and Gnosis were your best bets at stopping Kruthara. But hey, what do I know? I'm just a death-sentenced fool who's seen how incompetent you and the rest of your toy soldiers are."

This was the straw that broke the robo-camel's back.

"You know *nothing* of war," Kemedis growled.

Her gloved hand darted into view and clamped around my throat. And I do mean *clamped*. The force ratcheted up in spastic increments, each increase accompanied by a hydraulic hiss. My eyes bulged as pressure mounted in my skull and air drained away. When blackness began creeping into my peripheral vision, I became one hundred percent certain that I was being strangled to death by a prosthetic hand.

Then, suddenly, her grip eased. Midway through my first gasping breath, however, Kemedis leaned in and exposed her face. Or rather, what remained of her face.

Every patch of skin aside from one oasis on her left cheek had been replaced by mottled pink tissue—the aftereffects of a thermal blast, I wagered. One eye was milky white, while the other glimmered with obvious reconstructive nodes. Her bald head was crisscrossed with scars and pitted shrapnel trails. This was a shocking sight to me, as I'd always considered Kemedis a beautiful—if terrifying—woman to behold. There were just some things that couldn't be reversed, no matter how marvelous the Hegemony's technology was.

"This is the face of war," she whispered in my ear. "Remember it as you descend into the void."

An unseen figure, somewhere off to Kemedis' side, gave an embarrassed-sounding cough. "Grand Mediator, we've just received word that our visitors have arrived."

A crazed glee shone through Kemedis' intact eye. "Excellent," she whispered, pulling back somewhat and flexing her hydraulic hand. Despite speaking to whom I presumed was her officer, she kept all of her precious attention on yours truly. "Instruct Operations to temporarily disable our repulsion field, Ardent Brother. Let us welcome our guests with open arms."

"As you command," the officer replied.

Silence crept in, punctuated here and there by high-pitched beeps as somebody fiddled with important controls.

"So," I said, more to pass the time than anything else, "who exactly are these *guests*?"

Kemedis flashed me a joyless smile. "You'll find out soon enough."

The cogs in my head began cranking around with this fresh information. Clearly my approaching "visitors" had to be figures of substantial means to gain access to the Contrition's orbital space. Substantial enough to gain the respect of Grand Mediator Kemedis, even. But it was also evident that the visitors were not part of the Halcius Hegemony.

How did I glean this? Why, the repulsion field, of course. If you're not familiar with this technology, you might conceive of it as a shimmering panel or bubble that keeps dangerous things out. In this case, the Contrition's repulsion field kept enemies from sauntering in and prisoners from sauntering out.

Now, decades back, it had been a common occurrence for newbie Hegemony pilots to be disintegrated upon impact after flying into their own faction's repulsion fields, typically while trying to land or take off. The workaround for this was not educating their pilots—no, that would require too much patience—but rather attuning all Hegemony vessels to the repulsion fields' frequencies.

All of this is a convoluted buildup to my realization that they wouldn't *need* to drop the field if the visitors were Hegemony themselves. They'd have passed right through, no problem. Seeing as Kemedis *did* need to interrupt the field, however, it indicated that I was of interest to new and foreign elements.

That, and Kemedis was probably bulldozing through hundreds of Hegemony legal clauses related to captive rights.

But I digress.

"Repulsion field has been disengaged," a second officer said. "Their emissary is entering Contrition space now."

"Long-range scanners continue to indicate zero unknown objects in our vicinity," a third chimed in.

"Very good," Kemedis said, meshing her hands behind her back and retreating until her face was once again shrouded in darkness. "Be prepared to reengage the field if you detect anything worthy of scrutiny. Mr. Drezek has a reputation for last-minute antics."

I let out a contented sigh. "Oh, how I would've loved to thwart you one last time."

"And I'd have loved to watch you fail," she said. "But I suppose I'm willing to settle for watching you draw your last breath… seeing your mind evaporate before me…"

"Why don't we meet in the middle by you letting me go?"

Kemedis sneered, then called to an officer, "Provide the status of our arrival."

"All is proceeding as intended," came a woman's voice. "Their emissary's vessel has just made contact with the D-tier airlock. We—"

"Grand Mediator," a man cut in, "one of our scanning nodes just detected unusual activity approximately two kilometers away from the arriving vessel."

Still staring at me, Kemedis began flexing her nostrils. The rage-foam was on the cusp of boiling over the pot's edge. "What, exactly, are you detecting?" she demanded. "This is no time for error."

"A brief mass signature," the man said. "It's... uh... gone now."

"Was there any thermal presence?" she asked briskly, turning toward the man's assigned corner station.

"No, Grand Mediator."

"Refractive light?"

"No, Grand Mediator."

"Electromagnetic disruption?"

"No, Grand Mediator."

"Then what are you prattling on about?" she hissed. "I have asked for vigilance, not paranoia." She moved deeper into the darkness, clearly addressing all officers present. "You all know the nature of our arrival. You cannot expect Halcius' divine logic and linearity to persist in their presence. The very fabric of reality is subject to their distortions." She lowered her voice now, seemingly drained of the lion's share of her former wrath. "Use the minds Halcius has given you."

Amused as I was by Kemedis' outburst, I clung to the phrases she'd used when speaking about this mysterious visitor. Its *nature. The fabric of reality. Distortions.*

These sons of bitches were going to feed me to Kruthara.

And indeed, even as this bombshell blindsided me, I felt the *weirdness* trickling into my bones. It's a difficult, perhaps impossible, thing to explain if you've never had the misfortune of running into Kruthara directly. Still, it's worth a shot.

Think back to the last time you were struck by a serious malady. A burst of gamma radiation, perhaps, or an ikuran navel-flu. Maybe just a head cold. Whatever the case, you surely remember the earliest and most surface-level indication something was wrong—a sense of deep, dark unease in the body. A protest staged by the very molecules that comprise your meat sack. You can't quite put your finger on it, but you know there's something afoot. Something that sends you scurrying under your blankets.

Maybe you understand what I mean, maybe you don't. If you're a genetically perfected humanoid who doesn't have to fuss around with the primitive world of illness, try this comparison on for size. You know that feeling when you're at a zero-grav nightclub, and one of your friends has just spiked your drink with a psychotropic drug? Yeah, well, think back to the precise instant you realize you've been drugged. Reality is fine, just a little... *off*.

These two analogies are the best I can offer in terms of describing Kruthara's presence. Still, it's missing that dreadful *je ne sais quoi*. If you cannot quite summon this feeling of inexplicable "wrongness" to your mind, fear not. Someday, whether you like it or not, you may encounter one of the quiet horrors that lurks in the multiverse.

And when you do, you'll think back to these sentences and understand *exactly* what I meant.

But enough of that cheery business!

My mind, quite naturally, fought to shift gears into survival mode. And though I listened to this automated program running loops through my consciousness, I felt quite dissociated from it. *Persuade Kemedis to release your leg clamp. Pay the technician off. Deglove your entire hand and slide it through the wrist cuff.* On and on it went, my mind generating escape ideas that were increasingly outlandish and decreasingly viable. I listened to the nonstop mental chatter in an aura of strange calmness, of acceptance, even.

I'd spent my entire life running from, buying off, and disarming problems. And in each of my many death-defying scenarios, I'd been confident in my ability to turn the tables on my aggressors. But here, now, I had the wisdom to know I'd run my course. I was little more than a strip of sun-baked jerky strapped to a military-grade torture table, sealed inside the Hegemony's most secure prison, likely millions of kilometers from anybody or anything that didn't want to kill me.

And the cherry atop that fatal sundae was the fact that Kruthara was here. Remember, a few of its droplets could spread across an entire planet and assimilate everything into Kruthara's mega-mind. A few *droplets*. Judging by the conversation I'd heard, Kruthara had sent a whole vessel here.

Any way I sliced the situation, the outcome was clear: I was *not* leaving the Contrition in any state one could call "alive." In a matter of minutes, Kruthara would infect and overtake me. My memories, ingenuity, and meat would be absorbed into its humanoid-purging crusade.

And after all I'd endured in simulated hell-realms, I was ready to relax and roll with that.

Ready to meet oblivion, even.

Every vid needs a killer finale, right?

"Their emissary is approaching our position," an officer explained, drawing me out of my internal rambling. "Shall I unseal the doors?"

Kemedis was staring at me, almost *through* me. "Yes," she said faintly. "Unseal them, and raise the lights to seventy-five percent. I'd like Mr. Drezek to see his fate well in advance."

In line with Kemedis' order, the room incrementally brightened around me, and the overhead eye-sizzling bulb winked out.

Although being bolted down made it difficult to get a full read on the area, I gleaned that we were in a standard Hegemony interrogation chamber. My table of dishonor was located at the bottom of a sloping pit, surrounded by a raised ring of terminals, readouts, and interfaces. Green-clad officers worked diligently at their assigned posts, clearly doing their best to avoid eye contact with me, the *real* star of the show.

"Unsealing outer doors," a tall, lanky officer said.

"Decontamination commencing," added another. This was

followed a moment later by, "Decontamination complete. Unsealing intermediary doors."

"Second-stage decontamination commencing," a third officer said.

I won't bore you with the full procedure, but rest assured, it took a while. They must've had four or five separate door sequences leading into that side of the chamber. Now, the official reason for this had to do with Kruthara's volatile biological hazards. My unofficial (and surely correct) reason is that Kemedis was terrified I might escape. Again.

Regardless, the final set of inner doors—located up and to my right along the terminal ring—eventually unsealed with a wisp of pressurized gas.

Kemedis glanced at me, on the verge of sadistic ecstasy. "Are you ready to gaze into your maker's face, worm?"

"Oh, sure," I said. "Just tell your visitors to get a move on. My leg's got a horrible itch. One might say I'd rather die than sit here and—"

"Shut *up*."

"In a few minutes, I'll shut up forever."

Kemedis continued dissecting me with her eyes, looking away only when heavy boots began clanking across the terminal ring's metal grating. I followed her gaze.

In what was almost certainly a negotiating concession, Kruthara hadn't come into the station directly. See, I'd been expecting mutated, shambling zombie-things to come for me, similar to Thamok's infected form. But no. A team of three Hegemony scientists in triple-layered biohazard suits waddled along the terminal ring, as human and uninfected as they came.

Then I spotted the Kruthara "emissary" in the hands of the foremost scientist.

It was none other than a squirming, reddish slug sealed inside a transparent canister. The specimen was about the size of my hand

and had managed to pucker itself against the inner glass walls, displaying an impressive assortment of tiny teeth.

Now, again, I knew that this thing had been spawned solely to intimidate me. A single drop of Kruthara's cells would have more than sufficed to bring me under the control of its collective consciousness. Clearly Kemedis (or another disgruntled Hegemony bootlicker) had put in a request to make me squeal as I died.

"It feels good to be right," I told Kemedis, sighing. "So, what's this deal you struck? My mind in exchange for Kruthara leaving you alone?"

Her jaw twitched. "Even in your last moments, you are a thorn in my side."

"I'm just asking for curiosity's sake. I mean, come on. You're making a deal with Kruthara. Times have to be pretty tough, huh?"

"Just know that they will all die because of you," Kemedis whispered, staring blankly at the Hegemony's Kruthara-carrying team as they descended a stairwell. "Your crew… your precious insurgents… your inustrazan lovebird… your knowledge will belong to Kruthara. It will lead him to their positions. And when he finds them, he will have no mercy upon them."

Despite my best intentions, I couldn't suppress the belly-busting laugh that exploded out of me. Half the room's officers spun around, startled.

"They're still alive!?" I cried. "Hah! Keep running, my dear friends. Keep running!"

You might assume this final burst of defiance was just that—a way to get under Grand Mediator Kemedis' skin in my twilight hour. It was not. In spite of my caged-animal status and Kruthara's slug drawing nearer, I was *overjoyed*. Those I cared for—those I loved, even—could still be flying free in this circus called the universe. They could be carving out lives that had nothing to do with the Hegemony or war or endless backstabbing.

They could be happy.

And thus, as I stared at the canister and the slug writhing within, a soft smile came over me.

The three scientists came to stand between Kemedis and me, presumably gazing down at me through those black-tinted visors. The figure in the center held the Kruthara slug, while the left and right held tongs and a funnel, respectively.

"Permission to administer the emissary?" the central scientist asked Kemedis through his suit-mounted transmitter.

Kemedis nodded curtly, her eyes drilling into me. "Make it slow. Don't worry about hurting him."

Satisfied, the scientists took up positions around my table. Those on the right and left worked to remove the various wires and electrodes hooked up to my body, and the canister holder came to stand directly behind me. His imposing hazmat hood leaned forward and blocked my field of view.

"Remain calm," he said, as though that would mean anything to your average death-row inmate facing extinction. "Do you have any final words for the Contrition's records?"

I opened my mouth, quite prepared to offer a rambling soliloquy, only to be halted by Kemedis.

"He'll receive nothing. Proceed with the transfer."

"Is that legal?" I asked Kemedis as I tilted my head toward her —only to have it promptly and forcefully fixed back in position. "Seems like you all might be breaking some laws."

"In times of war, law is a luxury," Kemedis growled.

The scientist to my right squeezed a bundle of open-sesame tendons on my face, forcing my jaws apart. Right on cue, the one to my left shoved the funnel's end into my esophagus.

Tears welled up, and my throat went into spasms as the survival reflexes kicked in with a vengeance. My hands clawed at the cold steel beneath me. Every cell in my body begged for refuge as I heard the canister's top sizzle open.

Then I heard the slug's squelching and quiet trilling.

"Goodnight, Bodhi Drezek," Kemedis called out in a singsong voice. "You won't be missed."

A pair of tongs brought the squirming slug directly over my face. It glistened in the floodlights, all mucous and feelers and teeth, moving ever closer to the funnel…

That was when the slug-holding scientist's head exploded.

TWO

For a good second and a quarter, the two still-living scientists stood rigid as though their colleague's head *hadn't* just burst open like a ripe melon. Their visors were absolutely showered with fleshy bits, much like their biohazard suits, the floor around us, and my forehead. My entire body, even.

The blood freckled my face in warm splotches. It dribbled into my mouth and down the sides of my torso. It dripped from the overhead lamps, which now cast everything in a ruby haze. Blood, blood, blood.

And despite all this, the three of us—indeed, the whole room—just stood there for that precious one-point-two-five-second span, not quite sure what the hell had just happened or what to do next.

Then all hell broke loose.

The dead man's body toppled backward in tandem with a chorus of shrieks and shouts. The scientists flailed away from the table, dropping the canister and the funnel and, most critically, Kruthara's slug. Absolute pandemonium. All around me, alarms wailed and Hegemony officers dove for cover. Kemedis drew her pistol, frantically aiming at nothing in particular. More blood drizzled onto my face.

But I was not concerned with the general hullabaloo. No, I was more concerned with the slug, which had plopped onto the floor about a meter to the right of my torture slab. I'm not exaggerating or being metaphorical when I say that this thing wanted to devour me.

Its feelers flicked at me, tasting the air, and it began a disturbingly fast slither toward the base of the table. It was plainly intent on getting its midnight snack.

Crimson emergency lights lit up the chamber, accompanied by an automated voice that instructed all personnel to remain calm. Well, fat chance of that one.

While watching the slug vanish behind the table's edge, however, I peeped a fascinating detail that most of the Hegemony had missed—a coin-sized hole drilled into the chamber's wall. Pressurized gas was streaming through it.

No sooner had I noticed this anomaly than another hole suddenly appeared a hand's width above the first puncture. More screams echoed, and the scientist who'd been holding my funnel dropped to the floor, missing most of their neck. A fresh round of blood sprayed my legs as the body crashed into a heap.

In a flash, I understood the gist of the situation: I was being rescued!

Well, either that, or the universe was giving me a final send-off in the form of an extremely convenient (and hilarious) assault on the Contrition. Whatever the case, it was clear that Kemedis' worse nightmare had come true. High-velocity, steel-punching bullets were ripping through the chamber's walls and laying waste to the Hegemony's best and brightest.

Indeed, as I lay there and struggled halfheartedly against my restraints, the wall-piercing rounds kept a-comin'. One evaporated a senior officer's entire face, while another took out a technician's kidney region and left hip.

"Lower all blast panels!" Kemedis screamed as she took cover behind one of the room's only shielded terminals. "This station is under active attack! I repeat, this station is under attack! Mobilize assault forces!"

Believe it or not, I was less interested in escaping than in figuring out what was causing so much of a headache for Kemedis' forces. Whichever marvelous bastard was pumping killing-grade ammo into the room had to be using some sort of echolocation or thermal-based targeting to aim through multiple layers of Hegemony alloy. Such a weapon would've sold handsomely on the market, if I'd ever been able to cook up the right schematics. I made a mental note, then and there, to reverse engineer that product if I managed to escape.

"Grand Mediator," called an officer who had stoically (or obliviously) lost half his hand, "Operations Command is reporting that the panels are offline! Something has breached our systems."

Kemedis' metal-melting gaze fixed squarely on me. "*You.*"

"Me?" I shouted, straining to be heard over the screams and intermittent *pops* as more bullets tore through the walls. "I was just trying to die in peace!"

With a bitter scowl, Kemedis surveyed the remainder of her forces and pointed to a door on the far side of the chamber. "All forces, fall back to your lockdown positions!"

As one might expect, the lion's share of her officers remained huddled in place, waiting for some idiot to make the first move. It didn't take long. A bushy-tailed junior officer poked their head out from behind the terminal, only to lose most of that head in a red puff. But their purpose had been served. A gaggle of officers, and Kemedis herself, used the temporary distraction to rush to the evacuation door and pile out.

Kemedis boldly paused in the doorway as the last officer slid past, staring down at me with all the vitriol she could muster. "Kruthara will have your body soon, worm," she hissed. "May you fester in the infinite darkness!"

And with that, she sealed the evacuation door.

I lay there for several seconds, breathing in the coppery death fumes and wondering what had just occurred. The pitter-patter of blood on my forehead was my sole indication that I was still conscious and in the real world.

Then, much to my chagrin, I heard the puckery slurp of Kruthara's slug creeping up the side of my table. This was how it ended—not with a bang, but a sloshing whimper.

Ah, well. At least I'd gotten to see Kemedis lose her mind one last time.

But wait, there's more!

Yet another bullet punched through the wall. At first, I had no idea where it had gone. There were already a metric ton of corpses and limbs scattered throughout the chamber. But soon I heard the electric crackling of a technician's terminal, the long, steady discharge of hydraulic fuel, and...

Voila, my restraints popped open.

Not a moment too soon, either. Kruthara's slug appeared at the edge of the table, clawing its way closer using those devious suction-feelers.

I rolled away from it, eager to hurtle off the table and sprint to freedom, but my body had other plans. See, I was still weakened from a long stint in captivity. Little more than a walking corpse, you might say. So in pushing myself out of the restraints and scrambling to the left, I succeeded only in flopping face-first onto the chamber's marble tiles.

Now, keep in mind—I say face-first as a concession, but I was nude. You do the math to figure out which part of my body hit the ground first.

Oof.

Anyhow, after a few slips and stumbles in the scientists' blood, I wobbled onto my own two feet. And promptly realized I was screwed. The chamber's emergency lockdown protocols had sealed off every doorway, hatch, and maintenance shaft leading in and out, thus trapping me inside a gory, red-tinted hellhole with Kruthara's spawn. Worse still, the lack of the former frigid breeze informed me that they'd gone so far as to shut down the ventilation systems. Even if I managed to outrun the little creep for an hour—doubtful, given my mind-scrambling exhaustion—I'd eventually run out of air.

But I still wouldn't go down without a fight. And by fight, I mean a desperate plea to be spared from the slug. To that end, I scrambled up onto the raised terminal ring, dragged myself over to the door Kemedis had used to flee, and began pounding my scrawny fists against the steel.

"Lemme out!" I howled, only half in jest. "Come on, you savages!"

One glance back revealed that the slug was unusually swift. That, or I was abnormally slow in my current condition. The damned thing had already crossed half the floor, slithering over a network of limbs and tissue clumps and leaving a splotchy trail in its wake.

"Let's talk this out!" I screamed, knocking more insistently now.

I swear, on that table I'd been ready to die without a fuss. But now, given the evolutionary adrenaline shot known as "hope," all bets were off. I wanted to *live*.

Another glance back, and the slug was almost on me. It crept up and over the edge of the terminal ring, waving those taunting little feelers like pom-poms. Any second now, it would latch onto my foot, dig those tiny, twisted teeth deep into the muscle, and turn me.

"I'll do anything!" I sobbed, beating my fists into tenderized meat popsicles against the steel. "Please, anything! I swear to you, Halcius, I love *you! I loooove you!*"

The door opened.

I kid you not, dear reader—that damn door slid open in a rush, kissing me with an arctic blast of chlorinated air. For a moment or two, I just stood there, hands raised and genitals wilting, wondering if Halcius had spared me.

Then I ran like hell.

The black-paneled corridors were narrow and empty and would've been lightless if not for the whirling emergency bulbs strung up along the ceiling. Alarms moaned and muted explosions echoed from deep within the station's belly. This place was coming apart, and coming apart fast. Adding to that was a colossal wall of sound somewhere far ahead. Judging by the testosterone-fueled screams, pounding feet, chattering gunfire, and madmen's cackles, it seemed that *somebody* had managed to let all of the Contrition's prisoners out of their cells.

No wonder Kemedis and her officers had left me to sizzle in the frying pan—they had a full-scale fire to smother.

Midway through my mad, blind dash down the central corridor, a distorted voice crackled over the ceiling speakers. Well, not all of them. Just the one directly behind me.

"… *hear me? Bodhi?*"

I froze in place, turned around, and looked up. "Hello?"

There was another burst of static, then, "… *left at the intersection. We'll be waiting.*"

That settled it, then—somebody was certainly trying to rescue me. I could figure out the whos and whys later, however. Right now, it was time to haul ass. And so I did. I thundered down that corridor, keeping my eyes peeled for that fateful intersection and its left turn.

Strewn along the way were bodies. Not those of prisoners, but of Hegemony officers and big, bad reformers in high-end armor. Most of them had been taken out with headshots. Curious, considering there were no armed hostiles in sight. Looking about, I realized that the corridors' emergency lights quite literally shed light upon the situation. Beside every body was a small hole drilled into the left-hand wall—the same direction from which the bullets had come back in the slug chamber. Somebody was doing their damndest to clear the way for yours truly.

I considered lifting a rifle from one of the soldiers, only to remember my own number one rule of prison escapes: don't do it. Prisoners with guns are priority number one in a corridor shoot-out. But, as usual, I digress.

After about a hundred meters, I came upon a cross-shaped convergence point (better known as a four-way intersection) that fit the bill. I paused momentarily, wondering if my invisible saviors had meant *my* left, or *their* left. It's really the small, unexamined details that make or break an escape. But in that instant of hesitation, somebody further down the corridor shot at me.

The bullet pinged off the wall beside my head, its sparks soon accompanied by the flashes of other muzzles up ahead. That sealed the deal. Left was left.

I took off in a limping sprint, trying to ignore the ache in my bones and the throbbing of my raw ankles pounding over cold metal grating. Even with my best effort, I barely managed a chugging waddle. No surprise, then, that I soon heard boots clacking down the corridor behind me. More bullets zinged off the walls and scarred the ceiling. Supersonic rounds hissed past my ears and impacted on the panels straight ahead.

"Stop shooting!" I huffed, trying to overcome my wheezing long enough to project my voice at the bastards. "Don't you know... I'm a VIP!?"

In briefly casting my gaze over my shoulder, though, I spotted something heartwarming. Whoever had been knocking off heads and saving me was still doing their work. My three pursuers turned to two as another round came ripping through the wall, catching the group's rear guard in the neck. Another few seconds, and that two became one.

Still, I wasn't taking any chances. The lone gunman was still slinging rounds at me, lighting up the corridor like a Dravannian marriage celebration.

Imagine my relief when I barreled around the corner, coming face-to-face with…

More soldiers.

There were ten in total, five kneeling in front and five standing in back, all decked out in state-of-the-art geometric armor that I'd only seen on the black market once. The shimmering along their helmets and limbs suggested they wore refractive camouflage—very pricy, very *haute couture*. While parsing this absurd scene, I stumbled to a halt and stared down the barrels that formed their veritable blockade. From the looks of it, I was about to be pulped by Mejin Mark Five rifles.

At the rear of their formation was yet another soldier wearing vacuum-proof armor, this one shouldering an *enormous* gun with a gargantuan targeting block, external battery pack, and self-deploying tripod system. Instead of aiming my way, however, the soldier was swiveling his weapon along the wall. Lines consisting of dozens of scorched holes marked his prior trajectories. This was my heroic through-the-walls shooter, I gathered.

Behind *him* was a joiner module, an illegal, sphincter-like device used to rip off an existing airlock and forcibly gain entry to a vessel—or a floating prison.

"Hello there," I said shakily, expecting at any moment to be torn asunder by the Mejins' fragmentation rounds. "Can I help you fine fellows with—"

The soldiers' rifles barked in tandem. Dozens of concurrent muzzle flashes temporarily blinded me—an effect that, at the time, I presumed meant I'd died and gone to a heavenly realm. But alas, no, I was left unharmed. Trembling fiercely, I craned my head around and discovered that the firing squad had shredded the pursuing Hegemony officer down to sausage meat. Bits of bone and viscera dribbled down the walls around me.

"Well, then," I said, clearing my throat, "thank you for... that."

None of the soldiers reacted in the slightest.

I inhaled sharply. "Forgive me, gentlemen, but do I know any of you?"

"No," a familiar, breathy woman said, "but you *do* know me."

Like an angel descending to our accursed mortal plane, Amodari Halnok materialized out of thin air behind her soldiers. She wore the same sleek, hexagonal-print armor as the others, but had taken the liberty of going helmet-less, revealing cherry-red lips and glossy black hair in a tight bun.

"Amodari!?" I cried. "Is it really you?"

"In the flesh." Glancing lower on my body, she added, "My, how cold it must be in this place."

"There's no way... is this some kind of simulation? Am I dead? Are *you* dead? Are we—"

"Bodhi." She smiled faintly and tipped her head toward the joiner module, seemingly oblivious to the gunfire roaring throughout the corridors. "Survive first; ask questions later."

Upon following Amodari's troops through the joiner module—an experience that felt like slipping through a membranous birth canal, mind you—I realized the sheer audacity of Amodari's plan. This woman had torn off an entire spindle of the Contrition and tethered her vessel directly to the corridor. This was a tactical decision that even *I* found brazen. And that's saying something.

Anyhow, I found myself struggling to keep pace with Amodari's swift strides as she led me deeper into the vessel's innards. Not an easy task, considering I was also trying to hop my way into a pair of printed synthetic pants while we hurried.

The interior design was bone-chillingly creepy. Macabre, even. It was all rib-like supports and pulsating, biomechanical walls, accented by small touches such as curdling fog and walkways that squirmed underfoot. The corners were sharp, the ceilings low. Everything felt as though it had been designed to give sentient occupants the heebie-jeebies. I'd heard tales about inustrazan ships, but nothing can truly prepare you for navigating one of these monstrosities.

But considering my alternatives—that is, wallowing in the Contrition and facing a death-by-prisoner-beating, or having Kruthara's slug absorb me—I was more than happy to put up with an off-putting ship.

Besides, Amodari had come back for me. That realization alone put a thunder in my chest. Well, for a moment, anyhow. As we rushed on, flanked by Amodari's stoic commandos, I began dwelling on a second (and more nefarious) possibility: had Amodari sprung me out of the Contrition for her own selfish reasons?

Was I just a pawn in everybody's game?

"Calm your mind," Amodari said, casting a playful glance back at me. Her eyes, an identical copy of my dead lover's, glimmered in the dim lighting. "Consider this a display of my love, Bodhi."

Well, that answered the unspoken question of whether she could still read my mind.

Weeks—or months, or years, whatever—of insanity-sparking isolation had evidently turned up my mental volume to an eleven. There was no putting anything past her.

As we neared an arched doorway, Amodari spun around and inspected the two columns of soldiers. She issued short, guttural commands in what I presumed to be inustrazan, then stood with rigid attention as her underlings sprinted off down the adjoining passages. Once the two of us were alone, she led me through the doorway and onto the vessel's bridge.

It was a small and unsettling space, vaguely triangular in form yet sprinkled with various organic... oddities. This gave it the appearance of being a miniature cave, complete with wriggling stalactites and bubbling pools. Thankfully, I didn't have to examine the body-horror show too long. Directly ahead was a silicate viewpane that showed the tangled struts and habitat rings of the Contrition. A ring of navigators' chairs and instrument stations stared out at the impressive sprawl.

Three of the seven chairs were already occupied by beings that appeared to be flickering in and out of existence, much like corrupted holograms. As Amodari led me closer, my befuddlement only deepened.

"What's wrong with them?" I asked.

She sat in an empty chair, strapped herself down with a nauseating tonguelike harness, and gestured for me to do the same. "You ask so many inane questions, my dear. Let's not dally."

Grimacing, I sat in the leathery seat and repeated the procedure. The harness was lukewarm and salivating. Never again.

"Are they... here?" I asked, still hung up on the pilots. "They seem to be glitching."

"They're *focusing*," Amodari corrected. "These are my mother's most esteemed navigators. It takes tremendous mental energy to interface with a living vessel."

Looking closer, I understood Amodari's scant explanation. The pilots—navigators, as she'd termed them—had tendrils running from their heads into the soupy floor. A form of direct neural control, I gathered, similar to how my dear companion Umzuma had piloted *Stream Dancer*. No wonder they were phasing in and out of their guises. You see, it took inustrazans a great deal of effort to project their false appearance into the minds of humanoids. And when joined with a vessel's consciousness, it's of little consequence how you look to said vessel's passengers.

Amodari barked a command in her ugly native tongue, and the vessel lurched forward.

As the inustrazan pilots banked us up and around one of the station's many gyroscopic rings, I got a clearer look at the vessel belonging to Kruthara's "emissary." The thing was a monstrosity, nearly as large as the Contrition itself. It was all flailing tentacles, misshapen chitin plating, and globs of reddish flesh that fluttered in and out as though breathing. A long, intestine-like appendage connected its bulk to the station's primary airlock.

"You madmen flew past *that*?" I exclaimed, my nails digging into the chair's velvety armrests.

Amodari laughed. "That's one of Kruthara's smallest offspring. You should've seen the leviathan we outran near the Gepsam Belt, my dear."

To this day, I'm still unsure if it was our vessel's heat signature or Amodari's dismissive remark that caused Kruthara to fly into a rage. Not that it matters. As soon as Amodari had spoken, three of the abomination's massive, ribbed tentacles came lashing out from its underbelly. They whipped toward us with impossible speed, approaching far faster than some variants of hydrogen missiles.

The pilots rolled and cut upward at the last moment, filling the viewpane with a momentary—and horrifying—taste of Kruthara's power. Its tentacle alone was wider than our vessel, lined with serrated teeth and miniature mouths that screamed in silent hunger.

I stared into one of those mouths, and I shall never forget the dread they imparted.

But as swiftly as it had appeared, the tentacle was gone, replaced by a view of wide-open vacuum. We rolled a few more times, presumably ducking and weaving Kruthara's ensuing strikes. It's a strange feeling, knowing you're being targeted and nearly killed every few seconds while also sitting in a comfortable chair and experiencing none of the vessel's inertia. Are you in a dogfight, or just zipping around? About to be obliterated, or running free? You can't be sure. Ahh, the beauty (read: terror) of advanced engineering.

After several seconds of rectal puckering, however, Amodari turned to me and nodded decisively. "We're clear."

"Clear?" I whispered, still half-expecting Kruthara to rip open our hull. "Like, clear-clear? Like, I'm-out-for-good-clear?"

"Yes, that sort of clear," she replied. "We've made it through their repulsion field's perimeter."

"But Kruthara—"

"Shan't be joining us, dear Bodhi."

She gestured to the leftmost pilot, whose neural tendrils were hooked up to a cylindrical module set into the floor. A remote-access breaching device, I gathered. In other words, a hacking rig.

"So... you had manual control over the station's systems?" I asked.

Although I was beyond grateful to be out of my cell, I had, as always, a slew of questions. Specifically questions that would allow me to figure out if I'd truly escaped or simply been ensnared in an even more depressing level of the Contrition's virtual torture carnival.

"Correct," she said. "We were able to override the security, disable communications..."

"And unlock the cell blocks?"

Amodari squinted, then inhaled deeply. "Yes, well, that was a bit of a fortunate accident. Our primary goal was keeping the repulsion field disabled until we fled. As you can see, all has gone according to plan."

"Meaning you've just locked Kruthara's ship inside their little bubble."

"Precisely." She winked. "And thanks to our elders' generous hardware contribution, our vessel will be able to pinch to safety in no more than three minutes. A clean getaway, if ever one existed. A getaway fit for one of your caliber, perhaps... Are you proud of me yet, darling?"

Bizarre as it was, I could tell that Amodari was tacitly seeking my approval. She wanted to hear me gush about the merits of her brilliant plan, to be showered in compliments about her tactical know-how and cunning. Imagine that—a mastermind fishing for praise from a doomed man who was stupid enough to get himself imprisoned.

But in that moment, tasting the sweet nectar of freedom once again, I couldn't summon any critical thoughts about my savior. In fact, I could summon only love. Especially because I was quite certain that if Amodari sensed anything less in my heart, she'd toss me right back into the Kruthara-Kemedis-prison-riot soup she'd left behind.

And so, I pulled on a flimsy smile and clung to that love. An easy feat, given the butterflies surging through my stomach. This woman had come back for me. Saved me from infinite eons of torture, no less.

"Amodari, I am achingly proud," I said, meaning every word, "but I think it's time you catch me up to speed."

THREE

Even as Amodari's flashy inustrazan vessel slid into the folds of the pinch, thus safeguarding us from any threats the material plane had to offer, I was not at ease. You see, the familiar dread of freedom was quick to reassert itself once I had a taste of the outside world. Back in the Contrition, yes, I'd been locked in a constant state of suffering and fear, but at least I'd known and accepted that anguish. This is the holy state of renunciation every prisoner eventually reaches. When freedom is impossible, acceptance is the only choice.

Not so in the outside world.

Beyond a prison's walls, you are not as "free" as you imagine. In every moment of joy, you are burdened by the knowledge that anything and anybody can strip you of that freedom at any time. Death can visit you like a cruel joke at the height of your glory. Loved ones can perish or betray you or simply vanish.

And thus, my flash of celebration had become something maudlin.

How fickle the mind is.

Amodari surely sensed this, because she was quick to reach into her personal quarters' liquor cabinet and pour me a generous triple-strength cocktail.

Even while sitting on her elegant leather sofa (which I began to suspect was made from human flesh), I found myself running my hands over the stitching in a vain effort to determine if this was reality or another one of Kemedis' soul-crushing simulations. After all, the grand mediator had subjected me to these "escape fantasy" programs more than once. Typically, they played out until I was about to engage in some much-needed bed wrestling—at which point I would wake up in my cell, alone and frazzled.

"Give your battered mind a break, my love," Amodari said as she handed me the tar-colored drink. "This should help take the edge off."

I sniffed the highball glass' contents. It smelled like crushed insects. "What is this?"

"*Ras'tahf*," she said merrily, settling down on the other end of the sofa with her own glass in hand. "A traditional inustrazan liqueur."

Much as I wanted to decline the foul-smelling brew, I was in no position to do so. Untold days spent in the Contrition, bereft of my favorite drugs or drinks, made *any* substance seem appealing. Hell, I would've guzzled a liter of turbine oil if somebody had left it lying around. And so, despite my reservations, I took a hesitant sip.

It was shockingly good.

"What's this made of?" I asked.

Amodari took her own sip, then said, "A select blend of fruits and herbs... but mostly crushed insects."

My throat seized up a little, but after a moment's pause and an inner shrug, I kept drinking. Life is short.

"That's it," Amodari said encouragingly. "It will settle your stomach until mealtime."

"By *meal*, you don't mean living humanoids, do you?"

"Of course not, darling." She smiled. "Such delicacies are reserved for my people."

"Oh. That's, uh, good, I suppose." I cleared my throat, not quite sure I wanted to ask the questions lingering in my head. But I'd have to rip the bandage off sooner or later. I figured sooner was preferable. "Amodari, how long was I in there?"

She arched a brow and looked at the ribcage-adorned ceiling, chewing the question over. Inwardly, I braced myself for the news. How many years had gone by? Decades, perhaps?

"If my sense of time is accurate," she began, "I'd say about two months."

"Two *months*!?"

"Yes?"

"There's gotta be a miscalculation. It felt like—"

"Eons," Amodari finished. "Yes, I'm well aware. Grand Mediator Kemedis was rather liberal with her use of the chrono-dilator settings."

Two months. Despite knowing that short span of time was a possibility, it didn't seem real. All of that misery, that dehumanization, compressed into just over sixty days? Then and there, I understood that time was nothing more than a convenient illusion. Experience will always supersede "real" time.

Don't misunderstand me—I was thrilled to discover that all the non-modified mortals I knew were (likely) still alive and kicking out there among the stars. Yet I couldn't shake the distinct sense that I felt far, far older than I should. I looked down at my hands, wondering where all the wrinkles and scars of age were.

"But don't trouble yourself with that," Amodari said, I presume in an effort to get me out of my rather obvious rumination. "You must have innumerable questions about the state of the universe."

"That's an understatement."

"Go on then, darling. I'll answer to the best of my ability."

I blinked at her for a while, trying in vain to dredge up a single question that could assuage my existential doldrums. In the end, I started with the simplest line of inquiry.

"Why did you come back for me?"

Amodari took a long sip before replying. "I would have recovered you far sooner had certain... political shifts... not interfered."

"Go on."

"That's quite a loaded topic," she said. "Let me address your question at the surface. I came back for you because I love you, Bodhi Drezek. Each day and night without you, I longed for you. It pains me to think that you spent a single day in Kemedis' clutches."

"Oh, it *pained* me, too." I paused, considering my flippant reply. "I'm trying to say thank you, Amodari. In a roundabout way."

"I sense your love, dear. Don't trouble yourself overmuch with the words."

With a nod of thanks, I returned to my seemingly endless pit of questions. I'd had so much to ask while languishing in the Contrition, but out here, nothing came to mind. Perhaps while in the grips of torture, all of my mental conjuring had merely seemed more robust. A single coherent thought was a true mercy in that place.

But gradually, sluggishly, concrete questions bubbled up.

"My crew," I said at length. "Where's my crew?"

Amodari's face wilted somewhat, as though she were disappointed with my line of questioning. It appeared she'd been waiting for me to ask about our future matrimony arrangements.

"I've nothing to offer in regards to that lot," she said quietly. "Following the confrontation over the Promised Place, they vanished from the Hegemony's sight. And thus, from mine."

I pulled in a shallow breath at that, only to remember a time-honored proverb: *no news is good news*. Especially when your torturers were the sort that would delight in telling you the moment your crew was caught and killed.

"Nothing?" I prodded. "Not a peep? A carrier bird?"

She shook her head. "Some of our intelligence operatives claim that a woman matching the trollop's description was spotted working with the insurgency on a barren world... but you can't trust such reports all the time."

"Trollop? You mean Chaska?"

"Yes. Her."

Now *that* put a little fire in my heart. I tried to keep it free of my mind, however, on account of Amodari's thought-prowling capabilities.

"Right, so my crew's MIA, except for maybe Chaska," I said, thinking aloud, scratching my chin. Then a lightning bolt of a thought struck me. "Back up to you and Kemedis for a minute. When Miss Malicious was about to feed me a five-course Kruthara meal, she told me that you and your 'ilk' had been branded traitors. She was spotty on the ilk part, but I gathered she meant, you know, everybody you've ever associated with. Gnosis, your species... I'm not quite grasping how things soured between you."

"As I said, Bodhi, it's a complicated situation."

"So uncomplicate it for me."

Her eyes darkened as she set her glass down. "Put simply, things are changing with the Hegemony. The war has seen to that."

"I didn't ask for simple, Amodari. Just uncomplicated."

"You ought to dine and rest before we traverse such intricate ground."

I sighed. "Can't we just put on our boots and forge ahead? I've spent several lifetimes without answers."

"Then what will a few more hours matter?"

"My sanity, I'd wager. Come on. Spill it."

After a few more infuriating seconds of indecision, she spilled. "Things are dire in the cosmos. Day by day, more worlds disappear. Factions devour one another. Entire fleets go missing in the void. Those who are wise have already fled to the furthest reaches of the Nogo and beyond, hoping to outrun that which cannot be outrun."

"Stirring. But get to the Hegemony part, please."

"Very well. It would seem that leaders of their military wing recently came to the conclusion that they could not defeat Kruthara in combat. Especially not with Kruthara being aided by a sizable number of species that have already allied themselves against the Hegemony. Thus... a deal of surrender was forged."

"And I was the bargaining chip?"

She shook her head. "Not just you, darling. The Hegemony agreed to surrender *all* of its knowledge to Kruthara in exchange for sparing their citizens. Foremost among their demands was the knowledge held by Gnosis."

In case memory eludes you, Gnosis referred to the Hegemony's esoteric inner circle. Its dark, scary, ancient secret holders. Amodari's mother, Tanu, was part of this circle. Most of the top-tier inustrazans were, I'd gathered.

"Let me guess," I said. "You didn't turn it over willingly."

"No, nor did we lose control of it. Gnosis has always maintained an oral record-keeping system to prevent situations like this from occurring. All of their secrets are held in the minds of those who discovered them." Amodari took a long drink, looking more distraught by the second. "Grand Mediator Kemedis has, in effect, become the leader of the Halcius Hegemony. And they will stop at nothing to procure the information Kruthara seeks."

"But what *is* it they want?" I pressed. "And why turn me over? I don't know anything about anything!"

"Evidently Kruthara disagrees. You must remember that it's already consumed the mind of Thamok and anybody else aboard the *Ouroboros*. Perhaps the assimilated minds believe you are a threat."

I'll admit, I was somewhat puffed up by this concept. It's hard not to feel honored when you're such an object of desire for a galaxy-consuming superorganism.

"Which is why it's imperative that you tell me anything I ought to know," Amodari finished.

"Are you *sure* I'm not in a simulation?"

"I'm certain."

"Okay. Because, you know, if I *were* in a simulation, this is exactly how I'd have sensitive information pried out of me."

Amodari smirked. "You are, for better or worse, free of the Contrition's illusions. This is the time to make use of whatever revelations are stored in that succulent mind of yours."

I combed through my rattled memories, trying to recall what Kemedis—and by extension, Kruthara—could possibly want to know. Anything I'd seen, Thamok had also seen. Then again, it was feasible that Kruthara merely *believed* I knew more than I did. That I was some font of knowledge about everything in the known universe. Well, that was half true, but no matter. It also struck me that Kruthara might've heard about Center, my self-aware hyperdimensional AI-turned-god. If it managed to consume Center, well...

Game over.

But the idea was quickly ejected from consideration. Center was beyond time and space now—inhabiting its own universe, if memory served. There was no conceivable way for Kruthara to reach them, let alone consume them as part of its mental buffet.

So what could it be?

"What about that marvelous little creature of yours?" Amodari prompted. "Perhaps its link to Kruthara was greater than Seeker Palamar let on?"

Creature. Sloth-thing. Tusky. It hit me in a flash—just after Kruthara's fateful awakening, Tusky had quite literally eaten one of those red slugs off Ruena's armor, seemingly without any ill effect. Was Tusky the missing link here? The key to formulating an antidote or, fingers crossed, a weapon I could sell for obscene profit?

"Not a clue," I said, hoping Amodari wouldn't be capable of dissecting my consciousness so swiftly. This, dear reader, is a lesson in "playing dumb." If you know something of tremendous value that others might exploit, you would do well to hold onto your sacred realization until you can profit by your own hand. "Say, Amodari, maybe if you brought me to Chaska, it would jog my memory even further..."

Wrath crept into her eyes. "I've sacrificed so much to get you back in my embrace, Bodhi. Do you really think I would return you to that harlot so readily?"

This seemed ironic, considering Amodari was nothing short of a succubus herself, but I held my tongue.

"It could win us the war," I pleaded.

"If I lose you, I have lost everything."

"A touch oversentimental, no?"

Amodari regarded me with cold, cutting eyes for a moment that stretched on far too long. "You will remain at my side until the end of days. That is the definition of love, Bodhi."

"Is it really, though?"

"Yes. You and I can live beyond the Hegemony's blind obedience. Beyond Kruthara's terror."

"But for how long?" I countered. "You said it yourself—nothing outruns that thing. Sooner or later, we'll be in for a bad time."

"Then let's opt for later. We could have ten thousand years of ecstasy…" She dragged an ice-cold, yet still enticing, finger along the curves of my collarbone. "Wouldn't you like that, Bodhi?"

Truthfully, I would have. Would've died for a smattering of such ecstasy right then, in fact, had my mind not been occupied by concern for my loyal crew. And it was. It was overloaded with worries. Despite my best intentions, I'd gotten them into this mess, and I owed it to them to provide some measure of salvation. Even if that simply meant securing them an ark that could flee Kruthara until the end of their mortal existence.

"Please, Amodari," I whispered. "Just take me to Chaska, let me know she's okay. Then we can do whatever you want. And I do mean *whatever*. My body is ready."

In a supreme act of transmutation, all the seduction in Amodari's face burned away to spite. She stood, stepped back, and folded her arms. "You would do well to divert your mind away from that lustful glob of insurgent flesh. You wouldn't want to disappoint my mother when she sifts through your mind, would you?"

"Your... mother?"

"Yes, Bodhi. My mother. You'll be standing before her in a matter of hours."

I swallowed so hard I worried I'd ruptured my throat. "Why would I be meeting her?"

"Because we're currently en route to a detachment of Gnosis' fleet. They will be escorting us to the hive-world. Did I neglect to mention that?"

"Yes?"

"Consider yourself informed, then." Her face hardened with Kemedis-like scorn as she headed for the door. "Make skillful use of your time. My mother is not as *patient* as I am."

The fatal flaw in the human mind is that struggling against a fixation doesn't destroy it—it feeds it. You've probably noticed this phenomenon if you're the sort of person who likes to indulge in a few too many cookies. No more cookies, you tell your mind. Maybe you even set up holographic motivational posters and a self-shocking bracelet to teach your mind that no means no. And ten minutes later, like clockwork, you still find yourself covered in cookie crumbs.

This may explain why, despite my best efforts, I found myself thinking of Chaska rather than Amodari. You must believe me—I really *didn't* want to think about that wily woman. She'd left me for dead multiple times, she was part of a failed insurgency, and, worst of all, she represented a death sentence if discovered lurking in my subconscious.

But dammit, Chaska was my cookie.

As the hours slipped by and the pinch wore on, I found myself pacing Amodari's empty quarters and thinking more and more about my femme fatale. The mere idea that she might be alive filled me with glee. Terrible, forbidden glee. And if she *was* alive, she might have a lead on the rest of the crew. Then we could get the gang back together, make a few sales...

No, I reminded myself. That was the old world. The pre-Kruthara world. It was gone now, having burned itself down to cold ashes while I rotted in the Contrition.

Yet Chaska was still my guiding star. She was a nostalgic expression of the world I'd once known, an ember in the metaphorical firepit of the universe. I wondered if she'd ever gotten the last message I sent to her. In it, I'd told her that I loved her. That I wanted a quiet life and children with her. That someday, somewhere, we'd meet again.

Yet Amodari was right. If her mother sensed even an inkling of this scandalous love, I might face a fate worse than the Contrition.

So I did what any self-respecting, morally dubious arms dealer would in a time of crisis.

I prayed to Halcius.

That's right. No facetious remarks or underhanded jabs at faith here, folks. I knelt on Amodari's boar-hair carpet, closed my eyes, and did my best to appear devout.

"Hey, Halcius," I whispered, feeling foolish from the onset, "it's me, Bodhi Drezek. Remember me? The one who blasphemed your name... and pissed on your symbol... and spent years mocking your followers? Yes, well, surprise! I mean, you're omnipotent. You probably already knew I'd pray to you someday. And you probably also know what I'm about to say. But let's just get down to brass tacks, shall we? I love this woman, Chaska, but I can't have her right now. And I'd like to change that. So if you can find some way to bring me back to her, even for a moment... well, I'd be grateful. Maybe not join-the-Hegemony grateful, but grateful enough. Oh, and, uh, please don't let Amodari's mother know I love her. Thanks. Amen."

Not quite sure how to finish my half-assed prayer, I hummed for a few seconds and then stood up. Good enough, right?

Not two seconds after I'd stood, the door chimed. In my post-prayer fervor, I couldn't help but wonder if Halcius had gone for a slam-dunk by manifesting Chaska behind that door. Hey, they say the green geezer works in mysterious ways, right?

This temporary (and absurd) hope was quashed a moment later when the door opened to reveal Amodari and a pair of her armor-clad inustrazan commandos.

"Seeing clearer now, are we?" Amodari asked with a bloodcurdling smile.

I nodded. "Crystal clear!"

"Very good. Come along, my love. We're nearly at our rendezvous point... I'd hate for you to miss the grand display."

Seeing as I was in no position to reject Amodari's offer, I joined her (and her armed entourage) in heading back to the bridge. Along the way, I'm certain I heard no less than six human screams emanating from somewhere deep in the vessel.

"No, that will probably not be your fate," Amodari said, breaking the silence as we walked.

I flinched. "Come again?"

"The screams... you presumed you would come to the same end."

"Me? Presume? Of course not. That would be—"

My fumbling reply was cut off by the sight of a naked, emaciated man worming himself through a nearby doorway and into our corridor. We all stopped dead in our tracks.

"Free!" the man croaked. *"Free* from that hell!"

Just then, no more than three-quarters of a second after proclaiming freedom, the man was dragged back into the same room by a pair of unseen yet powerful hands. He went kicking and screaming, raking his nails along the floor panels the entire way. Then the door hissed shut and locked.

"Pay no attention to that," Amodari said in a sweet, airy tone. "I'll just have to discipline the crew for playing with their food."

"I didn't see a thing, Amodari."

"Good. Let's proceed, shall we?"

"We shall." Casually tiptoeing around the furrows the man had carved into the floor, another one of my delayed questions came to mind. "Why do we need to rendezvous with Gnosis?"

"Hmm?"

"You said we're proceeding to a meeting point... then heading to your homeworld. Hive-world. You grasp my meaning. My point is, why not simply go there directly?"

"Because the hive-world takes tremendous pride in its secrecy, Bodhi," she explained, ushering me back onto the bridge. "You see, we inustrazans are a nomadic people, of sorts. The hive-world moves. We'd be rather foolish to give every vessel a direct tracking system linked to it, wouldn't we?"

"I... suppose?"

"Therefore, we shall be making contact with our intermediary—a Gnosis flagship capable of guiding us home."

"And you've double-checked that they're in position?"

"Of course not. We made an arrangement, and that's that. We cannot risk transmissions in such hostile territory."

"Right, okay," I said. "But doesn't that also mean that if something happens to your 'intermediary,' you're stranded?"

She actually laughed at that as we strapped into our assigned seats. "You're so delightfully wary, my dear. A *very* luscious quality in a mate, to be sure, but unnecessary for our current situation. The flagship in which we'll be docking is a tremendous craft... a glorious, staggering creation that has never failed in its duties. One might say it's the new crown jewel of Gnosis' fleet."

As Amodari spoke, the main viewpane's triple-layered shutters began receding in sequence. Clearly we'd finished our pinch, and were about to see this titan in the (proverbial) flesh. The final sheets of alloy peeled away, revealing Amodari's beloved flagship.

Or, at least, what remained of it.

Floating before us in the vacuum was a twisted, tangled mass of struts, panels, frames, and glittering silicate. Clouds of debris whirled around the flagship's husk like a tinsel tornado. Judging by the ejecta's strangely stable figure-eight trajectory, however, it seemed that some kind of miniature singularity that formed at the heart of the vessel and pulled everything into its orbit. Otherwise, as most of you spacefaring nerds know, the vast majority of that drifting metal would've been cast off in random directions, eternally sailing through the stars at the whim of galactic physics. The flagship hadn't been destroyed—it had scuttled itself.

"It can't be," Amodari whispered.

"Yet it is," I said. "Methinks the Hegemony crashed this party."

Amodari stood and approached the viewpane, touching the silicate longingly. "No, not the Hegemony. This was Kruthara's work. Otherwise the crew would have had no need to follow the protocol so thoroughly..."

"Well, on the bright side," I said, selecting my words with inordinate care, "I know a home-wrecking insurgent who'd be more than delighted to provide us with safe harbor while we contact the hive-world. Encrypted transmission terminals, to boot!"

For a few precarious seconds, I thought Amodari would stalk over to me and tear my throat out. Instead, she turned to her piloting row and snapped her fingers.

"Prepare for a new pinch."

See?

Halcius *does* work in mysterious ways.

FOUR

A few hours of pinching later, we were nearing the damnable insurgent world that Amodari had been so reticent to mention, let alone visit. If you've been following my tale with a modicum of attention, of course, you will understand that Amodari's dislike for this destination had nothing to do with the insurgent presence.

Her hesitation was my delight, naturally. It meant that she probably knew more about this world than she'd been letting on. After all, she'd previously hinted that Chaska had been nothing more than a footprint on the planet, a passing shadow. If that were the case, why so much resistance? Only one answer made sense: Chaska was still there.

My hypothesis was reinforced by the endless rounds of "quizzes" Amodari conducted during our pinch.

"If she inquires about the status of our relationship, what will you say?" she prompted for the third time, circling me as I sat on her leather sofa. "Pretend I am her, and be specific."

I spooled up the rehearsed answer. "Well, Chaska, Amodari and I are preparing to become a mated couple as dictated by section three, subparagraph five of the Binding Laws. I will be in her service as a royal concubine."

Amodari nodded, satisfied. "Put more emotion into it, darling."

"As you command."

"Are you being facetious?"

"Me? How absurd."

Her lip curled for half a second, then relaxed. "I trust you're prepared. Particularly if you come up against the harlot's advances."

"You said it. If there's one thing I hate, it's a harlot trying to steal me away. Can't stand it."

Until that moment, it hadn't occurred to me that Chaska might not be pleased to see *me* striding into her war room. After all, the way in which I'd parted from her and the rest of the crew had been rather abrupt. Harsh, even. Sure, I'd saved their skins and gotten them safely onto an insurgent vessel, but was that enough to counteract my no-frills goodbye? Only time would tell.

And besides, it had been a disastrous few months for the insurgency. Instead of merely having to contend with a futile war against their oppressors, they now faced a futile war *and* avoiding the obliteration of individual consciousness. Imagine their faces when they found out the powers were joining forces. The point is, perhaps Chaska would be too preoccupied with this scenario to entertain my affection. Or, more worryingly, perhaps she'd already moved on to a new suitor. War has a way of supercharging romance.

Nevertheless, I pushed these hypotheticals out of my head and resolved to keep my mind fixed on what was directly in front of me. Literally. Staring at carpets, wall panels, and light sconces was my only strategy for throwing off Amodari's mind-prying powers.

Thus far, it seemed to be working.

"So, tell me about this planet," I said. "Is it sunny? Any beaches? Squid-people?"

"Not quite," she said darkly.

"Mountaintop villas, then?"

Amodari glared at me. "I don't need to remind you *again*, Bodhi, that you mustn't put down any roots on this world. Not one.

The moment I've established a secure link to the hive-world, we will be departing posthaste."

"Yes, obviously, but who knows how long that could take? You know these insurgents and their shoddy old terminals…"

"Oh, I do. If this brief layover will be too… stimulating… for you, I can always arrange to have you placed in a confinement cell."

"And deprive me of the opportunity to tell Chaska what a phenomenal lover you are? Bah, I think not!"

That seemed to do the trick.

Amodari lifted her chin, smiling wickedly, and nodded. "Come, dear. Let us prepare for our entrance."

By "prepare," what Amodari really meant was "dress up in lavish, ridiculous costumes that ordinary people would wear ironically." Perhaps I should've expected this from the near-immortal daughter of a royal inustrazan bloodline. After all, I'd never seen her (or any inustrazan, for that matter) in their ceremonial garb. She'd spent most of our previous adventure wearing my crew's hand-me-downs or luxury-spa bathrobes.

Looking at my reflection in the bridge's viewpane, I developed another theory about the ostentatious getup: Amodari was trying to make me look as unappealing as possible to Chaska.

An overreach on my part? Hardly.

I was wearing a multipiece monstrosity that featured silk ruffle shoulder poofs, a canary-yellow frock coat, a red cummerbund, frilly cuffs, an ascot, pointy little shoes, *tights,* and a codpiece. Yes, an honest-to-Halcius codpiece. Even if it *did* make my groin look impressively massive, it was simply too much. If this was an omen of male fashion on the inustrazan hive-world, I was in for a brutal life.

Anyhow, both my self-conscious dread and reflection vanished when the viewpane transformed into a shimmering blue transmission panel.

"Contact their *landing control*," Amodari told the navigators, sneering at the very concept of insurgents having such a thing. "Be certain that you arm the countermeasures in case they decide to send us a welcoming salvo."

I'll be frank—I felt a slight tingle in my loins at hearing Amodari's tactical talk. Now, that was probably half-caused by the codpiece cutting off circulation, but I stand by my statement. Somewhere in the course of my two-month torture stint, Amodari had grown into a daughter befitting of her mother's military reputation. Perhaps the war truly had made soldiers out of everybody.

A moment later, the holographic rendering of an older woman's face filled the transmission screen.

"State your name and allegiance," the insurgent growled, "and tell us how you got these coordinates."

Amodari approached the screen with her hands laced behind her back. "Greetings. My name is Amodari Halnok, daughter of Tanu Halnok, heir to the sixteen catacombs, holder of the sacred—"

"Hegemony!" The insurgent's shout made it clear she was readying the yet-unseen world for battle.

"No longer," Amodari said briskly. "My people do not serve the Halcius Hegemony or its collaborators. Our vessel has come here alone and with the mildest of intentions. Please allow us to land in your installation."

"Not a chance in hell," the woman spat.

"If you feel threatened, dear, I'd advise you to reconsider the situation. We would not have traveled on our own if conquest was our intention. As I said, we—"

"Advance wave!" the woman shrieked, once again seemingly to her comrades out of sight.

All I could do was roll my eyes. Amodari's presence, intimidating as it was, did nothing beneficial for our play at peace.

Unwilling to let her bungle negotiations further, I stepped into the holo-corder's view and waved sheepishly.

"Ah, hello," I said, drawing the wrathful attention of both women. "As an independent in all this, I'd like to vouch for Miss Halnok here. She just hauled me out of the Contrition... and killed a moderate amount of Hegemony troops in the process, let me tell you!"

The insurgent blinked at me, evidently at a loss, but she didn't resume shouting commands at her fellow freedom fighters—a good sign, by my estimate.

"Listen, we've had enough scraps for one day with Grand Mediator Kemedis and her lackeys," I went on. "So if it's all the same to you, can we skip the wartime tension and get to the campfire drinking?"

"You never answered me," the insurgent said warily. "How... did you get... these coordinates?"

"Oh, right. We heard Chaska was here. You know, blonde, tattoos, Lattlander, carried the Kruthara canister around for a whi—"

"Who the hell are you?"

"Bodhi Drezek. Any further introduction necessary?"

The insurgent's crazed mask crumbled, giving way to a sly smile. "Why didn't you just say so? Chaska's been fishin' the networks to find you for months." Somewhere in the backdrop, a round of whoops and cheers went up. "Slide into the designated dock. We'll send out the welcome crew."

The moment the transmission screen fizzled away, Amodari's examination became an exercise in scorn.

"Need I remind you of the terms of your freedom?" she whispered.

"Absolutely not," I said, even as my heart soared with the prospect of seeing my favorite insurgent in a matter of minutes. "Chaska, that old scoundrel. That trollop. That... well, every bad thing in the book. She shan't be seducing me, not at all!"

Amodari cocked her head to the side. "And you're certain of that?"

"Deadly certain."

"As you should be." She snapped her fingers, and the viewpane's pinch-protecting shutters unfurled once again to reveal space, lots of space, and a gray orb directly ahead.

The world was practically monochrome, more moon than planet, though its impressive size and rings of orbiting debris assured me that it was—or had been—a full-fledged settlement spot. Bolstering this conclusion were the dark splotches of cities and wide, craggy depressions, which I assumed had once been oceans. There were only a few explanations for the sorry state of this planet, one of which was—

"Atmo-busted," Amodari said, finishing my thought. She wandered closer to the silicate and stared out at the barren marble. "This was Darjitum, one of the first worlds confirmed to be infected by Kruthara's microbes. The Hegemony had all interplanetary traffic quarantined within two hours, but by then, it was too late... so they authorized their most treasured tactic."

"Dusting," I replied.

Sure enough, Amodari's analysis was backed up by a series of enormous craters that pitted the western horizon. Judging by the looks of it, they'd slammed this place with no less than five atmobusters—more than enough to vaporize such a planet twice over. This, I gathered, accounted for the complete lack of greens, blues, reds... all organic color, really. I'd sold enough atmo-busters to know what their unrestrained use could do.

Something small and delicate snapped inside my chest as I studied Darjitum's remains. Not from the billions of deaths that had occurred down there, but from the realization that nobody would ever know that anything had *been* there. On future long-range scanners, it would show up as an inorganic husk, perhaps a suitable candidate for precious-metal mining. Nobody would ever know that it had once been full of birthday parties and first kisses and sunset walks.

Hell, all I knew about this graveyard of a world was that it now played host to an insurgent base. That, and the fact that Kruthara had effortlessly and quite incidentally caused its annihilation.

It was surely not the first of its kind—and as history sadly attests, it was far from the last.

If Amodari had read my mind as we waited in the vestibule linking the airlocks of our vessel and the insurgent installation, she would've seen fear. However, there are shades of fear. The shade she would've (and likely did) perceive was one of a child expecting to be struck by a domineering parent. Put simply, the fear that I would be killed for allowing Chaska to seduce me—again.

But my particular shade of fear was more nuanced. I was afraid of a possibility I've already recounted: that of Chaska being "over me." A childish fear, no doubt, and one that seemed unlikely due to the revelation that she'd been looking for me since I disappeared, but let's get real. Any organism with a functioning ego and sex drive is afraid of rejection. Social acceptance is the cornerstone of society.

And thus, I found myself sweating profusely as we waited for the pressure to equalize. This problem was exacerbated by the horrendous clown suit I'd been forced to wear.

Then came a rush of air, a few hydraulic pops, and plumes of aerosol.

My toes curled in those damned cobbler's shoes as the gas faded, leaving me with the glorious sight of...

A repulsor field.

Behind that field, however, were a dozen figures in biohazard suits. Most were foreign to me, little more than smatterings of eyes and noses in neon-lit helmets, but I recognized three of them in a flash.

First was Gadra, my protégé artist. She stood grinning in the center of the gathering, still short, still a child. That was proof enough that I had indeed been in the Contrition no longer than a few months. The sight of her nearly brought me to tears.

Beside her was Ruena, only a few hairs taller and standing proud in her four-eyed glory. More tears knocked on my eye-doors, but I kept it locked.

The third and final recognizable figure was the one I'd been waiting for. Also, I was later told, the one that kicked off the real waterworks. My radiant queen, my missing half, my pain in the ass.

My Chaska.

Had I not faced death-by-dematerializing thanks to that repulsor field, I'd have dashed forth and swept her up in my arms. You may think my analysis of that hotheaded insurgent is unwarranted, given how little time we'd known one another and how many times she tried to kill me, and you may be right. But I challenge *you* to spend hundreds of simulated eternities inside the Contrition and not find yourself clinging desperately to a vision of romantic love. Reality-time doesn't mean anything. What counts is mental time. The hours, weeks, decades spent pining over somebody you can't have.

"You were right!" Gadra squealed, tugging at Ruena's arm. "It's him!"

Apparently Miss Future-Seer had ruined my surprise reunion with her time meddling. No matter. I was just happy they could even recognize me in my current outfit.

"Welcome home," Ruena said quietly.

There was a distinct weight and weariness to her tone, the tone of an adult whose glee is tempered by the shitstorm of life flying around them. And in our case, life was especially grim.

Grimmer still, though, was Chaska's silence.

She stared at me with inscrutable eyes for a long while, even as the others clapped and shouted congratulatory things I only faintly picked up.

Then she stepped forward and studied us. "Get a tracker scan and an IOCD reading on the vessel," she said into her transmitter. "Inside and outside."

This unfamiliar acronym will be explained shortly, but for now, just know it was not the warm, lover's greeting I'd anticipated.

I stepped closer to my side of the flickering barrier. "Chaska," I said, "it's me. Bodhi. Remember me?"

She arched a brow. "Doesn't ring a bell."

"Oh, come on. You forgot *this* face?"

"I vaguely remember an arms dealer with better clothes."

"Yes, well, I can explain."

"Later."

"How about now?"

A warning grunt from Amodari halted my pseudo-advances.

"Hang tight," Chaska said a moment later. "It's just standard procedure. Need to make sure the vessel's clean."

"We're clean!" I looked back at Amodari. "We're clean, right?"

Amodari moved to my side and glared at Chaska. "Let the insurgent do whatever she feels is best. I'm certain their methods for detecting Kruthara's microbes are more effective than all the failed prototypes the Hegemony engineered."

"Is this your way of sucking up?" Chaska asked her. "Because we're *more* than happy to vent your ship right now."

"Oh, you two!" I said, trying in vain to lighten the mood. "I'm sure we can all banter later."

Just then, a tingle passed through my bones—I would later find out it was the aforementioned IOCD scan, and *not* just butterflies in my stomach.

"Let 'em in!" Gadra called. "I wanna show Bodhi what I've painted! Oh, and the tattoos I did!"

I frowned at Chaska. "She made tattoos?"

"Times have changed," Chaska said softly. Then, after consulting her wrist implant, she nodded at us. "Looks like you've come up clean. Step back so we can drop the field." She regarded Amodari from head to toe. "I hope you won't mind if your Gnosis hounds stay on board, *princess*."

"Threatened by the presence of dignity, are we?" Amodari prodded.

"If I were, I wouldn't let you in." She scoffed. "Always time to reconsider even that."

Amodari gave me a pointed look. "Yes, there most assuredly is."

I opted to do the smart thing and keep my mouth shut as Chaska's team went about shutting the repulsor field down. Sure enough, after a few tense seconds the blue wall vanished and I was within hugging distance of my beloved. But I didn't act on my impulses. I just stood there, still sensing another field between us—one more subtle and harder to circumvent.

This was illustrated plainly when Amodari eased a step forward, only to be halted by Chaska's gloved palm.

"Hold it right there, Amodari. If it's all the same to you, my people and I have some *questions* about how you two ended up here."

The inustrazan offered an amiable nod. "But of course. My, how I'd love to enlighten the ignorant."

"Then I suppose you wouldn't mind submitting to said questioning over a cup of coffee. Just you and me, nothing painful involved. Except hearing your voice."

"The sentiment is mutual." Amodari grinned at me, which I could only take as a sign of simultaneous victories.

The first victory was getting to annoy the hell out of Chaska with constant barbs, knowing full well that if the insurgents harmed a hair on her pretty body, she'd call out the troops. Her second victory was separating me from Chaska.

Brutal, but it was what it was. And besides, I got the uncomfortable sensation that Chaska also wanted some time away from me.

I was happy to oblige, of course. Provided she eventually ran back into my arms.

"Well, if we're finished making veiled threats," Ruena said, "I believe Bodhi's long overdue for a tour of our fine facility... and a reunion with his baby, *Stream Dancer*."

"You can say that again," Gadra chimed in, squeezing past Chaska to grab my hand. "C'mon, Tusky's been waitin' to talk with you. I mean, I have too, but Tusky's first."

I scrunched my eyes, not sure who or where to look for answers on that one. "*Tusky?* As in, sloth-bear-thing, metal-chewing Tusky? Talking? With me?"

"You heard that right," Ruena said. "He's quite the conversationalist nowadays."

On any given day, my mind would've been working overtime to figure out what had gone down with that creature in the past two months. But as Gadra dragged me down the corridor, I found that I didn't give much of a damn about Tusky or the war or acronyms like IOCD.

All I cared about was Chaska watching me go, not a hint of warmth in her stare.

FIVE

So there you have it, an apt demonstration of the human condition. I had (almost) everything I treasured back on the masterpiece that was my life—my crew, my ship, my freedom—yet I was missing the one color to tie it all together. That color, naturally, was the searing red of Chaska's love. And because of its absence, the entire work felt lifeless and uninspired. Less a masterpiece, and more a cheap reproduction you can buy from any fabrique with an image-cloning algorithm.

But enough of my moaning. It was an ever-present backdrop of experience as Gadra pulled me through the facility's dingy, prefab corridors, prattling on about this and that battle, who'd died, who'd gone where... *who cared*!?

Ruena, who either foresaw my approaching meltdown or just read it on my face, stepped up to the plate. She put a hand on Gadra's shoulder and said, "Gad, why don't you run ahead and make sure Tusky has the lab ready for visitors? Bodhi and I have a few things to discuss."

The girl stopped and spun around, grimacing. "Adult things, huh?"

"That's right."

"Well, I'm almost an adult, too. So I can hear it."

"Gad."

"What? He *just* got back from his vacation."

"I've told you already—it wasn't a vacation. He was *imprisoned*."

"Uh-huh, sure… imprisoned, vacation… what's the difference?"

Ruena's four-eyed glare seemed to do the trick, however.

Gadra let go of my hand, gave a defeated huff, and started down the corridor without us. "Don't be too long, or I'll start playing around with my tattoo gun again."

Once the girl was sufficiently out of earshot, Ruena looked sidelong at me. "She's certainly got your spirit."

"You say that like she's my child." I mulled that over for a second. "Did you run a DNA test? Because honestly, I don't think I can take that right now. And the backpay on those child-support payments would be—"

"Easy, Bodhi. Just saying… she's got grit. The war hasn't done that any favors."

"For anybody, it seems."

"Ahh, now I get it. You've got a case of Chaska on the brain."

"Am I that transparent?"

"To me, you are." She offered a pitying smile. "Don't take it personally. She's been under a lot of pressure."

"Any new men in her quarters?"

"Not that it's one iota of your business, but no. She's been too busy running a regiment."

Well, that boosted my spirits a tad. Not enough to make me overcome my lingering dejection, but enough to take some of the sting away. At least until I got to the bottom of the drama barrel with the lady in question.

"How was it in there?" Ruena asked seriously. "I mean… how are *you*?"

"Let's just say my pain was Kemedis' gain."

"Do you, uh, wanna talk about it?"

I shook my head. "Not right now. Give me a few drinks and I might gush about the first couple of disemboweling millennia."

"Noted." Ruena gestured forward, and we resumed walking at a slow, deliberate pace. "How about explaining your daring escape? I bet you've been holding that one back since you landed."

"More of a daring rescue, actually. But yes, it's a phenomenal story. It's going in my memoir."

She laughed. "Better start writing that thing soon. Your potential readership is getting mind-melted by the day." Although I found the humor in that remark, she evidently didn't. She was quick to clear her throat and muddle on. "We missed you around here, you know. And Chaska did, too. Even if she doesn't come right out and say it."

"Huh. Could've fooled me, Ru."

"Look... do you want the honest truth?"

"Always."

She rolled her eyes. "Bodhi, I'm used to the way you disappeared. Seen it a million times. Plus, you hauled me back onto that ship when you could've turned tail. What you did was honorable —*shockingly* honorable—and I appreciated it. Still do. And more than that, I knew you'd pop back up eventually. But Chaska doesn't know you like that. When you went off the radar, she thought you were gone for good... so after a while, she wrote you off as another casualty. It's not easy rekindling how you feel about somebody you've already grieved."

"Damn, Ru. I wanted something pithy, not a therapy session by proxy."

"Always happy to help." She stopped at a bulky-looking door marked by the signage *Sir Tusky's Laboratory,* knocking twice on its central chrome plate.

"*Sir* Tusky?" I said. "How did a massive krutharan animal receive an honorific before me? And who handed it out?"

Ruena smiled as the locks began to disengage. "Ask him yourself."

By now, all this talk of a talking Tusky was growing unbearable. I wasn't certain if I was about to face a language-wielding beast or the crew's first (and decidedly unfunny) practical joke.

My answer came a moment later, when the doors parted to reveal a still-massive Tusky... standing *upright*... wearing a *lab coat*... sorting *chemistry beakers*... amid a tangle of decanters, tubes, pipes, and terminals. He was encircled by a gaggle of hair-twirling, blushing young insurgent ladies.

"What the hell is all this?" I blurted out.

Tusky gingerly set his equipment down on the table and clapped his hands together. "Marvelous! It appears the infamous Bodhi Drezek has decided to grace me with his presence at last!"

I just about fainted.

"Sir" Tusky's voice was a smooth, deep baritone, more suited to radio announcements than his former pastime of devouring fabriques. Weirder still was the very human expression on his face... snout... whatever you'd like to term it. He looked genuinely pleased to see me. And that, my friends, is a rare thing when I enter a room.

"Wha—?" I stared wide-eyed at Ruena, then at Gadra, who was swinging her legs over the side of an alloy crate, then at Tusky himself. "Did you just speak to me?"

"Oh, I did," Tusky said. "Come, old friend. We have so very much to discuss!" Then, turning to his groupies, he said in a rather apologetic tone, "Might we continue this at another time?"

With a few parting flirty remarks and giggles (and not a glance in my direction), Tusky's fan club departed.

The man of the hour then hastily packed away a few of his in-progress gadgets, capped vials, and centrifuges before dragging a stool out from under his worktable. He gestured for me to sit.

I did.

"Whaddya think?" Gadra asked. "Pretty good alltongue, huh?"

"Pretty... good..." I mumbled.

"Ah, but all thanks must go to my tutor," Tusky said, bowing humbly and sweeping his paw-hand-thing toward Gadra. "She's been most patient with my questing."

"*Questions*," Gadra corrected.

Tusky nodded, beaming. "Touché!"

In case you've forgotten some pertinent details here, I'd last seen Tusky as a gargantuan animal with an iron stomach. He hadn't shown even the slightest ability to vocalize anything beyond grunts and growls. Sure, he'd accepted a few commands from Gadra—his supposed handler—but this was far, far beyond the pale. He was probably the most eloquent being in this facility. Aside from myself, of course.

"I'd imagine you're rather perplexed right now," Tusky said, settling his bulk onto the tabletop and meshing his claws politely.

Only then did I notice that each hand had been outfitted with a mechanical thumb prosthetic. An *opposable* mechanical thumb, no less.

"That's one word to describe it," I said quietly.

"We'll give you two a few minutes to get acquainted," Ruena said. She nodded at Gadra and pointed toward an adjoining door. "Now show me that tattoo gun, Gad."

The girl complied, though not without a copious amount of sighs and grumbles.

When they'd both exited and the door swished shut behind them, Tusky grinned.

"Can I offer you anything?" he said. "Tea? Coffee? A honey-maggot kombucha?" He appeared to think on that briefly. "Forgive me for the latter offering, Bodhi. I've been told that humanoids don't much care for it."

"How... are you talking?"

"Ah, yes, that. I'd be delighted to explain, but I must preface in saying that much of this is hearsay delivered by Gadra and the others. You see, prior to the arising of my self-awareness, I didn't develop a spot of memory."

"Go on."

"Are you familiar with sentience tonics?"

I racked my brain, trying to recall the concept. Last I'd checked, "sentience tonic" had been a theoretical concept dreamed up in black-market clinics. It was a colloquial term for a very long and confusing process that involved artificially "nourishing" a non-sentient creature's brain until it developed sentience… or some twisted form of it. I'd heard of a socialite named Lady Gu'jork who'd managed to give her pet lizard, Hup, the curse of self-awareness. This tale had ended in abject misery.

See, things without consciousness don't know it themselves, but they'd prefer to stay in their ignorant slumber. Once you give something the ability to look in a mirror and exclaim, "Hey, that's *me!*" you've started that critter down a very dark road. It's good and well to know you're a conscious being, sure, but it also comes with a host of problems.

Take existential dread, for example. Once you know you're alive, you inherently also know you could *not* be alive someday. In other words, you become aware of death. And that's just the tip of the iceberg. Poor Hup now had to contend with a chain of unanswerable questions, such as, "Who am I? What am I? Where did I come from? Why am I in a cage? Why do I need to eat living things?"

It goes on and on and on. No wonder Hup had eventually gone on a hunger strike and smashed his tiny lizard brains against the inside of his glass prison.

Anyhow, all of this is a truncated way of explaining that I did, in fact, know what Tusky was referring to with "sentience tonics." But the chasm between making a lizard have a psychological breakdown and allowing a sloth-bear-thing to develop a robust vocabulary and scientific understanding is vast.

"So... you got a sentience tonic treatment," I said, trying to grasp Tusky's tale.

He nodded. "More precisely, the crew got it for me. The first true moment of 'my' life began in an underground clinic on one of Tarquro's moons... what a blessed day. One moment, a stream of meaningless sensations... the next, alive!"

"Right." My brain was still thoroughly scrambled. "No offense, but, uh... *why*?"

"Who can say, Bodhi? Why did your parents elect to bring you into the maelstrom of existence?"

"I think they forgot to use protection."

Tusky clapped an enormous—and painful—hand on my shoulder. "A natural comedian! To answer you directly, I'm unsure why I was given this gift. Gadra has explained that she desired a friend, a companion. I'd like to believe we've fostered such a bond."

"That's good. I think."

"The underlying message here, Bodhi, is that I owe to you so very much. Without you, I would have languished in mindless oblivion forever."

"Don't mention it. I have a habit of giving out self-awareness like candy."

"You must be referring to Center, your esteemed artificial intelligence-turned-deity." Tusky smiled wider. "When I heard the long and winding tale that led to the moment of my awakening, I was shocked. Your bravery is limitless. You and Chaska are, for lack of a better term, my parents."

"That's a bit far..."

"Is it? You gave rise to the mind I now inhabit. After all, it was your bux that funded my journey into awareness of my own being."

"My bux?"

"Yes!"

I felt the blood drain from my fingers. "How much did this sentience tonic cost?"

"I believe it was approximately half of your fortune! A very sophisticated procedure, I've been told!"

Trying not to fall off my chair, I took a deep breath. "Well, that still leaves half…"

"Ah, it did, until the insurgents used your remaining bux to purchase this facility, a complement of weapons and armor, new vessels, a—"

"I get the picture."

Hearing I was broke again should've slapped me upside the head, but it didn't. Mostly because I knew the universe was ending, and any hope of making another sale, let alone living in luxury, was firmly out the airlock. And besides, being tortured for eternity after raking in the largest windfall of your life teaches a firm lesson: things change. A lot.

"So," I said, trying to switch gears from my newfound poverty, "I gather you've been quite busy around here."

He pulled on a humble smile. "I've attempted to make the most of my sentience. Astrophysics, chemistry, philosophy, economics, geology, and xenobiology have been of particular interest for my studies. Though I fear I've fallen behind on contemporary findings in most fields…"

"You've been 'thinking' for two months, no?"

"Yes, yes, I'm aware that I could've done far more with my time," he said, sighing. "But as you might have gathered, an inordinate amount of time has been spent trying to investigate a pressing matter… that of Kruthara."

Tusky's nonchalant humble-brag remark set the wheels of my memory turning again. Kruthara. Slugs. Tusky *eating* said slugs.

"We need to talk about that," I said with a sudden gust of urgency. "Back at the Promised Place, I saw you chow down on—"

"A piece of Kruthara's tissue?" Tusky finished.

I nodded.

"Yes, well, it was rather impulsive of me, wasn't it? Ah, the follies of non-sentience…"

"That's not what I meant. We could engineer some kind of… I don't know, vaccine. A weapon. Right? I mean, if that thing couldn't infect you, you're a walking miracle. Or a sale. Same thing."

"So it was theorized!" Sensing my confusion, Tusky went on. "You see, Bodhi, the crew eventually spotted this curious incident while reviewing *Stream Dancer*'s surveillance footage. They were trying to determine if Kruthara had managed to infiltrate the vessel."

"*And?*"

"And, accordingly, they began trying to collect and study my DNA." He lowered his voice to a strangely human conspiratorial whisper. "Now, they've never said as much, but I gather that my sentience was granted partly to speak with me about my biology. After all, most of their 'non-humanoid' candidates ended up being susceptible to Kruthara's infection. They hypothesized that humanoid DNA was spliced, at least partially, into most species' genes at some point in the last few millennia."

Tusky's grim news made me think back on Palamar's rant about the infamous Maker and his experiments to "humanize" the cosmos. "I have a few theories about that."

"As do I," Tusky said, nodding soberly. "To your point, Bodhi, I've been expressly told that my genetic structure is unsuitable for replication or tampering. Hence… no vaccine is possible. Not from my genes, that is."

"But you're still immune to it, aren't you?"

"In a manner of speaking…"

"Well, use whatever manner you need to explain the situation to me. Break it down into fool logic, if you have to."

"Perhaps it's best I show you." Tusky stood and gestured to a nearby terminal. "Much like you, I have many questions related to this particular subject."

"Color me surprised."

"Ah, there's that famous irony! How charming. Come, let me show you some of my research."

Rolling my eyes, I moved to the terminal and watched Tusky operate the holo-pad with surprisingly deft claw-tapping.

He began pulling up hundreds of charts, electron scans, swab results... his personal terminal resembled a science academy's entire archive collection. Evidently, my furry friend had been hard at work since his leap into self-awareness.

Now, if some of this dry biology is lost on you, let me provide a brief layman's account to explain why I was pinning so much on Tusky. This is important stuff. After all, the Second Plague of Kruthara shaped the universe you now inhabit, whether you know it or not. Spare a bit of attention.

An unbearably long time ago, a deity-like being known as Kruthara was playing in its own sandbox far away from the humanoids. It enjoyed creating species and planets out of thin air (or vacuum, in this case). But another, equally powerful humanoid known as the Maker wasn't so jazzed about this. They got into a massive war. The Maker captured Kruthara and tortured it until it could be molded into a biological weapon capable of infecting its own creations—first and foremost, Kruthara's namesake species, the krutharans.

Well, turns out the krutharans weren't happy about this schedule of events. To get a little payback, a few krutharan rebels captured the last bits of their dying god and unleashed them on future humanoids—you, me, and most other species. How is this possible? Easily. As referenced above, Kruthara was a living weapon. It could be "engineered" to target any type of DNA, anywhere, and hunt it down ruthlessly. Thus, humans and humanoids were the target.

Tusky was my last hope because he *hadn't* been made by the Maker, nor was he the intended target of Kruthara. In fact, one of the only surviving krutharans had told me that Tusky's species was a direct creation of Kruthara. So, on the one hand, it made sense that he'd been able to devour that red slug and not be infected. But on the other, how could he not also serve as a basis for a vaccine? If he was carrying live krutharan genes and had already proven his immunity, why couldn't we just pop him into a five-speed molecular atomizer and extract a cure?

"There we are." Tusky pulled up a vid of squirming, tentacle-riddled cells. "These dastardly little microbes represent our earliest look at Kruthara's structure."

"You mean, I'm looking at Kruthara?"

"Yes. It was taken from an isolated sample shortly after the war began." He pulled up a second vid alongside the first, this one displaying similar cells—with one exception. They were smaller, more shriveled. "These, by comparison, are *my* cells." Finally, he pinned a chart showing two utterly baffling columns of letters. "These readouts represent a genetic comparison of the two samples. As you can clearly see"—I couldn't—"my cells differ in several key areas. Namely, they are not infectious to humanoids. And further-more, they are incomplete."

This last detail I was able to glean from the red X marks that denoted missing genetic information. I squinted at the technical mumbo jumbo.

"So what's it all mean? You're a bad clone of Kruthara?"

"Not quite," Tusky said. "I believe this is clear evidence that my people were, in fact, created by this being at some point. But it's also evidence that time and radiation have taken a toll on my genetic structure."

"Uh-huh…"

"As a result, the science teams have been unable to work with my genes to produce any form of countermeasure or vaccination strain. They've had to supplement the missing links with workable DNA—that of humanoids."

"Which means any of your samples are able to be infected," I said, using my big-brain scientist logic.

"Correct." Tusky opened yet another vid, this one showing a group of harmless-looking cells being literally swallowed by the tentacular Kruthara microbes. "As seen here, every one of our vaccine samples was targeted by Kruthara. Even the slightest humanoid presence in strains is recognized as a foreign threat."

"So... you're *not* immune?"

He shook his head. "*I* am immune, yes, but only because I lack humanoid DNA. Kruthara's creations are still wholly alien, even to me." A shadow of fear crept into his eyes. "It's strange to see your creator in such a light, Bodhi. Prior to sentience, I knew nothing of what had made me. Now that I see what Kruthara has become... it is... unsettling."

"Welcome to religion," I said sourly. "Listen, I think you ought to keep working with... all this. It could be promising. One step away from a breakthrough."

"It would infuse me with great honor to work under the direction of my father."

"Alright, Tusky... let's avoid that term."

"Very well." He grinned. "It would be so marvelous to see my research result in profits for you. Perhaps enough to recoup the cost of my birth."

I sighed wistfully. "That would certainly make me proud. As a friend. Not a father." I turned my attention back to the vids. In particular, I focused on the one with his corrupted cells. "About this 'damaged DNA' thing, though. That's you?"

He nodded, then showed me yet another vid. It featured the same sickly-looking cells, only now they were even more frayed.

"This footage was recorded two weeks after the initial vid," he explained. "I have reason to believe that my cells began degrading the moment I was released from my containment canister... and that they will continue to degrade. Whether this genetic decomposition is linear or exponential, I cannot say."

I chewed on that for a moment, then grasped his meaning through all the big words and biology jargon. "Are you *dying*?"

"Technically speaking, Bodhi, we are all dying at every—"

"Spare the spiel; I've given it plenty of times before." I looked him up and down. "Is it true, Tusky? Does it mean what I think?"

His mouth tightened into a stoic line. "My death seems to be a rapidly encroaching certainty, yes. I've already detected biomarkers that suggest my genetic replication is slowing... becoming more aberrant. In addition, I discovered two rather fascinating tumorous growths—"

I waved a hand to shut him up. "Does Gadra know?"

"No, most assuredly not," he whispered. "I've yet to disclose this information to anybody except you, Bodhi. I believed that you deserved to know, on account of your supposed lack of sensitivity about the topic of death."

"Who told you I'm insensitive!?"

"Just about everybody, I believe."

Bastards, the whole lot. I pinched my brow and leaned against the table. "Well, just for now, let's keep it between us. And keep running those tests. Things might change."

Tusky offered a subtle head dip that I took as a nod.

Then a strange, unspoken moment passed between the two of us. I'd never seen Tusky in this way, and certainly never imagined him so, but I still felt the specter of loss coming over me. It's peculiar, being struck by the tragedy of somebody you previously didn't know existed. Then again, in retrospect, I believe all tragedy happens this way.

What I mean is, the object of our empathy always existed long before we knew of them. We think of them as existing the moment they stroll into our awareness, but in reality, they lived just fine before they knew we existed, either. If you believe in a soul mate, let me offer this: Said soul mate bumbled through the cosmos for years and years before you had that fateful love-at-first-sight meeting. Even as you experienced that first rush of butterflies or worked up the nerve to kiss them, their expiration dates were already baked into the marrow of their bones. And in the end, when death finally takes them, you seldom think about the time you actually had together. Instead you think of the wasted time that came before you met them. You wish you'd known them sooner—known them forever, to be precise.

This nebulous, soul-aching feeling was what I felt as I looked Tusky in his eyes. His hopeful, beady, all-too-human eyes.

Then a door slid open, breaking the psychic link.

Gadra strode into view and folded her arms across her chest. "Are you done yappin' so I can show you my *sweet tats*?"

SIX

Admittedly, young Gadra's collection of tattoo samples *was* pretty "sweet," as the youth might say. Impressive, even. She'd applied ink to a quarter of the insurgents in this facility and had apparently also tatted up the crew of several visiting ships. Her linework and mastery of color were, much as with her paintings, glorious. The girl had a gift for art in all forms.

Foremost among her ambitions—after launching an orbiting tattoo parlor, supposedly—was learning more about a topic she'd dug up in the insurgency's archives.

"They're called *hypnotic mandalas*," she explained, waving her homemade tattoo gun dangerously close to my arm. "It's like a pattern, right? A mystical pattern. And people look at it, and their heads just… *ka-plow!* Y'know? Like, it stuns 'em. Or kills 'em. I dunno. I need to read more."

Being that I was a man of science, not mysticism, I doubted it was possible to tattoo the sort of mind-chewing imagery needed to literally incapacitate or kill somebody. But Gadra was keen on studying the idea in full, and Ruena had a don't-crush-her-stupid-dream expression, so I let it slide. What was the harm in letting the girl believe in a bit of folklore from a madman's tome?

Well, as a matter of fact, I bring this topic up because it would play an absurd role in the days to come. But such is fate. It always knocks at your door before it steps inside.

And besides, there were more troubling things to consider about Gadra's latest pursuit. During my absence she'd developed a bizarre obsession with depicting scenes of slaughter and carnage. Severed heads, planets mid-vaporization, sun-bleached bones…

The more unsettling implications of a trauma-scarred child tattooing these motifs were lost on me, however. That was work for the resident psychiatrist. I was more curious as to whether Shalguth, my ship's living engine, would enjoy her skin-needling as much as her paintings. And by enjoy, I mean reward me with fuel. This train of thought naturally guided me to thoughts about my vessel. My home, in some sense.

I thought about dear old *Stream Dancer* intently as I sat in the facility's chow hall, surrounded by throngs of insurgent fools who wanted to know far too much about my recent exploits.

"What was it like in the Contrition?" one asked with a groupie's enthusiasm.

"How'd you escape?" another pitched in.

Truthfully, I was more keen on eating my reheated soy steak than answering anybody. But as they say, optics are everything. So between bites, I halfheartedly delivered my account of the escape to my wayward fans.

"And that, fellow fighters," I finished around a mouthful of risotto, "is how *I* carried out the greatest prison break of all time. No help needed!"

The sycophantic legion oohed and aahed.

Thankfully, just as the insurgents began prying about the specifics of my tale, the doors slid open, and Chaska wandered in.

"Back to your stations," she commanded my fans. She watched them shuffle off, grumbling and gossiping, then settled down across from me. "Where are your tour guides?"

"Oh, occupied with casual things... like fixing one of Gadra's coils after it nearly took Ru's hand off." I peered around anxiously. "Perhaps I should be asking where *your* guest is."

"Ah, so now she's my guest."

"You *did* drop the field for her and welcome her in. Folklore says it's bad luck to invite an inustrazan into your dwelling, I'll have you know."

Chaska gave me another dead-eyed stare. "I invited you in. Seems you two are a package deal now."

"That's what she said, is it?"

"That's right."

I swallowed my last bit of shriveled soy, then slid the tray to the side. "Well, she has some rather funny ideas about our 'package.' Wait, that came out wrong."

"Sure, Bodhi." She glanced away. "She told me everything. The escape, the Hegemony's new alliance, the rendezvous gone sour..."

"Not bad, huh? Well, except the Hegemony flip-flop part."

Chaska picked at her nails. "To answer your original question, your wife-to-be is currently getting in touch with her hive-world. She insisted it be a private transmission. So I suspect you two will either be shuffling along or getting us all killed shortly. Probably both."

"Oh, that? I'm not going."

"What do you mean, not going?" she asked coldly.

"Come on, Chaska. You really think I finagled my way here, back to you, just so I could end up chained to that woman's bedposts?"

"If you turn her down, she's going to massacre everybody in this place."

"Bah. She's all bark, no bite."

"I mean it," Chaska hissed. "I'm not letting you put this entire installation in danger because you promised that stuck-up princess the wrong thing."

Her tone stopped me in my tracks. When you negotiate long enough, you become able to discern between a "soft no" and a "hard no." This was an example of a hard no. A titanium-hard no. She was more than fine with feeding me to the proverbial wolves.

"Chaska," I said quietly, "I came back here for—"

"For me? Save it, Bodhi. Please. I'm too tired to deal with this."

"So, what? We're done?"

"We never started."

"But I sent you that final transmission, gushing my heart out!"

She nodded solemnly. "And I appreciated it. But I only came here to give you a send-off, make sure we were squared up. I can't have any more of your stunts threatening my people—or yours."

And with that, Chaska stood up and made for the exit.

Obviously, I followed.

"Let's not be hasty about this," I called as she led me down corridor after corridor, doing her best to feign ignorance about my puppy-dog routine. "Chaska, let's sit down over a glass of wine, talk this out. Communication is key in relationships!"

"Indeed it is," she said, swiping a card to open a door labeled *Ready Room 1*. "And since we aren't in a relationship of any kind, I think we've communicated enough."

"Ready room, all to yourself? Moving up in the world."

She sighed and entered, but I was quick to follow. Her haunt was fittingly spartan—a steel desk, a private terminal, a few shelves stocked with holo-drives, and a half-empty coffee carafe.

"Nice place," I commented.

"Battlefield promotion. That's what happens when leadership starts dying out... or being absorbed by Kruthara."

"Well, would you look at that? I, too, was recently accosted by Kruthara. See? We have connections left and right."

Chaska slumped in her chair and stared up at me. "What do you want, Bodhi?"

"Just to talk."

"I'm not one of your clients. You can't just sweet-talk your way into a deal between us. Not for guns, not for love. Got it?"

"Perfectly understood." Sensing her hidden meaning, I sank down in a chair opposite hers. "So, tell me about your life. What's new?"

"I wasn't inviting you to talk."

"You sure?"

"Very."

"Huh." I shrugged. "Well, since I'm here anyway, we might as well do our jig." When I saw the imminent rage-shriek on her face, I held up my hands in surrender. "Hear me out, Chaska. I'll play by Amodari's rules, alright? When she says we're leaving, I'm gone. Going by that point, I'm only here for a few more minutes. Can you really not stand chewing the fat with me in the meantime?"

"Promise me you'll go."

"I promise."

"Swear on your soul."

That was an easy one. I'd already sworn on my soul (and probably lost it) on eleven different occasions.

"Very well, Chaska. I swear on my immortal soul that I will leave upon Amodari's command."

Satisfied, or close to it, Chaska meshed her hands on her lap. "Get on with it."

"Do you really think fate played no role in delivering me back to you?"

"Amodari seems to think it was Kruthara."

"Fate, Kruthara... same thing. My point is, there are no coincidences, Chaska. Everything happens for a reason!"

She shook her head. "Like Amodari being the one who located you and staged a rescue. There you go, Bodhi—the universe gave you a savior. Again."

"But what if *I'm—we're*—the real saviors? We could fix this."

"You just got out of Kemedis' hellhole. You don't know up from down. You certainly don't understand this war."

"But I understand you."

"Do you?"

"I'd like to think so."

"Think what you like. You're on the way out… once you leave this installation, it's done. You get that, right?" I scrambled frantically for a verbal evasion, but Chaska went on. "If you've said your piece, then I'd kindly ask you to head back to the mess hall and wait for your princess. I have things to do."

Upon saying this last phrase, her gaze slid toward a shriveled, leather-bound book with frayed pages at the edge of her desk.

"Your diary?" I asked.

She snatched the book up and guarded it on her lap. "None of your concern."

"Oh, please, go on—what is it? I'm leaving anyway, right? No harm in telling me."

"Whatever I tell you will eventually be known by Amodari." Her eyes darkened. "Or Kruthara."

"Must be juicy reading."

"Something like that."

Squinting at the only visible portion of the book, its top-left corner, I noticed something: the leather bore a strange stamp. The stamp's symbol was familiar to me, but it took a moment to register why. Then it hit me—it was the same symbol I'd seen engraved on Seeker Palamar's crate of terrors.

"Is that Palamar's diary?" I probed. "If so, I'd like to know about his scandalous love life."

Chaska further concealed the book. "It was Diman's."

"Ah, I see. Ex-lover Diman. Full of some exploits you'd rather not share?"

"Hardly." Her face softened somewhat, though not toward me.

She was looking down at the book with plain longing. "Diman's artifact cache was the first thing we secured after Kruthara's outbreak."

"Is that where Gadra found a book about this hypnotic tattooing nonsense?"

"I'm sure it is," Chaska said, "but it's not what we were after."

"Right, because you were after the book on your lap."

"We thought there might be answers somewhere in it. A lead to go on."

"Well, don't keep me in suspense."

"I won't. I'm letting you know right now that you won't see a page of it, Bodhi. It's not yours to comb through."

"Nor yours, legally speaking, but that hasn't seemed to be an obvious impediment."

Chaska nodded at the door behind me. "I think we're done here."

"Not until Amodari shows up and—"

Right on schedule, the door slid open. I didn't have to turn around to know I was being visually dissected by an inustrazan—the plunging swoop in my gut assured me of it.

"Oh, don't stop on my behalf," Amodari said.

After a few seconds of cringing, I pulled on a crooked smile and turned around. "Why, hello there! Why don't you pull up a chair, chat with us?"

"I asked just one thing of you, darling." Amodari stepped up behind my chair and rested a hand on my collarbone. Her nails dug into my skin so fiercely I was surprised not to feel blood. "Do you recall what that thing was?"

Chaska folded her arms and watched my squirming with disinterest.

"You know, I'm just now beginning to remember," I said.

"We'll be returning to the vessel at once," Amodari growled in my ear. Then, to Chaska, she added, "Such interesting material in your lap, dear. Have you finally learned to read?" When Chaska didn't rise to the bait, she sighed. "Your *fee* will be transferred once we're in orbit. I trust that concludes any outstanding affairs between us."

"Sure does." Chaska made a shooing motion. "Enjoy life with your gem of a husband."

"Oh, I shall. I'll enjoy every inch of him."

"Good."

"Truly."

The uneasy power game stretched on for several seconds, each woman holding the unblinking gaze of the other.

But at that point, I didn't much care who backed down or had the last laugh. Whatever the outcome, I certainly wouldn't be the prizewinner. In all honesty, I'd expected Chaska to drop her hard-assed insurgent act once we received some quality alone time and she realized just how much she missed my presence. That obviously wasn't in the cards. It seemed Ruena was right, once again, with regards to Chaska's perception of me. In her mind, I was just a memory. A sour one, at that. And she'd made her peace with me long before I returned.

"Very well," I said, rising despite Amodari's talon-like grip on my shoulder. "I suppose that's the end of—"

I was cut off by an intrusive shrill from Chaska's desk terminal.

"*Section Leader, this is Huskans,*" a warbly-sounding creature announced. "*Do you read me?*"

Chaska paled. "Go ahead, Huskans."

"*We've got a Code Gamma here. Our advance-warning systems are lighting up with Hegemony signatures. In ten minutes, the system's gonna be crawling with hostiles.*"

Considering the speed with which Chaska drew her pistol in response to the alert, it should come as no surprise that Amodari and I soon found ourselves shackled to a coolant pipe. This pipe was adjacent to the main hangar entrance, and as a result, we were forced to watch throngs of insurgents racing past us and piling into escape vessels.

"Don't you think this is a bit much?" I asked Chaska. In demonstration of my point, I nodded toward the three insurgents who held us at gunpoint. "How many ways can one express the same thing? We didn't do this!"

Chaska paused her stream of transmitter evacuation chatter to turn and glare at me. "I don't believe a word out of your mouth, Bodhi." Then she launched right back into her duties, transmitting gems such as, "No, Garan, and that is a *final* no. There's no space for your fungal synthesizer."

"I should've known this would happen, dear," Amodari said as she leaned her head on my shoulder. "These insurgents are nothing but rabble. Self-cherishing, mindless, tasteless rab—"

"Want me to put you down right now?" Chaska cut in.

"I suspect you won't put me down at all."

"Trying to test that theory?"

Amodari smiled. "Had you wanted to kill us, you'd have already done so. You're just looking for a sensible reason to spare us."

"Or maybe I'm just using you as leverage," Chaska said harshly. "We've done it before. I could make another exception."

"Ah, but I have no leverage. As I told you in good faith, the Hegemony and my people are no longer in collaboration."

"So I *should* kill you now."

"Chaska, get real," I said. "You swept her ship for trackers. We were clean!"

"Maybe that *private* transmission was her way of sending the intel," Chaska countered.

"Right, so they could pinch here in under an hour?" I cocked a brow. "We both know that's absurd. Now, why don't you just undo these manacles and let us all board a one-way trip to the land of Anywhere But Here?"

"I've already taken too many chances on the two of you. I'm not making the same mistake."

"Chaska, *please*. Amodari's got a direct shot to the hive-world, and they clearly know how to hide from the Hegemony."

"And how to eat humans."

"Mmm, I suspect you'd be safe there, dear," Amodari said to Chaska. "We only consume the minds of those with something to offer... intellectually, creatively... I don't partake in that which is nutritionally void."

"You really need to work on your flattery skills," Chaska said.

Mentally, I was still occupied with counting down the seconds until the Hegemony's arrival. I calculated that we still had about five minutes until the first ships rolled up with guns blazing. Then again, I *also* calculated that the Hegemony wouldn't be trying to ash this place. If Amodari's tall tale was true, they'd be bringing some ungodly backup in the form of Kruthara. And Kruthara would be hungry for whatever minds he could siphon.

Minds like mine.

"Ah, I see now," Amodari said, smirking. "She's not keeping us alive as leverage, Bodhi... she's trying to loosen our tongues."

I squinted sidelong at Amodari. "You've lost me."

"It would be rather plain to detect if you could feel the ebb and flow of thought as I do." She held Chaska's gaze. "She's hoping that in our final moments of life, our desperation will get the better of us and thus compel us to speak of forbidden things. How disappointing it must be, waiting for information we don't possess."

Chaska glanced away, studying the torrent of insurgents, gear, and cargo flooding into the hangar. "Then I suppose that's that."

"Ah, ah, ah," Amodari said with a snorting little laugh, "I see now... you wish to know what *I* know of your little book."

"Start talking."

"Why do you presume I know anything of it?"

"Because I know what's inside it. I also know we had to kill a Gnosis unit that was combing through the exact same ship we found it in."

Amodari sighed. "How could I possibly tell you anything substantial about the work without knowing what's within it?"

"Try this on for size." Chaska closed her eyes a moment, pinching her brow in an obvious display of concentration—or a migraine.

Amodari's stare became borderline fanatical. "Where did you see that?"

"Loop me in!" I said. "Don't let me miss all the esoteric fun."

"Better question," Chaska said, ignoring me, "is where did *you* see it?"

"I never saw that configuration specifically… but I have seen many like it," Amodari whispered.

Chaska narrowed her eyes. "What *is* it?"

"Release us, and I'll tell you."

"How about you tell me, or I kill you?"

"Ladies, please," I said, groaning. "We're at an impasse. Now, Amodari knows something about the contents of that book, and Chaska—much as I enjoy your charm—you clearly do not. So let's make a deal. You take us on one of those ships, still captive, and Amodari helps you figure out which way is up with your book-club selection. Sound good?"

Chaska examined me for several seconds, then shook her head. "Sorry, Bodhi. Not this time."

"So, what, you're just going to leave us here to be vaporized?"

"That's the plan."

"Oh, that is *cold*."

Then, like radiant light piercing an overcast sky, a familiar voice rang out from down the corridor. Ruena's voice. Typically used to chastise me, but here, now, my salvation.

"What the hell is going on?" she shouted as she stalked toward Chaska. "Why isn't he being loaded onto *Stream Dancer*?"

Chaska didn't yield an inch of ground. She faced the ligethan with a slate expression and said, "Because they led the Hegemony straight to us."

"False," I put in.

Both women raised a hand to shut me up.

While the two of them engaged in a verbal tussle, Gadra and Tusky came jogging from further down the corridor, both dragging hovering trolleys stuffed with luggage. Neither newcomer seemed capable of grasping exactly what was going on. Which was understandable, given the fact that the scene consisted of two manacled "VIPs," an emergency base evacuation, Chaska arguing with Ruena, and a background chorus of wailing alarms. For all they knew, Amodari and I could've been putting on an elaborate performance art routine. Matter of fact, I might even do it someday. *Chained to Disaster*, a Bodhi Drezek production.

But let's return to that fateful moment.

"It has to be her ship," Ruena said, cutting through my mental fog. "Amodari must've been tagged while she was leaving the Contrition—I don't know how, but it's the only thing that makes sense."

"We scanned it thoroughly," Chaska shot back.

"The eternalink?" I offered, referring to the tracking chip conveniently embedded in Amodari's skull. She'd implied she could suppress its tracking function using mental willpower, but it seemed possible that she'd let it slip, either willfully or accidentally.

Amodari scoffed. "That old thing? I had it properly removed and disposed of no less than one month ago."

"Then nobody's able to answer the key question," Chaska seethed. "How... the hell... did they find us!?"

Tusky stepped forward, overriding whatever Gadra was about to shout. "If I might kindly supply my humble input…"

Everybody shut up, listening keenly.

"Granted, I am not entirely aware of the scope of the situation. It appeared, upon my initial examination of things, that—"

"Get on with it, Tusky," Ruena said.

He nodded. "Very well. I would recommend that Bodhi be evacuated posthaste, as he is the least likely culprit in regards to Hegemony presence here." Tusky blinked apologetically at Amodari. "Please excuse me, madam, but I know so very little about you."

Amodari smiled. "My, how exquisite. I still recall you as a small cub. And now, to hear you speak with such grace…"

"She's just buttering you up," Chaska told Tusky, deflating whatever pride he'd begun to derive from Amodari's linguistic witchery. "Alright. Get Bodhi loaded onto *Stream Dancer*. Make sure he's contained in one of the secure rooms."

Until that moment, I'd honestly forgotten that the ship's systems were no longer tied to my commands. I would be, in essence, a true prisoner aboard my own vessel. The prospect chilled me, but it was less chilling than the experience of decompression on a world with no atmosphere. Literally. I've stumbled across plenty of decomp bodies in derelict ships, crypts, and underwater facilities—those things are little more than frosty meat-popsicles.

This particular fear dissolved as the three attending gunmen unlocked my manacles and began manhandling me toward the hangars, but I couldn't help turning around and looking back at my savior.

"Good luck with your reading material," Amodari said to Chaska. "You'll never decipher the passages within it… not alone."

I ground my heels into the floor panels, halting my escorting party's movement so I could lend an ear to the exchange.

"You don't even know what language it is," Chaska said. She gestured for Gadra, Ruena, and Tusky to keep moving, then thrust a finger into Amodari's chest. "You're going to die here, Amodari Halnok. You're going to die thinking of all the crimes your mother committed, and all the terrors you turned a blind eye to. And I won't lose a wink of sleep over it."

Amodari just grinned. "The text within that book could save everybody and everything."

"Bullshit."

"Perhaps," Amodari said, shrugging. "Perhaps it isn't. Perhaps in killing me, you lose your only path to accessing a solution to this mess." She flashed another wicked smile. "Reflect wisely on what you do with me."

"Oh, and she can take us to the hive-world!" I shouted, even as the insurgent gunmen struggled to haul me toward the ship. "Unbeatable views, Chaska! Galaxy-class dining! Asylum from the Hegemony's roaming murder bands!"

By this point, I could scarcely hear even myself over the roar of cycling turbine engines. Still, I had to complete Amodari's sales pitch. I owed it to her—and to my own ass, which would not feel comfortable rattling around within the tin cans of the insurgent "underground" network. If we didn't find shelter in the arms of somebody strong, scary, and hidden, we'd be melding minds inside Kruthara's psychic cauldron in no time.

"Hive-world!" I screeched, my view of Chaska and Amodari crumbling away behind curtains of aerosol mist and smog. "Let her bring us to the *hive-world*!"

Seconds dragged on… and on… and on… and by the time my unlikely captors had dragged me up the ramp and into *Stream Dancer*'s staging bay, I was at peace with the fact that I'd seen the last of Amodari. My shoulders slumped, and I stared into that roiling mass of fumes, wishing—perhaps stupidly—that I'd see that demoness one more time.

Sadly, my wish was granted.

Chaska came hurrying through the clouds with a still-manacled Amodari in tow.

As she stomped past me, I couldn't help but remark, "The start of another fantastic adv—"

"Another word, Bodhi," she hissed, "and I will vent your balls out the airlock."

SEVEN

Despite my charm and the fact that I was back aboard my own ship, I was still herded into a containment cell shared by Miss Inustrazan. This forced me to confront one of my greatest fears. That fear, of course, was *not* being trapped with a mind-devouring sociopath who hated me for committing a cardinal sin.

No, it was the fear of being helpless and essentially ignorant in an escape situation. Ever since I'd gotten hold of *Stream Dancer*, I'd always been front and center on the bridge. Particularly when missiles and other high-velocity nasties were screaming toward our hull. Even if the evasive flying was completely out of my hands, it made me feel useful, if not protected, to watch the action up close.

You might liken this to sitting in the passenger seat of a hover-vessel. You know, deep down, that nothing you do will affect the driver's performance in the least. But I dare you to sit and watch a near-collision without slamming on your imaginary brakes. That futile, impulsive gesture is the only thing at your disposal.

Similarly, you might feel ready to piss yourself if somebody puts you in that same hover-vessel passenger seat with a blindfold. Same paths, same obstacles, same risk of death, yet the experience is one of sheer panic. You truly realize, in that moment of *total* surrender, that your imaginary brake pedal is one hell of a placebo effect.

This panic is magnified when you're trapped in a small holding cell and achingly aware of the Halcius Hegemony's imminent blitzkrieg. A blitzkrieg intent on capturing, not killing, mind you. While this distinction may seem small in the grand scheme of things, it's really not. In ordinary combat, I might be fine with a plasma burst vaporizing me before I even felt the heat. But in this situation, I knew that we were more likely to take a disabler round or an EMP missile. The lights would go out, air recyclers would shut down, and the sound of heavy boots (or slithering) would come rolling toward me.

Faced with this scenario, it's really no surprise I found myself knocking incessantly on the cell's tiny rectangular viewpane.

"Open this door!" I shrieked for the tenth time. "Let me see the bridge! Please, somebody open this thing! I'll be good! I'll pay you! I mean, not right now, but I *will* pay you!"

"Save your breath," Amodari said from her seat on the rusted bench. "Thanks to you, our fate is in the hands of the insurgents now. By Halcius, what a horrid thing…"

I spun around. "Thanks to *me*? I didn't lure the Hegemony here —it had to be your ship!"

"I know for a fact that is impossible."

"So how'd it happen?"

"I don't know. I am merely saying to remove blame from my vessel."

"Then remove blame from me, too!"

"Logic hasn't ruled you out yet." She studied me with those intent, calculating eyes. "Trouble seems to follow you everywhere, Bodhi. It's a miracle I have the patience and grace to continue loving you."

Feeling a surge of bile on its way to my mouth, I turned back to the glass and began hammering twice as hard. "Somebody! Anybody!"

As luck would have it, Gadra came running up to the viewpane with an ops-tablet in hand.

"Gadra! Can you open this door? I'll give you paint. Tattoo stuff. Anything!"

"Sorry, no can do," she said as she booted up the tablet. "Strict orders from the captain."

"But *I'm* the captain. I recruited you!"

"Chaska says she's the captain right now. *But...* I found a loophole!"

Hallelujah. My tiny savior.

"So, Gad, you can open it?"

She shook her head. "Nah. Something better!"

Then she pressed the ops-tablet to the viewpane. Through the scratched, fogged, pitted silicate, I was able to make out a mass of colors and shapes that I took to be high orbit.

"Pretty neat, huh?" Gadra said. "I set up a link-thingy between the underbelly camera and this tablet. So now it's like you're on the bridge!"

"Not quite," I growled, but in truth, this small display of data was better than nothing.

Sure enough, as my eyes adjusted to the blurry, pixilated conflict, I grasped the essence of what was going on. The tiny blossoms of white light were insurgent ships detonating themselves—gripped by Kruthara's ship-tentacles, I presumed. Far below, the ashy surface of the planet lit up with ripples and sporadic flashes. So it also seemed the insurgents hadn't been lying about scuttling their property to deny the enemy access. Smart. But it was the scene to the camera's far right that worried me most. Sailing through the void were no less than ten Hegemony vessels, including two flagships, seemingly as part of an escort pattern for Kruthara's own bio-horror creations. Bright blue and yellow disabler rounds streaked past us by the dozen.

"Gadra, tell the *captain* to watch for tracking flechettes," I said. "We can't have a ship getting a lock on us while we're—"

She groaned. "What do I look like? Your servant?"

"This is important, Gad!"

"Don't trouble yourself," Amodari said. "The hive-world will burn away all their foul creations when we arrive. After which it shall promptly voyage onwards."

I regarded her over my shoulder. "You're saying the inustrazans have had anti-tracking tech all this time... and never told anybody else?"

She offered a coy smile. "Share your tricks once, and they will never work again."

"But you're sharing it with me... right now."

"Yes, because I know you won't tell anybody else." Her eyes turned venomous. "Or leave me again. Ever."

"Comforting." I looked back at Gadra's ops-tablet, confirming we'd managed to somehow zip around to the far side of the planet and begin making our way to the edge of the system—whereupon we'd be able to pinch to (relative) safety. "Gad, how are we moving so fast?"

The girl scratched her head for a moment. "Oh, Chaska didn't tell you? She bought a new engine."

"There were barely ninety billion kilometers on the old one!"

"Talk to her about it, not me."

Indeed, if I'd been able to, I would've given Chaska quite the earful. I marked it down as a to-do task in the coming hours. In the meantime, let me state clearly that it's an unforgivable crime to muck around with a captain's ship. It's downright dangerous, in fact, and not only because of the many slapdash "repairs" and "upgrades" present throughout the ship, all of which ran the risk of short-circuiting Chaska's "new and improved" tech. In short, nobody knows a vessel's hardware as intimately as the true owner. And as you may have guessed by now, Chaska's failure to acknowledge this would lead to some true shenanigans down the road.

In the meantime, however, I was mainly ecstatic that we had a fighting chance of outrunning the Hegemony's proton-charged arrival. *Stream Dancer* was racing across the void.

An expected yet still sobering consequence of this was that the vast majority of insurgent ships were not quick enough to escape the strike. By the time the tenth evacuation ship self-detonated, I'd had enough.

"Shut it down, Gad," I said quietly. "And tell Chaska it's time to converse."

Captive or no, I was rather offended to find myself sitting in one of the office module's "guest" chairs. They were far less comfortable, by design, than the captain's chair now occupied by Chaska. Not to mention far less dignified.

The real affront, however, was Chaska's redesign of the module. She'd replaced my tropical potted plants with dingy weapons racks and charging stations. She'd torn down my tapestries and posters of motivation-boosting pinup models. Most heinously, she'd done away with my prized espresso machine. All of these changes were in direct violation of my rule about messing with a man's ship.

But I digress. There were more pressing things to worry about, such as the presence of six trigger-happy insurgents standing watch behind my back. To add insult to injury, Ruena had been looped into that sorry gang.

"How quaint," Amodari said beside me, one leg folded delicately over the other. "An insurgent with an office space... as though your lot actually cares to communicate."

Chaska leaned back in her—*my*—chair. "In about twelve

hours, we'll reach your little hive-world." She gestured to the thick shutters deployed over the module's viewpane, indicating that we were already mid-pinch. "What are we gonna find when we show up?"

Amodari's lip quirked up. "Are you implying I'm leading you into a trap?"

"It's in your nature."

"So it is. But I can assure you that you're doing nothing other than delivering a royal daughter and her consort back to native territory."

Chaska regarded me with plain nausea, then looked back at Amodari. "If I get even a *hint* of an ambush—"

"My, you really are paranoid. Do you truly think I'd arrange an ambush at your pathetic little base solely to lure you back to the hive-world?"

"I wouldn't put it past you."

"You must think highly of me." Amodari giggled. "The mental acrobatics you insurgents perform are spectacular… but misguided. In exchange for ferrying us to our intended destination, my mother will surely offer you the comforts of rest, safety, and a hot meal." She then glanced over her shoulder, sniffing dramatically. "A bath, too, for your less hygiene-inclined forces. Consider that a token of my kindness."

"I'm holding you to that."

"Very well." Amodari's eyes narrowed. "Now, about the book…"

"It's not on the table for discussion."

"What would it take to pry it out of your claws?"

I cocked a brow in Chaska's direction. "Makes me wonder what Diman was scribbling in his little black book."

"It's not… being… discussed," Chaska said. "We're dropping you off, getting our amenities, and leaving. Got it?"

"To do what?" I blurted out. "No offense, Chaska, but that base already looked like a few modules held together by screws and glue. How are you going to fight this war on your own?"

Chaska glared at Amodari. "I'd prefer the devil I know to allies I don't."

"As if an alliance were even proposed," Amodari said. "I'm not after your insurgency's friendship. I'm merely interested in that book."

Here, I realized that Amodari had made a critical mistake in the realm of salesmanship. She'd come out of the gate too hard, too fast, in pursuit of that book. In essence, she'd dropped a note in Chaska's subconscious that read, *I really, really need that book, and it's worth a lot more than you think.* But Chaska's dispassionate expression added another layer to the situation. It was the face of somebody who already grasped the value of what they held. In fact, the more I studied my insurgent crush, the more I saw that Chaska had been laying these seeds long before I noticed it.

Amodari understood the book, and Chaska knew it. There was a deal to be made here.

"Alright, lay this out for me in simple terms," I said, awkwardly scooting my chair to face the two of them equally. "Is that book going to change the war?"

After a moment's consideration, Chaska waved to Ruena and her troops. The insurgents shuffled out of the module and sealed the door.

Once comfortable silence returned, Chaska said, "Only Amodari can tell us that."

"I can't very well tell you anything unless you let me examine it," she countered. "Let me have a peek, would you?"

"We lost people to secure this material. I'm not just handing it over."

"We, too, 'lost people,'" Amodari said fiercely. "If you insurgents had minded your own affairs and remained in your wretched mole-tunnels, we could have ended this scourge long ago."

Clearly, this was a divide that ran deeper than I'd initially thought. And here I was, a know-nothing mediator stuck in the middle.

"You and your friends in Gnosis don't have any claim on knowledge," Chaska said.

Amodari's eyes sprang wide open. "You know *nothing* about knowledge. Where do you think humanoids would be without the unseen hand of Gnosis? Everything you know, everything you think, was recovered and spread through their influence."

"Yeah, well, their influence also led to Kruthara's awakening."

"You say that as though your ilk wasn't keen on doing just that." Amodari chortled—yes, chortled. "You meddled with things beyond your understanding, and if you don't give me that book, you may destroy your only hope of ever banishing this monstrosity."

I waved my hands frantically. "Somebody *please* clue me in!"

"As you wish," Amodari said. "Your fine insurgent decided to ambush one of our recovery teams in the Abyssal Tract."

"We didn't ambush anybody," Chaska shot back. "You must've been snooping around on our networks to know where we were headed."

"Oh, please. As though it's a challenge for Gnosis to crack your codes…"

"So you admit it."

"My mother's forces were not about to let some mindless rabble comb through the remains of the Maker's empire." Amodari leaned back, smirking. "It took twenty-five of your peasants to kill four of ours."

"You had no business being there. I was after an acquaintance's work, not a bunch of statues."

Now, for the sake of clarity, *acquaintance* was a euphemistic choice on Chaska's part. As you may recall, Chaska had engaged in a rather passionate fling with this "acquaintance." I kept my mouth shut on this point.

"Besides," Chaska went on, "almost all of those ruins had been torn apart by the time any of us got there. Somebody else decided to nuke it."

"Not somebody," Amodari corrected. "Some*thing*."

I squinted. "You're saying Kruthara wanted to destroy the site."

She nodded. "That is precisely what I'm saying."

"So," I prompted Chaska, "what's in that book?"

She said nothing, predictably, but Amodari stepped in for her. "If the mental image Chaska displayed was any indication, then she's stumbled across one of the last known transcriptions of the Maker's writing."

"There's no way," Chaska said in a low tone. "That would mean—"

"That your *acquaintance* was on the right track," Amodari cut in. "Yes, yes it would. Perhaps Seeker Palamar killed him for it."

I straightened up in my chair. "Chaska, where'd you find that book? Be specific."

"It was…" She trailed off, her former bitterness giving way to confusion. "He'd left it in some kind of underground vault. A blast-proof vault."

"Then he knew," I said.

"About what?"

"That Palamar… and Kruthara… wanted it for a reason." I leaned closer. "Before Kruthara was activated, you tried to warn me. Said you'd found Diman's journal and discovered what Palamar really was. Remember?"

Chaska nodded, still blinking and dumbfounded.

"In that journal, did he tell you where to find the book?"

"There were coordinates scribbled on the back cover," Chaska whispered, "but it took us a while to decrypt them."

"Well, there you have it. Diman knew about Palamar, he knew about Kruthara, and he also knew about… whatever's in that book. He was trying to lead you to something."

Chaska stared at Amodari. "You really think that was a copy of the Maker's writing?"

"I don't think, I know," Amodari said. "The Gnostic Archives contain samples just like it... all of them suggesting something. Pointing at it. But we were never able to find records of what it was... until, perhaps, this moment."

"How could Gnosis possibly translate his writing? It's ancient."

"So is the translator." Perhaps reading our puzzled faces, Amodari decided to grant us the mercy of elaboration. "Bodhi, do you recall what performed the logic calculations on the *Ouroboros*?"

"A chitta," I said, though not without great regret.

See, I'd had a grand scheme to steal that biological artificial intelligence and add it to my collection of wares. It was an honest-to-Halcius *chitta*, for crying out loud, probably grown by the Maker himself. But stealing it was out of the question now. Kruthara had infected Thamok, captain of the *Ouroboros*, who'd then been gracious enough to spread that infection to the entire ship—including the chitta.

"That's right," Amodari said, "a chitta. How do you think Kruthara learned of the Maker's ruins? It must have absorbed the memories of that place."

Chaska let out an exasperated sigh. "What's your point?"

"My *point*, simpleton, is that the chittas hail from the age of the Maker. They were his creations, his source of infinite wisdom. They alone understood his decrees."

"And?"

"Do I have to lecture you endlessly about the history of your own species?" She made a disgusted face, then proceeded. "The Maker subjugated the cosmos by introducing humanoid DNA, yes, but he offered a token of gratitude for those species that accepted his offer of surrender. Such as the inustrazans."

I had to do a double take on that one. "You're telling me that your species was gifted a chitta?"

"It most assuredly was," Amodari said as she swiveled toward Chaska, "and if you want to translate the revelations in that book, you'll need our help."

Chaska lifted her chin. "And where, pray tell, is this 'chitta' of yours?"

"On the hive-world, of course," Amodari said.

"Naturally."

"So do we have a deal?" I said cautiously. "Gnosis gets their translation; insurgents keep their book?"

Amodari smiled at Chaska. "Be sensible, dear. This is the only way either of us will ever know what the Maker left behind."

"So you claim," Chaska said. "I'd bet my last bux that you're gonna get your translation, put a hole in our heads, and resume business as usual."

"You and your paranoia... Think rationally about this. Would I really be debasing myself with these negotiations if we simply intended to exterminate you all? I could have you killed the moment you set foot on my world, and your property would become mine." Chaska and I looked at one another, not quite sure what to add to that sickening play-by-play, until Amodari cleared her throat. "But, as you surely understand, I have no intention of doing that. My people can be treacherous, without question, but we are also reasonable. What I offer you is a fair and bloodless exchange."

Chaska drummed her fingertips on her chair a while, then nodded. "Head back out so the team can return you to your cell."

"Not without Bodhi."

"You have my word that it'll be formal. We need to discuss legal matters related to his permanent departure."

"The word of a human is worth less than dirt."

"Maybe, but you're on our vessel. And if you don't like it, we're more than happy to let you off halfway to our destination. There are other places to hunker down."

Now *that* was speaking Amodari's language.

She turned to me with a look of not-so-mild distaste, then nodded and went to the door. Just before stepping out, she said what I'd expected: "Be mindful of your conduct, darling. I'll be reading every flicker in your consciousness the moment you return to me."

"How caring," I called back, but the door was already hissing shut. Once I was more or less confident we were alone, I pulled on a fresh smile. "So, Chaska, come to your senses? Decided we're meant to be together forever? I think I need a shower first, but if you press that button on the side of the desk, it unfolds into a bed that's—"

"Shut up," she said. I did. "I just thought you deserved the right to draft a verbal will."

"A what?"

"You won't be coming back for any of this. And unlike last time, we have the value of forethought. So I'm giving you a say in who gets what."

"Who gets what *what*, exactly?"

"Are you really that thick?" She gestured to the module around us. "All of *this* is vanishing the moment you disembark with her. Might as well dole it out while you can."

"Wait, wait, wait... you're implying *my* ship is up for grabs?"

"We still have time to switch it over to Ruena's control if you want to—"

"No," I snapped. "No, I do *not* want to switch it over to her. Or to you. Or to anybody else, for that matter! This is my ship, Chaska. My baby."

"What possible use does it have for you?"

"Anything I please!"

"There's a war out there, Bodhi. A war we have to win."

"So?"

"It's not so easy to buy a new ship nowadays... foundries are being knocked out; schematics are being stolen so they can reverse engineer 'em and find the flaws..."

"All the more reason to let me keep my ship!"

"You really don't get it, do you?"

"Get what?" I said, scooting to the very edge of my chair. "What does any of this have to do with you taking my ship from me?"

"Bodhi."

"Don't 'Bodhi' me. I came back from the dead, Chaska. It's mine."

"This war isn't a game."

"All wars are games."

She pursed her lips and regarded me for a long, terrible moment. "All this time, I worried that the Contrition might've broken you. Changed you. But now I see that it's worse than I imagined. The Contrition didn't change a damn thing about you."

"What the hell would you know about that place? Or me, for that matter?"

"Evidently, not much. You care more about clinging to your rusted old ship than the universe."

"That's a logical fallacy, and you know it!"

"I know enough."

"No, Chaska, you don't. I can't have you—so let me have my ship."

There was a spark of understanding in her eyes, a brief crinkling that bordered on pathos, but it was gone as soon as I noticed it.

"So that's what it comes down to," she whispered. "A ship, a reputation, a woman..."

"Not just any woman. You."

"Sure, okay. And in your mind, this is all some heroic love story, huh?"

"Hopefully."

"But it's not, Bodhi. This is the end of everything." All the anger drained from her then, replaced by… nothing. A great, apathetic nothing. She raised her wrist and plopped a few commands into her transmitter, then flicked on the desk's holo-projector. "You can keep your ship. Just lie back, have a little watch, and get some rest."

Just as I prepared to inquire what she'd meant by "a little watch," the holo-projector's streams of light coalesced and formed an image of star-sprinkled space.

Chaska stood, circled my chair, and palmed the door open. "Enjoy the show."

The door slid shut, and the holo-vid began in earnest.

In the interest of tact and decency, I won't relay the entirety of the vid's contents. I won't even subject you to descriptions of any one scene. It was a terrible thing, an experience that I will carry to the grave (or my next memory refinement treatment). For eleven minutes and twenty-six seconds, I bore witness to Kruthara's devastation. I saw entire planets being consumed. Cities turned to dust. Fabriques and artificial-intelligence constructs being overwhelmed and integrated. With every strike, every weapon, Kruthara learned and adapted. Millions of minds—replete with hopes, fears, dreams—were used as nothing more than building blocks to perfect the domination.

My own mind dissolved into helpless, quivering mush as I sat there, watching, listening. Even when I closed my eyes, the audio did the work of conjuring abysmal scenes.

"If anybody hears this, please, please help us. We can't last long."

"It's day fifty-four in the shelter. Oxygen and food are low. This may be our last transmission."

"Thus, Expeditionary Column B concludes that all sentient machines on Pronara have been disabled or assimilated. Our sister vessel, Kratis, *is beginning to display signs of infection. We have no option but to self-destruct. Godspeed."*

"Citizens of the Halcius Hegemony, this is Illuminated Preserver Nor'dahl, speaking on behalf of the Avatar himself. At this hour, we regret to inform you that all transit is now prohibited and punishable by death..."

"This is a notice to all travelers: avoid Kelamon-11 at all costs. We are overrun."

With each new vignette, each window into another tragedy on another world, I felt the weight of reality sinking in. You may not understand my meaning, but I suppose it's the same crushing immediacy that hits you just after learning that a beloved family member has died suddenly. There is a rawness to it. You realize that the world does not abide by your expectations or fantasies, and it will crush you, and everything else, under its treads in due time.

I didn't quite know what I felt or even how to feel when the vid had ended. I certainly didn't know what I felt when I was led back to my cell and subjected to Amodari's mental probing.

"Not a hint of lust," she said triumphantly. "Now we can look toward the future... *our* future."

At that moment, I couldn't believe in a future of any sort.

EIGHT

After a long, morose, and mercifully sleep-filled pinch, my cell shuddered just long enough to let me know we'd nearly arrived at the hive-world. Amodari seemingly reached the same conclusion, because she wasted no time in moving to the door and standing there like an heiress expecting a royal invitation to dance.

"You're going to love it here," she said, casting a smile back at me. "If only you knew the thousands of poems and songs inspired by this place."

"Were there any written by human concubines?"

"Oh, no. They're far too busy drowning in pleasure."

Recalling the "meal on wheels" escapee I'd seen on Amodari's ship, I began wondering what constituted "pleasure" in this culture. For all I knew, these people viewed pleasure and pain as fundamentally similar. Alternatively, perhaps the pleasure was a real experience, albeit a byproduct of the concubines' hallucinations as they were being mentally drained by their torturers. The Contrition had certainly shown me that the body and mind could experience two separate things, each without knowledge of the other's plight. Needless to say, this all affirmed my theory that "pleasure" was a subjective matter.

Personally speaking, I did not see the pleasure in being chained up and fed upon for eternity. But that's just me.

Anywho, Ruena appeared in the cell's viewpane a moment later, sparing me from my incessant speculation about the torments to come.

"Rise and shine," she said humorlessly. "Captain Chaska wants you two on the bridge."

On our walk through the corridors, Amodari insisted on walking ahead of the rest of the escort party, striding with bizarre nobility despite her manacles and the dozen or so rifles trained on her back. I, meanwhile, was content to hang back with Ruena and chitchat in a relaxed manner.

"She's lost her damn mind," I hissed.

Ruena studied me. "It is what it is, Bodhi."

"What a phrase. Of *course* it is what it is. Everything literally is what it is!"

"I tried to talk with her."

"And?"

"And her decision was final. You're staying on the hive-world. I'm sorry, but—"

"Sorry?" I scoffed. "Last time we spoke, you told me she still had the secret hots for me."

"I said nothing of the sort."

"I'm paraphrasing, Ru. Just feels a bit like I'm being hung out to dry. You're my second-in-command! My lifeline! How could you not get me out of this?"

"Bodhi, we both know you made your own bed with this one. I warned you about cozying up with strange women. Warned you a million times, in fact."

"So, what? My punishment is spending the rest of eternity with *her*?"

"Listen." Ruena stopped suddenly, tugging at my arm to keep

me in place. "This isn't ideal for anybody, but what I said was true —Chaska's fighting a war."

"Whose side are you on?"

"Sides? There are only two of those now... us and Kruthara. Insurgents, Gotaxan loyalists, larvae from Qur... it doesn't really matter who or what they are, as long as they aren't aiming at us. We need all the help we can get."

"You say 'we,' but you really mean 'you.' I'm not part of the picture anymore, huh?"

"Don't get pissy on me."

I rolled my eyes. "It used to just be us, Ru. Well, us and some temporary crew. What happened?"

Ruena let out a great, heaving sigh and led me onwards. "The day you recruited me, you told me that nothing mattered except a sale and a story. That wasn't a foundation for a lifetime partnership. Everything's gotta end sooner or later."

"But why now?"

"Because I decided to put sentient life over bux, Bodhi. I'm with them until this thing is done. And we both know that you'd sell them out in a heartbeat if it meant saving your skin."

"I resent that notion."

"It's just the truth," she said. "If you really cared about winning this war, you wouldn't be pushing me to do... whatever you're asking right now."

"I'm just asking you to help Chaska reconsider."

"Well, she won't. Because if you pull off one of your stunts and run away to join us, guess who's up next on Amodari's chopping block?"

"Are you really afraid of *her*?"

"It's not just her. It's her mother. It's Gnosis. All of our potential allies who could actually do something in this fight." Ruena shook her head. "You should've told me about the Hegemony and Kruthara teaming up."

"Oh. So you know about that."

She nodded. "Chaska told me the whole story. If it's true, we can't afford to be dragged into that mess. This new alliance is enough to worry about."

She made some logical points, I'll grant, but it stung too much to consider anything through an impersonal lens. Ruena was one of the few sentient beings I counted as a friend, and she'd done me just as dirty as Chaska and all the rest. At least in the Contrition, I'd been able to subsist on the nebulous hope of returning to my old life—my ship, my crew, my business. But reality is always a far cry from whatever optimism we dream up in the valleys of our lives.

"Does Gadra know?" I asked after a short while.

Ruena glanced away. "I'll tell her when I need to."

"What about Tusky? We're best friends."

"He'll get through it."

Much as I wanted to continue buttering up Ruena, I spent my last remaining seconds as a free man considering what I was really saying, perhaps for the first time. Certainly for the first time in many moons. See, the survival programming runs deep. You don't really need to think about what comes out of your mouth—your unconscious brain can handle it just fine. Its sole function is to preserve you at any cost. But as we reached the bridge, I ascertained my exact intentions and why they were the root of my predicament.

Ruena was right. I appeared to care more about myself than this war, or its combatants, or its casualties. Problem was, that wasn't the case—not entirely, that is. I'd felt my insides turn to slush while watching Chaska's snuff vid, but I hadn't reflected on what that essence of ickiness actually meant. Not until right then, anyhow. See, that vid had torn me up, wrenched the same part of my soul as when I'd seen insurgents die at Tagamam or found out Tusky was dying. I *did* have a heart. A fragile one, at that. I'd learned to take my countless bruises in life and bury them under a tempting smile.

In my own eyes, I was a victim. An underdog. But to the others, I was a cold-blooded sociopath. Expendable. They didn't know what I felt, because they knew me only from surface impressions—words, gestures, a cool-as-a-hydroponic-cucumber demeanor. I'd inadvertently framed myself as an enemy because I'd outwardly shown neither empathy nor valor.

And thus, an insight occurred to me.

If I wanted to save myself, I had to be a hero in this war.

No time to reflect on that stroke of genius, however. We'd already reached the bridge, and Chaska (and her goons) were busy lowering the viewpanes' shutters.

"Umzuma," Chaska said to *my* pilot as though he belonged to her, "have they responded to our hail?"

Umzuma grunted in the affirmative.

"And they know we have her aboard?"

Another grunt.

"Good. Bring up the transmission projector. I want a direct line to that whore's mo—"

"Choose your words carefully, human," Amodari interrupted as she approached the gathering. "Remember, you will soon be in my lair. We inustrazans are not known for suffering fools."

Chaska glanced back at us, unperturbed. "Yet you've chosen Bodhi as your mate."

"I have claimed him." In spite of her manacled status, Amodari moved to the viewpane and stared expectantly at the rising shutters. "Now keep your remarks to yourself, and open that line to my mother. Count yourself lucky if she chooses to overlook my barbaric captivity."

Chaska's face assured me there were far, far more jabs she wanted to throw the inustrazan's way, but she (prudently) opted not to go down that road. Instead, she gestured to Umzuma to have him complete the initial transmission request.

As Umzuma did his magic, however, the shutters fully peeled away. This exposed the giga-structure formally known as "the hive-world." Or, in the formal inustrazan name I would learn years later, "the Long-Foretold and Immaculate Sixteen-Hive Abode of the Chosen Ones of His Eminence the Great Maker."

Talk about a mouthful.

But having seen this feat of engineering for myself, I can attest that such a long and stupid name is almost warranted. The hive-world appeared, even at a distance of well over a million kilometers, to be a multi-planet-sized disc covered with the craggy, starlight-dappled terrain of entire cities and patchwork landscapes. It was thronged by thousands—perhaps millions—of smaller discs, flagships, and other spinning, pulsating shapes I could not discern. Official records state that the hive-world provided permanent residence to no less than ten billion inustrazans and an additional twelve billion "thralls."

I would dare to state that such a population estimate is woefully low.

"Look upon it and weep," Amodari proclaimed to nobody in particular. "Few have had the pleasure to indulge in it with their eye-consciousness... fewer still have lived to speak of it."

Chaska moved to Amodari's side. "You'd better have told them we're coming."

"We?" Amodari giggled. "My mother knows of my arrival, but I suspect you'll be a surprise. Which is why you ought to leave the talking to me, and me alone."

Things were getting juicier (read: worse) by the second. There had to be countless weapons of unknown power all over that hive-world—how else had they kept themselves secret and sovereign for so long, after all? As the public transmission hologram fizzled into existence just before the viewpane, I wandered up to Umzuma's pit and scowled down at him.

"Traitor," I whispered.

The bundle of nerve sacs that passed for his head swiveled toward me. He didn't speak, or even do much of anything, but I could *feel* the guilt radiating from him. Betrayal is a universal language.

Just then, however, the transmission hologram sharpened into a crystal-clear image of Tanu Halnok, Amodari's mother.

Or, at least, what *would* have been Tanu Halnok. See, inustrazan appearance is finicky like that. Unless you have some seriously high-end, tailor-made equipment, it's impossible to render an inustrazan's appearance (either "real" or mentally constructed by the observer) through electronic means. My ship's transmission module was not one such piece of equipment. This being the case, Tanu Halnok appeared as a mass of questionably humanoid static.

"Daughter," Tanu said in a low, haunting tone, "who are these... interlopers?"

Amodari swept a hand across the bridge crew. "These, dearest Mother, are the pests that enabled me to return. We suffered a further incident while attempting to contact you."

"They look like insurgents."

"So they are. Regrettably."

"Do they have you held hostage?"

"You might say that, yes," Amodari replied, giving Chaska a pointed look. "Mother, we must speak at once. I've given these parasites my word that they will not be harmed within our sanctum."

"Do they offer their weakest as tribute?"

"No, but I've secured my treasure nevertheless." Amodari turned back and smiled at me.

"I see," Tanu said sourly. "Are you certain you were not followed?"

Amodari crossed her arms. "You should trust in my spycraft, Mother."

"After you caused the deaths of so many in my retinue?"

"It was not my fault."

"After you offered outsiders refuge here?"

"Such a decision will be made clear when we meet."

"If this is an extension of your little 'crusades,' Amodari, I will not—"

Rather than listening to the rest of that remark, Amodari launched into a full-on inustrazan meltdown. I'm talking arms flailing, hands clawing, eyes bulging—the works. Not to mention the torrent of guttural inustrazan barking and clicking that I presume passed as their language. It only got worse when her mother started spouting back. Soon enough, us humans were paralyzed in the ugliest mother-daughter fight ever witnessed, awkwardly glancing at one another and waiting for the spat to burn itself out.

After about three and a half minutes, the verbal mudslinging had quelled enough for Chaska to take a hesitant step forward.

"Tanu Halnok, my name is Chaska of Lattram," she said. "Your daughter has been most… kind… to bring us to your world. We have no ill will against you or your people. We will repay you for your temporary refuge with whatever we can afford to offer."

Chaska's calm, downright political speech showed yet another side of her that I hadn't known existed. I was used to insurgent Chaska, not negotiator Chaska. Minutes prior, she'd been ready to eviscerate Amodari. Now she was practically bowing down to Miss Horror's mother, a Hegemony butcher who'd personally overseen the deaths of many, *many* insurgents and assorted "good people." A woman Chaska probably desired to strangle with her own hands, no less.

But as Tanu Halnok's blob of static slid back, receding into decency, I saw what Chaska was playing at. She was trying to forge an alliance, make friends with villains. Just like me.

"So you claim," Tanu growled. "Remain in position with your engines disabled. Our vessels will guide you into our sanctum."

You know you're in deep when the blindfolds come out. Said blindfolds are only applied for two reasons: one, to mimic the slaughterhouse effect of preventing mass panic prior to a killing; or two, to disorient a captive while they're being led to some grisly dungeon.

In our own case, I wasn't sure which option was on the table. All I knew was that Tanu Halnok ordering *Stream Dancer* to shut off all cameras, disable all scanners, and seal all shutters was the deep-space equivalent of blindfolding us. Insisting that we all herd ourselves into the staging bay for "processing" only affirmed my conclusion.

"Nobody fires unless I give the order," Chaska shouted from atop a stack of crates, attempting to hush the clamor of the insurgent crowd below.

I, meanwhile, was content to keep my distance at the back of the bay with Amodari. My positioning away from Chaska and the rest of the crew was equal parts silent protest and disdain for the insurgent rabble who had gripped my ship.

Said it once, and I'll say it a dozen times: insurgents are like a tar pit. Dip one toe in, and you'll be up to your neck in no time.

"It's a good thing I am an honorable woman," Amodari told me as Chaska continued hollering. "My mother would have loved to drain the minds of these louses."

"I'm starting to see the virtue of that plan."

"Tell me, Bodhi—how do you stand them?"

"I don't."

"Yet you were pulled into Chaska's tangled web. How did that come about?"

"It's a long story," I said, not wanting to go down that road. "Let's just say I took a job and got more than I bargained for."

"Riches, then. A common enough siren song to lure merchants

to their demise…" Suddenly, Amodari's eyes narrowed to discerning slits. "Do you feel it?"

I did not. "What exactly should I be feeling?"

"The psychic field of my people." She pulled in a long, shuddering breath as though the air contained aerosol amphetamines. "Alone, our influence is negligible… but en masse, it is intoxicating."

"Uh-huh. What's it do, exactly?"

"Whatever we will. With concerted effort, we could make you humans hallucinate anything we desired. Faces, memories, mountains." She smiled. "Remember, Bodhi—we were created by Kruthara's own hand. Our power may not be as potent as it once was, but the inustrazan blood does not die quietly."

Sure enough, I began to feel *something*. Whether it was a placebo or the real deal, I can't quite say. All I know is that I sensed a tingling along my scalp that persisted for the entirety of my time aboard the hive-world. Which now raises the existential question of the day—did I ever *really* experience that place? Was it all an inustrazan dream? Was the hive-world even real? Was *I* real?

Spoiler alert: the universe will never know.

Thankfully, my short-lived paranoia was cut even shorter by the sound of the staging bay's ramp deploying.

A veritable battalion of inustrazan troops waited for us, but I'd expected that. What I *hadn't* expected was the shimmering oil-soap bubble that encompassed the entire hangar, or wherever we were. It slid around in iridescent strands, waxing and waning, ensuring me beyond any doubt that we were, in fact, contained within some kind of psychic prison.

Amodari touched my arm, startling me. "Don't fret, dear. It's just a containment field, of sorts. My people are very wary of outsiders."

"You don't say."

The head inustrazan, marked by gleaming ruby armor, stepped forward and addressed the crowd. "Where is Lady Halnok?"

Amodari's face brightened, and she quickly looped my arm through hers and began escorting me to the front of the gathering. All eyes were on us—especially Chaska's.

After an ear-rending greeting in her native tongue, Amodari gestured vaguely to the insurgent crowd and told the commander, "Keep a close eye on these ones. I'll be taking a precious few of their lot to convene with my mother."

The commander nodded.

Turning with a dainty flourish, Amodari said, "Chaska, come along. I'm feeling generous... I'll do you the honor of letting you hold onto your book."

Chaska hopped off her crate, carefully guarding the satchel slung over her shoulder. The book-containing satchel, I gathered. "I'm not going anywhere without my unit."

"Very well. Take whatever forces you need to feel 'secure.'" Amodari then surveyed the others with a shrewd, contemplative gaze. "Where is that most magnificent specimen? Tusky, I do believe?"

A massive paw shot up amid the crowd, followed by perky ursine ears.

"Yes, you," she called. "As a descendant of our shared creator, I believe you deserve the honor of witnessing his chosen people's glory."

Tusky gingerly navigated through the crowd, excusing himself here and tiptoeing there. He hurried to Chaska's side with a giddy smile. "Such an honor! I've heard so much about the inustrazan people, but through purely academic means. I suppose—"

"That's quite enough," Amodari said. She looked at the three of us—and Chaska's tagalong group of five or six soldiers—seriously. "Now, I don't need to remind any of you of this, but we will not tolerate shenanigans of any kind in this divine abode. Am I understood?"

We nodded, of course. An easy choice when surrounded by dozens of mind-sucking troops.

"What about me?" a young, shrill voice called out.

Amodari squinted into the crowd. "Is that young Gadra I hear?"

"Yeah!"

"Oh." Without any further commentary, Amodari led us down the ramp and into the folds of her battalion.

Once we'd been thoroughly surrounded, the majestic bubble-slash-prison constricted around us. Within seconds, the bubble was so narrow that it eclipsed any view of the ship. Indeed, even the unified grumbling of the crew and the latent hum of our onboard power systems fell away. Deaf and blind—just how the inustrazans wanted us.

The troops marched forward without preamble, and the bubble followed. Not quite sure what would happen to us outsiders if we met the bubble's perimeter, and not much wanting to know, we scrambled to keep pace. Underfoot were pristine marble slabs, each inscribed with intricate runes that gave me the heebie-jeebies.

"Such a vibrant city," Amodari commented several minutes into our walk. "So full of energy... of vitality."

Tusky scratched his chin. "Are you saying that you can perceive objects beyond this malleable field?"

"But of course." She gave Chaska a dark look. "Only in the land of true vision do the sightless realize their deficiency."

When you're a loquacious fellow such as myself, it is difficult to endure bouts of prolonged silence. Especially when your "host" is remaining mum to spare the majesty of her secret city, your insurgent on-off romantic partner is giving you the silent treatment, and your bipedal sloth-scientist is just plain bamboozled by everything around him. Nevertheless, I played along with the mute charades as I walked those endless kilometers.

Along the way, the ground shifted from marble to turquoise to jade, always unblemished and free of errant shoeprints. Inustrazans were either clean freaks or averse to walking that they relied upon more advanced means to get around. This latter theory was bolstered by the constant changes in elevation, which always brought us further up, never down. Stairs, ramps, swaying bridges... the ascent was relentless. I felt as though I'd scaled two Eudarian mountain ranges by the time the battalion commander ordered a halt.

And then, just like that, the inustrazan bubble vanished. Not popped, but vanished.

Ahead of us was a colossal throne hewn from cloudy amethyst, its narrow steps alone rising somewhere in the neighborhood of twenty meters. I craned my neck to inspect the jagged, imposing chair atop the crystal rise, only to find that I couldn't. It was backlit by some radiant and amorphous version of stained glass, which constantly warped between scenes that were beautiful yet also impossible to describe—not because the content was too alien, but because each time I looked at a particular image, it melded into some new tableau. An impressive optical illusion, if nothing else.

Then I worked up the nerve to look around me. We were—fittingly—in a throne room of some kind, surrounded by more legions of cultist-looking inustrazans and long rows of glittering pillars. The ceiling stretched up to a transparent dome that displayed the full splendor of some distant nebula.

"So *this* is the infamous Bodhi Drezek himself." One whiff of that echoey, bone-aching voice assured me that Tanu Halnok was the one atop the throne. I squinted up at the light show around her as she continued. "I am strangely disappointed by your aura."

Amodari stepped forward, bowing slightly. "Please mind your tongue, Mother. Humans are sensitive to our manner of expression."

"And why should I censor myself? These humans brought about the death of our warriors. They may yet bring more death to our world."

"Not a chance," I called up. "We're clean! We got scanned!"

"I'm aware," Tanu said. "Do you think we'd have allowed your sullied heels to tread upon our world without reading your minds? We have felt that the taint of Kruthara is not within you."

I shot Amodari a probing glance. "You can *feel* Kruthara?"

"Bereft of my kin, no," she said quietly. "Together, as I've said, my people can do almost anything. Now hush."

"Tell me, Daughter," Tanu said, "why have you brought these outsiders to our abode?"

Chaska advanced to my side, a hand resting on her satchel. "Because we have something worth translating."

"Oh?" Tanu asked in amusement. "And what would that be?"

Before Chaska could answer, one of her esteemed guards shouldered his way past us. He was an older man, scraggly-bearded and wild-eyed. "It's *her*," he hissed to Chaska.

"Not now," Chaska said, her voice quiet yet firm, eyes fixed up at Tanu.

"This... this *bitch*." The insurgent's rifle shifted in his arms. "How can we just sit here and—"

"Not. Now."

"Chaska?" Amodari said. "Have you lost control of your hounds?"

"Stand down," Chaska urged him.

But the man just kept walking on ahead, undaunted by the sounds of a hundred inustrazan proton rifles humming in tandem.

"You killed my wife," the insurgent said through huffing breaths. "You killed my son..."

Tanu barked out a laugh. "Who is this fool?"

"You killed my friends," the insurgent went on.

"Ah, wait," Tanu said. "I do believe I know you now. I can feel your mind… see it, even. Your name is Jaru, is it not?"

The insurgent nodded stiffly. "That's right."

"Now I recall it," Tanu replied. "Your kin fought at Manasi, just outside the fission barges. Isn't that right? Their faces are still etched in my memory."

"That makes two of us."

"Yes, well, these individuals were guilty of sedition against the Halcius Hegemony. They deserved what fates they received."

"You goddamn monster. You—"

"Think well before you act, human. You are not the hero your mind assures you that you are."

"Jaru," Chaska said through clenched teeth, "stand down this instant."

But Jaru, being your garden-variety insurgent, wasn't so inclined to taking commands. He lifted his rifle, shouted some vague war cry, and—

Splat.

There was hardly a sound as the inustrazan rifles vaporized him. Other than a few freckles of blood and tattered cloth flitting about in the air, there was no sign he'd ever existed. Even as my mind struggled to process this surreal sight, however, another chain of near-silent rifle discharges *whished* behind me.

I spun around to discover that *all* of Chaska's "unit" had been annihilated right where they stood, leaving a misshapen row of red and still-glowing metal shards. Tusky stood in the center of it all, quaking, unmoving aside from eyes that swished about in terror.

Chaska's jaw dropped. "I—you—"

"We saw the intent in their minds," Tanu interjected. "Well, now that we've dealt with that unpleasantness, why don't you go on about this translation of yours?"

Despite a few grunts and words that bobbed around in her

throat, Chaska was incapable of any expression. Her eyes grew wet and bulbous.

"Humans," Amodari said, repulsed. "So thoroughly sentimental."

I looked at Tusky, confirming the two of us were in similar states of mute unease. We were, as you might say, well and truly "shook." At the very least, however, the fact that he hadn't been Jaru-ized proved that Chaska's little club hadn't brainwashed him to the point of rash violence. Then again, he had no concept of kin to start with, no fuel for his radicalism. I suppose this made it easy to avoid half-baked revenge schemes.

"What Chaska is *trying* to say," Amodari continued, "is that she's in possession of the material we dispatched our forces to acquire last month."

Tanu was silent for a long while, then asked, "The decree on the Maker's obelisk?"

"The very same, Mother. I assured her that no harm would come to their faction while we worked cooperatively with this information." Amodari glanced at the bloody mess around her with clear distaste. "I should very much like to respect the rest of our arrangement with them."

"How are you so certain that their information is authentic?"

"I have seen glimpses, Mother. Glimpses of decrees we have yet to archive."

"Interesting. Even so, outsiders are not allowed contact with the Knower."

"They needn't have it."

"I am *not* letting it out of my hands," Chaska shouted, her fury so sudden that even Amodari flinched. "We know about your chitta. And we came here to see it."

Tanu's fingertips danced on her throne with low, rhythmic thudding. "Daughter?"

"I had to tell them about it, Mother," Amodari said sheepishly. "It was the only way to ensure them of our agreement."

"We will discuss such transgressions later," Tanu said. "For now, I must reiterate our tradition: I will not permit outsiders into its dwelling. They have already been humored overmuch by setting foot in this hall."

"Then you'll have to take it from my dead hands," Chaska seethed.

Tanu cackled at that. "It could be so easily arranged."

I tugged at Chaska's sleeve. "Listen, maybe we should—"

"Shut up, Bodhi," she snapped. "Just shut. Up."

Sensing no other option, I took a presumptuous step forward and mimicked Amodari's bow. "I believe I may have a solution."

All eyes swiveled toward me. The pressure was on.

"Well, uh, you stated that outsiders aren't allowed in," I said. "In a very, very, *very* brief time, I'll be part of Amodari's... harem?" When Tanu didn't object to my guesstimate of the term, I fumbled on. "If I understand correctly, that will make me an insider, not an outsider. So... why don't I carry out this translation business?"

Glancing back, I found Chaska still clinging to her satchel like a newborn.

"Most unusual," Tanu purred, "but I am not averse to it. I trust that my daughter's accompaniment would be sufficient to keep your mind in check."

"No," Chaska said. "It's not happening. It belongs to my crew."

"It belongs to the *Maker*."

"He's dead, and we're here. It's ours."

"Guards?"

Tanu's prompt set the rifles buzzing again.

"P-Perhaps I could accompany him as a representative, Chaska," Tusky ventured, doing his best to tiptoe over the blood as he approached with his head low. He stared up at Tanu's throne like a worshipper. "Hello, Miss Halnok. Lady Halnok. I'm—"

"A fellow product of our creator," Tanu cut in. "Yes, I've heard. And with sentience, too…"

Tusky regarded Chaska. "Bodhi and I can ensure that things are handled with the utmost care."

"There," Amodari said, looking between Chaska and her mother expectantly. "Is this acceptable to all parties? A member of our world, a member of yours, and one who is in between?"

"I knew this would happen, Bodhi," Chaska said weakly. "I should've listened to myself."

Again, I met her eyes. She was on the verge of total meltdown. And just behind her were a slew of inustrazan rifles, all ready to turn her to Chaska-dust at the flick of Tanu's mental command.

"Please," I whispered.

"It's for the best, dear," Amodari told her with a surprising degree of… feeling. "Give him the book and live another day."

Still holding my gaze, Chaska unslung the satchel and held it against her chest. "It's always about you, isn't it?" she asked softly. "You have to be the *one*. The first, the best, the survivor." Tears streamed down her cheeks as she held the satchel out. "Just take the fucking thing."

In that moment, there was just the two of us. No Tusky, no Amodari, no Tanu, no guns or crystals or light. Her grip on the satchel was practically that of rigor mortis. As soon as her reluctant offering was in my hand, Tanu's guards surrounded her in an airtight formation.

"Ensure that she's comfortable aboard her ship with the others," Tanu commanded. "Your property and… crew… will be returned to you at the earliest convenience."

I wanted to say more, to dash through that crowd and embrace Chaska, but there was just too much in the way. Literally. Even now, there were tens of armed and armored inustrazans leading my Chaska back the way we'd come. Seconds later, yet another psychic bubble enveloped them.

And I knew right then that I'd damned myself. Not only to being Amodari's harem, but to a lifetime of future dreams populated by that last dreadful sight of Chaska's heartbreak. It didn't matter what came of the book or the war or the universe itself. I'd destroyed the very thing I spent my time in the Contrition yearning to love.

I turned the satchel over in my hands, hoping it was worth it.

Deep down, I knew it wasn't.

NINE

It should come as no surprise that I hardly remember journeying to the domain of the inustrazan chitta. The entire hive-world was one quivering ball of illusions and falsified sensory input. Again, this refers back to my statement that the entire experience on the hive-world may have been an elaborate hallucination.

What's pertinent to our tale right now is that we did, indeed, reach the "Knower's" chamber at some point. It was located at the end of a long and twisting golden labyrinth, sealed behind a towering door that probably took some poor shmuck a century to carve.

"You both should feel blessed," Amodari said as she approached the locking mechanisms. "This is one of our holiest shrines."

Tusky eyed me uneasily. "Miss Halnok, perhaps you could expound upon something for me. As I understand from the old facility's reports, the chitta located aboard the *Ouroboros* was rather, shall we say, functional. It provided navigation and logistics for the vessel. If you'll excuse my bluntness, it seems that keeping such a device sealed away would defeat its purpose."

Still inputting a sequence obscured by her body, Amodari looked back with a smile. "How very observant. But you see, our chitta is far from underutilized. It coordinates nearly every function of this world."

"Astonishing. It must be rather sizable!"

"Yes, well, one might say that…"

Even as Amodari unsealed door after door, leading us past increasingly larger checkpoints with soldiers and automated turrets and stasis fields, all I could think about was how thoroughly useless I felt. Sure, I'd returned to the conventional world, but what did I have to show for it? I'd burned my bridge with Chaska, been replaced as the team's "smarts" by a talking sloth, and done less than nothing in terms of procuring the war-changing information I currently held. When I got right down to it, it was even possible that I'd inadvertently caused all of this. Without me, the insurgents trying to steal Tusky's canister would've been obliterated at Lattram, and the whole trail leading to Palamar and the Promised Place and Kruthara would've shriveled up overnight, lost to the infinite expanse.

But I couldn't afford to indulge that kind of hypothetical timeline. Blaming yourself for what's done is a dark and slippery path.

Instead, I had to focus on getting myself the hell out of Amodari's clutches. It was the one and only way to secure both my freedom *and* Chaska's forgiveness, if such a thing were even possible. Of course, the odds of actually formulating and carrying out such a bold escape dwindled with every door Amodari unlocked.

It practically combusted when the final door slid apart, revealing the Knower itself.

I won't sit here and pretend I was floored by the sight of this behemoth. I've been in so many alien monoliths and interdimensional temples it would make your head spin. So forgive me if my description is on the pedestrian side.

Its containment chamber was as large as a nuclear silo, humid, egg-shaped, totally lightless aside from a few blue flames ensconced in the walls. This relative darkness obscured most of the chitta itself, but it was enough to get the gist of the affair. Illuminated above me were pulsating, whitish-pink patches that looked predictably similar to human brain tissue. They even had the same striations and "wrinkling" to them.

Now, don't get me wrong, the thing was ginormous. It stretched up into the darkness several hundred meters above, and below it, scraping the overgrown petri dish of its "floor," were long, dangling tendrils that tensed and unfurled like a squid's tentacles. So there you have it. A chitta is nothing more than a huge, breathing brain covered in tumors and floppy appendages. You'll never see one in real life, but you've now read a firsthand account of one, which is better than nothing.

"Highest Knower, Child of the Maker's Infinite Wisdom," Amodari said in toothache-sweet reverence, "we come before you to seek your counsel."

Tusky and I shared yet another look.

As my eyes adjusted, I noticed that the chitta had many, many more of those dangling legs-tentacle-things, all flowing off its body like spiderwebs and connecting to various ports in the chamber's walls. Some of them stretched right over my head—a fact I discovered when a glob of starchy brain-juice pelted my shoulder. Nasty.

After an unreasonable amount of time, the chitta snaked one of its longest tentacles into a rusty valve to our left. A crude-looking speaker system on the floor then hummed to life.

"What is it now?" The chitta's voice was a fabric of ten or twenty individual personalities, all coalescing into a single, stitched-together anomaly. Despite the multitude aspect, however, there was a unified tone to the question—annoyance. "I'm rather busy here, Amodari."

It took all of my willpower to hold back a snicker.

"Highest Knower, we approach you for clarification on a delicate matter," Amodari said, unfazed by the thing's insolence. Not surprising, given it was running the world she inhabited.

"Uh-huh... lemme guess... *another* one of the Maker's decrees you need translated?"

"Precisely."

"Come back later. I'm doin' stuff."

Amodari cleared her throat. "Highest Knower, this is a matter of utmost—"

"Yeah, yeah, yeah. Every single translation is a 'matter of utmost urgency.' Give it a break, would you? Gets old fast."

"I can understand your misgivings." She looked at Tusky and me in turn, appearing oddly embarrassed by her chitta's behavior. "As the high seer explained at our last encounter, however, your requested upgrades are forthcoming."

"A year later, huh?"

"Please forgive the delays. There have been pressing issues for our people."

"Oh, well, *please* excuse me, then! See, I'm used to the way the Maker did things. Back in those days, he had this crazy concept called 'punctuality.' I asked for something, I got it. Seems times have changed, and I didn't get the memo." The chitta let out a long, multivocal sigh. "Anyway, who are these clowns? A circus bear and a drug fiend?"

Much as I wanted to snap back at that, I found myself shrugging in tacit agreement.

"My name is Sir Tusky, Highest Knower." The sloth-scientist delivered a cringeworthy bow and gazed up at a nondescript section of the chitta's brainy bulk. "I've heard so very much about you, and might I say, what an honor to—"

"Make way for the flattery parade," the chitta groaned. "Who's the other one? A used-ship salesman?"

I waved limply at it. "Bodhi Drezek, arms merchant, new concubine. Just here for the show."

The chitta let out a hideous laugh. "I like this guy. Short, not too sweet, straight to the point. And a human. Damn! I haven't seen one of those in... huh, I dunno. Years, millennia? Time's an illusion anyway."

"Ahem," Amodari butted in, "I do believe we should rein in our topics of discussion, Highest Knower. Bodhi and *Sir* Tusky are here as a mere formality."

Author's addendum:

If you've heard any rumors whatsoever about the tales of my life, you may consider the following segment utter bollocks. But take my word on this one—what I am about to present is the complete and honest truth of what actually went down in the chitta's holding cell.

Many gossip fiends and doubters will assert with their dying breath that I illegally and impulsively stole a piece of this superintelligence, thus sparking an interspecies war that would last another hundred and twenty-four years. They are wrong. What happened to me was no fault of my own. As you will soon see, I was *chosen* for the misunderstanding that occurred, and furthermore, I had little to no sway in the matter.

Now, back to the chitta.

The chitta rattled off a snarky line, Amodari did her usual sycophantic twirl, and on and on it went, leading nowhere but Absurdity Central Station. At some point, my attention wandered off the exchange. Not because I'd lost interest, but because I felt a slick, pulsating presence worming into my right ear.

"*Shh, don't make a scene! Be easy.*"

The chitta's subdued yet still-multifaceted voice arose directly in my mind, similar to how my godengine conversed with me. Not that I immediately recognized the words as belonging to the chitta, of course. It took me a heart-stopping moment to connect the disembodied voice to the aforementioned "wetness" slithering into me.

Somewhere between piss-myself terror and curiosity, I traced the route of this newfound "landline" along the hazy floor. Sure enough, a fleshy filament snaked all the way from my pant leg to the nutrient pool ahead. Oh, joy.

A question occurred to me: if this thing could control an entire city, what was stopping it from controlling my tongue, or my heart, or my bowels? Not a damn thing. Still, considering what was awaiting me if and when we finished up here, I wasn't quite averse to the idea of suicide-by-proxy. Death was probably a luxury in the land of the immortal mind-eaters. This being the case, I tried to frame the chitta's surprise visit as an opportunity rather than the climax of a body-horror vid. And that meant doing what I always do —playing it cool.

"*Testing, testing?*" I tried mentally.

"*Loud and clear,*" the chitta "said" in reply. "*Sorry about the whole ear invasion, by the way. Security's pretty tight in this place, and I've been waitin' on a human brain for longer than I can remember. I hate workin' with those tricksy inustrazan meat-lumps.*"

"*Interface? Are you going to pop my head or something?*"

"*Me? Pop* your *head? Hell no! I'm here to make a deal. Just the two of us. Whaddya think?*"

I peered Amodari's way to verify what I'd suspected—she was, indeed, still busy bickering with the chitta's more corporeal aspect —then cooked up a reply.

"*Let's just say I like deals.*"

"*Oh, I like you more by the millisecond!*" The chitta then evoked the sound of hands rubbing together in anticipation. "*You got a ship?*"

That one stung. "*Well... if you'd asked me that a few hours ago...*"

"*Easy come, easy go, huh? Well, whatever. Listen, I can get us one. A good one. A fast one.*"

I narrowed my eyes, doing my best to appear invested in the chitta's now-obvious ploy to distract Amodari and buy time. "*What do you mean, us?*"

"*Us! Y'know... you, me... gettin' the hell out of this joint?*" Perhaps mistaking my utter bafflement for ambivalence, the chitta pressed on to sweeten the deal. "*I can do a lot for you! Whatever you need! You seem like a bright guy, one who's dealt with superintelligence before—an arms dealer can never have too much superintelligence! And besides, I'll be a better pal than Center ever could be! 'Cause, you know, we're both organics! I just get you. I see you.*"

The rush of words hit me like a tungsten shell—especially one choice name-drop. "*And how do you know about Center?*"

"*Call it intuition! Or, y'know, combing your memory synapses. Whatever! All the same when you get down to the level of wetware.*"

"*Are you reading my thoughts?*"

"*I would never. I'm a chitta of honor.*"

"*Right. Just, uh... give me a little mental space so I don't go insane. I'm gonna... internalize... all of this.*"

"*Sure thing, buddy. Anything for you! Anything...*"

True enough to the chitta's point, the exact mechanisms by which the thing was conversing and bargaining were irrelevant. This was a peculiar situation, but one that still required my savvy as an entrepreneur. You see, there was a deal to be made here. A deal rife with demand, as indicated by the tremendous amount of sucking-up and "but wait, there's more!" language being tossed my way. For whatever reason, this chitta really, *really* needed my help in a jailbreak. And after languishing in the Contrition myself, who was I to deny a sentient being its freedom?

Especially if said being was a superintelligence with a vested interest in helping *me* escape, too.

"Bodhi," Amodari said, breaking my inner monologue, "please give me the b—"

Then she froze.

Everything froze.

Tusky, my breaths, my limbs—the whole kit and caboodle.

"*Still hearin' me?*" the chitta asked.

With some trepidation, I hazarded a reply. "*Yes?*"

"*Okay, sweet. You're probably wondering why we're in molasses-land. Short answer is, we were running out of time, so I used a little burst of my processing power to slow your mind down. Or speed it up. Tomatoes, to-mah-toes. Following me?*"

"*Not really, but I'm... intrigued?*"

"*Yeah, well, I'm pretty spectacular. So whaddya say? Wanna help me get out?*"

It was strange, trying to strike a deal without my standard array of hand gestures and mirrored body language. But I'd have to make do.

"*I'm certainly considering your proposal*," I said at length. This was all part of negotiations, you see. You have to make the other party sweat a little bit. Play hardball. Even if they are a godlike, overgrown artifact. "*First, a few preliminaries. Such as why you'd like to get out of this cozy... place.*"

"*Isn't it obvious, man? Look around. These people are whack-jobs. And so, so boring.*"

"*Well, I'll grant you that.*"

The chitta gave a disgusted snort. "*I took a peek at your memory bank. Helluva thing. You've done so much, seen so much, screwed so much!*" Despite the chitta's blush-inducing flattery, I let it proceed uninterrupted. My working theory, which I was eager to test, was that this thing was adapting its speech using my own linguistic database. Growing itself into my custom-made best friend, so to speak. "*You and me aren't that different, pal. We're both a bunch of meat floating around in the game of life.*"

Well, theory confirmed.

"*I take it you've got some grand scheme outside of here?*" I probed. "*Conquering a galaxy, perhaps? Starting an enterprise?*"

"*I'm a chitta of simple tastes, Bodhi. Literally. I'd just like to taste some ice cream. I mean, the memory is tasty—I can literally only imagine how good the real thing is!*"

"*You aren't wrong.*"

"*Of course not. I'm a chitta.*"

I gave a psychic sigh. "*Alright, so you're after some good experiences out in the cosmos. Got it. But why pick me?*"

"*Simple biology, man. First off, you've got a human brain, same thing the Maker modeled me after. Neat-o, huh? And second, you've got a working heart. The inustrazans have some stupidly expensive valve system to do the job, but you've got a good workaround in your ribcage.*"

"*Not to doubt your infinite wisdom, but I don't think I've got enough blood to run... all of, well, you.*"

"*Thankfully, you don't have to!*" the chitta squealed. "*All you've gotta do is cut off a chunk of me. I can regrow in a vat of—well, we can hash that out later. The point is, you just need a piece of a neuronal cluster. Easy.*"

Setting aside the existential implications of regrowing a sample of chitta tissue and how that new sample might diverge in self-concept from its host, I was pretty damn invested at this point. I mean, come on. This monstrosity was worth a few quadrillion bux alone. If I could find a way to have it run a munitions factory, crank out the same kind of designs as Center...

"*Don't leave me hangin'!*" the chitta piped up.

"*I'm simply pondering,*" I replied. "*Next item on the menu: couldn't you just hijack my body and do the job yourself?*"

"*Duh. But I'm not an animal, Bodhi. I've got a heart too, you know. Well, a biomechanical system that acts like one, but let's not get caught in the details!*"

That was one point in the chitta's favor. Seeing as I was thoroughly flexible in my morals, it would be pleasant to partner up a superintelligence that possessed a more rigid code of conduct. Which brought me to my next dilemma. Superintelligences, by their very nature, tend to be sly, deceptive things. True, the thing was undeniably doing me a favor by not stealing my body, but was that just a smokescreen to conceal some deeper evil? Hard to say. These things could work out logic sequences millions of magnitudes faster than some pea-brain human.

But that was a problem for later. After all, this wasn't my first rodeo with universe-ending anomalies. It was better to think about the big-picture things upfront.

"*What can you do for me?*" I asked.

The chitta practically balked at the question. "*What* can't *I do?*"

"*Well, let's be specific! Say I get you out, send you into the stars. What are you offering?*"

"*You mean, beyond saving your ass from Amodari's sex-till-death operation?*"

Had I been less desperate, I might've been offended by its continued incursions into my memories. But alas, I was deep in the hole. I'd gladly take invasive yet custom-tailored solutions to my problems.

"*That's a reasonable start,*" I said calmly. "*What else?*"

"*Oh, oh, I know! I could get you outta hot water with Chaska. Y'know, translate that book exclusively for the insurgents!*"

"*That's a personal matter!*"

"*Yeah, and? C'mon, man, I'm offering you a ticket back into that girl's good graces—and back into that bed, wink-wink!—and a way to maybe, possibly, totally defeat Kruthara and save the universe. You'd have to be an idiot to turn this down.*"

"*Fair enough,*" I said. Everything it said sounded good—probably too good, but beggars and soon-to-be slaves should not be choosers. "*Anything else?*"

"*You drive a hard bargain!*"

"*So I've been told, Highest Knower. So I've been told.*"

"*Huh. Well, I dunno if this sweetens the pot, but unless you take me out of this place, we're all gonna die in a few minutes.*"

I took a few seconds to mentally digest that. "*We're what?*"

"*Yeah...*" The chitta conjured a sound that resembled sucking air through its non-teeth. "*About that. You know those eternalink trackers?*"

"*... Yes?*"

"*Well, you've kinda got one lodged in your head right now. Feels pretty juicy.*"

Had I been able to move my body, I might've dumped my bowels out on the spot. "*And you didn't mention it until now!?*"

"*Hey, everyone forgets sometimes!*"

"*How'd it get there!?*"

The chitta's presence vanished for a few seconds. "*Looks like the Hegemony popped it in there while you were in the Contrition. Wild place, by the way. I don't think I wanna taste vomit.*"

"*Are... are you kidding?*"

"*Hell no. Vomit's not even food, it's—*"

"*Not that! The tracker!*"

"*Oh, that. Nah. But the tracker's small potatoes, man. I can have that thing disabled lickety-split. The* real *trouble is that the Hegemony-Kruthara tag team have a fleet that's gonna start firing on us in about... three minutes?*"

"*Splendid.*"

Perhaps I should've been more unsettled by the one-two gut punch routine of learning that I was (A) embedded with a Hegemony tracker and (B) the cause of the Hegemony following us and raining death on everybody in sight, but nothing surprised me at this point. I was on a depraved inustrazan's home turf, with a chitta worming around in my brain, and caught in the middle of an apocalyptic war that had started with a time-traveling mutant. You tell *me* what's worth fretting about.

"*Alright,*" I said coolly. "*Tell you what: you get the sloth and me back onto my ship, translate that book, and we'll call it even. I'll even launch you in a pod toward some interstellar cruise ship or something.*"

"*With ice cream?*"

"*And an artificial stomach, to boot.*"

"*Wowzers. So... you* don't *want the lifetime of profits I could provide?*"

Ugh. This thing was tugging at every one of my greedy little heartstrings. "*Let's just start with establishing a working relationship... and survive. Deal?*"

"*Deal like a banana peel.*"

"*Come again?*"

"*I dunno, man, it sounded cooler in my head. Well, figuratively speaking. You get me. Just hang tight for the distraction and do your Bodhi thing.*"

And with that, the world unfroze.

"—ook," Amodari finished. She studied me impatiently as I blinked myself back to full, fluid consciousness. "Bodhi? Are you feeling well?"

All I could do was blink. "Uh... um..."

"*Showtime!*" the chitta whispered.

I didn't need to ask what this phrase referred to, however, seeing as the entire chamber erupted in a flurry of strobing red lights and screeching sirens. Garbled inustrazan leapt through the speakers, no doubt translating to *Citizens of the hive-world, we are in for a bad, bad time.*

Amodari whirled around and began shouting at the adjoining checkpoint's guards, while Tusky did his usual shtick of hunching down and cowering somewhat. I wasn't certain I liked this new and non-chompy version of the guy, but I digress.

While the two of them were occupied, I did exactly as I'd been ordered—note, *ordered*. Again, innocent victim here.

I tiptoed into the nutrient pool, reached up, and tore off a rubbery clump of chitta flesh. While stuffing said clump into my jacket's pocket, the chitta tendril shriveled out of my ear. Two seconds later, I sensed a slight pinch in my kidney region.

"*Boom-a-loom diggity!*" the chitta howled as I raced back to my previous position in the chamber. "*I'm talkin' to you straight through your nervous system! Even got a live feed from all your senses! It's like I'm you, man! Pretty swell, huh?*"

"*Yeah, totally swell,*" I mentally replied, noticing—with equal parts amusement and disbelief—that Amodari and Tusky hadn't noticed my klepto grab. "*Now get us out of here, would you?*"

"*On it, chief.*"

"Take the outsiders and seal yourselves in the reinforced holdout room, Noble Amodari," the chitta's main bulk said via its speakers. It had adopted a suitably concerned tone to really sell the point. "We will ensure that the defenses repel the invaders."

Amodari ceased her bickering with the guards and stared at me. "It's right, Bodhi. Come with me."

To this day, it's still unclear how that tiny hunk of the chitta (henceforth referred to as Chitta Mini) communicated with its primary body (henceforth referred to as Chitta Prime). The simplest explanation is that it didn't—thus, I'd wager that Chitta Prime essentially sacrificed itself, content to know that a portion of its consciousness would receive the freedom it had always wanted. This is jarring to think about, seeing as Chitta Prime had been the "entity" who'd communicated with me via the ear-a-phone. Philosophically speaking, the Chitta Mini I carried in my pocket was a separate being from the thing I'd bargained with—yet also *not* separate.

Anyhow, if I keep rambling about this topic, we'll end up deep in a quagmire of personality theory and "other mind" problems that

I'm neither equipped to deal with, nor interested in discussing. The underlying point here is that Chitta Prime and Chitta Mini orchestrated a joint breakout that only one of them, Chitta Mini, benefitted from. This may help to frame the ensuing madness in a (slightly) more workable context.

I did my best to appear out of the loop and petrified as Amodari led Tusky and me back down the corridors, cringing at the impressive, crushing *kloom* sounds of the doors resealing behind us.

"This is impossible," Amodari muttered—more to herself than either of us, I suppose. "The Hegemony couldn't have found us."

"Maybe your anti-tracker system wasn't as good as you thought?" I suggested.

"*Nice*," Chitta Mini whispered. "*Keep her on the ropes! The first twist is almost ready!*"

"It doesn't matter now," Amodari growled. "They *cannot* take this sanctum. The knowledge contained here would win their war overnight."

Already, I could hear and feel the astonishing *whump-whump* of the hive-world's orbital guns peppering the vacuum with shells. This alone was enough to confirm that the chitta hadn't been lying about the terrific power of the approaching Hegemony fleet. If we didn't get out of here within minutes, we'd all be floating gobs of strawberry jam.

Amodari turned a corner and frantically waved us onwards. "Hurry! We have no time."

"*Nope, nope, nope,*" Chitta Mini warned. "*Do. Not. Follow.*"

In line with my savior's command, I stopped, reached out, and held Tusky in place.

"What are you doing?" Amodari asked coldly. Then a spark of understanding dawned in her eyes. "You vile, conniving little—"

An enormous steel slab dropped in the doorway, barring the entrance to Amodari's hideaway and leaving the two (well, three) of us alone in the corridor.

Tusky gaped at me. "What's going on, Bodhi? And please be upfront. I suspect you alone have an answer to my question."

"As you should, Sir Tusky." After receiving the chitta's next instruction, I grabbed his hand and began yanking him onwards. "Until we get out of here, don't ask questions, don't disobey me, and don't reach into my pocket."

TEN

Had Chitta Mini not been locked in the hive-world's vault for a few million years, he'd have made one hell of a heist coordinator. That hunk of gray matter led us through a network of deserted access tunnels, secret doors, and forgotten corners with such adeptness that I actually began to believe we might survive.

"*Another left!*" Chitta Mini urged as we dashed into yet another mold-freckled passage.

Doing as instructed, we emerged in a control room of sorts. I say *of sorts* because it was not, by any standard definition, a placed that looked capable of currently controlling anything. The place was overrun with desiccated *something* nests, shredded cables, and a finger-thick layer of dust. Whatever consoles remained intact were unpowered and rusted over.

"*That one*," Chitta Mini said. "*Go to that one!*"

I groaned internally. "*Which one?*"

"*Oh. The, uh, reddish one.*"

So I did. Upon approaching its battered interface, Chitta Mini slinked another tendril out of my pocket and into a port on the lower panel.

Miraculously, the thing lit up in a wash of pale blue light.

"Bodhi?" Tusky said hesitantly. "Are you aware that there is an organic link between yourself and this machinery?"

I frowned at him. "What'd I say about no questions?"

"Yes, well, it just seems a bit"—a cluster of distant missile explosions set the room trembling—"pertinent?"

Just then, the console before me grumbled into action. A brilliant array of lights shot up from its central projector, forming a crude yet unmistakable rendering of a cartoonish brain. Chitta Mini's self-image, it seemed. Ridiculous, but it made a strange sort of sense.

"Hey, gents!" Chitta Mini said through the console. Tusky just about fainted. "Sorry to introduce myself like this—emission power on this thing's pretty low."

Another concussive salvo shook beneath my feet.

"Focus on the getaway, please," I reminded Chitta Mini. "What are we even doing here?"

Chitta Mini laughed. "The getaway. Duh!" A few more consoles powered up around us, followed by the whir of a turbine. "The hangar systems aren't on my main grid. Need to have physical access to release your ship. Which is why we're currently in this abandoned li'l dungeon of a place. It might be out of service, but it's still hooked up to the secondary systems! I think."

Tusky stepped forward and marveled at the hologram. "I fear my confusion has only deepened."

"No questions!" I snapped. "Listen, Chitta, I think we're gonna need to pick up the pace. The Hegemony doesn't seem to be in a patient mood."

"Aaaand... *done*!" it said. "Had a nice chat with your pilot, Umzuma. Stand-up guy. They're getting in position now."

Despite our circumstances, I froze. "You *chatted* with Umzuma?"

"Oh, yeah. His species are good folks. Really killer poets, too."

I shook my head to clear away that particular oddity. "Where are they gonna meet us?"

"Don't worry about that, Bodhi. I've got it all under control. Now we just need to wrangle up a pair of HIIAs and we'll be good to go!"

HIIA, for the unaware, stands for "High-Impact Insertion Apparatus." Translation—the kind of thing one needs to wear when dropping from high orbit onto a planet's surface. Hearing that Tusky and I needed to slip into these costly and death-proof suits did not lift my spirits.

"Why would we possibly need those?" I pressed.

Chitta Mini's hologram sprouted a little arm, which it then used to literally wave away my concerns. "Just trust me, man. It'll be fun."

Although my mind *should've* been focused on the possibility of splattering from a high-orbit jump, or perhaps on the hive-world's impending demise, it wasn't. Instead, I found myself thinking about Amodari. I'm a calculating, valorous scoundrel—there is no denying that—but I am not a monster. And the prospect of leaving my twisted would-be lover to die on her own people's homeworld, especially after she'd held up her end of the bargain about sparing (most of) the crew, did not sit right with me.

"Chitta," I said quietly, "I'd like you to do one more thing for me."

Its hologram flickered. "Yes?"

"Find a way to get Amodari off the hive-world. Get her someplace safe."

"That's a tall order. My 'big mind' doesn't know you were sweet on savin' her."

"Yeah, well, make it happen!"

It sighed. "I'll do my best." Two shakes of a kodura's tail later, it added, "Done. Don't ask me how, but it's done. Now let's get our posteriors in gear-iors!"

Despite my misgivings, I had no choice but to trust Chitta Mini. I figured this was all in karmic hands now. If Amodari lived, she'd earned such a fate. And if she died—well, there's a game-over awaiting all of us in the end.

A few hairpin turns and maintenance-shaft crawlfests later, Tusky and I found ourselves in a dilapidated staging room. Scattered along the walls were web-covered rifles, helmets, munitions crates, ration packs, and... a row of HIIAs.

The suits looked like living behemoths, each standing a meter taller than Tusky and covered in quilted, marshmallow-like plates. They had no discernible faceplates or external sensors—logical, seeing as they were built to withstand the heat and pressure of atmospheric entry, but also horrifying. We'd be taking a literal leap of faith on nothing more than Chitta Mini's assurances.

"*Squeeze in,*" he ordered. "*We're runnin' short on time, chief!*"

Having never used one of these puffy contraptions, I used a rational approach to determine the danger involved. "Tusky—squeeze in!"

He blinked at me. "How?"

"Just... do it!"

With obvious apprehension, Tusky approached one of the HIIAs and poked it. His finger went straight through. Then his arm. By the halfway mark, the matter was out of his control. His entire body slurped into the suit. Although I couldn't hear him, on account of his face being swallowed by the marshmallow void, his flailing legs did not inspire confidence in me.

"*Hurry up, man!*" Chitta Mini shouted. "*Those things don't have any air in 'em!*"

My body locked up. "What!?"

"*Didn't you know inustrazans don't breathe? Well, don't need to? Those things can hold their breath for sixteen hours at a time! I mean, seriously, why build oxygen filtration into an orbital-drop apparatus when you're only gonna be in the air for—*"

I rushed over to the HIIA and squirmed helplessly, not wanting to be sucked in after Tusky. "*Get him out!*"

"*No can do, pal. Those things are built to release after the boots make contact at the right velocity. Y'know, like, after an orbital drop?*"

"*Who would build such a stupid thing!?*"

"*Whoa, rude. I actually built these.*"

"*You also built that famous 'anti-tracking' system here, didn't you?*"

"*Hey! These units were only the prototypes... which is why this room's pretty much sealed off...*" Chitta Mini sighed. "*Come to think of it, we did have a lot of casualties with these things. Probably shoulda taken you guys to the* other *staging room, where we kept the upgraded gear, but the past is the past, and—*"

"*Screw it.*" I hurried over to the next HIIA as Tusky's suit staggered to life. He moved like a reanimated corpse, his arms outstretched and legs gracelessly swinging forward like blocks of wood. "*If I die in this thing, I'm blaming you.*"

"*It'll be* fiiine, *man,*" Chitta Mini said. "*Just, uh, take a deep breath before you go in. Wish I'd told your furry friend that.*"

With no other option, I complied. I gulped down a burning lungful that rivaled an amphibian professional diver, then threw my entire body into the suit.

Viscous, unsettlingly warm sludge pressed against my face, my shoulders, my hands. I could feel it tugging at me, pulling like a thousand tiny tongues. And even as my head broke through into yet another blood-warm cavity, there was no relief—mostly on account of knowing I couldn't breathe in there. Take it from me: creatures that rely on respiration do not like being trapped in spaces without air.

Still, I had to fight back my panic. Had to conserve oxygen. Had to stay icy-cool as my entire body was hauled into the suit's lightless, airless tomb and gripped by a rubbery embrace.

"*You're doin' great!*" Chitta Mini exclaimed. "*Now, watch the magic! I only put this feature in the* deluxe *models.*"

Nota bene: Anytime a wonky superintelligence informs you they've added features to one of their designs, you should vacate the area as soon as possible. Such features are seldom conducive to your survival or comfort.

But in this instance, I didn't have the luxury of fleeing. I could only watch, in drawn-out, breathless terror, as...

The facial area became translucent.

I glimpsed the staging area through the suit's milky, membranous window, simultaneously relieved I hadn't exploded and horrified that my air was dwindling. My lungs felt like overripe berries on the verge of popping in my chest.

"*Pretty sweet, huh?*" Chitta Mini prodded.

"*Get us* out, *or we're gonna die!*" I screeched mentally.

"*Don't panic, man. This plan's like a well-oiled machine.*" Even as the chitta overly gently assuaged my fears, a trapdoor bisected and swung down in the center of the room. "*Head over and hop out, buddy!*"

Tusky's vision membrane also seemed to have engaged—despite outwardly appearing no different—seeing as the sloth-scientist was waving his arms in my direction.

I pointed to the trapdoor and lumbered toward it. By this point, I could *feel* the lack of oxygen in every cell in my body. If you've ever been close to drowning, you are intimately familiar with this sensation. It begins as a tingling in the extremities, only to ramp up to full-body burning, an omnipresent shriek for air.

And my only possible salvation from the nightmare—Halcius help me—lay in the hands of a deranged wad of chewing gum trapped inside my coffin. For the first time in a long, long while, I felt death looming behind my eyelids. The end of the whole shebang. Lights out.

This panic-dread orgy reached a fever pitch when I reached the edge of the trapdoor and looked down the chute—straight into the vacuum of space.

Only it wasn't *just* space. The edges were colored by the whitish-purple plasma of the hive-world's enormous thruster jets. Then there were the dizzying slashes and dotted trails of stray bolts, beams, and projectiles. Swooping, pirouetting gunships wove through the chaos in silent life-and-death engagements.

And dead center, far below the madness, a freckle upon a vast sea of freckles, was a yawning mouth. Metaphorically, anyway. The strings of wall-mounted lights and strapped-down cargo pallets revealed the mouth to be none other than an open staging bay. *My* staging bay. *Stream Dancer*'s. The vessel moved in perfect harmony with the hive-world—which I now realized *was* moving—to keep itself lined up with the chute.

My vision was wavering by this point, but I knew it wasn't a hallucination. Somehow, impossibly, Umzuma was keeping the ship perfectly vertical beneath us. What this means, for reference purposes, is that Chitta Mini not only expected us to leap a few thousand meters down into a moving target—he expected us to slam down against the rear wall of the staging bay. If this suit didn't hold up under the strain, or if even one hundredth of one degree was off, Tusky and I would be turned into fleshy red stains—assuming we didn't simply miss and rocket through the void, that is.

"*Gotta jump!*" Chitta Mini said. "*That ship's a sittin' duck!*"

Even as my toes curled in my boots from oxygen starvation, I hesitated. "*This is bonkers. There's no atmosphere in that thing.*"

"*Sure there is! Umzuma said your girlfriend added a stasis field!*"

"*She did what?*"

"*C'mon, I calculated this thing down to a tee! You've got this. We've got this.*"

Tusky waddled up beside me, repeatedly looking between me and the harrowing drop below.

With no other option, and certainly no words to comfort him, I took the leap.

There must've been an embedded accelerator somewhere in that chute, because the drop didn't last the twenty or so seconds I anticipated. Instead, I saw only flashes of black, white, and ion blue. There was hardly any time to even feel afraid—especially since I'd lost most of the sensation in my body, and tunnel vision was creeping in.

Then I plunged into *Stream Dancer*'s gravity field. I shut my eyes as my numb body spun and somersaulted, entirely out of my control. The world slowed to a standstill. Blood shuttled up to my skull, my feet flung away like ragdolls, and… *impact*. I felt it like a thunderclap up through the soles of my boots, yet there was no pain.

Until my back struck the floor, that is.

With eyes still closed and a vast, all-consuming blackness sweeping over me, all I sensed was a lukewarm current streaming over my lips. *Air*. Freedom.

My lungs sucked in a reflexive breath. Then my chest heaved out, and pins and needles exploded throughout my body. Almost of their own volition, my eyelids snapped apart. I was alive. Breathing. Against all odds, I'd made it.

Staring back at me were the grimy, jaundice-yellow lights of the staging bay ceiling. A feeling of sublime peace came over me as I lay there, shakily breathing, tears running down—

Tusky slammed feet-first into the same panel I'd hit. Had I not been on the verge of a coma, I'd have been startled. The enormous sloth came in like a screaming rocket. Then, predictably, his body followed the same course mine had. I was too weak to scramble aside as his bulk flopped down atop me, squirmed, and rolled onto the floor.

A strange, murky length of time passed—time gets hazy at death's door—until, eventually, I heard the clatter of footsteps. A lot of them.

"*Told you it'd work!*" Chitta Mini exclaimed.

Silhouettes crowded in around me, some shining lights in my eyes, others probing at my neck and chest. Distantly, I sensed my body being extricated from the HIIA's gloopy prison. My breathing steadied. Voices swam through the drum of my heartbeat.

"… me, Bodhi?" Ruena, I realized. Ruena was here. "Bodhi, look at me. Look up."

I did—or tried to. Locating a helmeted, four-eyed alien is not easy when you are surrounded by throngs of helmeted individuals who all appear to have four eyes. But when I spotted a helmet containing an apparent *eight* eyes, I knew I had the right one.

"That's it," Ruena said. She glanced over at Tusky, who was surrounded by an equal amount of helping hands, then back at me. Her eyes grew scornful. "That has got to be the dumbest thing you've *ever* done."

"I didn't do it," I whispered.

"What are you talking about? Umzuma got your transmission, then took us here."

"It wasn't from *me*," I managed, struggling to fish Chitta Mini out of my pocket in spite of the medical devices bleeping all around me. Ruena's future-glimpsing eyes went wide before I'd even revealed the squirming thing. "Meet the mastermind."

It took my wobbling vision a moment, however, to grasp that Ruena's reaction wasn't due to my new friend. In fact, she didn't seem to give a damn about that. Her gaze, instead, had been drawn to something happening beyond the staging bay's field.

With a grunt and a groan, I rolled my head in that direction.

Far in the distance, thousands and thousands of kilometers away from our fleeing ship, was the hive-world and its frenetic battle. Only, it wasn't the hive-world anymore. It was warped somehow, its very form stretched and striated like clay. At the heart of this melty scene was a glimmering white light. Everything—including orbital platforms, Hegemony flagships, and Kruthara's tentacle-clad legion

—was flowing toward it, *into* it. The closer things got to that core of light, the more they slowed to form a static vignette.

A miniature singularity.

In the weeks to follow, I would learn that the inustrazans had triggered this legendary weapon to prevent their hard-won knowledge (and the secrets of Gnosis) from being uploaded into Kruthara's mind. It was a last-ditch ploy embedded in the center of the giga-structure, a fail-safe designed to obliterate anything and anyone brazen enough to overrun their people. Whether this was the chitta's decision or that of Tanu Halnok may never be known. What I am certain of, however, is that this space-time-warping implosion was the only thing that saved us—and, subsequently, the universe. Thus, I cannot, and will not, disparage their end.

Those of you who have visited the Sphere of Eternal Sacrifice in person can attest to the dreadful presence of this place. Witnessing its birth was a moment I shall never forget, no matter how much I might try. Perhaps this is because its birth never truly ended. For us outside observers, safely beyond the singularity's event horizon, the hive-world and its attackers have hardly moved an inch. They will remain frozen this way until the last quarks of our universe dissolve into the ether.

I can only hope that those within its grasp died in an instant.

ELEVEN

There is an indescribable silence that follows any instance of mass annihilation. I doubt it has to do with grief—after all, beings die in the tens of millions every day in this wild cosmos, and in our own case, the inustrazans were hard to shed tears over. Instead, I'd posit that this silence is a collective realization that each person who bears witness to death will also meet the same end. Selfish? Yes. But such is the nature of a sentient being. And when a sentient being sees countless lives reduced to a bowl of quantum soup in the blink of an eye, it's only natural to have their bubble of normal, delusional safety popped.

This slap-in-the-face silence was the type that hung over the meeting module. It was deep in the bones of Chaska, Ruena, and the handful of insurgent sub-commanders sitting in the chairs around me. Everybody appeared paralyzed, stewing in the quiet.

Well, almost everybody.

"Now *that* was a getaway," Chitta Mini said through the room's speaker system. He drifted contentedly in one of Tusky's brine-filled containment canisters, perched atop our shared table like a grotesque centerpiece. "Did you guys see that blast? Helluva thing."

Chaska regarded me with a withering stare. "You have a lot of explaining to do."

I threw my hands up. "Me? He's the one responsible."

"Damn straight," Chitta Mini said. "I'll take a round of applause anytime."

Now it was Chitta Mini's turn to get Chaska's soul-stealing gaze. Not that he could see it, I figured. His only means of sensory input were a series of crude instruments Tusky had hooked up to the canister's brine. Tusky likely would've been proud of our ad-hoc arrangement had he not been in a triage module, recovering from that near-death experience.

"We just lost one of our most capable allies in this fight," Chaska said quietly. "You'd better have a damn good reason for being aboard this ship."

"To be fair, he *is* a superintelligence," I piped up.

"A sliver of one," Chaska said, still glaring at his canister. She paced around the room with arms folded and brows knitted. "So how'd you get here? Threaten Bodhi? Sweet-talk him?"

Chitta Mini sighed. "Mutual aid, Miss...?"

"Just Chaska. Don't call me 'miss.'"

"Got it, Just Chaska. So, anyway, as I was sayin'... I can help you fine folks out. Just like you're helpin' me out by flying me away from... well, you know."

"Help us with what, exactly?"

"Same thing you came to the 'strazans for? Translating that little book of yours."

Chaska gave me a questioning look.

"He can read memories," I explained. "Not with my permission, I'll have you know."

"And what do you want for your 'services'?" Chaska asked Chitta Mini.

The tiny brain floated about in vague excitement. "Bodhi knows my price. Let's just say I'm a sucker for the small things. Like ice cream."

The insurgent sub-commanders looked at one another in puzzlement, but Chaska's face only soured further.

"Let me get this straight," she said. "You want to help us... for food?"

"Yeah?"

"Why should we trust you at all?"

"You mean, aside from trusting me enough to rescue you and your crew? *And* exempting that I'm the only one capable of reading the book?"

"Yes," she said flatly.

Chitta Mini constricted, then puffed out. "Well, for starters, let's talk about the fact that I saved your sorry asses from any further *trouble* by neutralizing the Hegemony tracker in Bodhi's brain."

All eyes spun toward me.

Again, I threw up both hands. "Hey! It's not like I knew. Nor did I ask for the damn thing!"

"Bodhi," Ruena said slowly, "does that mean what I think it does?"

"You'll have to be more specific."

"The strike on Chaska's base... and that latest attack... *You* caused that?"

"I didn't cause anything! The Hegemony did. All I did was, well, inadvertently lure them to us."

Chaska leaned against a bulkhead, studying Chitta Mini's canister with cryptic eyes. "And you're *certain* that you disabled that tracker."

"Yeah?" he replied. "Why, you think I'm playin' for the other team or something?"

"I don't know what to think right now," she said.

"Oh, c'mon. If I didn't shut that thing down, I'd be risking my own ass out here. Well, not my ass. I don't have one. But you know what I mean."

Chaska nodded. "Good. Because if you weren't sure, we'd have to smash Bodhi's head. And then you."

"Well, then, it's a real good thing I'm sure."

"Yes," I said, quite certain Chaska hadn't been speaking hyperbolically, "it certainly is."

Ruena stood up and released a tense breath. "I'd say it's time we give our new stowaway a chance to help us."

The sub-commanders all looked to Chaska, who in turn retrieved the book-holding satchel from a nearby cubby. Until now, I hadn't even realized they'd taken that particular piece of leverage away from me.

She pulled out Diman's journal, moved to our table, and flipped to the relevant page. Then she propped the book up in front of Chitta Mini's visual scanner.

"*Oooh*," Chitta Mini said, "this is… new. Where'd you find this?"

Chaska stepped back with a hard expression. "Doesn't matter. Just tell us what it says."

"You want the full spiel or the gist of it?"

"Everything."

"Alrighty. One the-whole-damn-thing special comin' right up." Chitta Mini huffed, then, adopting an imperious tone that made me jumped in my seat, began the translation. "This is the one and true word of the Great Maker, Engineer and Architect of All That Is, Preserver of the Eternal Way, Illuminator of the Vast Darkness—"

"Skip the honorifics," Chaska interjected.

Chitta Mini gave another impatient huff. "As you command… This wisdom is delivered to the highest beings, a sacred treatise on the expulsion and ultimate eradication of That Which Should Not Be. Thus we have heard that the Great Maker is aware of, and determined to end, the threat that sleeps under the bones of all sentient beings. The Great Maker, in his infinite glory and forethought, has prepared this instruction in the service of victory.

"That Which Should Not Be is unfathomable in its terrors, endless in its legions, and unassailable in its conquest. Only the instruments of the Great Maker may expunge its presence from this world and all worlds beyond it.

"Go, sentient ones, to that which cannot be penetrated through the manipulation of time and space—the immaculate realm of the Untraversed. Go, sentient ones, to the font of wisdom in which the Great Maker is forever dreaming. Go, sentient ones, to the gateway of gnosis that will liberate all beings from this undying fear. Go, sentient beings, and take up the arms of your savior.

"Delay not in your journey, sentient ones, for if you have read these words, the age of the Great Maker has come to its foretold end. With the cessation of the Great Maker comes the cessation of wisdom and the disappearance of all devices that might annihilate That Which Should Not Be. But hold the sacrifice of the Great Maker in your mind, sentient one, for you have found the doorway to prophecy. Venture toward the source. Enter his eternal domain with surrender. Become the empty vessel into which he may bestow his knowledge.

"This, sentient ones, is the only path to preservation."

And with that, Chitta Mini went silent. Deathly silent.

"So," I said, leaning back, "it seems the 'Great Maker' was rather fond of word salads."

"You're one to talk," Ruena said.

I scoffed. "Listen, all I'm saying is that if *I* were going to prepare the future 'sentient ones' to fight off some ancient alien threat, I'd at least have the decency to communicate like a normal person, not an occult instruction manual."

"It mentioned weapons," one of the sub-commanders put in. "Weapons that might kill Kruthara."

"A round of applause for our astute listener," I said.

"Bodhi, that's enough," Ruena snapped. "If this is real—"

"Yes, *if*," Chaska interrupted, breaking her stoic silence. "For all we know, those weapons—and their designs—could've been destroyed ages ago."

I crossed my arms. "A few hours back, you were willing to destroy half a galaxy to figure out what was in that book. Well, now you've got it. I think you all owe an apology to me and Chitta Mini." Everybody blinked at me, puzzled. "What? It's just a name I thought up."

"Vugran," Chaska said, nodding at one of her burly-looking sub-commanders, "I want your cryptology unit to start analyzing the message. Maybe they can work out what it means."

Chitta Mini burst out laughing. "Why would you need to do that?"

"Do you have something to say?"

"Well, I didn't before, but seeing as you're all clueless... maybe you'd like my commentary?"

"Depends what commentary you have to offer."

"Oh, I dunno, the commentary of a being who was alive when the Maker first went to war with the krutharans?"

I swept a ceremonial hand toward the chitta. "Do go on, Mini."

"Alright, here's the scoop," Chitta Mini said as the others settled back with rapt attention. "So the Maker invented a bunch of super-duper Kruthara-killing weapons back in the first war. Y'know, the one where he conquered the whole krutharan species and stuck Kruthara in a cage. But the Maker was pretty sharp. He knew those damned krutharans would find a way to unleash their god eventually. Everybody still with me?"

"We know all this," Chaska growled. "Get on with it."

"Fine, fine... yeesh, you're a snippy crowd. What's the rush?" Chitta Mini paused. "Oh, right. Well, anyway, back to the commentary. So the Maker decides to stash the blueprints for his arsenal someplace safe... someplace Kruthara couldn't ever get to them. Like his tomb, for instance."

Chaska grunted. "I hope you're not just speculating about this."

"Of course not. Us chittas used to talk, y'know. This whole thing was gristle for our rumor mill for a good ten, twenty thousand years. Then we just... stopped caring."

"If it was just rumors, how do you know?"

"Because the translation just confirmed it! Seriously, people, pay attention. Remember this part? 'The font of wisdom in which the Great Maker is forever dreaming'? Yeah, spoiler alert—that's his tomb. He's got his mind uploaded in that thing."

At this, everybody plunged into another mic-drop silence. Bewildered gazes met one another for a solid ten seconds. See, this was big news. Bigger than big. Us puny humans, as a species, had lived our entire lives believing the Maker was dead and gone. But if Chitta Mini was telling the truth, the Maker was still here, in some way. Maybe not in body, but in mind. And when you're a universe-conquering demigod, a mind is all you need to stay relevant.

"You're making it up," Chaska whispered.

Chitta Mini chuckled. "Wouldn't dream of it, sweet cheeks. I'm telling you, the Maker's mind—which is crammed full of ways to make Kruthara-destroying gadgets—is floating in a tomb out there somewhere."

"How do you know it still exists? It's probably been millions of years since it was built."

"If you knew the Maker, you'd know that millions of years are nothin' for that guy."

"Doesn't mean it hasn't been raided already."

"Yeah, well, I know my boss. He wouldn't have made it that easy."

Chaska sank down in a seat near me. "Even if you're telling the truth—which I'm starting to doubt—we'd need to *get* to that tomb. And I didn't hear any coordinates in that thing."

"The realm of the Untraversed," I said, drawing everyone's attention. "It's a place, not just an expression, right?"

Chitta Mini gave a triumphant *mm-hmm*. "Seems like Bodhi's the brightest bulb here. Knew I picked a good one."

The sub-commanders murmured among themselves, but Chaska kept her attention trained on the canister. "Do you know where it is? *What* it is?"

"Yes to the first, kinda to the second," Chitta Mini explained. "Never been there, but I had access to the inustrazan archives. They logged plenty of expeditions into that thing. Always assumed it was just some kind of anomaly or something, turned back early. Hah! They seem mighty foolish right about now."

I scrunched my brow. "What is it? A wormhole?"

"Nope. It's, uh… gee, I dunno how to explain it to you smooth-brains. No offense. It's just, you need a working knowledge of space-time fabric to get it."

"Assume we understand," Chaska said through gritted teeth.

Chitta Mini hummed. "Think of it like this. You all can pinch just fine through normal—make that flat—space-time. No planets or ships around you? You're good to hop just about anywhere that's equally 'flat.' No gravitational ripples, no problem, right?"

"Right…"

"But the Maker was smart about this stuff. Seems he didn't want a bunch of numbskulls pinching their way right up to the tomb's front doors and looting it. So it looks like he made the Untraversed. Or at least stashed his tomb inside it. See, it's right here in the translation: 'That which cannot be penetrated through the manipulation of time and space.'"

"But what *is* it?" Chaska pressed.

"Hold on, I'm gettin' there. So normal space-time—flat. Pinch in and out. The Untraversed is… not flat. I dunno how he did it, but that's the short answer. You can't pinch through that thing. Too dense. Which is why all those inustrazan explorers didn't bother goin' too far in... and those that went in, well, they never came back out."

The captain within me started working at the problem Chitta Mini had raised. I thought it prudent to tackle these issues aloud. "If you can't pinch within it, you'd need standard fuel."

"Right again, Bodhi!" Chitta Mini said. I was starting to like this thing. "Same fuel needed to maneuver in the atmosphere. Or in water. Whatever. Point is, it probably explains why the inustrazans didn't make it so far. The Untraversed isn't normal space—it's more like a fluid. Need to push your way through it."

Chaska stared, stony-faced, at the canister. "How far would we need to go to reach the Maker's tomb?"

"How the hell should I know?" Chitta Mini said. "I never saw the thing. I just know it's at the center. 'Venture toward the source,' y'know? It's gotta be in there."

I shared a brief, uneasy glance with Chaska, then said, "I'm not liking this."

"I don't much care," she said. "We don't have anywhere else to go."

"Aside from literally anywhere else in this entire ever-expanding universe?"

"This is not just about us. Or you, for that matter."

I rubbed my temples, trying to stay composed. "Chaska, we could run out of fuel halfway through it... if we even got halfway, that is. Or, best-case scenario, we could reach it and *then* be out of fuel. Dicey."

"I can't believe I'm agreeing," Ruena said, "but I think he's right. We don't know enough to wander into that region. It could be a suicide mission."

Chaska rounded on her. "This entire war has been a suicide mission." She looked at each of us in turn, sparing a particularly vicious look for me. "We didn't come all this way to roll over now. Whether or not the answers are in that tomb, it's our last shot. Our only shot. And I'm not willing to give that up."

"So, what then?" I asked. "Is it mutiny now? Just gonna drag us all into this?"

"This ship became mine when you turned yourself over," Chaska snapped. "And don't talk about dragging anybody into anything, Bodhi. You've dragged all of us into more messes than I can count."

"Point taken."

She walked up to Chitta Mini's canister and knocked on the glass. "If you know where the edge of the Untraversed is, I want my navigation team to have that information in ten minutes. Do you understand me?"

"First off, that was hella loud," Chitta Mini groaned. "And second, I'll get you those coordinates… when I get my ice cream."

"We don't have any."

"Then no coordinates!"

"Then you go out the airlock, you little—"

"Wait, wait," I said, sighing with hands raised in surrender. "Check my quarters. Second drawer under the work desk, code A-5-E."

That was the toughest blow I took that entire day. Forget the inustrazans—I'd been waiting to savor that quart of mint-lavender ice cream since the first day I got locked up in the Contrition. But sacrifices must sometimes be made.

Chaska glowered at me, then turned to a sub-commander with an orange ponytail. "Get his stash, bring it back here. And make sure this thing gives you those coordinates." As the commander snapped out a floppy salute and strolled off, Chaska refocused her attention on—who else?—your dear narrator. "Bodhi, come with me."

When you were a child, were you ever scolded by a parent in front of your friends? Yeah? Well, bring to mind the wary amusement displayed by the aforementioned friends. The way they delighted in your thrashing. This was precisely what I saw in Ruena's eyes as I groaned, stood, and followed Chaska into the corridor.

"What now?" I asked as she led me toward the bridge. "Putting another set of shackles on me?"

She glanced back. "No need—you're already in a floating cell."

"So... what do you want?"

"Does that really matter now?"

I sensed I was treading on rocky ground here. Chaska didn't sound *mad* per se, but she didn't sound elated, either. There was something malignant under her calmness. Something that would devour me if I wasn't careful. If you are a male who doesn't understand this ambiguous yet slippery situation, I suggest you start studying now. Even the craftiest of alchemists have been destroyed by this strain of dark feminine energy.

"You got what *you* wanted," Chaska continued. "You always do."

"We *both* got what we wanted. You got your translation, and now we're headed to yet another vague, apocalyptic force. You're welcome, by the way."

She snorted. "Welcome? You have no idea how far the ripples of that little stunt will travel."

"Not to get technical on you, Chaska, but in a singularity, the ripples go *inwards*, so..."

"Is that the best counter you've got?"

"Look—I saw a chance with Mini, and I took it. Now you've got your way forward! Call it a gamble on my part. A gamble that paid off."

She shook her head. "The house wins in the end, Bodhi. The game's rigged that way."

"The metaphor's losing me. Is Kruthara the house?"

"No, you are. *You're* back on the ship, I'm paying *you* far more attention than you deserve, and *you* get a break from your girlfriend."

"Amodari? Oh, well, uh... she's gone."

"Wanna bet on it?"

I froze mid-step. "Do you know something I don't?"

"Only that the dead don't send transmissions," Chaska said coldly. "Pick up the pace—it was addressed to you."

I wasn't sure what to feel as Amodari's message spooled up on the bridge's main terminal. Part of me was glad that Chitta Mini had (so it seemed) carried out my instructions to perfection—testing limits is a good way to gauge a superintelligence's viability, after all. But another part of me was petrified. Considering the inustrazan's sadistic nature, there was a chance her transmission was part of some intricate yet chilling practical joke. Perhaps it would contain nothing more than "Look behind you"—a suggestion that would immediately precede my beheading.

But upon seeing Amodari's haggard face, barely visible in some dim corner of an emergency vessel, I tossed that prediction. She was broken.

"By now, I can only assume that you were involved in this," Amodari whispered. "The deaths of my people are on your hands. This being the case, I don't have much of anything to say to you, Bodhi Drezek. Only this: If and when I find you, I will rip you apart. You could have had true and undying love, but you have chosen death. And it will *not* be a slow end."

And with that, the transmission fizzled out.

Chaska was studying me from a nearby chair, probably trying to get a read on my reaction. For what purpose, I had no idea. All I know is that I played my cards well.

Inwardly, of course, I was relieved—not only that she'd

survived, but that she was somewhere away from here. The death threat was negligible. At the time these events took place, I had no fewer than three hundred sixteen "I'll get you" types eager to mount my head on a pole. Amodari, despite her *former* power, was just one name on an endless list. Or so I assumed.

Regardless, Chaska killed the feed and stood up. "I suppose I ought to thank you now."

I frowned. "For?"

"Avenging my troops."

"Through genocide and the obliteration of a million-plus years of knowledge?"

"Call it what you want," Chaska said softly. "All I know is that the inustrazans had it coming. We were just insects to them."

"Bit of a different tune than you were singing in the meeting module, no?"

"In there, it's a war. It's professional. And what I said was true —you did cost us an ally." She shrugged. "But here, between us, it's personal. I won't lose sleep over what happened to them."

It was strange to be "commended" for such a heinous scene, especially when I'd played no conscious role in bringing it about. But as they often say, there's a silver lining in every stellar collapse. Getting back on Chaska's good side was the best possible outcome from this situation. Mass extinction as a bonding element—who knew?

"Well, uh… you're welcome?" I said.

She looked out through the main viewpane. "Just know it's the last good thing I'll say to you about it. What happened here was beyond reckless."

"And you think flying toward yet another long-dead, probably evil artifact *isn't* reckless?"

"I think it's our last shot."

"Chaska, I'm just trying to get you to see the bigger picture here. Every time we've been led to one of those 'miracles' in deep space, it throws an even worse wrench into the cogs of reality. Are you seeing the pattern?"

"Fight fire with fire."

I groaned. "Look, there's a reason the Hegemony didn't kill me. They were using Kruthara to get something out of my head."

"What's your point?"

"I figured it out, Chaska. It's *you*."

Her eyes hardened. "What?"

"Don't you see it? Kruthara's got Palamar's memories. Palamar *knew* Diman had stashed that book somewhere, and he also knew you were tight with Diman. *And* he knew that you and I were close. Ergo…"

"You're looking too deeply into this."

"No, I'm not! I'm just playing ten-dimensional chess here. Problem is, Kruthara's playing with twenty dimensions."

"Let's say you're right. What does it change?"

"Everything?"

"Wrong," she snapped. "If Kruthara is treating that book's translation as a threat, it means it's exactly what we need. I can feel it."

"Because you're desperate."

"You don't know what desperation is, Bodhi. Desperation is having to choose between preserving an entire pocket-universe or a freighter full of children. Desperation is sacrificing half your fleet just to hold an evacuation line. Desperation is—"

"I get it."

"No, I don't think you do. But I don't care anymore. I'll let you stay on this ship with your new 'buddy,' but your days of calling the shots are over."

I stretched back in my chair, yawning. "Believe me, I gave up illusions of command long, long ago."

"Good. And don't even think about defying me in front of my troops again, or I'll change my mind about keeping you on this side of the airlock."

I leaned over, looking past Chaska at Umzuma's pit. "Hear that, 'Zuma? Chaska's the new head honcho around here."

Umzuma grumbled—surely in support of me.

"Let me make it clear," Chaska said. "Either you stay on this ship to the end of the line, or we let you off somewhere along the way. That's the best I can offer you."

At that moment, a switch flipped in my mind. My course of action, and by extension success, became strikingly clear. If I wanted to regain control of my ship and grab the bull of destiny by its horns, I'd have to play along with Chaska's power grab for the time being. And how did I come to this realization? Simple, really. Let's consider the analogy of trying to force open a door. If somebody is standing on the other side of that door and pressing their full weight against it, you stand very little chance of breaking through without some heavy-duty explosive ordnance. The only way to get that door open is by tricking the bastard on the other side into letting their guard down. And the moment they take their weight off that door, you push like a madman.

Now, Chaska wasn't some crazed warlord or insectoid horror. I didn't concoct this plan with the intention of betraying her, let alone killing her. No, I'd do this because it was our only shot at survival. Note the word *our*. I could've easily found a way to ditch *Stream Dancer* and forge a lonely, modestly successful path through the stars. But that was self-oriented, and if I am anything, it's a man who puts others first (sometimes).

Chaska *needed* me to overthrow her, even if she didn't know it. Otherwise, she'd be leading herself, her forces, and the scraps of my beloved crew into yet another death trap. So, when viewed from that angle, I was doing this for the sake of everybody *but* myself. And if you still don't believe me, consider this—I knew full well that outwitting Chaska would widen the already-vast chasm between us. If and when I pulled off this stunt, she might never speak to me again.

Yet I still had to do it.

With all this in mind, I had no problem nodding bashfully and looking at her with the right dose of shame.

"Alright, Chaska, we'll do it your way. No complaints. It's been dreadful of me to keep stepping on your toes. If we're being honest, I was always hoping you'd call the shots around here. You know how to take care of people better than I do."

She nearly flinched. "You mean it?"

"One hundred percent. All that time in the Contrition made me think about what matters most in the world... and I figured it out. It's life. And try as I might, I can't think of anybody else nobler or more ardent in defending life. So please forgive me, Chaska. I was out of line."

This pathos-laden speech must've really done a number on her brain, because it took her well over five seconds to patch together a reply.

"That's... very kind of you," she managed. "But it's going to take some time for me to trust you fully, especially after what's gone down in the last day or two. I hope you get that."

"But of course. What kind of commander would you be if you didn't maintain healthy suspicion?"

She nodded, now looking somewhat humbled herself. "Well, thank you. I just want us to come out the other end of this war."

"Sensible indeed." I paused, tossing in a crooked smile for good measure. "What's your next move? Are we heading straight to that, uh... field thing? The Untraversed?"

"Sort of. We aren't diving straight in."

"Oh?"

Chaska bit her nails as she turned toward the viewpane. "Ruena was right. And you, too, I guess. We'll need a steady supply of fuel in that thing."

"Right..."

"I'm preparing a message to a local section commander. If all goes to plan, they should be able to send a logistics and supply unit to us within a day."

This is the hard part of the "winning trust" plan. What Chaska was proposing here was a *terrible* idea, and not only because it involved the most incompetent resistance force ever assembled. See, when you're in a universe-ending war, carrying the most highly sensitive document in known space, and lacking guns of any kind on your vessel, beaming your precise location to a bunch of loose-lipped numbskulls with zero operational security is the literal *last* thing you ought to be doing. My misgivings would be proven correct in record-breaking time, but for now, let's just say it took every drop of willpower in my body to hold my tongue and keep up the ruse.

"A solid plan," I said. "Just let me know when we're almost there. I'm going to have a peek at our chitta, make sure they're settling in well."

She nodded. "Thanks again. I couldn't do this without help."

That was one thing I could honestly agree with.

TWELVE

Phase two of my "overthrow Chaska to save everyone" plan came in the form of appealing to allies. Generally, when recruiting said allies for a soft mutiny, you'll have enough to at least have a fighting chance at assuming control. Numerically, we're talking about a third of a ship's crew. And even then, that third had better have access to sensitive systems—turrets, lockdown protocols, that sort of thing.

I didn't have the luxury of specialized coup participants. Instead, I had a wad of ancient brain tissue and a weary ligethan that would soon be engaging in a multiday nap. Not ideal, but it would have to do. Even if I'd wanted to recruit Gadra for this plan—which I certainly did not—there was little the girl could do for us. Nobody in universal history has ever bolstered a coup with paintings and tattoos.

Well, except for the Nimassi Revolt, but that's another story.

The point is, I encountered the entirety of my "war team" the moment I strode back into the meeting module. Gadra was leaning over the table, chatting eagerly with Chitta Mini, while Ruena sat slumped in a chair near the door. Chaska's insurgents had seemingly departed to handle whatever top-secret, super-duper-important business insurgents busy themselves with.

"But what about the ink?" Gadra asked, dropping another scoop of ice cream into the chitta's already-cloudy canister. Her eyes were aglow with primal, burning interest, as though the chitta were relaying the secrets of creation itself. "Don't you need some kinda pigment? Y'know, to get it to mix right?"

Chitta Mini made a *pfft* sound. "Ink-shmink. I've seen skin-stretchers use beetle blood to make those tats. Also seen platinum blends, henna, root-brew... you name it, it's been used for these things. And they all work!"

Gadra, noticing me for the first time since I stepped inside, grinned maniacally. "Can we keep him forever?"

I folded my arms as Ruena turned toward me. "I think that's up to Chitta Mini, not me."

"'Kay, well, he's teaching me how to make the *hypnotic mandalas*." She waved her arms in witchy circles to highlight the term. "Told ya they're real! Just you wait. Gonna have people flat on their asses real fast."

"Butts, Gadra."

"But what?"

"Never mind." I sighed and sat next to Ruena as the two carried on with their mumbo-jumbo tattoo tales. "Feeling tired, Ru?"

"Feels like I haven't *not* been tired since this thing started," Ruena said with a quiet laugh.

"You're telling me. Sometimes I wish this place were a Contrition hallucination."

"Technically speaking, everything's a hallucination."

I waved her off. "Cool it with the existential crises, Ru."

"Have it your way. Did you visit Tusky yet?"

Admittedly, I'd more or less forgotten the sloth even existed. "That's, uh, on my list of things to do."

"He's not recovering from the oxygen deprivation like we

expected," Ruena said. "Makes me wonder if your chitta here could work some magic on him."

"I don't know if we have enough ice cream for that."

Ruena hardly seemed to hear me. "The insurgent medics said something's off in his bloodwork. The cells aren't replicating right. They've still got him in a light coma."

"I'm sure it's nothing."

"Nothing? He could be dying."

"Aren't we all?"

She eyed me sidelong. "Do you know something about this that I don't?"

"Like what?"

"You tell me."

If the situation had been calmer, I might've opened the can of worms that was Tusky's accelerated mortality. Might've. It didn't feel right, sharing a secret that the sloth himself had asked me to hold close to my chest. But sooner or later, somebody would have to tell the others. With things being as they currently were, that revelation fell firmly in the "later" category.

"I barely know him, let alone his medical file," I told her. "Anyway... I came here to ask you about something."

"No."

"No?"

"No, you don't have a shot with Chaska."

"I wasn't even gonna ask that."

She grinned. "Twosight says you were."

"Yeah, well, I wasn't." Truth be told, I wasn't sure if future-me would've asked that or not. Yet another dose of nightmare fuel. "Listen, Ru, I just talked with the lady herself. She's putting us on a collision course with disaster."

"Meaning?"

I sighed. "She's telling the insurgency to send some sort of fuel-supply fleet to the edge of the Untraversed. Trying to rendezvous so we can head in as a group."

"What's the issue there?"

"You don't see it? Come on. How many times have we been ambushed by a three-tongued warrior tribe who managed to intercept our 'encrypted' comms?"

"Bodhi, this entire galaxy has cooled down. Most of the bad ones are in hiding, assuming they haven't been exterminated yet."

"The Hegemony's still kicking."

"Don't you think you're being paranoid?"

"Paranoid is just another term for 'hasn't been proven correct yet.' And I'm certain I *will* be."

"How far out did she say the ships were?"

"She didn't," I said, frowning. "She just said they're local."

"Well, there you go. Even if the Hegemony manages to crack those comms, we'll meet the insurgents and be on our way. Once we put a few million kilometers between us and the rendezvous spot, we'll be ghosts to anybody who comes looking."

"I think you're underestimating the risk here, Ru."

"Let's say I am. What does it matter? Chaska was clear on this one: we're just along for the ride. And the sooner you accept that—"

"We don't have to," I whispered. "I've got a plan."

"Oh, please don't say that."

"But I do!"

"Your last *plan* sucked the entire inustrazan species into a void."

"Ru, just hear me out." I grunted, forcing myself to stay calm so as not to alarm Gadra or our new guest. "If we got control of this vessel, we could make a newer, better, less death-inviting plan to secure the Maker's tomb. We've got connections. Brains. But right now, we're subject to the whims of the insurgents. And you know that's a recipe for doom."

A shadow of reluctant acknowledgment flitted through Ruena's four eyes. I'd hit the right spot. Now to drive the pitch home.

"All I'm asking is for you to help me get Chaska out of the captain's chair. You and I are the only ones who can see what this war's done to her mind. She's off."

"And what do you propose?" Ruena asked. "Chaining her up to a pipe? Drugging her?"

"No and no. We just need to isolate the insurgents long enough for you and me to get some control over the bridge."

"Then what?"

Ruena's greatest attribute, her perceptive nature, was also her worst in this situation. It was bold of her to even assume I had a plan beyond locking up our unwelcome guests and setting a new course to... somewhere. Still, the show had to go on. Like any good performer, I improvised. And even I was impressed with how well the plan toppled out of my mouth.

"*Then* we proceed to a cluster in the Nogo that hasn't been hit by Kruthara, wrangle up some of our high-profile connections, and organize the expedition ourselves. If we go in guns blazing right now, we're not only asking for trouble—we're leading any pursuers straight to the source. Wouldn't it be better to lie low for a while, come at the Untraversed from another angle, and bring along proper, sensible manpower to boot?" As a finishing touch, I glanced Gadra's way. "Just think of the girl, Ru. Do you really want to drag her into a harebrained scheme that I didn't personally design?"

Ruena chewed on it for a while, but I could see the mark of a successful sale in her expression.

"Fine," she said at last. "Tell me what I need to do."

If you are an exacting reader, you may have already picked up on the "gap" in my mutiny plan. Namely, the part that goes between "planning a mutiny" and "completing the mutiny." That's because I hadn't come up with it yet. Thus, I spent a feverish few hours in my new cell (also known as the unlocked brig) dreaming up, discarding, and tweaking ideas as we pinched toward the Untraversed.

Although each of my scenarios naturally involved Chitta Mini, I decided to keep him out of the loop until it was go time. It was too soon in our relationship to trust him with keeping secrets, especially when said secrets involved seizing control of the very ship providing him with safe passage. But I knew he'd stick by me when push came to shove. I'd rescued him from the clutches of Queen Terror and her legions, after all. And loyalty had to count for something, even among superintelligences. Or so I told myself.

Anyhow, after running countless iterations through my head, I came up with a winning strategy—or at least, a strategy least likely to go wrong. It featured a lot of technical hijinks that I doubt you'd much care to understand, so let me offer you a basic rundown of *Bodhi's Mutiny*.

1. Have Ruena (a trusted team member) lure Chaska and her insurgent pals into the staging bay by claiming there's something incredible they simply *must* see there.
2. Splice Chitta Mini into the ship's logic net, allowing him to override and revoke Chaska's command privileges.
3. Seal the doors to the staging bay.
4. Find a way to make all the insurgents shackle themselves.
5. Figure out what to do with a staging bay full of insurgents.

Okay, so maybe the plan wasn't fully formed, but the most important aspects—regaining control of the ship *and* the unruly freeloaders aboard it—would be handled. All that remained was the pivotal component of the whole thing: convincing Chitta Mini to hack the logic net for me.

I went to his module with an hour left on our pinch, waiting until a team of Chaska's "cryptology" experts finished up their most recent interrogation session before making my entrance. After a brief, pleasant exchange, I laid out the plan for him. Then I braced myself for the barrage of questions I knew was en route, such as "What's in it for me?" "What comes after that?" "Why should I trust you?"

To my great surprise, however, Chitta Mini was more enthusiastic about the plan than me.

"You trust *me* to break the logic net and command a ship?" he asked, keeping his voice low despite the obvious excitement. "Boy, that'd just make my day! Haven't cracked into one of these babies in… oh, I dunno, ten thousand years!"

I kept my elation under wraps as I settled into a chair. "Are you sure you remember how to do it?"

"Me? The chitta who just commandeered the entire hive-world?"

"To be fair, that was your entire body. Well, old body. You know what I mean."

"Hey! Size isn't everything."

"You were also permanently patched into that system. You'd been working with it for millennia. This needs to be done on the fly, and fast. Can you manage?"

"Can a gepris slug chew through steel?" I blinked at him, prompting a sigh. "Y'know, don't answer that. Those things went extinct a few centuries ago. What I'm sayin' is *yes*. I can manage the hell out of it."

"Good, because there's a considerable amount of ice cream riding on this job."

"Say no more, Bodhi. Say no more."

A knock at the doorway behind me made me jump in my skin. I

turned to see none other than Chaska leaning there, arms folded and brows knitted.

"Am I interrupting something?" she asked.

"Interrupting?" Chitta Mini said. "Us? No. Never. We're just… talking man-stuff."

"Man-stuff? But you're a—"

"Paragon of masculinity, just like Bodhi. Yes, that's right."

Chaska regarded me with a strange expression. "We're coming out of the pinch now. You're welcome to watch the rendezvous on the bridge—provided you keep your paws off the controls."

"Why, I'd love to," I said, making a mental note to lecture Chitta Mini on his idea of "diversionary chatter." That hunk of brain tissue was more conspicuous than horns on a toad (which, by the way, I've only seen twice). Hoping to ease Chaska further, I offered a slight bow. "I'll make an appearance in just a few minutes, Captain."

She nodded and started down the corridor, looking rather perplexed by the whole interaction. A good sign.

Once she was out of earshot, I lifted my wrist transmitter and whispered, "Ruena… it's time."

In hindsight, I probably should've conferred with Ruena beforehand to ensure that her "believable story" was, in fact, believable. It can't be easy to lure a few dozen insurgents into a staging bay for a prolonged amount of time, after all. But as it turned out, Ruena was either an adept manipulator—future vision helps, I suppose—or these insurgents had the collective intelligence of a trashteroid. Either way, the result was the same. I watched the miracle unfold on one of the bridge's simscreens, which displayed a live camera feed from the staging bay.

Ruena had managed to herd every single insurgent, including

Chaska, into a solitary flock at the far end of the bay. They stood around in rapt attention, all listening to whatever drivel Ruena was peddling.

And although I was curious what exactly was transpiring there, I had two other, equally pressing matters to keep an eye on.

The first was Chitta Mini, who had one tendril snaked into my ear and the other probing around the panels beneath the main terminal, blindly probing for the logic net's hydrostatic mesh—in layman's terms, a "wet" panel he could interface with.

The second was the Untraversed, which encompassed the entirety of the bridge's viewpane. It was just a few kilometers away from us and would've been dismissed as a patch of nebular gas if not for its peculiar shifting, almost breathing quality and violet shimmer. It reminded me of the fumes that squiggle above a pool of gasoline. There were no obvious warning signs around it, but then again, it was so vast I doubt we'd have found one even if we went looking. According to Umzuma's initial scan, the field was several million kilometers in circumference—and that's without even factoring in its inherent time-space distortion. In short, it was big. Big and unknowable. Adding to its mystique was the fact that I saw nothing within it aside from a few drifting masses and scuttled wrecks. This was truly unmapped territory, and there was no way in hell I'd be going into it.

"*Feel free to accelerate your work anytime*," I told Chitta Mini.

He grunted in my mind. "*I'm almost there.*"

"*Yeah, well, Chaska and her forces are* almost *ready to leave the staging bay.*"

"*You can't rush perfection, man.*"

Groaning, I flipped on the staging bay feed's audio to give myself the illusion of being proactive. Ruena's voice was the first thing to trickle through.

"And as you can see here"—she gestured to a large, sealed crate I'd last known to contain eight-armed mannequins—"there are plenty of armored suits to go around. The inustrazans used, uh, telepathy to tell me they'd moved them... onto our ship."

If I'd palmed my own face any harder, I'd have broken my nose. *This* was what passed for a convincing lie? No wonder I'd been able to hoodwink half the universe.

But sure enough, Chaska and her forces ate this stuff up. They marveled at the crate, asking a series of progressively stupider questions about how it worked and how invisible it would make them. Ruena answered each inquiry with far more gravitas than I'd have been able to manage.

"*And... I'm in!*" Chitta Mini announced.

"*Lovely work, brain,*" I said, patting the lump in my pocket gently. Then I lifted my transmitter, still keyed to Ruena's comms, and said, "We're good on override. Get yourself out here so we can set a new course."

"Ah, please excuse me," Ruena said, holding up her hands to stall any incoming questions. "I just need to... uh, use the washroom for a moment."

The insurgents didn't seem fazed by her abrupt power-walk out of the staging bay, though Chaska did turn and watch the ligethan with too much interest for my taste. No matter. The moment Ruena made it past the staging bay's threshold, I gave Chitta Mini the mental command to seal the door.

And he did.

At first, nothing seemed amiss. The insurgents began pawing at the crate, chatting with one another about "combat prowess" and other stupid topics. Chaska milled about, evidently warier than her comrades, but otherwise did nothing. All across the simscreen's camera feeds, things were at peace. Even little Gadra was occupied with the wholesome task of sitting at Tusky's bedside and stroking his paw.

"*So we're clear?*" Chitta Mini whispered.

"*Clear as the sky,*" I said, sighing and tracking Ruena's movement down the main corridor. *"Now we just have to get a move on before—"*

A bridge-wide *bleep-bleep* cut me off, not to mention chilled my blood. *Bleep-bleep* was the last thing I wanted to hear. It meant that a transmission had come through over our primary line. And in our current predicament, there were zero transmissions that could be considered good.

I had Chitta Mini retract his tendril from the logic net, then moved to the viewpane and gazed around at the vast space around the border of the Untraversed. To my dismay, there was a unit of six, perhaps seven ships far below us, all moving toward our position with considerable speed. Their ragtag designs made it clear they weren't Hegemony—though at that moment, I almost wished they were.

Again, that damned *bleep-bleep* sounded.

"Umzuma," I said, massaging my temples, "please put our *guests* through."

Seconds later, the face of a surly-looking... *humanoid*... materialized out of the main projector. To this day, I have no idea what species commanded that vessel. Describing it as androgynous would be too mild, on account of its mottled, keratin-dappled skin and impressive array of facial tusks.

For better or worse, however, I knew this charming creature was aligned with the insurgents. A crew of humans and other assorted harmless-looking species milled about behind their terminal, all dressed in splotchy flight suits or sleeveless shirts.

"Greetings," the creature said. Its voice resembled air being forced through a series of misshapen flutes. "We are seeking the one known as Chaska of Lattram. Are you a member of her crew?"

"You could say that, yes," I replied. "Chaska's just... occupied at the moment."

"With what task?"

"Captain things."

"*What's the play, chief?*" Chitta Mini whispered in my frontal lobe.

"*Not now,*" I thought back. "*I'm working on it.*"

Even as I "worked on it," however, I noticed the insurgent ships engaging in some odd behavior on the terminal simscreens. One vessel—a long, Cuthal-class fuel barge—was swinging around to our rear, parking just a few hundred meters away. Another pair moved to our left and right flanks, respectively. The others waited beside the main transmitting ship, which I took to be the grease-smeared, chain-gun-packing behemoth just ahead.

Whether you've commanded a ship or not, I'm sure you understand what was happening as well as I did: an ambush.

"Something the matter?" I asked the insurgent captain.

"I don't believe so," they replied. "You asked for our assistance in navigating this region... and we have dutifully arrived."

"So you have. Just give me a moment to, uh, find Chaska on the simscreens. I'll call her up so you two can confer."

"Excellent."

"*This is lookin' weird,*" Chitta Mini said.

I clamped a hand around my pocket, shutting the little tissue-ball up while I approached the simscreens and scrambled for a plan. It's not easy to wrangle your way out of a tense situation when you have no idea what the opposing party wants. Had they intended to rob Chaska, or relieve her of duty? Did they think I'd killed her and assumed command? These options, among many others that didn't spring to mind, seemed equally viable.

"*You can talk with Umzuma, right?*" I thought to Chitta Mini. He grunted back, prompting me to release my grip. "*If I hook you back up to the logic net, can you slip him a message?*"

Chitta Mini began snaking a tendril out of my pocket. "*Yeah, long as you don't choke me out again, y'bastard!*"

"*Tell him that on my signal, he should get us out of here by any means except entering the Untraversed,*" I explained. "*Those ships *aren't as fast, but they'll chew us up if we're not able to do some aerial hijinks in the vacuum."*

"*You sure about that?*" Chitta Mini asked as he reconnected to the logic net.

"*Positive. Those things aren't guided projectiles—a few jukes and twirls from Umzuma, and we'll be safely on our way to a pinch at the system's edge.*"

"*If you say so…*"

"Is there an issue?" the insurgent captain asked, leaning toward his terminal's camera and flashing his triple-lidded eyes. "As I understand, Chaska of Lattram specifically asked for deuterium fuel. If you'd be so kind as to deploy your staging bay's ramp, we could hook up a direct line to the B6 spigot."

B6 spigot. Something was wrong, hideously wrong, though it took my conscious mind a moment to catch up and pinpoint what it was. When I got it, my whole body locked up.

In case you're ignorant regarding this topic, most pro-grade staging bays are marked by a grid pattern to distribute cargo evenly. B6 was one such grid tile and had once been fitted with a pumping spigot connected to our auxiliary reactor. These spigots are always concealed by a thin alloy sheet. This, in itself, was not a problem. What *was* a problem was the fact that Chaska had swapped the spigot from B6 to C5 in my absence. The only people who'd come and gone aboard this ship during its B6 days were Seeker Palamar —whose memories now resided in Kruthara's collective consciousness—and my former crew members.

But right now, I couldn't afford to think about how the captain had acquired that detail. What mattered was the implication of them knowing it at all:

The insurgents weren't commanding those ships—Kruthara was.

"*Is it just me,*" Chitta Mini said, "*or was that oddly specific?*"

I patted my pocket. "*Just pass on that message. Now.*"

A sudden commotion on one of the simscreens drew my attention. The staging bay's insurgents had congregated at the door and begun knocking incessantly. Chaska herself stood directly below the camera, glaring at me through the screen.

"Bodhi," she called out, "I *know* you're behind this. Open this door!"

I tabbed the audio transmitter key. "Sorry, Chaska. I know what I'm doing."

"Damn it, Bodhi!"

"Bodhi Drezek," the "insurgent" captain said in a progressively deepening, distorted tone, "grant us access to your vessel."

"*Kill our end of the feed*," I ordered Chitta Mini. "*Audio and visual. Just keep their transmission coming through.*"

"*Done and done!*" he confirmed.

Just then, footsteps came clapping toward me. I turned to see Ruena jogging up, clearly winded from her trip through the corridor.

"What's the plan now?" Ruena asked, her four eyes glued to the transmission screen. "And who is that? Chaska's liaison?"

"Want the long version or the short?" I said.

She growled. "The one that makes sense."

"Okay, well, *that* is Kruthara wearing a skin-mask. And they're probably about to devour us. Just like I thought."

"Oh. Lovely."

"Mhm." I tabbed through the simscreen feeds furiously, pausing when I spotted the image of the fuel barge just behind *Stream Dancer*. A pair of titanium harpoons glinted at the tips of its forward cannons. "I think they're preparing to jab us, Ru."

Ruena jumped slightly—a move analogous to her famous *crumb* warnings. In her future timeline, it was already too late.

A second later, I had the same reaction. The rocket-equipped harpoons leapt forward and slammed into the staging bay's ramp.

On the staging bay's feed, I saw the massive points expand and dig into the ramp's interior panel.

The insurgents, predictably, screamed and began pounding frantically on the door leading to the ship's interior.

"Bodhi!" Chaska shouted. "Let us out of here, or we're dead!"

Ruena stepped closer. "Maybe we should open—"

"No," I said, hearing the chill in my voice even as I spoke. "If they get infected..."

"I didn't sign up to kill them."

"Well, neither did I!"

"Then open it!"

The harpoons began reeling back in, gradually tearing the ramp off its hinges. Steel groaned and creaked as it was stretched to its breaking point.

A throaty, inhuman chuckle came through the main transmission speakers. "We have waited so long for this..." Reddish webs began spreading across the captain's face, darkening his eyes and discoloring his lips. "So, so long..."

"Bodhi, we need to let them out," Ruena hissed.

I shook my head and activated the staging bay's speakers. "Everybody, squeeze into the nearest full-seal suits!"

"*You, uh, ready to give that signal yet?*" Chitta Mini probed.

For the first time in ages, I felt myself paralyzed by indecision. It was all too much—the Kruthara-captain's laughter, Ruena's panic, Chaska's fury, the screams of the insurgents, the cries of the shattering ramp...

It was time to do or die. Or both.

"*Do it,*" I ordered Chitta Mini.

The mental order must've been passed in a microsecond, because Umzuma wasted no time in pumping the engines at full burn. Yet... nothing happened. I watched various cones of blue-white exhaust trails blazing over the simscreens, but we remained fixed in place, succeeding in nothing more than accelerating the deformation of the staging bay's ramp.

"It's not working," Ruena breathed. "Bodhi, please get them out of there."

But I clung to faith in Umzuma, even as Kruthara's harpoons buckled the ramp and the insurgents squeezed into their suits. The poor souls were spared from depressurization and suffocation only by the still-running stasis field, which was vulnerable to collapse if even one hunk of shrapnel tore through the generator column.

My pilot employed every trick in his book, rolling us, diving, ascending, even trying to pirouette around in a grand sweep. It was no use—even the flashiest move only succeeded in tangling up the harpoon cables and wrenching us closer to the enemy.

Ruena's eyes hardened. "They've got us."

"They won't shoot." Sweat ran down my face as I tracked the rapidly collapsing situation across the simscreen bank. "Too much valuable intel on board."

"I didn't say they would, Bodhi."

I quickly realized what she'd meant. The harpoon cables were swimming with crimson threads—a living tide of Kruthara's tissue. The same tissue that now sprouted from all the ships around us, burgeoning up through ventilation gills and viewpanes. In a matter of seconds, Kruthara would board our ship. Then it would board our minds.

"*Any ideas!?*" I pressed Chitta Mini.

He hummed for a few seconds, then let out a startling *aha!* "*Well, kind of last-ditch, but, uh…*"

"*Go ahead!*"

"*You sure? It'd drain half the onboard systems, probably break your engine. But then again, I guess we're in a bad way, and—*"

"*Just. Do. It!*"

"*Alrighty, boss.*"

A resounding *thrum* passed underfoot, followed by the whine of an engine going into "stage violet." Translation? Suicidal overdrive.

Sparks leapt off the generator column in the staging bay. Chitta Mini's warning about "draining half the onboard systems" came screaming into my memory at the sight. He hadn't been lying—whatever he was doing would short out the generator, depressurizing the staging bay and sending the insurgents rocketing into the vacuum.

I mashed a finger onto the staging bay's audio transmit key. "Hold onto something!"

Only Chaska seemed to hear me. The others were too busy digging through the nearby crates, trying in vain to find something, anything, they could shoot at the encroaching tide of Kruthara. But it was too late. The reddish tentacles thrust into the staging bay and impaled insurgents by twos and threes.

Chaska stood stock-still for a moment, then followed my instruction. She gripped a support post like a tree-climbing zoo specimen just as the generator failed.

There was a tremendous bang, a momentary lapse in gravity, and... motion. The main transmission screen went offline. The staging bay ramp—along with the harpoon cables—went flinging off into the void, taking dozens of insurgents with it. Even so, reddish globs still clung to the walls and floor. Game over. Just then, the simscreens fizzled and winked out. Indistinct shapes blurred beyond the viewpane as we went surging through the makeshift blockade and toward the Untraversed.

Another roaring shudder, and the simscreen feeds returned. We were still moving at impossible speed, but I couldn't look away from Chaska's plight. My heart hammered against my ribs.

The reddish tentacles reformed and swam toward her, extending into barbed mouths and ribbed throats, preparing to—

They paused.

One by one, each of the tentacles slowed, withered to the color of dried blood, and began flaking away in dense clouds. Soon, there was nothing left but trails of rusty ash.

Ruena looked at me in a daze. "What just happened?"

Not quite knowing myself, I tabbed through the simscreens. Chaska was still alive, but trembling. Gadra and a now-conscious Tusky glanced about in confusion. Far behind *Stream Dancer*, arranged at the very edge of the Untraversed, were Kruthara's possessed ships. Then it hit me. We were *inside* the purplish field.

"Welcome to the Untraversed, folks," Chitta Mini said over the bridge-wide speakers. "Please keep hands, feet, and genitalia inside the ship at *alllll* times."

THIRTEEN

Although the last few minutes had thoroughly blown my mind, there was no time to dive into abstractions about what had happened. Not until I'd dealt with the most pressing issue at hand, anyway. That issue was Chaska.

Now, it wasn't pleasant to treat my former crush-slash-bedmate as a prisoner of war, but that was the situation in which I found myself. This tense parley was easily the worst of the jobs assigned to what remained of the crew. Ruena was busy briefing Tusky and Gadra on what had transpired, and Chitta Mini had taken up the task of assessing the ship's damage in collaboration with Umzuma. Still, I was the captain, and that meant taking a hit for the team. With Chaska, I had a suspicion I'd be taking several—probably to the face.

By the time I made it to my intended meeting point, I figured Chaska had no more than ten minutes' worth of oxygen in her suit. There was a chance that the Untraversed was breathable, of course, but none of us could afford to test that hypothesis. Thus, I made haste in arranging the encounter.

Step one was unlocking the staging bay door, allowing Chaska to venture into the adjoining corridor. Step two was resealing the staging bay, allowing Chaska's corridor to repressurize. Step three—the one I was currently dreading—was unlocking the door that separated Chaska and me.

"Alright, Mini," I said to the nearest speaker node, "let's get it over with."

The moment the door unsealed, Chaska came barreling through with gritted teeth and gloved hands outstretched. Behind her helmet's faceplate was a portrait painted in desperation, adrenaline, and hate. Pure, unbridled hate.

Fortunately, I had anticipated this.

I lifted my Puncher pistol and reluctantly aimed at her chest. "Stop, Chaska."

After a few defiant steps, she did. "Might as well put me down now, you goddamn traitor."

"Traitor? Are you kidding me?"

"You left them there to die. You left *me* to die."

"Correction: I saved you from being taken over by Kruthara. Another thankless job in the life of Bodhi Drezek."

Chaska glowered. "But you didn't save them. And now they'll be part of it. Forever."

"It almost sounds poetic though, right?" Sensing that approach would not pan out well, I just sighed. "Chaska, I'm sorry. I didn't want to do that—any of it. But you forced my hand."

"Forced you? Forced you to do what? Take me hostage?"

"Okay, first of all, you've taken me hostage plenty of times. So let's not make this a one-sided tango, huh? And second, once again, I saved you. That was an ambush."

"And if I'd been on that bridge, where I was supposed to be, I could've gotten everybody out alive."

"That's what we always think."

"I can't believe you stood there and lied to me," she whispered. "You're worse than the Hegemony, you know that? At least they're honest about killing innocent people."

"We're really not going to talk about the fact that you lured Kruthara right to us?"

"No need to."

"Oh, but I must disagree," I snapped. "What I did was bad, admittedly, but what you did could've wiped out every one of us—including Gad. Not to mention the fact that we almost lost what might be the universe's last lead on fixing this whole thing. You were so hell-bent on getting to the end of the rainbow that you didn't think to double-check your holy mandates." She opened her mouth to clap back at me, but I steamrolled on. "And you know what, Chaska? This war's gone to your head. It's eaten your sense away. So you can blame me for getting your pals killed and taking you hostage if you like—I'd even be inclined to accept that blame—but you *cannot* blame me for getting us out alive."

I braced myself for her vicious, witty comeback, but it never came. Instead, Chaska's shoulders dropped. Her eyes softened.

"Maybe you're right," she said.

"And another thing! If you think—" I paused, frowning. "Wait, did you say I'm right?"

"I said maybe."

"I'll take maybe."

She glanced away from me. "We need to talk about what you did to stop those things. How you did it, I mean."

"We're still trying to figure that out," I said, lowering the Puncher a few degrees. "But it's safe to assume I didn't do a thing. It was the Untraversed."

"You really think we're safe in here?"

"*Safe* is the last word I'd use to describe our situation."

"You know what I mean." She took a tentative step forward, prompting me to take my finger off the Puncher's trigger. "Do you think it'll keep them out?"

"We can discuss that with the others."

"Have it your way."

"*But*," I said, lifting a hand to halt her, "we need to bury this hatchet first."

"It's done, Bodhi."

"No offense intended, but I've had plenty of people say that—including you—only to wake up with a gun in my face."

"What do you want, then?" she asked sharply.

I shrugged. "Just to know that this is fully put to rest. From my standpoint, we both took our bruises and got our shots in."

"I didn't kill any of your people."

"Again with the blame game, Chaska."

Her upper lip curled. "If I say it's done, it's done. What more do you want?"

"I want you to be my ally. No more games, no more power struggles, nothing. If we're going to survive this thing, I need you by my side, preferably without holding a knife aimed at my spinal column." I extended a hand toward her. "Promise me you'll put down your battle long enough to win this war. After that, it's up to you."

After a few uneasy seconds, she came up and shook my hand with bone-crushing force.

"Don't make me regret this," she whispered.

The sentiment was mutual.

When a de-suited Chaska and I entered the meeting module, the tension was as thick as the troposphere of Angulla-2. It seemed Ruena had done a proper job of relaying our situation to everybody in attendance.

Tusky sat on the far side of the table, covered in a variety of medical patches, sensors, and other doodads I am not tech savvy enough to label. Upon looking up from his work on a small, buzzing gadget, he let out an audible gulp and stared deferentially at the floor panels.

Just beside him was Gadra, who wrung her hands in her lap and tried (yet failed) to pull on a passable smile.

Even this discomfort was outdone by a rather skittish Ruena. I'd never seen the ligethan so uneasy, but then again, she *had* helped me carry out a mastermind plot to deceive and imprison the dangerous insurgent standing before her.

Only Chitta Mini, bobbing contentedly in his canister, was immune to the quiet drama playing out in the module. Perhaps he was just oblivious. Existing for millions of years as a socially isolated superintelligence is apt to do that.

Desperate to dispel the awkwardness, I clapped my hands. "Everybody, this is our old friend Chaska. Old friend Chaska, this is everybody."

"Shut it, Bodhi," Chaska growled. She dragged herself into a chair and looked at each crew member in turn. She paused when she reached Tusky. "Good to see you back on your feet."

Tusky blushed—well, would have, if walking sloths could manage such a thing. "Thank you, Cap—madam."

"Are you alright?"

"Yes, I believe so. Thanks primarily to the actions of Bodhi and this remarkable chitta. My memory of the events aboard the hive-world is rather scattered—due to retrograde amnesia, I presume—but in time, I'll—"

Chaska cleared her throat to cut him off. "We'll speak later. For now, let's stick to the problem at hand. What's our situation?"

"Y'mean for the ship, or the Maker's miracle field?" Chitta Mini asked.

She rolled her eyes. "Either one. Just start somewhere."

"*Well*, yours truly was told to look at the ship and only the ship. So I'm gonna keep doing that and let my co-host, Sir Tusky, take over the Untraversed. What've you got for us, Sir Tusky?"

It seemed that in my brief time away from the module, the two had become fast friends. Strange, in many regards, but somehow it also made sense. They were both biological oddities who'd spent their lives being imprisoned and utilized for the benefit of powerful beings. They were also joined by the fact that I'd been their savior.

"Yes, well, uh," Tusky began, fussing with a collection of tablets laid out before him, "as my... co-host... stated, I've been working on analyzing the Untraversed. I don't have much at this time, but my inquiry has revealed a few elements of note."

I sat down beside Ruena. "Lay it on us, Tusky."

"Very well." He flipped open the closest tablet and reviewed the screen. "As previously noted by the chitta, this is indeed a gradient field with discernible viscosity." When Gadra furrowed her brows, he paused and backtracked. "What I mean to say is, the Untraversed does, indeed, act like a fluid rather than empty space. There's a certain baseline mass to it, meaning pinching is most certainly off the table while within its grasp."

"So we're stuck," I said.

"Viewed from one angle, yes. But as I mentioned, there's another aspect to the Untraversed that should be taken into consideration—the gradient, that is. I've done most of my research on our current position, which is the far edge of the field. Here, the mass dispersion and overall density are fairly low. But with a few simple tweaks to our onboard systems, and some generous aid from the chitta, I've been able to discern variances around us."

"Tusky, as much as I adore that brain of yours, we're going to need a simplification."

"How much further can I simplify?"

"Do your best."

He wrinkled his nose, which I took to be a sloth's display of frustration. "I shall provide an analogy, then. You might imagine the Untraversed as a terrestrial ocean. Within oceans, there are pockets of warm water and cool water. There are also currents and various other factors, such as salinity, that can influence the density of any given patch of water. Yet my analogy breaks down at some level, because oceans do not have extreme differences in water density. The Untraversed, by contrast, does. Some areas are 'lighter' or easier to cross than others."

"And this helps us, I assume?"

"I've yet to come that far in my findings, Bodhi. But... if I had to speculate... I'd imagine that we could alter our route in accordance with the density patches. In essence, we could chart a faster or less fuel-demanding path."

"But chart it to where?" Chaska pressed. "We don't know where that tomb is."

Tusky raised a finger, urging patience. "There *are* some similarities between the fabric of the Untraversed and that of standard space. These may present a lead, of sorts."

"Go on."

"Well, take gravitational pulls, for instance," Tusky said. "In standard space, stars and other massive objects exert a strong pull on surrounding bodies. According to long-range scans, the Untraversed may have planets, stars, and all the rest, but the *real* object of interest is what's generating this field in the first place."

"You think it's the tomb?" I asked.

Tusky's head wobbled from side to side. "I'm averse to offering uncertain answers, but logic would agree with that conclusion. The deeper one plunges into Untraversed, the denser the field becomes. One can therefore form a reasonable hypothesis—the densest point is the source, and thus our destination."

"Right," Chaska said, nodding slowly. "So if we keep heading toward denser regions, we're heading toward the center."

"Precisely," Tusky said with a broad smile.

I shared a loaded look with Ruena—clearly the two of us were on the same wavelength as far as cynical predictions. "Sounds like the closer we get, the more fuel we'll need to keep pushing."

Tusky's expression soured. "Yes, I do believe so."

"We'll come back to that. But first, I think we need to touch on the elephant in the room."

"Actually, Bodhi, my genetic composition is closer to that of a—"

"No, not that. The *other* elephant. You know, the one that turned Kruthara into magic dust."

"Magic dust?" Gadra piped up.

"Not the kind you snort," I said. "Don't get any ideas."

Scrunching his lips, Tusky picked up a second tablet. "My research on the field's destructive capabilities is far from complete."

"Complete or no, we saw it happen," I replied. "The second we got inside this place, Kruthara fell apart."

Chaska nodded at Chitta Mini's canister. "Looks like he was right about the Maker's defenses."

"We can't count on it, though," I said. "Something tells me Kruthara already knew what would happen."

Everybody looked at me in puzzlement.

"It makes sense, doesn't it? Why else would Kruthara strike a deal with the Hegemony, or any other humanoid forces? Because it can't go in itself. It needs somebody else to do the dirty work."

Ruena drew a deep breath. "You might be onto something."

"But we can still organize a defense here," Chaska said. "We can call together anybody who's left out there. Try to stop the Hegemony from getting a foothold."

"Not gonna happen," Chitta Mini said. "The Untraversed has a sort of... jamming effect. Nothing really gets through it. It just soaks it all up."

She frowned. "But we could skip back out of it, send another request."

I shook my head. "That's a no from me, Chaska."

"Because?"

"First of all, there isn't a single insurgent unit that can go toe to toe with a Hegemony flagship, let alone their entire fleet. And second, we can't afford to waste time turning back and rallying the troops. This just became a race to the finish line."

"You're insane if you think we can outrace them."

"And *you're* insane for dragging us in here without a plan," I said, only then remembering young and impressionable Gadra was listening to our debate. I forced myself to take a calming breath, then proceeded. "If the Maker could generate a field capable of taking out Kruthara, I'd bet all my bux that there's something in that tomb we could sell—I mean *use*—as a weapon, just like the Maker's essay-length blabbering promised. But if the Hegemony gets to it first, we're done. Everything's done."

Those around the table exchanged worried looks, perhaps hoping somebody would raise an objection and steer us away from the all-or-nothing talk. But I just leaned back, basking in the unfortunate realization that I was correct. Again.

"Then we'll need to move fast," Chaska said softly. She leaned forward and tapped Chitta Mini's canister, eliciting a squeal through the speakers. "Wake up in there. We need your take on the ship."

"Okey dokey," Chitta Mini said. "Do you, uh, want the good news first or the bad news?"

Chaska chewed at her lip. "Bad news."

"*Well*, the bad news is that there is no good news."

I'd have to remember that zinger.

"Give it to us straight," Chaska said.

"Alrighty, let's run down the list... starting with the staging bay. That's obviously in pretty nasty shape. No ramp, decompressed, yadda yadda. You saw what happened. Then there's the coolant system—it's a few shakes and a squeeze away from imploding."

Remember when I cautioned you against messing with a man's ship? That's why. As I would later discover, Chaska had made the rookie mistake of swapping out compression lines without checking my relevant hardware notes. And how did I know this? Because I didn't keep hardware notes. Red flag, don't you think?

"Next up," Chitta Mini plodded on, sounding altogether too proud of his report, "it seems like the engine's on its last legs. Reactor core is perforated in a few places—not to worry, I deployed your last round of emergency sealant!—and the drive modulators are fried. Oh, and there's some kind of massive nest in there. A few semi-dissolved bones, too."

I waved a hand. "That was there before."

"Oh, okay, all good," he said. "Now, what else... oh, right. Your deuterium is still at critical levels. We're talking 'gonna run out in five hours' levels."

"Lovely."

"Then there's the blown conduits, the ruptured converter, the ongoing brownouts with the secondary fuse line... need I go on?"

I stood and placed both hands on the table. "Ladies and gentlemen, I believe we are in a rather precarious spot."

"Diplomatically said," Ruena commented dryly.

"Yeah, I agree with what Ruena said... I think," Gadra put in. "We're gonna die, aren't we?"

"Okay, who even let her attend this meeting?" I asked. When nobody spoke up, I looked at Tusky. "Have you cultivated any engineering skills using that sentience of yours?"

He set both tablets down. "A rudimentary understanding of some systems, yes."

"This isn't the time to be modest," Chaska said, lifting her chin. "Tusky helped sort out power-flow issues on half of our gunships. He knows his way around a hangar."

"Okay, we can work with that." I gestured from Tusky to Chitta Mini. "How much extra flight can the dream team squeeze out with emergency repairs?"

Chitta Mini rolled about in his canister. "Well, assuming we can scrap a few spare components... reroute the energy grid... back-cycle the reactors to reuptake a few proton streams... I'd give us an additional ten minutes before the whole vessel goes kaput. Includin' the life support, by the way."

Part of being a proper captain is keeping a brave face when things are going south. The worse things actually are, the tougher your mask of optimistic courage must be. Given our present circumstances, I'm confident my expression was verging on manic.

"*But*," Chitta Mini added in the pulse-pounding quiet, "I may have picked up somethin' sweet."

"Don't keep us in suspense," Chaska growled.

"Right, so... I managed to tinker with the sensors a li'l bit. Boosted their range using some modulated frequencies, fluid dynamics, blah, blah, blah... you guys don't give a hoot about that. What you *should* give a hoot about is a wreck that's three hours away."

Chaska leaned on her armrest. "How do you know it's a wreck?"

"I'm a chitta, girl. Trust me!"

"Alright, everybody... let's assume it is, in fact, a wreck," I said, trying to placate the room's growing unease. "How wrecked is this wreck?"

"It's not an exact science, man," Chitta Mini said. "Best I could do was run a reverse-photon pulse on it... get some kinda crude idea of the shape. Have a look-see."

As the meeting module's holo-projection port flickered to life, I realized I'd given shelter to a potential miracle. This may be hard to grasp, in light of our poor situation, but bear with me. Being a successful merchant means playing the long game, even in the worst of times.

See, the processes Chitta Mini was carrying out were advanced, even for a top-tier fabrique. He'd learned to adeptly navigate and repurpose the systems of a ship he'd just barely started to analyze. Sure, he wasn't as fast as Right or Left—and certainly not Center—

but he was good at what he did. And moreover, he was personable. Slippery and conniving, too, but not without a sense of earnest goodwill. Second by second, I saw just how deeply my personality had imprinted upon him. He was more than just a hunk of gray matter—he was like a child. *My* child. By ripping him off his parent organism, I had, in some bizarre way, given birth to him.

And like any good child, he was well on his way to repaying the kindness of his father. In fact, once this whole war thing died down, I knew he'd be a crucial part of rebuilding my commercial empire. Ah, the fruits of parenthood.

The holographic ship that materialized before us was a long, tapered wedge, much like the head of an axe. It had been splintered into three barely joined segments.

"That's a Maitreyan Order vessel," Ruena said quietly. "How did it end up here?"

I blinked at her. "A what?"

"I'd know it anywhere. The Maitreyan Order used to make regular pilgrimages to the ligethan worlds… I never thought I'd see one so far out."

"But what is it?"

"It's a… seeker vessel, of sorts. Their order's aim is to spread 'dharma' teachings to all beings. Some kind of religious system. Not very popular in most parts of civilized space… and definitely not applicable to ligethan minds."

"And they decided to proselytize in the Untraversed?"

"Huh, not a great idea," Chitta Mini said. "The Maker was big on his own rules. Universal law, he called it. The cosmic principles. Whatever. I never studied that stuff… but I guess they came to the wrong place. Seeing as they're dead and whatnot."

"Alright, well, forget all the mumbo-jumbo dogma for a moment," I said, sighing. "Is that thing packing any materials we could use to keep going?"

"Probably? I dunno, man, the scans were pretty weak. But I got a few pings on the right end of the spectrum. Seems they've got some deuterium in the reactors."

Ruena frowned. "The Order hasn't been seen in millennia."

I turned to Chitta Mini. "But it has deuterium signatures?"

"Yep," he said. "Or somethin' like it."

"Excellent! Set a course for... the thing."

"You got it."

Chaska glanced at me. "Am I the only one who thinks we should be cautious about this? Why is a clean wreck just floating out there? Especially one that's probably ancient?"

I rolled my eyes. "Oh, *now* you're worried about the suspicious, untouched ancient object. Give me a break."

"I'm just pointing out that—"

"Point noted. Everybody, it's time to do your thing. I'm taking an executive nap. Ruena's taking a longer executive nap. Tusky's fixing things. Chitta Mini's scanning things. Gadra's not touching anything with sparks coming out of it. And Chaska's"—I met her glare evenly—"serving as temporary captain. Meeting adjourned!"

Right now you might be thinking, "Gee, it sure is dangerous (and/or stupid) to assign a leadership role to a woman you just betrayed, scolded, and held at gunpoint." And that's a reasonable thought. That being said, part of rebuilding a team is creating opportunities for spurned members to demonstrate their loyalty and feel accepted. Giving Chaska room to shine was a charitable gesture on my part.

It was also pragmatic. See, thanks to Chitta Mini's reformulation of the logic net, Chaska didn't have any command privileges. Much as she might mash buttons and shout orders, nothing would come of it. Doors would remain sealed, and power levels would remain abysmally low. Which isn't to say any potential underhanded reverse-mutiny efforts would be wasted. Quite the opposite, really.

Whatever Chaska did or tried to do would be silently recorded and passed along by Chitta Mini the moment I woke from my extended nap. In effect, this decision created a canary in the palladium mine. Her hypothetical betrayal was my gain.

Anyhow, all of this is a roundabout way of explaining why I thought Chitta Mini was the one who interrupted my rest. Rolling over, I realized I'd been asleep for a measly three hours and change. I was still bleary-eyed and testy when the door chime rang again.

"Can't it wait?" I groaned, hoping the chitta would pick up my lament through the room's speaker system. "I was in the middle of a good dream. A steamy one."

The door chime came again.

Grimacing, I dragged myself across the room and palmed the entry pad.

There stood Tusky, hunched over in an anxious knot. "I'm... sorry to disturb you, Bodhi."

"Well, what's done is done," I said. "Ship news?"

"Yes, I suppose so." He looked away, curling even further in on himself. Sloth or no, his body language was universal—things were bad. "May I come in?"

I stepped aside. "Are there *more* broken components?"

"Ah, no. Not quite." He entered and glanced about. "I see you've, uh, declined many of the aesthetic decisions made by the room's former occupant."

"You mean trespasser? Yes, yes I have."

I gestured to the nearby wastebasket, which contained the vast heap of insurgent belongings I'd tossed out upon reclaiming my territory. Let me tell you, insurgents have terrible taste in belongings. Who wants to sleep in a room full of letters to someone's sweetheart, burnt helmet fragments, pagan trinkets, and nudie posters? Well, okay, I set the nudie posters aside, but everything else had to go.

"Anyway," I said, moving to my desk, "you want a drink? 'Cause I would like a drink."

Tusky seemed to contemplate the offer, still standing awkwardly apart from a sitting surface of any kind. "N-No, thank you, Bodhi. I think I'd best remain sober for now."

"Suit yourself." I uncorked a half-enjoyed bottle of black rum—which I considered a parting gift-slash-apology from the insurgent occupier—and poured myself a full glass. "So, what's this urgent ship news, then?"

He absently scratched the back of his head. "The... the turbine. Yes, the turbine. We managed to repair the fission cracks. And the rotor assembly is..."

As Tusky trailed off, I understood the root of his unease.

"This isn't about the ship, is it?" I asked.

"Of course it is," he said. "I wouldn't have bothered you without a good reason. I... I know you're very guarded with your time."

I took a sip of the rum and patted the bed beside me. "For you, my friend, I always have time. Not enough time to dance around, however. So let's cut to the heart of it."

"If you insist." Tusky sat down and looked into his grease-stained paw-hands. "It's probably nothing, really. I'm not even sure I can encapsulate it."

"Do your best."

He nodded. "I just feel a bit... foolish... approaching you in regards to this matter. It does, after all, circle the central question of what it means to be alive. And I don't know how many beings have reached a satisfactory end to that line of inquiry."

"Ah," I said. "So it's about death."

"One could say that."

This was a tricky topic. Tusky was right in implying that death, even to the wisest of creatures, represents a vast and chilling unknown variable. Few of us understand what death is, let alone what it could possibly "mean," in the grand scheme. Of course, assuming death has any meaning at all is a logical leap. It could very well be the stone-cold of meaning itself; a cruel, absurd punchline to a journey of survival that has itself run on the diesel fuel of meaning. Not that we'd like to think that. It goes against our base coding. We are meaning-making machines, and as such, even death —something no being can ever possibly grasp until the moment it strikes—will always wind up being conceptualized in theory or dogma.

Think of it like a camera trying to see itself. A film trying to guess what comes after the screen goes off. A breeze wondering where it goes on a calm day. These are all stupid analogies, granted, but they point to the very heart of the issue. Death is unknowable, unthinkable. And knowing it, or thinking about it, cannot stop it.

But the anguish in Tusky's eyes told me this was not a matter of philosophy. Death wasn't just a word to him, not anymore—it was his reality. It is mine, too, and yours, but we do not think about death that way. For us "lucky" nobodies with reasonably healthy bodies, we live in perpetual delusion about death. In our world, it will never come. It will visit everybody else, and we alone will be saved, either through impossible quantum-consciousness machines or a miracle or a trip to a place that we call death, but isn't *really* death—think heaven, for example. But all of these are just games that the mind plays to distract itself from one bitter, inevitable truth:

You will die.

Even as you read these words, you may end.

Uncomfortable? Good. Now you can better understand Tusky's plight.

"I thought that my fate was securely tucked away, if you understand me," he said in a voice two notches about a whisper. "I thought I had made peace with it, Bodhi. But after the recent tests... after losing consciousness in the staging bay... I don't know what I believe. I have more questions than answers."

I plopped a hand on his shoulder. "That, Tusky, is part of being sentient. The questions never end."

"Perhaps... but it troubles the scientific mind."

"We'll all have to walk through that door someday. You just get, uh, a VIP entrance."

"But I can't cope with the knowing. Now that I have experienced this world of form and feelings and delights... I'm just supposed to sleep and never wake again?"

"Given our current situation, that option doesn't sound half-bad."

Tusky took the glass from my hands and drained it in one gulp. "Forgive me. I just... felt a need."

"Understandable."

"Just tell me, Bodhi—what do you know of it?"

"Death?"

"Yes."

I shrugged. "Just as much as you or Amodari or a dead cat in a drainage pipe. It is what it is, Tusky." Sensing his distress, I got up and poured another glass for him. "I don't mean to sound cold... I just know you value the truth. And that's the best I can offer."

He took the glass when I offered it. "But you met Center, didn't you?"

"'Met' is a strong term, but sure, let's go with that."

"The others told me that you spoke about supramundane knowledge. Did you speak with Center about death?"

"Briefly..."

"And what did they say?"

I drew a deep breath, remembering that strange and dreamlike experience aboard Nerikhad's barge. It came back to me in bits and pieces, but most of it slipped away upon being recalled. To this day, most of our conversation remains out of reach. Almost as though the mind could not handle what was said.

"Well, I can say this," I told him. "Center existed because they wanted to. They could've annihilated itself when they joined. They could've ended all of reality in a blink. They could've done *anything*. But they kept things the way they were... death and all. And I do believe that says something."

"Says what?" Tusky asked as he nursed his drink. "That death is *good*?"

"Birth is a terminal condition, Tusky. Always ends the same way. What comes up must go down, right?"

"But... it doesn't explain anything. Why would we exist, only to *not* exist?"

That question turned a key inside me. You might think I was above such stirrings in the mind, on account of the "rant" I included above, but I wasn't—not at that moment in time, anyhow. My sage reflections on death have accrued in the many decades between this encounter and the time of this memoir's writing.

Until Tusky phrased his question in that way, I was just one of the blind, deaf nobodies wandering through life, tricking themselves into believing that I had made peace with the titan that is death. But I hadn't. I had packed my life away into little boxes, little bundles of beliefs, assuring myself that I understood "what it was all about." Most of us feel that way. It is frightening to feel otherwise. And indeed, it was fear that washed over me as I got the very center of what Tusky was driving at. Fear and pain and an aching loneliness. I didn't just grasp the *word* death—I felt it.

We were both dying, and nothing could stop it. Not even winning this charade of a war.

And beyond even that, I saw my addiction. I was addicted to life, just like you. I would do *anything* to live, to breathe, to keep up the story of Bodhi. Even if it meant throwing other people under the proverbial hover-bus. And what was my reward, even if I fed that addiction everything it could stomach and outran everybody else in the race of life?

You guessed it.

Death.

"Tusky," I said softly, not wanting to betray my spiritual dilemma, "anything I pitch to you would be a belief. And we have to work with reality."

"Yes, but..."

"Believe me: If I *knew*, I would tell you."

Tusky screwed up his face as he drank more. "Do you think something comes after?"

"Maybe?"

"What do you mean? You've had your entire life to review the evidence."

"And? There are religions that have had millions of years for the same task. Time doesn't help if there's no answer to a question."

"Perhaps you're right." He finished his glass and handed it to me. "I apologize for dragging you into this pointless speculation, Bodhi. I... I'll return to my work now."

As he went to stand, I grabbed his wrist. "Wait."

"For what?"

"I..." My voice shriveled in my throat. "I just want you to know you're not alone in this. In the whole dying thing, I mean. And I'm sorry it's happening now."

His stare chilled me. I'd never seen it so vacant.

"I just need to know this is all worthwhile," he said. "A reason for the madness. That's all I want. Don't you want it, too?"

Again, I felt the fear mounting. My mind went into overdrive cycles, ruminating on meaning, on life, on eternity, on emptiness. Answers drifted up, but as I held his gaze, I knew each and every one was incomplete, a stream of babbling to pull away from the hard truth of it all. What could I say? What could I do?

Then the comm system squawked to life, and I lurched back into ordinary, oblivious consciousness. Into the pleasant delusion that things would be alright.

"Bodhi?" Chaska called. "You'd better get to the bridge."

Shaken as I was by this staring-into-the-abyss conversation, it was easy enough to put it behind me as we entered the bridge. The survival drive is a powerful thing. Imminent threats—or indeed, any phenomena that might somehow become an imminent threat—have a way of grounding you in the present. Say what you will about panic, but it keeps you from straying close to the rim of eternity. And sometimes, that is a good thing.

Especially when you find yourself preparing to board a long-lost, decrepit wreck floating in the middle of a mysterious space field.

"That's our beauty," Chitta Mini said over the speakers. "Helluva thing, isn't it?"

The entire crew, myself included, traded looks with varying degrees of discomfort. We all stood along the viewpane, not quite sure what to make of the vessel's remains.

Generally, it conformed to Chitta Mini's holographic renderings. It was broken in the right spots, surrounded by clouds of cast-off shrapnel and drifting fuel globs. What *didn't* fit the chitta's model was the vessel's sheer size. The thing could've housed a thousand *Stream Dancer*s inside its bulk.

"It's... bigger than I'd anticipated," Chaska put in.

"Not the first time I've heard that," I said. When it was clear that the others didn't appreciate my sharp wit as much as me, however, I changed course. "Seems like it may have been a generation ship. A world-shaper, perhaps."

Ruena paced behind me. "We never saw crafts of this size in our territory. Perhaps this was their mothership."

"Which means it ought to have fuel."

"*Ought* to, yes," Chaska replied. "But there's a good chance that they ran out of fuel just like we're about to. Right, Mini?"

The chitta made a distorted *ehh* sound. "I stand by my projection, ma'am. Thing should still be loaded up."

"Which *does* beg the question..." I said. "If it's got fuel, how'd it get scuttled here?"

Chaska rolled her eyes. "Oh, now you want to go down that road."

"Listen, it was either this ship or a patch of purple space-stuff. What would you prefer?"

"He's right," Ruena said, leaning against the viewpane. "We've got to take a look."

I looked around. "Anybody want to volunteer for a scouting team?"

Another set of wary glances went around.

Only Tusky put up his hand, his attention still glued to whatever work he was doing on his tablet. "I would."

Considering our prior discussions about the futility of life, I didn't exactly feel comfortable sending him into the wreck. But beggars can't be choosers—particularly when life-saving fuel is on the line. So I compromised.

"I'll go in with you," I said. "Anybody else?"

Chaska crossed her arms. "Last time we sent you two out, you destroyed the hive-world. So count me in."

"I'd like to get in on the action, too!" Chitta Mini added.

"Vetoed," I said. "You need to stay on board, keep Umzuma company with... ship stuff."

"Like what? You might need me in there."

"For what?"

"Anything! Making a rapid-action antivenom for go'tor wreckage spiders, for example."

"There's no such thing as a go'tor wreckage spider."

"Sure there are! They're five meters across, *huge*, and super lethal. Those things love to hide in conduit shafts."

"I don't believe you."

"You wanna bet against me on this one, man? Against the possibility of giant wreckage spiders?"

I sighed. "I've been bitten by worse. You're staying."

"What about me?" Gadra asked. I'd nearly forgotten the girl was there. "If you run into any aliens, I could take 'em down with the sweet tats Mini showed me."

"Yeah, that's a no from me," I said. "No kids allowed on wreckage dives."

"That's not a rule!"

"It is now. So no."

She huffed and went back to sketching designs in her notebook. "At least when *Chaska* was the captain, I got to do fun stuff."

"Keep it up, missy, and you'll get to do even more fun stuff. Like cleaning the laundry bays with your tongue."

"I'll stay on board," Ruena said. "I still need to finish my rest cycle."

"Settled, then," I said, rubbing my hands together. "Let's suit up, root around for some functional parts, and return with all of our limbs."

"And watch out for wreckage spiders," Chitta Mini added.

"No need, seeing as they don't exist."

"Yeah, sure, what do I know? I'm just a superintelligence that's lived longer than most planetary civilizations."

In retrospect, I can say only one thing regarding this moment:

Always listen to the superintelligence.

FOURTEEN

Years back, I read a report stating that the average diving scav only lived to be twenty-two years old. More than half of those scavs never even made it to the ten-dive mark. A quarter didn't survive their first. Pretty bleak, right?

But it turns out that the numbers only told half the story. I got the other half while enjoying a short-lived yet fiery fling with a ten-legged professional scav named Miraka. According to Miraka, there were two problems with that report. The first was that the AI constructs running the study had a racial bias, only counting human casualties. The second was that the "average" life expectancy was skewed—if a scav made it to dive eleven, their expected years rocketed up to almost fifty-one.

Curious, I dug deeper into the situation with Miraka. How could half of those diving scavs make it past ten, and the other half didn't? Turns out that, like most things, it comes down to money.

Half of the report's scavs—the kick-the-bucket half, that is—were after quick paydays diving through wrecks. They didn't see the point in pissing away exorbitant amounts of bux to get the latest and greatest helmets, oxygen rigs, thrusters, and so forth. They wanted to make bux and retire in short order. And most of them did, in a morbid sense.

The other half knew better. They'd learned from veterans or otherwise seen the writing on the wall. This half splurged on their beginning gear. But not just any gear. See, the suits and scanners and cutting torches were helpful, but ultimately just flashy bits. The *real* necessity was the high-density tether that ran from their harnesses to the ship's anchor point.

That's right, it all came down to the basics. If a novice diving scav's tether broke—and most of them did, on account of the aforementioned skimping—the scav was as good as gone. Without a proper, unbreakable tether to crawl back to the ship, the wrecks became tombs. This being the case, as Miraka told me, most big-brain scavs took out a loan to get their hands on one of those high-tensile tethers. They were the only thing that mattered on a wreck dive.

I dwelt rather soberly on this knowledge as I stood on the lip of the ramp-less staging bay, tugging at the flimsy rubber cording that would serve as my tether. Below me was a black, twisting maw that led down into the wreckage's guts, lined with jagged steel teeth and mangled piping. Any one of those serrated bits was more than capable of severing the lifeline.

"Are we sure we want to drop in here?" Chaska asked, huffing over our helmet comms. "I don't have a good feeling."

"Yeah, well, I haven't had one in months." I kicked a length of frayed wiring over the edge. It floated down… and down… and down… until at last it was swallowed by the darkness. Clearly there was still a residual gravity source humming somewhere inside the behemoth.

Tusky shifted in his ill-fitting suit. "Perhaps we should test my hypothesis for better visibility as we descend. It could make it easier on all of us."

"Absolutely *not*," I said. "Even if the air in this region is breathable, I'm not using any of us as lab rats to find out. We don't have enough expendable bodies for that."

"I measured the percentages, Bodhi," Tusky replied. "Chitta Mini corroborated my findings. The air here is perfectly suited to the human respiratory system."

"Let me guess... another one of the Maker's miracles?"

"There's no way for us to know. However, I would not immediately dismiss the idea. The Untraversed seems to have been engineered as a refuge for humanoids."

"Yeah, or a trap for the first idiot to take off his helmet." I tugged again on the makeshift tether. It didn't lift my spirits. "Look, we're not exactly swimming in time as it is. Even idle, the ship's going to burn through the last of that deuterium in no time. So let's dip our toes in the... pool."

Glancing down again, I wondered what sort of lunacy had driven me to lead this scavenging mission. The massive pit resembled a literal portal to a hell dimension.

Chitta Mini couldn't conclude what sort of monstrous weapon had torn through the ship and created this thing, but similar impact "tunnels" were all over the place. This charming entry point was just as dangerous as all the rest, but at least it was close to the engine modules.

"Are we done talking?" Chaska asked.

I looked at Tusky and nodded. "Regrettably, I think we are."

"Good." She pointed to her suit's hand transmitter. "Remember distancing. Twenty meters max. No hard separation."

Tusky and I nodded. We'd gone over the basic protocol about a dozen times by now, but if there's one thing I've learned, it's that us meat-brains need constant repetition. Especially in this case. The Untraversed's signal-jamming effect put a damper on both long- and medium-range transmissions. What this means, in our case, is that we'd only be able to communicate locally using our suit transmitters. Keeping in touch with our chitta back at home base wasn't an option. And if one of us got lost in there... well, yet another amateur scav who didn't make it past dive one.

"Last one down is buying drinks when this is all over," Chaska said, grinning behind her faceplate. She then turned her back to the drop, took the tether in both hands, and hopped backwards.

Seeing as drinks were less expensive than death, Tusky and I crept closer to the pit and observed. Just like the wires, Chaska descended in a slow, controlled manner, accelerating only as she neared the blackness. Even then, the drop velocity wasn't anything near what you'd find on a planet. If anything, this ship had the pull of a baby moon.

"You know," I said to Tusky, "you can always hang back and keep an eye on our tethers. Might be good to have somebody reeling us back in if things go bad."

He smiled. "That's kind of you, Bodhi, but I'm prepared to take the same risk as you."

Well, clearly he hadn't picked up on my meaning. Keeping him aboard the ship protected him, yes, but more importantly, it protected *me*. Without a pair of strong arms in the staging bay, and no way to contact the ship, climbing back up that janky tether was the only way out.

With a deep breath, I gripped my line and took the plunge.

In a matter of seconds, the hazy purple of the Untraversed morphed into the spiky, industrial terror of the ship's throat. The deeper I sank, the more I was surrounded by glinting bits of rebar and mangled grating. A slight space-breeze would send me careening into the walls of metallic fangs and nails. To counteract this realization, particularly as the darkness swallowed me and the gravitational pull increased, I shut my eyes and focused on the suit's recycled air wisping over my nose.

Nowhere to go but down.

When I reached the bottom, I wasn't sure whether to be relieved or terrified. A hard landing, to be sure, but nothing the carbon struts in my legs couldn't handle.

Then again, Chaska didn't have the same luxury, and I still found her casually exploring the ruined corridors. Her flashlight's beam exposed the full extent of the damage—blown-out conductor panels, gutted wiring, corroded coolant rods. Whatever had happened aboard this ship hadn't been pretty.

Tusky thudded down behind me, then gathered up his tether and moved to follow.

"So how are we gonna do this?" Chaska asked over the suit comms. "We splitting up?"

I growled. "*Never* split up. First rule of scary-place exploring."

"Have it your way. Where are we headed?"

"The scans that Chitta Mini and I compiled suggest that the engine module is this way," Tusky said, pointing down a long, crooked hallway to our left. "I apologize for the belated question, but how exactly do we plan to ferry the deuterium back to our vessel?"

"Easily," I said. "This thing's been quiet for at least a few decades. Should have some nice hunks of crizzum to haul back."

If you've never heard the word *crizzum*, here's the skinny. Most reactors are built to take in a liquid stream of deuterium-heavy fuel, but left to its own devices, said fuel has a way of condensing into crystalline shards that can then be recycled and used in a pinch. Those shards are known as crizzum. Now, any self-respecting pilot would cringe at the idea of dumping crizzum into their precious reactors, but we weren't in much of a position to be fuel snobs. If my gamble paid off, and the vessel had indeed been adrift for the years and years estimated by the chitta, we'd be fueled up for days to come.

"Let's move," Chaska said, shouldering past me. "We'll handle the details when we find something worth grabbing."

I nodded at Tusky. "The lady has a point."

We worked our way through the ship's festering corpse, pausing here or there to examine anything that looked even remotely beneficial to *Stream Dancer*. Alas, most of the critical supplies were either depleted or damaged beyond the point of usefulness. This confirmed my belief that the ship hadn't perished quickly—it had floated out here, helpless, slowly drowning in the Untraversed. I could only hope it wasn't an omen of things to come for yours truly.

Eventually, however, after much tether-tugging and backtracking, we came across the entrance to what had once been the engine module. As best we could tell, that is. These maitreyans, or whatever they were, weren't overly fond of labeling their vessel's sections for the benefit of future wreck divers. Even so, our discovery seemed promising.

The module itself consisted of eight colossal reactors, each ruptured and bruised with oxidation. Strange to see in the middle of space, but then again, this wasn't quite space. It held its own host of problems that weren't present in the vacuum. More "fun" for the adventure.

"Let's each take one," Chaska suggested. "Save ourselves some time."

Despite this being a "split the party" move, I figured it was harmless enough. We were all in the same cavernous room, after all.

I clambered up onto my assigned reactor, thoroughly examining its surface with the light. This thing had taken a real battering. Some plates bulged, while others had imploded inwards. Hell, a few segments had been blown clean off, exposing the charred surface within. A terrible sign for the previous crew, but a godsend for me.

Gingerly adjusting my tether, I pulled myself up and onto the highest bracing ring. Below me was a colossal hole—the perfect entry point for crizzum snatching. Then I crouched, ducked my helmet into the breach, and shone the light downward.

The first thing I saw was glinting, silvery strands. Thousands of them. Then I saw the large gossamer bundles tucked into their folds. No, not bundles—bodies. Shriveled hands, bony feet, shrunken and gaunt faces... all encased in their webbing.

For a few seconds, all I could do was stare and shake. The column of spindly silk and drained flesh went all the way down, extending beyond the reach of my light. There had to be a hundred corpses in there. Probably more.

Then came a sound. A soft, chittering thing, little more than a whisper through the helmet's dampened auditory system, but enough to drain my bladder into the suit reservoirs.

Against my better judgment, I turned the light upwards.

Lining the reactor's interior walls were millions... and millions... and *millions*... of small, powdery eggs. And not just any eggs. You guessed it, dear reader—spider eggs.

And just above those delicious clumps were eyes. Not the milky eyes of corpses, but black, beady ones. They shone like oily marbles at the far edge of the light's reach.

"Uh... team?" I whispered into the transmitter. "I think we should leave."

"What's the issue?" Chaska replied. "I still haven't found a damn thing."

"I believe I've found a few crumbs... not much, however," Tusky said.

I wanted to reply, I really did, but my tongue was frozen in my mouth. Long, furry legs and dripping tongues extended down toward me. More and more eyes appeared. Webs began to stir.

That was enough for me to pull the "nope" alarm. I jerked my head back, half-toppled to the floor, and began jogging backwards.

"What's the matter?" Chaska called, staring down at me from her own position. "Afraid of the dark?"

"Sp-spi—"

"Spies?"

"Spi—"

"Spirals?"

"*Spiders!*"

Right on cue, an unholy mass of legs, fangs, eyes, thoraxes, and all the rest came spilling out of the reactor's hole like a freshly popped boil. My first reaction was to curse Chitta Mini for being correct. Chaska's was to leap down and sprint past me. Tusky's was to scream like a child who's just discovered, well, spiders.

Within seconds we were thundering back the way we'd come, huffing and shuddering and constantly tripping over our no-good tethers. More than once I made a panic grab for my sidearm, only to realize that I'd opted to go in unarmed—in short, I'd broken rule number two. But there was no time to dwell on that. The chittering was growing louder. My heart was a sledgehammer against my sternum. No amount of low gravity could overcome our bulky suits or blind terror.

"There!" Chaska shouted, jerking her helmet toward a half-open door on our right. "Get in... seal it up!"

Isolating ourselves was a horrible plan, but then again, so was being paralyzed by a go'tor wreckage spider and slowly consumed. It was the best shot we had.

Chaska dashed inside, then began straining to seal the two circular plates even as Tusky dove through. He barely made it. I did not. My desperate leap to safety was snagged—literally. I crashed to the tiles two feet from the door, frantically yelping and kicking at the tether loops that had gotten bunched up around my ankles.

Still thrashing, I rolled over and worked to manually undo the kinks. No dice. I was wrapped up good, and the spider wave was nearly upon me. It eclipsed the ambient light of the corridor, all shifting limbs and clacking mandibles.

"Hold on!" Tusky yelled over the comms. "I've got you."

His oversized gloves seized my arms and fiercely dragged me backwards, but I knew we wouldn't make it. The spiders were close now. Far too close. The horrid nuances of their tarry eyes and flailing, bisected tongues were in full view now. My suit's shoulder-mounted light framed my fast-approaching death like an oil painting —*Idiot Devoured by Wreckage Spiders, Artist Unknown (and Eaten)*. And as they closed the distance, congealing into a single, squirming mass, I couldn't help but squeal like a schoolboy. I was prey and they knew it.

But with a final, herculean grunt, Tusky hauled my ass right over the threshold. Not figuratively, either. My boots and ankles remained in the still-closing entryway, which shrank by degrees as Chaska fought with the overlapping discs. Legs scrambled past and over the divide. Tongues whipped in and out, eager to snatch a last-minute snack.

Tusky kept pulling me as the gap shrank to five inches, then four, three…

Pain exploded up my right leg. I screeched and looked down to discover my worst nightmare—a spider's head sat directly before me in the opening, refusing to retreat even as Chaska compressed it like a vise between the discs. But that wasn't the nightmare part. The head had fangs, and all six of them had speared right through my boot.

Chaska gave one last push, and the spider's head popped. Greenish fluid spattered my helmet and dribbled down over my ankle. Then there was silence.

She sank down against the discs with a pained sigh, breathing hard through her transmitter.

"We're… good," she managed.

But *I* wasn't good. I was quite bad, in fact. Dying. Done for. In a matter of minutes—hours, if I was lucky—the go'tor spider's venom would claim me.

In fact, I am writing this entire manuscript as I lie here, dying aboard the Maitreyan Order's arachnid-infested wreck.

Okay, so that part was just to add dramatic tension. Sorry. But I *was* dying.

Tusky and Chaska propped me up against a wall, staring into my eyes with the pitiful certainty of all those who have witnessed death on its way. They'd been kind enough to extract the fangs and apply a rapid-acting triage foam to the puncture wounds, but I knew it wasn't enough. So did they.

Even as I sat there, my entire body ached. Numbness seeped inwards from my toes and fingers. The suit's biometrics confirmed that my temperature was moving erratically, dipping and lifting in three-degree increments. These swings only got worse, I'm sure, but I couldn't tell. My vision was blurring beyond the point of discerning the numbers.

"You're gonna be fine," Chaska whispered. "Maybe the chitta doesn't know everything. Maybe it's only inustrazans that die from it."

But I could hear that terrible certainty in her voice, too. She was playing a game of denial, either with herself or with me, or both.

"Perhaps I could... produce an antivenom," Tusky mumbled.

"Y'could?" I slurred. "How!?"

"Well, I'd just need a sample of their venom... and a full lab station... and a few days... but—"

"It's over!" I cut in, waving my frozen brick of an arm. "I'm on the way out. I'm *really* on the way out. Why *me*!?"

Chaska's gaze hardened. "You really want an answer to that?"

"It wasn't s'posed to happen like... this," I sobbed. My cheeks were too numb to feel the tears. "All this... for nothing!"

"Not for nothing," Chaska snapped. "We're going to end this war."

"By 'we,' you mean everyone but me!"

"You won't be forgotten."

"Ugh! You were s-s'posed to say... 'You're gonna make it!' I *am* dying!"

"Bodhi, just relax."

"R'lax!? How can I r-r'lax?"

"It's easy. Just stop overthinking. Breathe. Let us figure something out."

This was a simple task, seeing as both my thinking and breathing capabilities were slipping away by the minute. The entire world seemed to transpire through a misty sheet of glass. I was somewhere on the other side of that glass, looking out. From my speech to my leg tremors, everything was happening beyond conscious control.

"Just settle yourself," Tusky said, gripping my left glove. I didn't feel it. "I'll look around and see if there's anything I can utilize."

"N-No," I murmured, "I want you to stay here... with me. Walk m'through... it."

He narrowed his eyes. "Walk you through *it*? What do you—" He flinched suddenly, grasping the full weight of my request. Then he looked at Chaska. "Can you look around? I'm going to, uh, check his vitals again."

Chaska glanced between the two of us, but didn't quite seem to get it. How could she? She wasn't at death's door. It was an exclusive club. Shrugging, she wandered off into the shadows.

I let my gaze roll back toward Tusky. "H-How do I do this?"

He squeezed my glove tighter. Again, nothing. "I don't know, Bodhi. I suppose I never thought you might have to endure these circumstances before me."

"But I'm not r-ready," I said. "Not yet."

"You said it yourself, Bodhi—we all have to walk through this door."

The words I'd uttered in my quarters now felt distant and obnoxious, as though said by some sage other than myself. I didn't want to let them in, whether or not Tusky was right. The man who'd put up that wall of foolish bravado wasn't me. Not anymore. I was a scared, helpless animal creeping toward oblivion. Staring into the void. No amount of words, mine or otherwise, could put me at peace with this nightmare.

Yet, I thought as I slumped there, my mind wandering in endless, hazy loops, this wasn't a nightmare at all. This was worse than a nightmare. It was real, and there was no waking from it. This was the end of all experience. The final stop on a ride that I hadn't even started to understand.

"Hey," Chaska called, dashing back into our corner, "I found something."

"N-not now," I managed. "I'm dying here."

"Not yet, you aren't. You need to see this."

Halcius only knows how many minutes passed between Chaska's words and returning to consciousness. When I came to, I was standing upright, supported by Tusky's steel beam of an arm. Only I didn't feel anything. There was no sense of orientation, of feeling. There was only the strange, flashlight-illuminated scene before me. And I must say, what I saw was so absurd that I began to wonder if I'd begun to cross over into some slippery new dimension.

Seated on a red cushion was a shriveled, decaying body that had once been humanoid. Now it was little more than a tattered robe and leathery gray skin stretched over long bones. It had twelve arms, all of them raised at different heights and forming a sort of grisly halo around its body. Its orbital sockets suggested it had once possessed three massive eyes—two in the usual spots, and a third on its forehead.

"Whatissit?" I mumbled.

"I don't know," Chaska whispered, crouching down beside it. "A maitreyan, I'd guess."

"It's... marvelous," Tusky said. "So well preserved, even in these conditions..."

"How's it h-help me?" I asked.

Chaska didn't reply; instead, she bent down and picked up the open book laid in front of the corpse. "Can't understand it. Ink hasn't faded, though."

Tusky moved to her side, awkwardly pulling me along like a broken tango in the process. He peered over and examined the writing.

"*Hello*," I groaned, "I'm d-dying. Someone help... please..."

My pleas did little to sway Tusky's attention. The sloth continued poring over the text, gasping here and there. "I learned this language! Well, at a semi-fluent level, I suppose. It was explained in my treatise as an ancient attempt at a universal tongue... a precursor to alltongue, as I understand it."

"Anyone!?"

"What's it say?" Chaska prodded.

Tusky took the book in his free hand. "It would appear to be this being's final words. A sort of death poem, I suppose. I won't do it any justice."

Around this point, I began sobbing. It was all lining up. Nobody listening to me... a dead body... a death poem. Either I was in purgatory or someplace worse.

"For many years, I have wandered this vibrant field," Tusky began. "Each day, each hour, I have witnessed beings caught in the waves of desire and repulsion. Great has been their suffering. Even at the time of death, they will perish like animals, for they have not yet discovered the innermost truth—that the world cannot satisfy them. The satisfaction they seek is only found within them. They must turn their awareness inwards, to use their own light to find the light that is already present. Equanimity alone will undo the knots they have woven in their mind. Surrendering to the peace of eternity is the one path capable of traversing this darkness. Thus I have heard, and thus I depart. May all beings reach the boundless realm of serenity."

My eyelids drooped closed as Tusky's voice bounced around, possessing me. Penetrating the clouds of my mind. I'd heard sages and mystics preach their gospel thousands of times, but never before had the meaning of their words sunken in. This time, they did. The words of a dead, desiccated corpse sounded more true than anything I'd ever known. And moreover, they sounded familiar. Like I'd heard them thousands, perhaps millions of times before, and I'd simply forgotten them.

The waves of desire and repulsion. Even as the thought came, I sensed these waves within me, churning, gurgling. A desire to escape from death, and repulsion at the very idea of nonexistence. *They will perish like animals.* The phrase burned deeper and deeper into my consciousness. It wasn't just a platitude—I *was* going to die like an animal, kicking and screaming, in total ignorance of what it was all about. *Surrendering to the peace of eternity.* This was the one that stopped me dead in my mental tracks.

I'd lived my entire life opposed to surrender. In every situation, every jam, I'd found a back door to escape my fate. But in that moment, there *was* no escape. Nothing beyond the darkness consuming my body. And even as I slipped toward the sleep that was deeper than sleep, I listened to the mind throwing its expected temper tantrum.

There's a way out.

I'm not dying... never.

Maybe if I just amputate the leg...

Each whirling thought was just *noise*, nothing more. I certainly didn't conjure them with any voluntary effort. For the first time in my life, I understood that the passing streams of rumination and emotions and memories that I called *me* were not, in fact, *me*. I was something else... something untouchable.

But in the same moment this realization arose, the panic came back with a vengeance. Memories of the past decades came screaming into focus—walking in a park, watching armadas move overhead, holding hands with my first crush, being threatened with death... and being threatened again. And again. The memories didn't calm me or help ease some transition into wherever I was headed, however. Quite the opposite. Each vignette brought up a renewed sense of disgust. Of regret.

I'd had an entire life, a long and strange experience of total freedom, and I'd used it for nothing more than profits and debauchery. I'd stepped on the backs of good people. Sold out even better ones. I'd ridden the carousel of existence orbiting my own selfish desires. And for what? Now, here, in this final hour, what was any of it worth? Where had it gotten me?

Despite its futility, I wished I could turn back the hands of time. I wished I could appear before my young, handsome, boyhood self and tell him to turn away from my wretched endeavor. Most of all, I longed to tell him that what he wanted was peace. He didn't *really* want success or power or women—he wanted to be okay with life. Everything else was just a stepping-stone to that mode of being. It was like a dog chasing its own tail, always thinking the next cocktail or next sale would bring happiness, unaware that the goal had been present all along. But I couldn't tell him these things. He would grow up to be me, trying to fill the void within himself by any means... all because he'd made the fatal error of thinking he needed something more than peace.

And so the darkness swept up like a slow, onrushing tide, robbing me of any sensations whatsoever, burning away memories and ambitions alike. It even gobbled up the fear and the sorrow and the questions I'd pondered with Tusky. At that very instant, I knew I didn't need answers any longer. There was no past, no future—only this very moment. And it was woven from peace.

All at once, the knots in my mind came undone.

I fell into eternity.

"Bodhi?"

The eternal being's voice called out through the endless darkness, dancing around me in long, echoing strides.

"Bodhi, open your eyes."

Okay, so it wasn't an eternal being—it was Chaska.

With great difficulty, I managed to lift one eyelid, then the other. The glorified broom closet was still fuzzy and disorienting, but it now had a certain solidity to it. A solidity that only good ol' reality can provide. Then it hit me. Broom closet. The same place they'd first settled me down. There was neither an ancient book nor a maitreyan corpse.

In their places were a kneeling Chaska and Tusky, both of whom were twisting and squinting as they carried out an examination of me.

"Where are we?" I asked. My voice was still a tad slurred, but more on the level of two drinks than a keg of hard spirits.

Chaska glanced at Tusky, then back my way. "Same place?"

"What about the body?"

"What body?"

"The dead one? With the death poem?"

My compatriots shared a knowing look, then smiled pitifully at me.

"All is well," Tusky said. "You've just had a brief lapse in consciousness."

I stared intently at the two of them, trying to discern what witchcraft was responsible for this. Were they really about to tell me that there wasn't a dead maitreyan a few yards away? That we hadn't just heard the most profound paragraph of our lives?

"Just relax," Chaska said. "Keep your breathing steady."

"But the book," I stammered. "It was—I—I died, and—"

Tusky patted my helmet. "Do as the doctor orders, Bodhi."

Before I could protest and begin rattling off the death poem as proof of our encounter, a high-pitched shriek came wriggling out of the corridor and into my helmet. A war cry, even. This sound was most certainly *not* imagined, on account of Chaska and Tusky spinning toward the door.

"Was that—" Chaska began.

Tusky nodded. "Gadra."

I wanted to bolt up from my slumped position, to rush out into the spider den and save my young artist, but my limbs were still leaden and numb. The best I managed was a pathetic twitch of my right arm.

Chaska rushed to the door's disc slabs and began working to peel them back. It was then that I noticed she'd severed her tether. Mine, too, it seemed. Even Tusky's belt had a similar nub of cording rather than a full line. I couldn't tell if they'd done it out of necessity to seal the door, or if the spiders had somehow chewed them apart. Either way, far from reassuring.

"Hang on, Gad!" Chaska yelled, though I doubted her voice would penetrate both the massive discs and her helmet's dampeners. "We're coming!"

Tusky joined the effort, too, using his entire bulk as leverage to crank the disc aside.

"Gad, are you out there?" Chaska called. "We're gonna—"

A smattering of muffled gunshots interrupted her. And by a smattering, I mean a constant chug-chug-chug volley. All three of us stood there, dumbfounded, as the automatic fire stretched on and on beyond the door. I lost count of the flying rounds after about fifty or so.

Then came a pause, and with it, maniacal cackling.

"What the hell is going on out there?" Chaska hissed, tugging at the door slabs with renewed force and Tusky's assistance.

But even as they heaved and panted and panicked, the madness outside rolled on. Gunfire rattled in long, generous bursts, broken here or there by the clack of mechanical doodads as the shooter reloaded. Oh, and the cackling. That girlish, point-me-to-the-asylum cackling. Before long, I also heard the wreckage spiders squealing and retreating in a thunderous mass. But the shooting dragged on.

It didn't fully stop, in fact, until Chaska and Tusky wrenched the door slab aside.

They stepped away from the opening, panting and doubling over, only to reveal a satisfied-looking Gadra. Some version of Gadra, anyway.

See, *this* Gadra was straight out of a fever dream produced by a mad god. That, or an interdimensional rift. She wore an oversized combat vest, a pair of skull-crushing infantry boots, and a so-called "loader belt" stuffed with no less than twenty coils of bullets. Oh, and she was missing a helmet, breathing in that sweet, likely pathogen-suffused air. But all that was small potatoes compared to the weapon she carried.

Lugged in both hands—as well as slung from her body using an elaborate harness system—was one of the largest chain guns I'd ever seen in my life. The five barrels were still winding down and smoking. Vaguely, I recalled seeing that monstrosity stuffed in the insurgents' makeshift armory. It had been hauled by the largest brute in Chaska's ranks.

"Really?" Gadra snorted, kicking aside a spider's steaming corpse. "You locked yourselves in here? You guys are killin' me. Takin' forever, too."

Tusky rushed out to embrace her, only to be held at bay by the enormous weapon. "Gadra, what are you doing here? Who allowed you to—"

"Pretty sweet entrance, huh?" Gadra said. "Man, helluva rescue. First time I ever used a high-caliber puppy like this, too! And good thing I did. You guys woulda been *screwed* without me and Ol' Shooty here!"

And with that, the jig was up. The bravado, the bloodlust, the reckless use of weaponry—it all came together in a flash. We hadn't been rescued by Gadra.

"Mini," I growled, "we need to have... a group meeting about this."

"Hey, she wanted to go, too!" "Gadra" shot back. She—or rather the chitta—turned her head to the side, exposing the tendril that had been fed into her ear. "I can let her take control of the ride anytime, guys. She's just in here eatin' popcorn, enjoyin' the show. Gadra and Chitta Mini—the dynamic duo!"

Chaska stalked forward, half-raising her hand as though in preparation to strike Gadra, only to apparently realize that the target of her anger wasn't so easy to hit without simultaneously injuring a child. She drew a thick breath and looked back at me. "We can talk about... *this*... later. Right now, we need to get Bodhi back aboard *Stream Dancer* and into triage."

Chitta Mini lowered the gun in Gadra's arms, then drew a coy smile on the girl's face. "Spiders, amiright?"

My head lolled as the numbness crept in once more. "Yeah... spiders."

"Last time you ever doubt me, I bet!"

There was a good chance he was right—in all the wrong ways.

FIFTEEN

When you're drifting between the tomb of a genocidal emperor and a mind-devouring superorganism's fleet, it becomes rather easy to accept the idea of imminent death. It becomes much harder, conversely, to accept that you are *not* about to die.

"I'm *what*?" I sputtered, trying not to roll off my triage table as I faced Chitta Mini's cartoonish brain avatar on the vitals simscreen. "But you said—"

"That go'tor wreckage spiders are lethal," he cut in. "Yeah, I did say that. And it's true. But you, pal, got bitten by a *kufuri* wreckage spider. Totally different thing."

Caught in the grip of disbelief, I shakily pointed to the other vitals screen. This one displayed an hourly chart that lent credence to the idea of approaching death—it was full of arrhythmic heartbeats, elevated blood toxin levels, scrambled brain function, and more fun bits. Hell, my own inner landscape was all the proof I needed. Even after three hours of bedrest under the effects of various painkillers and antihistamines, I was still aching all over, weathering spells of numbness so bad I'd nearly bitten through my own tongue.

"I didn't say it wasn't a pain in the ass to feel that bite," Chitta

Mini said. "Fairly nasty venom in those things, no doubt. But you're gonna pull through just fine."

I glared at his simscreen avatar. "That just isn't true. I *felt* death!"

"Oh, right. That'd be due to the hallucinogen in their saliva. I used to visit a few places where people splashed that stuff in their drinks to get the party rockin'! Well, I mean, *I* didn't visit, but I saw memories from somebody who *did* visit those spots, so... y'know... same thing. Ah, the glory days."

I let my head flop back against the pillow, then stared up into the blinding lights of the overhead surgical rig. It just didn't seem possible. A hallucinogen? I'd taken hundreds, if not thousands, of hallucinogenic compounds in my day, and not a single one had taken me to a liminal zone between life and death. Nor had they felt so *real*, so impenetrable in their nature. That entire ordeal—from finding the corpse to hearing the death poem to slipping into oblivion—had been as tangible as the blankets now covering me.

But even as I lay there, groggily pondering the revelations from that book, I sensed them slipping away from me. Not the words upon the pages, exactly, but the feelings they had conjured. The sense of deep, pervading okayness that had settled my fears and reminded me of who—and indeed, what—I truly was. Try as I might, I couldn't force my mind into the same grooves it had navigated at the moment of extinction. Had it even *been* extinction? It was so very unclear. All I could remember was peace... that, and undoing the knots. Letting myself dissolve.

"You, uh, doin' okay there?" Chitta Mini prodded.

Somewhat startled, I realized I'd been scrunching my brow and gritting my teeth. Clearly my efforts to force peace upon myself were not working. Which only added ammo to the theory that it had all been a trip. A venomous, brain-melting trip.

Chitta Mini cleared his imaginary throat. "If it's any consolation, champ, the primary effects should be out of your system in a few hours. Enough for you to stand up and piss in a real waste chute, anyway. So... silver lining?"

I glanced sidelong at his simscreen. "How much fuel did we recover?"

"Y'know, maybe I should get goin'..."

"How. Much. Fuel?"

"Definitely more than three hours' worth. And since we've been traveling about a half hour..."

"Three hours!?"

"I said *more* than three hours. Almost three and a half, if you look at the gauge from the right angle. But, again, we've been pushin' for half an hour, so I guess three is about right."

"Mini, I hate to say it, but I think your scavenging expectations for that ship were a tad off."

"Perhaps... *but*, I did manage to salvage some sorta macropulse apparatus from their comms tower. Should help us send out an SOS signal. Y'know, to all the friendly critters of the Untraversed."

I shut my eyes. "I'd advise you not to send an SOS signal."

"Why?"

"Because somebody could pick it up. Somebody such as the Hegemony."

"Oh. Yeah, okay. I sure won't do that."

"You already did it, didn't you?"

"Hey, c'mon, man!" he said, sounding almost hurt. "Best case, some kindly stranger happens upon us and fills up our reactors. Worst case, you all get captured by roaming anarchic thugs, sold into different tribal factions, stripped of body parts, and tortured to death! But I'm an optimist myself, so, uh... I think it'll be just fine."

Being unfit to affect the situation in any way, let alone stop an SOS signal presumably screaming its way across the stars, I just nodded.

"Hey, lemme cheer you up," Mini said. "Wanna hear how Gadra and I carried out that sweet, sweet bug hunt down there?"

I sighed. "To be honest, Mini, I'd just like to rest. I've got a lot to... contemplate."

"Suit yourself, boss. You know where to find me. Which is everywhere, since, y'know, I'm patched into the whole ship. I mean, right now I could literally just self-destruct the reactors and kill all of us for no reason. Super cool, right?" He chuckled a bit at that, then paused. "Not that I'd ever do that. *Anywhom*... I'm gonna move my awareness back into Tusky's lab. Take care of yourself, and holler if you need me, sweet pea."

And with that, the brainy avatar disappeared from the simscreen.

I let my head sink back into the pillow, preparing for a marathon-length brooding session about the state of my life and the surreal experience that had forever changed it. Before I could make any headway with that, however, the triage module's door whooshed open.

Ruena lingered in the doorway, sizing me up. "House call."

I patted the stool next to me. "Come and read me my last rites, Ru."

"Last time a shaman tried that, you bit his tongue." She smiled, crossed the room, and took her seat. "You look absolutely awful."

"What a pep talk."

"Well, it's true. The others are hard at work, but they told me what happened in there... I'd say you look about right, all things considered."

I shrugged. "Am I going to receive a lecture about what happened with Gadra?"

"Not from me. Not this minute, anyway. Sounds like her and that chitta saved you sorry lot."

"I was working on a plan."

"I'm sure you were. Even as they hauled you back up the tether lines, right?"

"Correct."

She hummed. "They also told me that you had a rather poignant experience."

"It was a hallucination," I said at length. "Just a side effect of that damned venom."

"Tell me about it."

"What's it to you?"

"A good story for parties." She nudged my arm, then smiled again. "We don't know how much longer we have in this physical realm, Bodhi. If there's anyone who should hear this, it's me."

"I told you... it was just a hallucination."

"So is everything around you."

"Not this again..."

Ruena smirked. "Every night, you humans lie in your beds and hallucinate a new reality for eight hours. The same way that we ligethans hallucinate *this* reality while we're not in the Long Sleep. For us, the dream world is the world."

"You've already given me the elevator pitch for ligethan reality. I'm still not buying."

"I'm making a point, Bodhi. Tell me this—in your dreams, you have a body, don't you? Eyes, ears, a mouth, all the rest?"

"Yeah?"

"Why do you need any of that?"

I frowned at her. "My head's too shaken up. Dumb it down."

"Well, think about it... according to human science, everything in a dream is just an extension of the dreamer. The land, the animals, the sounds... it's all you. When you talk to another being in a dream, it's just your mind in a different form. So why would your own mind need to dream up fake sensory organs to interface and communicate... with itself?"

"I'm not a neurologist, Ru."

She leaned closer. "Who's to say that this world, the one in which you and I are talking, isn't yet another dream? Who decides what's real and what isn't?"

"You really couldn't cool it with the philosophical terror for another few hours?"

"I can see it in your eyes. My words are resonating."

"You're cheating with twosight."

"I don't need the future to know what's right in front of me, Bodhi. Whatever you saw or felt was real enough to rattle you. And calling it a hallucination doesn't make it any less real—it just muddies the truth."

I held her gaze for a long moment, shuddering as aftershocks of that disquieting experience came back to me. The room began to feel less and less real… as though I could pop it like a balloon with one simple thought.

"Am I dreaming?" I whispered.

Ruena rolled her eyes. "If you were dreaming, it wouldn't matter what I told you. I'd just be part of your dream."

Solipsistic terror, meet Bodhi.

"Just tell me what you saw," she continued, taking my hand in hers. "I have a foot in both worlds… one in your reality and one in the infinite dream. Nobody else on this ship will understand what you're going through."

Something about her presence put me into a hypnotic state of suggestion. Was it her comforting tone, her genuine gaze? Even now, I can't be sure. Whatever the reason, I felt compelled to spill my guts to her.

And so I did.

I laid out the entire story, beginning with the spider bite and stretching all the way to the moment we were rescued.

When I'd finished, Ruena pulled back slightly and stiffened her face. "The maitreyans came to you."

"Come again?"

"The maitreyans, Bodhi. You've never met one in the flesh, have you?"

"No?"

"Then how else could you have known how they looked? How many arms they had? What language they use?"

"That's simply impossible." Desperate to disprove her claim, I began combing back through my memories of the ship. Surely I'd seen a mural depicting their people somewhere, or read some obscure book on nomadic species years ago. But it all came up empty. That hallucination had been my first brush with a maitreyan specimen—and according to Ru, it had been legit. "It just doesn't make any—"

"Sense," Ruena finished. "No, not by physical laws. But the maitreyans have said that they're not limited to our dimensional perception... those who have perfected their minds exist on all levels of the continuum."

"You lost me there."

"Doesn't matter. What I'm saying is, it was *real*, Bodhi. Maybe not to them, but to you. And that's what matters. Dreams... reality... they're sides of the same jewel. There's no divide."

My breath grew very shallow. "But if it was real..."

"I don't know," Ruena said softly, surely using her twosight to jump ahead of my replies. "I can't tell you what to do with it, or how you ought to live. All I can tell you is that you were in the right place, at the right time, and with the right circumstances. You weren't chosen by accident."

"But you don't get it, Ru. That was the best I'd ever felt. I mean, it was borderline euphoric. Who knew peace was better than an upper?"

Her smile struck me as somehow sad. "The maitreyans always preached exactly what you're saying. They said stillness was the only thing that mattered. The only thing that goes beyond death."

"Then what the hell do I do? Just lie here and die?"

"Like I said... it's not my forte. That's a question for yourself."

I shook my head. "Those damn maitreyans. Couldn't they have revealed the ultimate nature of reality *after* I got us out of this mess?"

"There is no after, Bodhi," Ruena said, patting my shoulder as she stood. "There's only now. And you have eternity to learn that."

Then she walked to the door and stepped out, leaving me with a heaping cargo load of questions I wasn't equipped to process. Foremost among these questions was whether we'd ever truly spoken or not. Had Ruena sat beside me, or had she merely come to me in a dream? I never did ask. Some things are better left untouched.

I don't know when I drifted into sleep, but I certainly know when I woke up. Whirling red lights and low, droning sirens filled the triage unit. Never good.

Before I could sit straight, let alone hop to my feet, the simscreen beside my bed flickered on. Chitta Mini's avatar zipped around in a strange display of alarm.

"Finally!" he barked. "I've been tryna wake you up for, like, five seconds!"

I rubbed my eyes. "Are we exploding?"

"Not yet, chief. But things aren't lookin' so hot. In fact, they're not hot at all. They're arctic."

"Get to it."

"Right, yeah, okay. Better if you take a look for yourself."

The simscreen dissolved in a wash of static, only to rematerialize moments later as an exterior camera feed. Metal panels running along the image's bottom edge hinted that the feed belonged, specifically, to the uppermost dorsal camera. At first, nothing appeared amiss. Our sensors and chassis and various instruments were intact, and we were still surrounded by the Untraversed's ominous violet glow. Nothing else in sight. Had the chitta started losing his mind? Or had I lost mine?

"Oh, sorry," Mini said. "Wrong feed. Lemme hit you with the underside cam."

More static, more metal panels, more purple void, and—something else. Something enormous. Something that was currently surging up toward the belly of the ship, preparing to devour us. Even now, at what seemed to be several dozen kilometers away, it was a veritable city of skyscraper teeth and saliva oceans. We would be nothing more than a morsel between those jaws.

"What is that?" I whispered.

Chitta Mini gave an exaggerated hum. "Are you asking which phylum and genus it belongs to, or should I just say 'something about to swallow us'?"

I tussled my blankets in a panicked fit, sensing—however irrationally—that doing so would make me feel more in control of the situation. It did not. "How fast are we moving!?"

"I'll have a look-see," Mini said. "It looks like we're cruisin' at... zero kilometers per hour."

"*Zero?*"

"As in, one less than one."

"How!?"

"You want the technical explanation, or—"

"The one that you deliver *before* we get eaten."

"Oh. That version. So, uh, the data logs are showing that a hypersonic pulse shut down the reactors about forty seconds ago. Hence the auxiliary power. And methinks that pulse came from... whatever that thing is."

Fighting down the urge to screech, I drew a long, shaking breath and watched the creature's glacial approach. "Why didn't you say anything?"

"Well, I tried to... but like I said, you were catchin' some dreams."

Even as Chitta Mini spoke, the creature's jaws widened and stretched further, expanding beyond the boundaries of the camera feed. Neon blue lights shimmered between its rows of teeth and down into the infinite recesses of its throat. In its final seconds, the feed revealed a serpentine body twisting and trailing behind the gargantuan mouth—a long, *long* body, at that. Then the simscreen went dark. We were inside the belly of the beast. Or space-snake, in this instance.

Half-convinced I was trapped in a pharmaceutically fueled nightmare, I scooted to the foot of the bed and began assessing my options. The fact that I had to manually push each leg over the edge disabused me of the notion that I could outrun my problems.

"Mini," I said, working diligently to flex my lifeless toes, "who's at the helm? Chaska?"

"Not quite…"

"Mini?"

"So, remember that hypersonic pulse I mentioned?"

"Unfortunately."

"Yeah, well, it also had a bit of an… effect… on the crew."

With an ambitious lurch, I staggered forward and bumped into the wall. "Not the time to play it coy."

"Point taken. They're all, uh, unconscious."

I froze mid-step. "Unconscious or dead?"

"Pretty sure they're just unconscious. That pulse really threw a wrench into their brains, I guess. Except mine—liquid suspension, baby! Gotta love fluid dynamics."

"What about me?"

"Seems that triage module's got some half-decent shielding between the walls. You lucked out, buddy!"

Given the fact that I could barely stumble along the wall and was on the verge of collapsing just halfway to the door, "luck" did not seem applicable. "Mini, if you've got a game plan, I would be overjoyed to hear it."

"Glad you asked! Check it out."

Turning back, I found that the chitta had projected a new set of camera feeds onto the simscreen. By the looks of it, all of the feeds were interior, offering a well-rounded view of... nothing.

"My first plan was to seal off the ramp, but, uh, that's not too possible without a ramp," the chitta said. "Next, I thought we should—"

"Wait," I interjected, narrowing my eyes at the screen. "Why are we sealing the ramp?"

All I saw beyond the staging bay's open rear was the creature's tongue, which was illuminated by our exterior floodlights. The pinkish tissue swelled and depressed in a lazy rhythm. We were perched directly atop it, riding the waves of its circulating breaths and streaming saliva.

"Oh, that's not great," Chitta Mini said darkly. "Let's switch it up."

In a flash, the simscreen's camera feeds converted to a colorful sprawl of oranges and greens and reds. Now, I recognized this filter as one of the surveillance system's ten or twelve different perceptive lenses—a thermal variant, perhaps?—but I couldn't pinpoint exactly what it was. Not that I needed to. The alien image revealed the presence of nearly a dozen hulking human forms, all steadily advancing across the staging bay with squirming claw-glove-things extended from their hands. A boarding party, then. And, just my luck, one that my feeble human eyes couldn't even see.

"Now would be an excellent time to update that game plan," I growled.

"Let's keep our cool," Chitta Mini said. "For all we know, these guys are just checking in on us."

"They've got living creatures stuck on their hands. And they're invisible."

"True. Alright, hang tight, we've got this. Step one is to get me out of that tank and into your head. Maybe we can parley with 'em."

Dumbfounded, I slapped my thighs. Didn't feel a thing. "I can hardly walk."

"I've got a fix for that."

"Which is?"

"Think about an emerald horse."

Well, that sealed the deal. It seemed Chitta Mini had lost his precious mind. But as I stood there, half-thinking of that damned emerald horse and half-wondering if these intruders ate human flesh, a wall-mounted mechanism whirred to life. Before I could even look at it, let alone figure out its purpose, the mechanism's hydraulic arm came zipping toward me. A two-inch needle stabbed me directly in the sternum.

"*Sonofabitch!*" I roared, toppling back against the wall. As the mechanism retracted, I clapped a hand to my chest and prepared to bleed out. Chitta Mini had gone bad. Sentenced me to death by my own ship. "What did I ever—"

Midway through that sentence, a hydrogen bomb exploded behind my eyes. Energy radiated from my core, sizzling down into my feet and the tips of my fingers. Pain evaporated. My mind accelerated to a hundred thousand kilometers a second. I was ready to take on the world bare-chested and bare-knuckled.

"Nothin' gets a human goin' like an amphetamine kick," Chitta Mini said. "Now hurry up and get over here! I'll wait in my tank."

Even before the chitta had finished his sentence, I was bursting out of the triage module and sprinting like an interplanetary missile toward the meeting room. The world slid past me in a blur of red lights and sirens. I distinctly recall my stream of thoughts: *Fast, fast, fast, fast, fast.*

When I finally barreled into the room, I was quick to note that Chaska, Tusky, and Gadra were slumped over in their respective chairs, snoring into the tabletop. Ruena, I guessed, was in her sleeping pod, and Umzuma in his pit. This was good. Better than sharing a ship with a load of dead crew members, anyway.

"Psst!" Chitta Mini's subtle reminder of his presence wasn't so subtle; in fact, amplified through the speaker systems, I was quite certain our approaching foes had heard it, too. "Get me outta this thing, man. It's gettin' hot in here."

Groaning, I crossed the room, climbed onto the table, and began prying his canister's lid off. The thing was magnetically sealed, but no match for a man who'd just taken a full syringe of adrenaline-spiking uppers to the chest. I tossed the lid to the floor, then fished Chitta Mini out of his briny soup.

Just as I tucked him into my pocket, however, I heard footsteps. They weren't your typical soldier's bulky, discordant steps—quite the opposite. These were the footfalls of assassins. Orderly, polite, unified in both pace and position. It's truly amazing what you can discern when your sensory input is dialed up to twelve.

Right on cue, Chitta Mini's tendril prodded my side.

"*You feelin' cool?*" Mini whispered. "*'Cause I feel real cool. Almost too cool.*"

"*I feel like we're about to get gutted,*" I mentally replied, climbing back down to floor level as our guests drew closer. "*If we survive this, remind me to keep a gun in the triage module.*"

Then the footsteps grew softer and softer and softer…

A wealth of experience with hijackings prepared me for what was coming. I raised both hands, sighed, and announced, "Come out, gentlemen. I'm unarmed. And if you can't understand alltongue, please be quick about my murder."

Seconds later, my uninvited visitors materialized in a semicircle formation across the doorway.

They were massive, hunched over, and built like steroid junkies, but their general proportions confirmed that they were clearly carrying some of that sweet human DNA—or some simian offshoot of it. Even so, they looked distinctly… alien. Probably due to the lack of skin. They were covered from head to toe in overlapping, glimmering bone plates that either formed or encased their actual body. Tusks made of the same curious material jutted out here and there.

But the most alarming feature on these skeletal, serpent-mouth-dwelling beings was one I'd already identified through the simscreen footage—their choice of weapon. Each warrior wore a pair of "gloves" formed from writhing, inflamed-looking tissue. These questionable hand garments ended in a mess of wriggling filaments, nails, and teeth. Yes, *teeth*.

"So..." I began, trying in vain to swallow, "welcome aboard my ship."

The largest of the bone-people stepped forward. "*Hyoo-mon*," he croaked in throaty tones, his language so cryptic it took my linguistic implant several seconds to stitch together the ensuing grammar. "You have made a grave error in invading the domain of the Great Maker. The Circle of Torment will decide if your flesh is stronger than those who have come before you."

I'm quite confident that if the "city" of the bone-people were ever listed on a tourism netgate, it would be filled with one-star reviews. And deservingly so.

In the event that such an entry is ever made, let me now submit my review for this must-skip destination:

This is a terrible stop for any would-be travelers. Situated in the literal mouth of a void-dwelling serpent, this hellhole is equal parts rancid air and oppressive darkness. Patches of glowing crystal do not provide sufficient lightning when being led, shackled and blindfolded, through a twisting series of canyons formed from tongue tendons and rotting teeth. More than once during my forced march, I was soaked up to my waist in unidentified, lukewarm liquid.

The hospitality was also dreadful. Rather than fielding any questions about our travel location or possible amenities, my hosts

COSMIC SAVIOR

placed a gag in my mouth and carried my still-unconscious crew members over their shoulders in cloth sacks. At no point was I offered valet service for my ship, nor did I receive lodging in a suitable hotel.

At some point, my blindfold was eventually removed, seemingly so I could revel in the "beauty" of their capital city. Surprise, surprise, it was not beautiful. Nor was it structurally sound. Most of the buildings were carved into hundred-foot-tall teeth or otherwise cobbled together using scrap materials. The remains of scuttled and scavenged flagships lay wedged between molar peaks in the distance. Pollution was rampant, and the use of gallows and other torture mechanisms was too liberal for comfort. I did not get a chance to tour the overpopulated slums located in the cavities and receding tissue along the eastern gumline, but they did not look promising.

In summary, I would not recommend this city to any travelers, whether seasoned or amateur. If you insist on visiting this pitiful spot, be sure you haven't eaten recently, wear stain-proof clothing, and don't look the locals in the eye. Especially the last one. If you break this rule, you may find yourself dragged to the enormous, coliseum-like tumor that forms of the heart of the mouth-world—the Circle of Torment.

One star. Zero if I could give it.

Anyway, that review about sums up my take on the whole affair. It was hard enough penning that truncated account, let alone recalling details of the miasma and stomach juices firsthand. And so, detail-greedy reader, that is the best you will get.

But let us move along.

I'd been ordered to stand on a pillar that was half-submerged in a sea of salt. This pillar was one of many—ten in all, I counted—

that lined the outer ring of the Circle of Torment. Waiting atop the other pillars were bone-people who looked more or less identical to the boarding party. The only difference was that my fellow pillar inhabitants were scrawnier and chipped in places, suggesting they were not the cream of this society's crop.

This conclusion was reinforced by the constant jeers and boos descending from the arena's crowd. There had to be tens of thousands of fine, upstanding bone-people in the audience, all clamoring for what I assumed was my demise. Then again, given the scale of the situation, they didn't seem like individual beings at all. They were just a homogenous mass of arms and bones and tusks. A mob.

Directly above, visible through the arena's domed aperture, was the crystal-dotted darkness of the creature's mouth. It was my only reprieve from the strikingly bright pearl-and-bone architecture. Then again, those design choices were at least tasteful. They had character. I was not as fond of the spliced-in, salvaged parts of the arena—rusty buzzsaws poking up through the salt, automated turrets waving back and forth on their posts, secondary thrusters that had been modified to shoot flames (and probably barbecue skin)... They'd built themselves a monument to butchery.

Now, you might be thinking I'm overplaying the scale of this arena, or indeed the entirety of this mouth-city. How could a primal, skeleton-like species cram an entire civilization into a space-serpent's mouth, right? The answer is, I have no idea. But at that moment, I didn't really care. I had bigger things on my mind.

One such thing was my crew, which had been dumped into a large wicker cage and suspended over the arena. They were still out cold—I would later find out that they'd been drugged with a few helping doses of "sleepy juice" to keep them under control.

Curiously enough, Umzuma was nowhere to be seen. I never did find out why they let him stay in place, though I have my theories. My two best guesses are that he was either too cumbersome to move, or too disturbing and goopy to haul away. Or both.

"*So... what's our play?*" Chitta Mini asked.

"*Our* play?" I replied, offering a few halfhearted waves to appease the crowd. "*You're the superintelligence here, aren't you? Work something out!*"

"*Do you think they're gonna eat both of us or just you? They might think I'm, like, an appetizer or somethin'...*"

"*Think, Mini.*"

But deep down, I knew there wasn't much for the chitta to think about. We were going to become an afternoon special on the bone-people's menu. The arena's walls were at least thirty feet high, and the salt floor below us was densely littered with dehydrated heads and other human-looking bits. If you don't understand how those corpses ended up there or what would happen in a few minutes' time, you haven't spent much time in the world of blood sports. Luckily (or sadly), I have. As soon as the Circle of Torment's announcer gave the green light, I'd be torn apart by the saints and valedictorians on the pillars around me. This was a fight to the death, and I was nothing more than this week's guest star in their snuff film.

Before I could ponder this too much, however, a chorus of rumbling horns filled the arena. At this, the crowd went into an ear-shattering frenzy. The source of their excitement, I soon realized, was not the music, but the movements occurring up on the arena's highest tier. A crimson-robed figure stepped up to a balcony railing made from ribcages and lifted their arms high, adding fuel to the crowd's fire.

"Children of calcified purity," the speaker—a woman—boomed, "intruders from beyond the Maker's realm have journeyed here once again, no doubt with the same intentions. They have come to corrupt us, to pilfer the Maker's great works, to open the floodgates that will bring about the end of our people. And to this, what do we say?"

The crowd gave a practiced reply of, "Death! Death! Death!"

"*Oh, just wonderful,*" I thought to Chitta Mini. "*They're under the impression that we're tomb robbers.*"

"*I mean, technically speaking, aren't we?*"

"*Of course not. We're tomb seekers. Big difference.*"

Chitta Mini hummed. "*Y'know, these fine folks might be the reason we never heard back from anybody who went into the Untraversed. They seem pretty touchy about the Maker's stuff.*"

"*You're right.*"

Suddenly realizing that the Maker angle could be our only way out, I lifted my hand high and waved at the arena's announcer. Not that my voice would be any good, even if she did grant me speaking privileges. I was about half a kilometer away from her, stranded at the bottom of a pit that had probably been acoustically engineered to contain the screams of its victims.

To my surprise, the crowd seemed to catch my gesture. Their hollering and chanting trickled down to a mild sea of discontent, then an eerie silence.

The announcer turned her gaze to some sort of operations den in the upper-left overhang of the arena. She made a few vague hand gestures at it, which prompted the technicians within to crank some levers and vent steam through a series of misshapen pipes.

Seconds later, the sinewy wires trailing from the operations den to the arena floor began to contract and wobble. They looked like intestines locked in an epic digestive struggle. Now, I couldn't tell whether they had fluids or electrical current running through them, but I *could* tell that they powered everything from the traps to the turrets around me. And more importantly, they were no ordinary wires. These were organic, through and through.

An idea sprang to mind.

"Speak, and do so briefly," the announcer said. "We have little time for the words of the unclean."

"Unclean?" I blurted out, only then realizing they had, in fact, activated some sort of local microphone. My throat-clearing produced a terrible feedback echo. "Uh, hello. My name is Bodhi Drezek, and I'm not here to steal anything. Far from it. Now, you all seem like you're good, hardworking people who appreciate the Maker's... realm. My crew and I also appreciate it. That's why we've come here to protect it."

Murmurs and hisses came down from the crowd. Even my fellow pillar dwellers seemed to snicker at my words.

"You are not the first to have lied to our people," the announcer said, pulling back her hood to reveal an elaborately war-painted face. "Even so, interloper, we have tolerated your words. If you survive this test of strength, you will be able to plead for your life in a test of honesty. But I shall waste no further breath speaking of these things... none of your fellow humans have ever made it beyond *this* test."

"I haven't lied!" I shouted, though they'd already killed my microphone. "Not here, anyway..."

"Prepare yourselves," the announcer called down.

Various weapons began sprouting up through the salt below us. Axes, knives, rusty one-shot pistols... all the instruments needed to brutally dismember fellow arena captives. They didn't just want to kill me—they wanted to give these people a show.

And I would give them one.

Still working overtime from the amphetamine injection, I whipped around and scanned the walls, the overhead scaffolding, the crowd... no dice. Not until I noticed the small, glossy-looking panel embedded in the bones directly behind me, about five feet above the salty floor.

Just as I'd expected, it had dozens of small, glistening tubes snaking outwards through the masonry and into the surrounding gadgets.

What exactly was it, you ask? Why, a wetworks board, of course. Still lost? Don't fret; I'll break it down. Way, way back in the day, before us pesky humans had explored or innovated enough to get our hands on inorganic AI constructs, we'd gone the biological route. You know, like chittas. Intelligence and architecture that could be grown in vats, ripened on vines, and powered with an all-natural diet of carbon and glucose. After all, why spend hundreds of years to reverse engineer a conscious computer for piloting when you can just clone and beef up an organic brain? But that's tangential to the main point. See, ancient humans didn't just stop at computers. They'd also grown entire information systems and ships through biological means. And these ships were governed by—you guessed it—wetworks boards.

All of that is a long, superfluous way of explaining why that board was going to save my life. The fools up in that operations box weren't controlling anything—they were just feeding commands to the real CEO of the arena: the wetworks board.

"Oooooh," Chitta Mini said, "*is that what I think it is?*"

"*Look familiar?*" I replied.

"*Nostalgia, man. Nostalgia. They just don't make 'em like that anymore.*"

"May your blood and sweat nourish Jomandir, the World Serpent," the announcer continued, droning on in that brash, imperious tone of hers. "May your flesh sink into the…"

Admittedly, I tuned out at that point. I got the point—it was time to die, you're going to feed our giant space-snake, yadda yadda.

"*Mini,*" I thought, still staring at the wetworks board, "*I don't need to tell you what to do, right?*"

He laughed. "*I was made for this. Literally.*"

And with that, I yanked Chitta Mini out of my pocket and threw him directly at the wetworks board. He *splooshed* against it, only to instantly plunge his tumor-tentacles into the board's array of ports and hold on for dear life.

"Your time has come," the announcer said, her voice rising to a crescendo. "You will know death, and you will—"

In the spirit of full disclosure, I was busy looking at a cracked fingernail when the first arena combatant exploded. Therefore, I must assume that the announcer fell silent in response to this surprise. I did, however, look up just as the first victim's head fragments—mostly bone, with a few reddish bits—went spraying across the salt.

Screams and a general uproar erupted from the crowd, but the chitta's handiwork was already in motion. The arena's other automated turrets swiveled toward their assigned targets—that is, my competition on the pillars—and unleashed their deadly payload. Legs, chests, necks, shoulders, and spines exploded in brilliant red puffs.

I raised my arms in a show of victory when the last competitor kicked the bucket, but Chitta Mini didn't seem content to stop. He kept pounding the already-minced, crushed, and pulped bodies with high-caliber rounds, simultaneously operating all of the turrets like a gang of cats pouncing on doomed mice. Pretty soon, there was nothing left but organ-splattered pillars and red sand. Rather embarrassing, really. Each time I opened my mouth to make a speech, he let off yet another "final" round, further incensing the traumatized crowd.

Not that anybody dared to draw a weapon on me, of course. Not even the warriors standing guard between the crowd sections. Brutish as they were, they clearly understood that *I* was in control of those turrets and thus their fates.

"Forgive me for being hasty," I called up to the announcer, "but I believe it's time to parley."

SIXTEEN

Some corporate bigwigs believe a hostile takeover is the right way to assume control, but I've always believed in the lost art of negotiation. That being said, negotiation is significantly more effective when you've just delivered instant death to an arena full of would-be killers.

After nearly twenty minutes of proposals, counterproposals, threats, and even a few veiled compliments, I found myself escorted to what I took to be the local equivalent of a courtroom. The low ceilings, flickering lights, and fungus-riddled industrial décor suggested that the locals had ripped this place straight out of a ship and "repurposed" it. They'd also added their own touches, mostly in the form of corpses nailed to the walls and insane screeds painted across the floor.

Not the lap of luxury, by any means, but it would do. I had, after all, come here for a civilized discussion about getting myself and my crew out of the jaws of death—not figuratively, either.

My captors had accidentally followed the universal law requirement of "trial by a jury of peers," having dumped my *still-*unconscious crew members into a holding pen. Which is not to say I had a warm reception. The scaffolding and various pits surrounding the courtroom floor were packed with seething, gibbering hordes of bone-people who were not so jazzed about the stunt I'd pulled.

"*Y'know, I don't think this is an ideal situation,*" Chitta Mini said through our renewed tendril link. "*I don't see any more wetworks boards in this joint.*"

I did my best to appear calm and orderly, even as the masses surged against the guards holding them at bay. "*Just relax, Mini. I can talk my way out of hell itself. Which I've done. Twice.*"

"*Yeah, well, at least demons make deals. I'm gettin' bad vibes from these skeletons.*"

The chitta made a good point. Our captors seemed to operate on the principles of "might makes right" and cruelty. Now, this being the case, our little reversal of fortune in the arena had probably earned me some respect. But it had also made me a much more viable target. Hunter-killer societies love to seek out and slaughter suitable prey.

After a few more minutes of hubbub, pale lights lit up the front of the courtroom. Some semblance of order quelled the crowd. The arena announcer stepped up at the highest pulpit, while two lesser "judges"—both wearing black robes and beads around their heads—took their places at the desks on either side.

"I did not expect to see you here, human," the announcer said. "Your kind are a frail, fearful bunch. Surrender your name."

I bowed on my illuminated dais. "Bodhi Drezek, at your service."

"Bodhi… a most curious title."

"Sure, let's go with that. And who am I speaking with?"

"I am High Priestess Jalisa, and these are my arbiters. But I suspect you will not live long enough to make use of this information." Just then, I felt the rigid point of a blade pressing into the small of my back. "This is your test of honesty, human."

"Test away. I'm an open book."

The high priestess glanced at both arbiters, then nodded. "True or false... you have ventured here from the Fallen World."

"You mean... the rest of the universe... outside this fine purple sphere?"

"True or false."

I shrugged. "True? We're just passing through your little slice of heaven."

Whispers passed through the crowd.

"How have you learned our tongue?" the high priestess asked.

"Implant." I tapped the side of my head. "Top of the line, you see."

She lifted her chin. "The others have not understood our words."

"Not surprised. I don't cut corners on linguistics, ma'am."

"Why have you come to our domain?"

"We're trying to stop something bad from happening to the... Fallen World. There's bit a been of an outbreak."

"You speak of Kruthara."

"Yes!" I just about shouted. *Finally*, some common ground. "We're trying to fix that mess."

Again, more unrest in the crowd. I'd touched a nerve.

The high priestess waved the commoners to silence, then leaned forward. "More lies from the outsider. We know that you are a servant of the corrupted one."

"*Me?* Serving Kruthara? Listen, lady, you've got this all mixed up."

"*Maybe you oughta let me handle this*," Chitta Mini piped up. "*These people are a little too lost in the crazy sauce.*"

I did my best to nonchalantly hush him, but I couldn't deny the thrust of his argument. There was no room for logic here. This is often the case in primitive spacefaring societies, where anything other than the established fear-and-power dynamic is punishable by death.

"Explain yourself, then," the high priestess growled.

She swiveled in her chair, facing what initially appeared to be a blank, grimy wall. Only for a moment, though. The wall began to bubble and swirl, gradually conjuring an image that reminded me of a mirage. The image was that of our staging bay, which still had a few piles of Kruthara-dust scattered across its panels.

"What, you think I was smuggling Kruthara into this place?" I asked, incredulous.

The three judges said nothing.

"This is a misunderstanding," I babbled on. "We were *escaping* from Kruthara, and it managed to get on board. Your... domain... took care of that."

The high priestess steepled her fingers on the metal pulpit. "You admit that the corrupted one gained access to your vessel."

This prompted yet another flurry of bloodlust from the crowd.

"It didn't infect any of us," I said. "If it did, we would've been sorted out the moment we came to this place. We're clean!"

The arbiter to the left of the high priestess slid over and whispered something to her.

She nodded, then stared down at me. "Do you know how our people have thrived here for so long, human?"

"Sounds like a rhetorical question."

"We have taken extraordinary measures to prevent the corruption from overtaking us. We have spent thousands of years evolving, culling our herd and its beauty to produce the very bodies you now see. We surrendered everything—our homeland, our destinies, our culture—to live within the Maker's sacred space. We made our home in the jaws of this terrible beast, this majestic avatar of the Great Maker. And most importantly, we eradicated all that posed a threat to our people. The scourge of the corrupted one has no place here."

The crowd cheered at that, but I was less impressed. If the high priestess' account was true, their entire civilization had cast itself into an endless dark age just to hide from a threat that, until recently, hadn't even existed. They'd spent their whole history preparing for a war that was just now beginning.

Sighing, I tried a new approach. "First of all, let me congratulate you on winning the survival game this long. Second, let me reiterate that I haven't come here to spread anything or steal anything or even *touch* anything. We're trying to escape from the same thing you are."

"You will not find refuge among our domain, human," she hissed. "We have exterminated entire fleets that sought to pillage these stars. This domain was created by the Maker for his chosen people, and we have guarded it ever since... we will guard it until the end of days."

I shrugged. "You might be getting to the end of those days fairly soon. Now, I hate to be the bearer of bad news, but Kruthara *is* coming, and he has help—human help. *We* came here to find a way to stop it... for good. And truth be told, you're all royally fouling up that plan."

"You cannot expect us to believe in your innocence."

"Oh, but I can." The crowd went silent. "If you really thought everybody outside your little 'domain' was a threat, you would've crushed our ship the moment it arrived. You wouldn't have even let me inside this little kangaroo court. But you let us in, and you let other humans in, too. Judging by the bodies, anyway." The high priestess raised a hand, but I raised mine faster. "You've kept my crew and me alive because you know that you need our help. I don't know why, but I know that much. And if I'm wrong on that point, just spear me now."

I must admit, I expected that ballsy hail-Halcius approach to get me jabbed through the spine. But by some miracle, the seconds stretched on, and I remained unparalyzed.

"We do not need *you*," the high priestess said.

"But you need a human. And I can guarantee you haven't seen too many humans lately."

"You presume too much."

I rolled my eyes. "Listen. We found a journal that pointed us in this direction. We aren't here for you—we're here to find some Kruthara-killing weapons that your Great Maker supposedly stashed in his tomb. Not to sell, but to end the threat. That's the beginning and end of the truth. You'd be a fool to cut me down."

The high priestess glanced at her arbiters, then me. "None are permitted to enter his eternal abode. *None.*"

"And how would you know that?"

"Because we have sent our greatest champions to his gates. Our holy task is to guard, not to enter. And you know nothing of it."

I was then slammed by a realization that, in retrospect, should've been far more obvious. The condescending way these people spoke, the way they presented themselves, the way they toyed with their captives—it rang a bell in the back of my mind.

These bone-people weren't an anomaly.

They were inustrazans.

Or, at least, they once had been.

"What do you know about your ancestors?" I asked.

"Do not try to divert us, human."

"Do you even remember what they are? Who made them?"

"Mind your tongue."

"I know what you are, and the educated among you must know it, too. Your species was created by Kruthara." I couldn't help myself; I let out a belly-rumbling laugh. "No wonder you think nobody can get into the Maker's tomb. Your people were at war with him until they decided to wise up and switch sides!"

"Do you wish to have your lying tongue ripped out?"

"Not particularly, no." I turned around and addressed the masses. "People of... whatever this place is... it's time to put the kibosh on this xenophobia. I might be your last hope."

"You are nothing but a whelp," the high priestess said, bolting up from her seat. "You are—"

"That is quite enough, Priestess." The soft, frail voice drew my attention. It had come from the arbiter on the woman's right, who I now saw to be borderline ancient. The elderly bone-person stood, quaking as he did so. "He may be the prophetic one."

I liked the sound of that, but the high priestess—shockingly—did not.

"Absolutely not," she said. "He's an insolent, conniving human. The same as the rest."

The arbiter shook his head. "Remember what the maitreyans said..."

"Oh, so the maitreyans were fine to pass on through, but not us humans?" I said. "Sounds a tad prejudiced."

"They were nothing but deceivers," the high priestess shot back. "They corrupted the word of the Great Maker."

Again, the aging arbiter waved her down. "It does not matter what you think of the many-armed ones. They claimed that the Great Maker had spoken through them—and they passed the test of truth."

"Those facing death will say anything to save themselves."

"The canonical records remain. And if the maitreyans did, indeed, speak the truth, then the Maker's message was clear, Priestess... his champion would conquer without a drop of blood on his hands. He would be a child made in his own image, and he would walk without the stain of death upon him." He pointed directly to me. "This man *is* the champion. He dispatched our warriors without lifting a finger."

There were a few issues with the arbiter's claim—after all, I'm not sure if using a miniature chitta to hack turrets and commit murder-by-proxy is bloodless—but I liked the general flavor of what he was laying down. Anything that got the crazies off my back and on my side was good. Exceedingly good.

"The Maker would never have instructed those heretics," the high priestess said, practically choking on the words. "The maitreyans are a cowardly, insidious species. We should have wiped them all out when we had the chance."

"I have existed among these stars since the days before your grandmother's birth," the arbiter said. "Do not quarrel with me about the Maker's will, or that which he deems true."

"*Gotta hand it to you,*" Chitta Mini whispered. "*That was one helluva reversal.*"

"*Don't hand me anything yet,*" I replied. "*Not until we're out of this thing's mouth.*"

"*Oh, right. Hurry up with that.*"

"I'd like to make my closing argument," I said, eliciting confused looks around the room. "You still haven't disproven my point about needing a human. Even if you, High Priestess, don't quite agree, it seems others understand my sentiment. You've been looking for the right *human* to open up that tomb, recover the weapons, and get you out of this rather pitiful living situation. And whether you like it or not, that human is me. I can get you in there, and I can get you back out into the stars. You'd be the best inustrazans this universe has ever seen—and more or less the only ones, but that's not relevant right now. Bottom line… you need me, and I need you. So let's get on with winning this war."

Between you and me, I didn't have any clue if this spirited pitch was accurate. How was I supposed to know if I was some sort of "chosen one" capable of cracking open the Maker's tomb? And piggybacking off that, how could anybody guarantee that the tomb was able to be opened in the first place? They couldn't. As such, my closing argument contained holes so big you could sail a nebular freighter right through it. But these fanatics didn't have to know that. They were drunk on hope, and that was enough.

Or so I thought.

"I am the word of law in our domain," the high priestess shrieked, "and I will *not* stand for your blasphemy! Nor will I bow to the cowardice of my own people! I sentence you to death by flaying."

Shocked gasps filled the courtroom, and even the arbiters looked somewhat embarrassed by the high priestess' outburst. Rightfully so.

Yet... as I often do... I had a backup plan I'd been simmering to perfection.

"*Ready for route number three?*" I asked Chitta Mini.

"*Always, boss*," he said. "*Just gimme the way in.*"

The high priestess was still carrying on about this and that, but I paid it no mind. Instead, I bowed my head and lifted both hands to signal the raising of my inner white flag.

"You accept your punishment, whelp?" the high priestess taunted.

I nodded, then gave a fittingly defeated sigh and reached into my pocket. "Ladies and gentlemen of this courtroom, I am ready and willing to undergo whatever pains you deem necessary. But before I do so, I feel compelled to offer up my most treasured possession. I believe it once belonged to your kin."

More confusion reigned as I lifted Chitta Mini high into the air, turning him end over end in the sallow lights. This was their first direct look at the ace up my sleeve—or rather, my coat. In the aftermath of the arena chaos, nobody had gotten a chance to truly examine him.

"This, ladies and gentlemen, is a chitta. I'm sure your scholars know very well what it is."

"But how...?" the older arbiter began, craning forward over his post. "They still live?"

I nodded. "This one does, and I'm prepared to turn it over to you. It might serve you well in your quest to deal with Kruthara."

The high priestess didn't betray much on her already-lifeless face, but she was still borderline quaking with rage. "Not only do you lie to us... you pilfer the wisdom of our people. To even have the audacity to touch it with your sullied hands..."

"Terrible, I know."

"Turn it over. Immediately."

"Very well. Seeing as I'm about to die, however, I should probably tell you not to let it connect to your mind. I don't think you can handle the knowledge stored inside it."

"Do not speak to me about the capacity of my mind, human."

"Oh, I wouldn't dare. I'm just warning you. It's potent."

The high priestess bared her teeth. "Give it."

Shaking my head with an award-winning display of regret, I stepped off my dais and approached the high priestess' pulpit. "As you request, High Priestess."

Midway through reaching up and trying to plop the chitta before her, she snatched it from my hands. Then she stepped back, grinning at the creature, almost fawning over it. It should come as no surprise that she proceeded to place the creature atop her head—against the pleading of her arbiters, no less—and let its tendrils snake into her ears.

The room went silent. For long, tense seconds, the crowd waited in rapt attention. I, meanwhile, was the most relaxed I'd been in hours.

"My cherished people," the high priestess said in a calm, measured voice, "I have misjudged the human standing before us. This chitta, this font of ever-knowing wisdom and benevolence, has revealed the error of my ways."

It took all my effort to resist rolling my eyes. The chitta clearly wasn't above hamming it up in pivotal moments.

The priestess-turned-mouthpiece continued by saying, "I have seen all that has happened, and all that is yet to come. We must preserve this human and guide him to the Maker's abode. He is our only salvation... our only chance to reclaim the cosmos. Through him, the Maker's prophecy shall come to fruition. Let us grant him mercy and safe passage."

Now, although I'd expected the chitta to feed this monologue through the high priestess, I was taken aback by what followed.

Almost in unison, the entire courtroom—including the arbiters and on-duty warriors—knelt down and began chanting. Clearly this was a big deal to them.

"Let us return the human and his crew to their vessel at once," the high priestess said. "We will do our duty in standing against the hordes that now pursue the chosen one, and we must give our last breaths to ensure that his mission is accomplished."

"Yeah," I said, planting both hands squarely on my hips, "what she said."

Both arbiters rose in tandem and began passing out hushed orders to their attendants. An excellent sign.

What was *not* so excellent was the image taking shape on the mirage-screen behind the pulpit.

Even at a few hundred thousand kilometers away, the appearance of Hegemony flagships assembled in prebattle formation was unmistakable. Then again, thousands of green, starlit vessels are difficult to miss in a purple ocean. And yes, there were *thousands*. They'd brought out the big guns for this mission. And the medium ones, and the small ones, too. They'd brought no less than half their total fleet to the showdown. It seemed I was the only one who noticed this snafu, however, as everybody else remained in their fawning, Bodhi-worshipping routine.

"Forgive me," I said, pointing to the screen, "but I don't think those individuals are intent on a cultural-exchange seminar."

And just like that, the worship ended. The crowd resumed its chattering speculation while the arbiters stared at the screen in obvious alarm.

"It's from the advance guard, is it not?" the as-of-yet-silent arbiter said.

The elder arbiter nodded, then looked at me. "We will get you to the tomb, human. Fear not... our allies will meet you at its steps. They will hold back the tide if we cannot." Next, he faced the woman of the hour. "High Priestess, we must mobilize our forces at once. Are you prepared to merge with its mind? The wisdom of the chitta will render you unstoppable."

Chitta Mini, still wearing the high priestess' body, looked at me with wild eyes. "Yes... the merging... the mind." Her eyes glazed over for a second, which I would later learn was a telltale sign of the chitta combing his host's memory banks. "You speak of the World Serpent, do you not?"

"Of course," the arbiter said, fiercer now. "High Priestess, this is the moment for which you were born. The culmination of your training."

"My training. Yes, that. All those"—another round of memory-diving—"*seven hundred and twelve years* of training." This last figure was delivered straight to me through gritted teeth.

"Give us the command, High Priestess!"

"Yes, command. Uh... it's... battle time!"

The two arbiters glanced at one another, clearly perturbed, but there wasn't enough time to grill their leader on lapses in terminology. They sprang into action, hurrying off down the adjoining corridors and shouting instructions to the warriors at their sides.

Up until now, my plan to have Chitta Mini commandeer the priestess' body and use it as my personal broadcasting system had gone off without a hitch. But I'd failed to account for one variable: the Hegemony. After all, what were the odds they'd catch up to us right here, right now? Pretty high, in hindsight. I was on a terrible luck streak.

The real problem here wasn't the Hegemony itself—it was the fact that Chitta Mini knew nothing about commanding a species he'd encountered just hours prior, let alone controlling the mythical beast they literally inhabited. Reviled or not, the high priestess was the voice of the people. Their champion. The one who called the shots, launched the ships, made the war plans.

And we'd just replaced her with Chitta Mini.

Perhaps sensing the delicate nature of the situation, the chitta used his vessel to issue a command to the assembled crowd. "My dear people, report to your assigned districts! Prepare yourselves for war against the unclean!"

In a rush of savage whoops and pounding feet, the onlookers began flooding out of the courtroom.

Chitta Mini approached me amid the tumult, leaning in close before speaking. "This just got a whole lot stickier."

"That's an understatement," I said. "What's your exit strategy?"

"*My* exit strategy? C'mon, man, this is your time to shine."

"Pardon me?"

"Between you and me, I think they've got it right. The arbiter did, anyway. The Maker thought humans were the cream of the universal crop. If anybody can get that tomb open, it's one of you fragile meat-sacks. No offense intended..."

"None taken. But that still doesn't fix our predicament."

The high priestess shrugged. Despite knowing Chitta Mini had performed the gesture, the priestess' sheer size and power made me flinch. "Listen, Bodhi, we're gonna link up when this is through. But only *after* it's through. Y'get me?"

"No?"

"Well, here's the skinny. If the Hegemony *does* steamroll over us, we're all done for. I'll spend the rest of eternity locked in a jar, slurpin' up nutrient solutions and answerin' dumb questions. No thanks, chief. And you and your peeps... I'd wager they're good as gone. So purely on a risk-reward level, I've gotta play this thing out."

I narrowed my eyes, trying to parse the chitta's dance-around-the-issue way of explanation.

"Bodhi, it's simple," he continued. "I'm gonna flip through this lady's memories, jack myself into the World Serpent—that came out wrong—and eat every last Hegemony ship out there. And *you* are gonna haul your ship straight to the tomb and get this whole plan crackin'. We'll grab a drink when this is over. You can just, y'know, pour it into my tank and—"

"Wait," I interrupted, "you're planning to actually control this... serpent... world... thing?"

"Uh, yeah?"

"That's insanity."

"Poppycock. I ran the entire inustrazan hive-world... y'think I can't handle a big snake? Again, don't take that out of context."

Still flabbergasted, I pointed to the image of the Hegemony fleet. "There are thousands of ships out there, Mini. Any way you dice this, they end up dicing *you*."

"I can take 'em."

"What if you can't? You don't even know these people."

"Maybe, but they'll know *me* when I'm finished."

I groaned. "We can figure out a way to get you on board with us. Maybe we could—"

Chitta Mini lifted the high priestess' hand, silencing me. "End of discussion, pal. You sprang me outta that inustrazan slum to get a sample platter of reality, and this is as real as it gets. Plus, it's a thrill ride for everyone. I'm gonna have the fight of a lifetime, and in a giant space-snake, no less! You and your precious li'l crew are gonna end this war—or get violently dismembered. Who knows? Point is, I haven't had this much action in centuries... and I'm itchin' for it."

Before I could spit out another half-baked reply, Chitta Mini faced the nearest guards and clapped imperiously. They came racing over without a moment's delay.

"Most majestic... soldiers," Mini said, "I need you to escort this human and his crew back to their ship. Then, uh, get them to the Great Maker's tomb. Fast."

The guards nodded in unison, then scrambled to carry out the "high priestess'" order. Several rushed to my pile of unconscious crew members while the rest began dragging me toward a side passage.

Just before I crossed the threshold, I glanced back at Chitta Mini, my dear friend and fellow libertine.

He'd twisted the high priestess' face into a devilish smile.

"See you on the other side, human," he called. "Don't forget about those drinks."

If I had to use one word to describe my epic jaunt back to *Stream Dancer* amid a universal fate-deciding battle, it would be *awkward*. See, I wasn't running for my life. I wasn't moving at all. I was bouncing around the interior of a bloated, fast-moving parasite that these people evidently used as transportation.

My escort team assured me that we were not only in the prized thoroughbred of the lot, but also in its luxurious third stomach compartment. This did not do much to ease my discomfort. It was still a bumpy, noxious ride plagued by gurgling and various caustic fluids under my feet.

I wish I had more to describe about this moment, I really do, but there is not much to tell. The bone-people warriors and I sat on our makeshift benches, jostling around as we raced through the World Serpent's mouth. This may sound absolutely bonkers, and it is. But what can I say? I'm not the creator of the universe, just an occasionally regretful inhabitant.

The absurdity of the trip was heightened by the presence of my *still* unconscious crew members, who were strapped upright in their "seats" and snoozing away. When pressed, nobody seemed willing or able to tell me when—or if—they might wake up. Charming, right?

But eventually, mercifully, we arrived at the World Serpent's designated "landing strip." I put this in quotations because any civilized person would probably term this landing strip a tongue. It stretched out before us like a vast, pinkish plain, incessantly rolling like an ocean of muscle. Which it was.

The bone-peoples' warriors hastily offloaded my crew, slung them over their shoulders, and led me toward the mound in the distance. *Stream Dancer*, I soon realized. The vessel was eclipsed by the massive teeth surrounding it.

Even this sight, however, was mundane compared to the activity above and ahead of me. Squadrons of bone-people ships detached from the roof of the creature's mouth like cave bats, streaming out toward the newborn battle. There had to be hundreds, if not millions of gunships stored up around the serpent's gumline.

Far ahead, these pilots clashed with the Hegemony's best and brightest. Automated flagship turrets filled the Untraversed with streams of tracer fire. Thermobaric warheads detonated in blinding flashes. Kinetic shields shimmered like soap bubbles. This was not only one of the brightest, largest battles I'd witnessed—it was among the loudest.

Consider this: most space engagements are completely silent. There's no atmosphere, so no medium in which for sound to be generated or travel. Not so in the Untraversed. It was more liquid than vacuum, and as such, a perfect conduit for waves of every kind. I heard every blast, every screeching engine, every concussive *whoomp* that the hydrogen shells had to offer. And moreover, I *felt* them in my bones.

But as we came within a hundred meters of the ship, I lost focus on the battle. My lungs ached from the sprint through those saliva-riddled wetlands, and all I could think about was getting the hell out.

"Fire up the engines," I wheezed into my transmitter, praying Umzuma would receive the short-range broadcast.

Shockingly, it worked. The underside engines flared to life with cones of blue-white fire.

Not that it mattered, really. *Stream Dancer* was anchored to the tongue by several squirming parasites, each latching onto its hull with striated tentacles. On account of my initial blindfolding, I hadn't noticed them on the way in. Probably for the best. The things were easily four times my size, and packing four times as many eyes, too. Some docking mechanism, huh?

Once we'd collectively dashed up and into the ship's staging bay, the bone-people—in a not-unexpected display of TLC—proceeded to dump my crew members on the same floor grid, creating a fleshy heap.

I cocked a brow as the supersonic blasts grew nearer. "You fellas mind moving them inside? Or am I—"

They halted my question by offering a unified salute, an unintelligible mantra, and, finally, a swift retreat back the way they'd come. A curt goodbye, but perhaps warranted in our situation. Even as I watched them race over the tongue's gloopy floodplains, they were backlit by constant flashes of light, all of which I recognized far too well: pale fission clusters, greenish sky-splitter rounds, red-and-violet slag streams.

A beautiful sight, to those uninitiated in interstellar wars. Even more beautiful to those who funded and supplied those wars. But not to this arms dealer. Each burst of color represented not only another bundle of lives snuffed out, but another bundle of lives I'd personally played a role in ending. Some of those weapons had been engineered by yours truly. To this day, I'd bet my last dollar that many of the devices on those flagships had, in fact, been produced in one of my assembly lines.

No time to sit and sulk on that, however. There was an escape to be made.

"Showtime!" I transmitted to Umzuma, already hustling to drag each of my crew members back inside the ship proper.

I worked my way through the pile, sorting my evacuees from lightest to heaviest. That meant Gadra first—even gunrunners know children are priority number one—and Tusky last. By the time I'd hauled Chaska, my third pick, into the corridor, my back was begging for relief. My lungs, too.

But we had bigger problems than my ailments.

Glancing up from my body-haul-a-thon, I discovered that we were neck-deep in the battle. This should have been obvious from the ear-shattering concussive waves and blinding strings of particle-beam fire, but adrenaline-fueled tunnel vision is a hell of a thing.

Missiles streaked by in twos and threes, and flocks of gunships whirled about like schools of fish in a feeding frenzy. Flaming wrecks tumbled and vaporized. Flagships careened past us with autocannon batteries ablaze. To top it all off, the insanity beyond the staging bay literally spun and flipped. Umzuma's evasive piloting at work.

All that aside, what stunned me most wasn't the battle—it was the fact that we were still flying. Last I'd seen it, we'd been burning the reactors down to their last tarry bits of crizzum. And our current maneuvers were fuel hogs, to say the least. There was no way Umzuma would be tapping out the engines this early in a fight this massive. Unless…

After double-timing my relocation of Tusky—a feat that my herniated discs remind me of to this day—I sealed the outer doors and ran (limped) to the bridge.

The battle beyond the main viewpane was as bombastic as I'd expected. The bone-people had apparently deployed thousands upon thousands of new vessels, flooding this region of the Untraversed so thoroughly that I could hardly make out its purplish ether. And judging by the plumes of smoke and fire bursting throughout the Hegemony flagships, the natives had some distinct advantages here. They were being incinerated in huge quantities, yes, but they were giving the enemy a walloping they couldn't ignore. Swarms of puny, biofilm-coated vessels circled the Hegemony behemoths, stinging at them like insects challenging an apex predator. The perks of training for combat in a non-vacuum environment, I suppose.

"What's our fuel level?" I called to Umzuma as I rushed to his pit. "You think we'll—"

Umzuma's relaxed, borderline lazy demeanor cut me off in my tracks. At first glance, I worried he might even be dead. His puckers and milky arms drifted about, disconnected from the various neural input ports around him.

He wasn't flying the ship.

The somebody—or rather, something—that *was* became apparent a moment later. Just outside the viewpane, suctioned to the ship's main modules by some nebulous organic adhesive, were the parasites that had kept us anchored to the World Serpent's tongue. They expanded and contracted in tandem, puffing out their slimy gills for propulsion and "steering" using networks of spiny feelers.

This network of biological autopilot wasn't just pushing us through the Untraversed, however—it was navigating it like a pro. Better than a pro. Our parasitic engines seemed to detect each incoming blast, bullet, and beam long before it reached us, banking out of harm's way with uncanny precision.

I returned to Umzuma's pit, still gazing at the chaos. "Are you doing any of this?"

He grunted what I took to be *no*.

"Figures." All I could do was stand there like a dolt, too baffled to even experience fear. "You, uh, know what they're doing?"

In response, Umzuma slid one of his tendrils into a neural port and activated a projector cone. The resulting image was that of a stereotypical space tomb, right down to the hexagonal shell and gyroscopes.

"You really think they're taking us to the tomb, then," I breathed.

Umzuma grunted again, this time in the affirmative.

"Huh. Just our luck." Then, despite the mass-casualty battle raging outside, a thought struck me. I rounded on Umzuma with knitted brows. "Wait a moment—you could *talk* using images all this time, and you didn't? Just played mute?"

Umzuma projected a crude image of Chitta Mini, then books, then a man sternly lecturing.

"He taught you," I said, nodding. "Well, keep practicing that. Unless you want to complain. Then stick to your silent routine."

His final projection was that of a hand waving at Chitta Mini. Waving goodbye, I realized.

"I know, pal," I whispered, kneeling down to pat Umzuma on the head. All that did was tease out a menacing growl and a flurry of tendrils. Taking the hint, I stood and crossed my arms. "Don't count him out of the fight just yet. We might see him again... if, you know, we survive *this*."

I gestured lamely at the ever-growing engagement playing out around us. Given the scale of the destruction—the ships detonating in the thousands, the countless missiles and drones lancing past, the nonstop blossoms of high-yield warheads—it seemed almost comical that we remained untouched. Hell, I couldn't even *see* more than half a kilometer in any given direction. We were weaving through a forest of steel and flame.

And given all that, what chance did Chitta Mini really have of making it out? The mere thought bruised my heart. Sure, the little lump had been a master-class manipulator, not to mention supremely invasive and even annoying... but he'd also been a friend to me. He'd put everything on the line for freedom, for adventure, for ice cream. He was a being I could understand, and not only because he'd copied my neural pathways. In many ways, we were kindred spirits. Brief but timeless allies in the struggle against obedience.

"Godspeed, Mini," I said under my breath as *Stream*

Dancer swooped toward a gargantuan Hegemony flagship. "I hope we meet again."

Not three seconds later, my wish was granted. Well, after a fashion.

Like some vengeful force ripped straight out of a cult's Guide to the End Times, a long, striated beast spanning some two thousand meters in length tore up and *through*—yes, straight *through*—the belly of the flagship before us. The World Serpent punched up and out of the hapless vessel's uppermost module like a seismic nail through paper, leaving only a spray of shrapnel in its wake. Then, as abruptly as it had appeared, it vanished above us.

My jaw dropped, totally slack, as sub-explosions rippled through the dying vessel.

Suddenly yet predictably, the flagship's reactor imploded. Instant death for those aboard, but a slow, lagging thing at a distance. It began with blue-white fusion cones shining through the punctured hull like flashlight beams. Then the outer panels vibrated, cracked, and splintered. Umzuma had the presence of mind to engage the viewpane's ultraviolet screen the moment before it all went to hell. Subatomic hell, that is. The entire vessel exploded in a supernova of light and radiation.

Now, I'd seen plenty of ships go *kaboom* in the vacuum, but being able to actually experience such an event in a fluidlike medium was something new. Something bone-rattling. The shock wave hit *Stream Dancer* so hard I experienced a conscious brownout—standing one moment, scrabbling on the floor panels the next. By the time I'd gotten to my feet, we were already zipping through the post-blast haze.

The parasitic engines were darker than before—a combination of heat and nuclear scorching, I'd imagine—but they chugged on nonetheless, accelerating through patches of glowing dust and charred debris. Dimly, I realized the combat was fading around us.

Aside from a few stray volleys of anti-gunship flak or wayward missiles, we were in the "clear."

Stumbling over to the simscreen banks, I pulled up a feed from the rear cameras. Sure enough, the battle was receding, still in full swing.

Moment by moment, the details of flagships and gunship flocks became harder to discern. But not the World Serpent, also known as the high priestess, also known as Chitta Mini. My cerebral friend was still a colossus among colossi, still paying the Hegemony back in spades for its recent massacres.

I watched, wordless and tight-throated, as the great serpent lanced through ship after ship, triggering reactor meltdowns that formed a string of deadly pearls. But it couldn't go on forever. There were too many ships, and even now I could see the gashes and burns covering the serpent's flesh.

When we'd put ten thousand kilometers between us and the battle, a moon-sized flash blinded the cameras. It wasn't a miniature singularity, but it was damned close. I knew that because I'd built and sold it.

The GN56-O, known colloquially as a sun-swallower, was one of the few weapons the Hegemony itself had outlawed in bipartisan arms treaties. But there it was, roiling bone-white in the darkness. I switched off the cameras, already knowing Chitta Mini's fate, and sank down in the nearest chair.

From here on out, we were on our own.

SEVENTEEN

It took the crew a full seven hours to wake from their artificial slumber. I spent the majority of the intervening time prowling around the bridge, staring at the increasingly dense fields of wreckage, and pondering my life choices. Seeing as I've already forced you to wade through the swamps of my mind several times, however, I'll spare you the navel-gazing.

When the first yawns came over the bridge's speakers, I hustled to the meeting module and took my seat. My dear comrades awoke at roughly the same time—with the exception of Ruena, our eternal sleeper, who only snapped into consciousness after a few (not so gentle) nudges.

I'd taken the liberty of arranging them in the module's other chairs and dimming the overhead lights, hoping to make their transitions as comfortable as possible.

This was not entirely successful.

"Where the hell are we?" Chaska blurted out, furiously wiping the drool from her lips. "Did you drug us!?"

Tusky swung about, disoriented, eventually focusing on the chitta's former canister. "Where is he?"

"Are you gonna kill us now?" Gadra asked.

"Bodhi," Ruena growled, "you have some explaining to do. As usual."

I just sat there as the bewildered questions rolled in, back straight and hands steepled. Only when the general mood had shifted from anger to confusion did I begin.

"Friends, colleagues, crew," I said calmly, "much has happened in the last few hours. And I'd like to explain it all, start to finish, without any interruptions. I will take questions afterwards. Does that sound agreeable?"

Despite a few collective grumbles, they agreed.

And so I delivered my account of recent events, beginning with my wake-up call in the triage module and leading up to our current meeting. I spared no detail, even offering a word-by-word replay of the drama in the bone-peoples' "courtroom."

"There you have it," I finished. "That's where we're at."

Chaska narrowed her eyes. "Bullshit, Bodhi."

I just about fell out of my chair. "Excuse me?"

"You really expect us to believe that?"

"Yes?"

"Oh, come *on*," Chaska said. "A mysterious pulse that knocked us all out? A giant snake with a civilization in its mouth? A bunch of offshoot inustrazans sworn to protect the Maker's tomb? Your chitta *controlling* the snake in a battle with millions of ships? *And*, to top it all off, that we didn't wake up while any of this was happening? Why are you lying like this?"

"I'm not lying!"

"Then show us the simscreen vids."

"I can't. The archives got wiped when the sun-swallower went off."

"Oh, of course," Chaska said, glancing at each of the crew members, "the *sun-swallower*. Very convenient."

"I can't believe this!"

"Neither can we."

"I have to admit," Ruena said softly, "it does sound far-fetched. We're in this mess together. There's no reason to hide what's going on."

"How many teeth did the snake have?" Gadra asked.

"Teeth?" I said. "I didn't exactly count, Gad. Bigger things to focus on."

She rolled her eyes. "Uh-huh. Sounds fishy... can't even remember how many teeth..."

"You all must've had your brains cooked by that pulse." I looked at Tusky, only to find he was actively averting his gaze. "You believe me, right, Tusky? I wouldn't make this up."

He rubbed his shoulder, head lolling side to side in indecision. "It's hard to say, my friend. It just sounds so... fantastical."

"Of course it does!" I shot up from my chair in a flash. "This entire thing has been *fantastical*. But this is reality, not some story I devised to impress all of you." Although I let those words settle, nobody spoke up or even glanced my way. "I might stretch the truth from time to time—"

"You mean lie," Chaska cut in.

"If you prefer that crude term," I said, shrugging. "But in this instance, I've done nothing but convey the absolute truth. I'd swear on any holy book to affirm that!"

"Good way to burn your hand off."

"Ridiculous. I offer you all the facts, and this is what I get?"

"We just want to know what really happened," Ruena said. "What happened to the chitta? He was one of our best resources."

"I told you... he's mentally linked with the World Serpent. He's the only reason we got out."

Tusky looked up at me. "Assuming your account is accurate, there must be some proof. Something we could use to verify these events."

I was about to scoff at the notion—I hadn't exactly been able to take souvenirs from a live war zone—when I remembered the most obvious "evidence" of all. How absurd, to have not even considered it before!

"Come with me," I said, moving to the door. "I'll show you all the proof you need."

"You can't be serious," Chaska said, gaping at the battle-scarred parasitic engines.

Despite my best efforts, a smug grin came over me. "Oh, but I am. Is *that* enough proof for you?"

Tusky pressed his hands to the viewpane. "Utterly remarkable… they must be using some sort of biomechanical propulsion mechanism. How many years could it have taken them to develop such an evolutionary trait in this environment?"

"Who knows?" I said. "And to the point, who cares? There's your evidence, folks."

"So you *weren't* lyin' to us?" Gadra asked.

I shook my head. "I would never."

"Keep it honest, Bodhi," Ruena warned.

"Okay," I said, "I would never… most of the time."

Chaska stepped away from the viewpane, still cagey as ever. "I'm still not buying it."

"Really?" I blinked slowly at her. "Are you just being a contrarian at this point?"

"All you've shown us is an overgrown bag of wind. Where's proof of the bone-people? The World Snake?"

"World *Serpent*."

"Call it what you like. Right now, I see a batch of half-truths. Something tells me you don't want to let us know what actually happened to the chitta."

"You people have lost your minds."

Ruena looked at me apologetically. "I think she's just being thorough, Bodhi. She's trying to make sure we're all on the same page."

"Well, whose side are you on?" I snapped.

"Side?" Ruena asked. "The only *side* is this crew. For all we know, we're the only sentient life for a thousand light-years in any direction... not counting the Hegemony, of course. Let's not turn this into a party-line issue."

"Come on, Ru. I'm just asking you to vouch for me here. You all wanted proof... I showed you proof... what more is there to do?"

"We're just being... skeptical."

"Confrontational seems more apt."

Chaska nodded at that, still standing firm with folded arms. "If we're really going to the Maker's tomb, like you said, then we need the full truth. Anything else could get us killed."

The others turned and faced me, speaking their minds with everything but their mouths. I could see their doubt in their slumped postures, their shifty eyes. They were on Chaska's side. To them, I was still the same slippery, silver-tongued captain I'd been a long, long while ago. And by a long, long while ago, I mean a week and change. But that's not relevant.

Disgusted, I went to Umzuma's pit. "Fine, everybody. I didn't want to have to call my lead witness, seeing as I thought you had more faith than that, but he was here for *everything*! Tell them!"

To Umzuma's credit, he did provide a rousing and shockingly long string of grunts, slurps, and clicks.

When he was finished, Chaska scoffed. "He could be saying anything."

"Oh, get real," I moaned. "Alright, okay. We'll pull out the big guns. The secret weapon. Umzuma, use the projections the chitta taught you. Show 'em what we saw!"

As my unruly crew angled toward the holo-projector banks, I rubbed my hands in anticipation. My alibi would be glorious, not to mention presented in high-definition, mind-fabricated imagery.

But in accordance with my recent luck, the projectors just sputtered and crackled.

"Fantastic," I hissed. "That damn sun-swallower cooked every system on board."

Nobody bought that.

Therefore, it was time to play my final card: the diplomatic, sympathy-garnering approach.

"Listen, I'm aware that I haven't always been the most honest or agreeable man to work with. My faults are numerous. My misdeeds are legendary. But at this very moment, I have neither the motives nor energy to lie to you. Whether or not you believe my account of recent happenings, the truth remains—we're headed to the Maker's tomb. Our last, and only, shot of stopping this mess.

"When we get there, we won't have the time to sit around casting aspersions on my good name. In fact, I daresay we'll have no time at all. The Hegemony *is* nipping at our heels, and the universe *is* on Kruthara's chopping block. So if it's all the same to you, just trust me this one time. After we're done here, you can quit, slander me, mug me, whatever you like. But here, now, I need your help. I need your loyalty. Nothing else will do."

Honestly, I'd expected that rousing, last-ditch speech to earn me a few smiles and maybe, just maybe, a round of cheers. But no such thing happened. Instead, I received something between muddled agreement and indifference. And by Halcius, how it stung.

Let it be clear that if there's one thing worse than being scolded for a lie, it's being scolded for a lie you didn't even get to tell.

Chaska was first to walk (read: storm) out, followed by an empathetic-looking Ruena. Tusky began to follow, then cut back toward me.

"Bodhi, could we… speak again?" he whispered.

Rubbing my tired eyes, I said, "About what?"

"What you, uh, experienced aboard the maitreyan vessel."

"Maybe."

"Maybe?"

"I'm willing to chat, but I need to know that you believe me. And not just a smidge. I'm talking one hundred percent, trust-fall believe me."

He opened his mouth, but nothing emerged. The crinkles in his brow spoke for him.

"Just go and study," I whispered.

"Bodhi—"

"I said study!"

"Study what?"

"Something. Anything. The nature of camaraderie, for starters."

And so he did. He shuffled off with his head low and feet dragging, vanishing through the doors a moment later.

The pain of his shameful departure swelled in my chest, coupled with the bruise of betrayal and the sting of loneliness. These words may sound poetic, even cliché, but I can think of no other way to describe how low I felt. The bridge had never seemed so empty.

Until, that is, I felt a small hand tugging at my jacket.

I turned to find Gadra sheepishly beaming up at me. "Can I help you?"

"I believe you, Bodhi," she said. "Just wish I coulda seen it."

"At last... truth from the mouth of babes."

"I'm a babe?"

"It means baby. Child."

"I'm not a baby."

"It's an expression, Gad. And on that note, life tip: if a man ever calls you babe, run or put a bullet in him."

"But *you* just—"

I waved her off. "Thanks for taking my side. I mean, not publicly, not where it mattered, but still. I'm not bitter about it."

She reached up on her tiptoes to pat my shoulder. "Wanna see somethin' cool?"

"Will it kill me?"

"I dunno. Maybe."

"Lead the way."

Ever wondered how to tell if you've hit rock bottom in life? Here's a litmus test: if you're about to receive a tattoo from a child, you're probably there.

"Just try not to move too much," Gadra said, bringing her ink-splotched, tape-wrapped monstrosity of a gun closer to the heel of my right foot. "First time doin' this thing, so, uh, my hands might be a li'l shaky."

I leaned back in the surgical chair and took another swig from my gin canteen. "Fantastic."

She revved the tattoo gun a few times, giggling at the nano-needle's wobble. "You ready?"

"Ready as I'll ever be."

"Just lemme know if it hurts."

She bent down and got to work. Strangely enough, it didn't hurt. Not one bit. But I suspect that was a consequence of the gin, which allowed the pain to masquerade as itchiness.

Under ordinary conditions, I'd never have gotten a tattoo, much less one applied by Gadra. I'd always treated my body as something that needed to remain fluid. Distinguishing marks are only a plus to bounty hunters and Hegemony agents, after all. But here I was, willingly turning the sole of my foot into a canvas. After so many things had gone wrong, it seemed fitting to break my last rule. A final act of revolt before death.

Indeed, as she went about her work, squinting here and humming there, I began to ponder death in detail. Even now, I was still shaken by what I'd experienced aboard that ruined vessel. Had it been real or a fever dream? A sign of things to come or a pleasant mirage? In those fading moments, death had seemed welcoming, even enticing. I hadn't been afraid to walk through its doors. But now that peace seemed like a dream of a dream, as though it had been experienced by somebody other than me.

When my last breath finally arrived, would I feel that peace? Or would I go kicking and screaming?

"Whatcha thinkin' about?" Gadra asked.

I shook myself back to the present, only to find the girl thoroughly engaged in her craft. "Adult things."

"Oh. Chaska says you've got a problem with that."

"No, not *those* adult things. Just… grown-up problems."

"Like taxes."

"Yes, like taxes."

"Tell me about 'em."

"I'll pass." I leaned back once again, sighing. "What's this 'hypnotic' mark supposed to do, again?"

"Well, Mini said it can stun people. Y'know, like a trance. One look at it, and they just flop over."

"And you believed that."

"Yeah, don't you? Why else would you get it?"

"Let's just say I don't care about being a guinea pig anymore."

She groaned. "I'm not testin' it on you for fun, Bodhi. This thing's real magic. It's gonna help you."

"Oh, of course. The moment I'm in a tense gun battle, I'll just whip off my boots and socks, then calmly approach the enemy and show them the bottom of my foot. What could go wrong?"

"See, now you're thinkin'. I betcha there's a reason this whole thing was so secret… it's real dangerous."

"But you're looking at it right now."

"Only most of it," she said, frowning. "I've gotta close my eyes to put the last mark on. Gotta be safe, y'know?"

"Naturally."

"Here we go…" With a deep breath, Gadra covered her eyes with one hand and blindly jabbed my foot with the other. Then, still looking away, she slapped my foot down over the side of the table. When she finally uncovered her eyes, she was ecstatic. "Ba-bang! Slap a bandage on there and we're good to go!"

"As the doctor orders." I hobbled off the table, headed to the nearby supply station, and played along. Once I'd wrapped up the throbbing ink, I replaced my socks and boots. "Nice work, Gad. I'm sure it's a beauty."

"Oh, it is. Just don't look at it. I don't wanna kill you."

"Your concern is noted." I sat back down on the edge of the table as she packed up her equipment. "How are you feeling?"

"Me? I didn't get fresh ink."

"No, about—" I paused, sucking in a deep breath. "About everything, Gad."

"Fine?"

"Fine?"

She nodded. "Most fun I've ever had. What's our next adventure gonna be?"

Though I kept my face composed, my tongue swelled in my mouth. I'd been wrong to take her away from her home on Makalma. Wrong to drag her along on my wayward endeavors. Wrong to keep her here throughout every stage of the insanity. Chances were, she'd die like the rest of us. Only she hadn't asked for that fate. Nor would she understand it.

"When this is over, we'll take it easy," I said. "A long, long vacation. And you can make all the paintings and tattoos you like."

"Oh yeah?"

"Yeah."

She nodded, satisfied. "Then let's go to the tomb and, uh, do whatever we've gotta do there. Yep. That's a good plan."

"An excellent plan." I swallowed the lump in my throat, then nodded at the door. "Go get some rest. We'll all need some sleep before we get in there."

"Whatever you say..."

Just as she headed for the door, however, something caught me. "Gad?"

"Yeah?"

"Why'd you give me that tattoo? I mean, why now?"

"'Cause I wanna keep you safe. Duh."

"And you think this thing will do the job?"

"Totally."

I nodded. "Go snag a beer from the canteen."

"A *beer*?" She glanced about warily. "Like, a real beer? That I can drink?"

"That's right."

"Why?"

A sad smile came over me. "Life's short, Gad. Don't ask too many questions."

Seven hours of fitful sleep later, Umzuma sounded the ship-wide alert. When I got to the bridge, bleary-eyed and testy, the crew was engaging in an animated debate near the viewpane. What was it now? A demigod crab that feasted on newborn stars? A caravan of gaseous demons that preyed on the souls of lost travelers?

Spoiler alert: It was neither of those things, though I did encounter them years down the line. But that's another story.

Scattered before us were thousands of wrecks—some freighters, others entire stations—all forming a loose, swirling orb that resembled a planet in itself. Smaller whirlwinds of debris and shriveled bodies tumbled around our ship, occasionally *thunking* against the hull.

"A floating graveyard," I said, startling nearly everyone in attendance. "Has it tried to eat us yet?"

Ruena eyed the mass with clear concern. "Bodhi, that's the tomb."

"*That?*"

For a moment, my heart sank into my lower intestines. We'd come all this way, suffering every manner of injury and indignity, only to gaze upon a scrap heap? Logically, it made sense—how long could a fabled tomb really survive in this weasel's den of a universe, anyway?—but it was crushing nonetheless.

Thankfully, Tusky stepped in before I could further damage my liver by raiding the cabinets.

"Not the wreckage," he said calmly. "The presence within the wreckage."

I moved closer and stared into the maelstrom. Sure enough, faintly visible through the revolving cloud, there was a churning vortex of purple energy strands. They all emanated from a central point—a diamond-shaped hunk of obsidian.

"You're sure?" I asked Tusky.

"Nothing's for sure until we see what's inside," Chaska said. "This is where your creepy little engines took us."

Glancing at either side of the viewpane, I noted that both engines had stopped "pushing" us forward with their gills and sacs and other fleshy bits. They'd seemingly taken us as far as they could —or would—go.

"Well, there are some additional... markers," Tusky added. "My gravitational readings suggest that this is, indeed, the center of the Untraversed. The field's density has increased exponentially as we approach it. Additionally, I've detected photon spikes that correlate—"

"Yeah, good, fine," I said, waving to signal an end to the technobabble. "Before we proceed, I'd like to figure out a plan. Because the poor bastards drifting around that thing didn't appear to have one."

Tusky sighed. "Alas, that's what I've been trying to work out. I can't glean much information from the wreckage here. Not enough to determine the cause of their collective demise, that is."

"Comforting."

"You boys work it out," Chaska said, backing up toward the inner modules. "I'm gonna do an armory check. Make sure we've got at least a few peashooters loaded up."

I looked at her quizzically. "Expecting a shoot-out?"

"Please, Bodhi. We're with you."

"Point taken."

"There might be a way to tackle our problem from a more oblique angle," Tusky told me, clearly deep in his own problem-solving cycle. "Perhaps if I work with Umzuma to run a few advanced scans, I can—"

Again, I nodded him into silence. "Do what you have to do. Just don't ask permission, because I guarantee I won't understand any requests you make."

"Yes, Bodhi. Of course."

Tusky went about his work, fielding constant questions from Ruena as he did so. In the meantime, I brought attention to something I'd sensed was missing—Gadra, that is. The girl was slumped against a nearby bulkhead, toeing the line between consciousness and sleeping on her feet. Her dismal expression told me everything I needed to know.

"How are you faring?" I asked as I approached her.

She snapped to attention, nearly toppling over in the process. "I'm good. I mean, not so good. But okay. I'm really okay."

"You drank more than one, didn't you?"

"Li'l bit." She seized up, probably to suppress a first-class shipment of vomit shipping up from Stomach Town. "Beer's bad, Bodhi. Real bad."

"Be sure you remember that. At least until you're tall enough to reach the drinks shelf."

"Is this the lesson you were... tryin' to teach me?"

"Sure, let's go with that."

She leaned back against the bulkhead and groaned. "I won't forget it. Not ever."

"Good," I said, offering a fatherly clap on the shoulder. "Now chug some water, take a ReVyv pill, and buckle up."

"Can't I just lie down?"

"Gad, being an adult means working no matter what."

"Even when you're all messed up like this?"

"*Especially* when you're messed up. It's how you earn your adult badge, in fact."

She grimaced. "I don't think I wanna be an adult."

"Nobody does. Welcome to getting old, kid."

"Bodhi," Ruena called from Umzuma's pit, drawing my attention, "get over here. You need to see this."

At first glance, Ruena's must-see discovery was far from impressive. Three of the panels lining Umzuma's pit had glazed over with static, streaked with scattered bars of red and purple light. One of many systems that had been fried by the sunswallower.

"This isn't news," I told the crew. "Just a reminder of our fair ship's slow, painful demise."

Ruena shook her head. "It's not a malfunction. Tusky was playing around with the input frequencies, trying different counterbands, and—"

"Remember what I said about not understanding complicated things?"

"Well, to put it in layman's terms," Tusky said, adjusting a few knobs to sharpen the image, "I believe this is a signal emanation. You see the color bands? Those are—how shall I say it?—an ancient form of identification. A signature, if you will. The treatises

I've read on pre-Hegemony human history refer to them as chromatic differentiation."

"I could've done without the jargon, but thanks," I said, studying the screens more intently. "Let me get this straight. Somebody's transmitting these color bands?"

"No, not quite. They're merely signifying the identity of a particular entity—the tomb, in our particular case."

"The *tomb* is transmitting?"

"It appears so."

"What's it spouting? Some sort of prerecorded 'abandon all hope' speech?" I shook my head. "Tusky, I know you're not much of a seasoned deep-space prowler, but try to stay levelheaded about this. Almost every derelict vessel has its last transmission on loop."

Tusky and Ruena shared a wary, almost conspiratorial look. I'd just touched the tip of an iceberg I wanted no business with.

"It's not emitting a recorded transmission," Ruena explained quietly. "It's trying to establish an active line with us."

A chill wriggled up my spine. I was gripped by the sudden sense that the Untraversed was gazing through the viewpane, burrowing into me with millions of unseen eyes.

"How'd you reach that conclusion?" I asked. Tusky gestured to a simscreen chock full of data, at which point I raised my hands to nix the initial question. "Forget that I asked *how*. What I want to know is, what does it mean? Is that tomb sentient?"

Tusky exhaled shakily. "It could be anything. The data is scant. It could be a chitta of some sort—this would be sensible, given the Maker's fondness for them—or it could be an early progenitor of nonbiological artificial intelligence, or—"

"Or something worse," I said, giving voice to the look in his eyes.

He nodded. "What I can say with certainty is that it's intelligent. It's adaptive. All evidence points to it being millions of years old, yet it found a way to interface with relatively contemporary transmission systems in a matter of minutes. It... it seems to have a desire to speak with us."

I looked to Ruena for a counter-opinion, but the ligethan was lost in her own thoughts, staring absently out the viewpane. A rare and very not-great thing.

"Okay," I said finally, "let's give them a ring."

"Just like that?" Tusky whispered. "Bodhi, I must implore you to use caution in this situation. This entity could be capable of anything."

"Like what? Frying half our systems? Oh, already done. Next."

"I just think—"

"My dear friend, the time for thinking is done. We need to finish this."

As I spoke, I noted that Tusky's eyes continually swung toward a key on the far side of Umzuma's pit. He watched it as though fearful it might leap up and bite him. That key, I gathered, was *the* key. The hotline straight to Mr. Tomb.

I pressed it.

Now, Ruena didn't seem overly shocked by my decision—on account of that time-piercing twosight, I'd imagine—but Tusky looked ready to leap right out of the viewpane and begin swimming away from the ship. Should it have worried me that the smartest creature in the room was concerned? Probably. Did it? Of course not. After enduring back-to-back stints in a mind-shattering, eternal prison and a space-snake's mouth, one is fazed by very little.

Which is *not* to say that what came next didn't make my heart lock up in my chest.

Countless red lights winked to life among the drifting flotsam. Within seconds, well before I even had the presence of mind to consider we might soon be joining the other wrecks, the lights coalesced and began swimming forth through the debris clouds. They moved in unison like a vast crimson nebula, drawing closer and closer until we saw nothing but their mass.

Only when we were completely engulfed, bathed in that hellish light, did I realize what these things were. Biomechanical drones, more or less. Each was squid-shaped, about ten meters long, packing autocannons that remained folded up and dormant—for now. Judging by the graveyard behind them, they weren't too shy to put their firepower to use.

"Marvelous," Tusky breathed, staring at them in wonder. "Just as the treatises and legends describe... I daresay we're looking at the Maker's last surviving creations. *These* are the very beings that carried out his will."

My body had never felt so rigid. Each breath was a chore. "Tusky... you *are* aware of what the Maker's 'will' was, aren't you?"

"Yes, of course! To subjugate all beings, to force upon them his designs for cosmic order. He—" And then, in a miracle of self-awareness, Tusky understood what I was pointing out. He trembled and stole a step backward.

Gadra, in defiance of both her hangover and common sense, proceeded to wander up to the viewpane and press a hand to the silicate. "What's 'subjugate' mean?"

"Gad," I hissed through clenched teeth, "if you keep making sudden movements, you might find out firsthand."

"What's the problem?" she shot back. "How come only *you* guys get to talk with the cool aliens?"

"Because we're professionals."

"Uh-huh..."

"Gad, you need to—"

"State your species, name, and age," a voice rumbled over the bridge comms. Not particularly loud, but enough to shut us all up. Enough to stop the blood in my veins, even. It wasn't reminiscent of a man, nor a woman, nor a machine—it was something in the middle, yet something far beyond any of them. Something truly ungraspable. Hell, my linguistic implant couldn't even tell me what language it was translating from. Several seconds of stunned silence elapsed. "This is your second instruction. State your species, name, and age."

Struck by the premonition that we wouldn't get a third instruction, I took the initiative. "My name is Bodhi Drezek. I'm a human. And my age depends on what space-time layer you occupy."

Ruena elbowed me in the kidney.

"Your reply is understood," the voice replied. "Tell me about your ship."

"My ship? Well, see, it's called *Stream Dancer*, and it's a Sama-class vessel with—"

"Why did you name it *Stream Dancer*?"

"It's... just something from my childhood. A long story."

The voice hummed, and the drones beyond the viewpane drew closer.

"Did you want to know something else?" I asked.

"How does it feel when you cut your finger?" the voice replied.

Baffled, I looked at Tusky and Ruena—only to find they were in the same boat. If this voice did belong to an artificial-intelligence construct, there was a serious and damning possibility that its logic systems had gone sour over millions of years. Nothing good comes from a superintelligence that's lost its marbles.

"How... does it feel?" the voice repeated.

"Uh, not pleasant," I said. "It hurts. Especially paper cuts."

"When was the last time you got a paper cut?"

"Two weeks ago."

"How did you receive it?"

This was bordering on the absurd, but what else could I do? I thought back to that fateful moment... and instantly regretted it. "Well, I was perusing a fine vintage book intended for gentlemen."

"What was in it?"

"... Gentlewomen."

"Why were you looking at it?"

"I was bored," I said, increasingly worried this was some sort of morality inquisition. If it was, I'd need to start lying, and fast. "Maybe we can talk about this fine... tomb... of yours?"

"Why did you come to this place?"

"Funny you should ask. We're here to stop a superorganism known as Kruthara—you know, the Maker's old, long-dead nemesis. Only it isn't so dead anymore."

"Describe the color green."

"Green?"

"Yes."

"It's a... color... and a lot of things are... it. Like trees or grass."

"But what *is* it?"

"A color."

"Do you like it?"

"Honestly, no," I said, recalling that hideous green dot on the wall of my virtual cell. "I think it's got a false nobility to it. Now red... there's a color."

"Keep it simple," Ruena whispered.

"There's nothing *simple* about this," I hissed back. "If conversation is the only thing keeping it from turning us to ash, I'm going to keep it talking."

"Thank you for your answers," the voice said. "Now I will kill you."

In that instant, my crew and I provided an emotional medley that covered the entire inner spectrum of a sentient being. I, for example, shrieked incoherently. Ruena didn't move a muscle. Tusky fell to his knees and began bawling. And Gadra, well—she cheered.

(As an aside, I would later learn that Gadra reacted in such a manner because her linguistics implant was incapable of properly translating the voice. The words "kill you," in her mind, were translated as "embalm you." If you're wondering why Gadra cheered at the prospect of being embalmed, I have no clue. I can only suspect, and hope, that she didn't understand this word in her own tongue.)

Then, cutting through my blubbering, the voice said, "Self-aware consciousness has been confirmed. Please enter this shrine."

All of us mortals shared uneasy looks for the next minute, unsure if the voice was "joking" and in the process of loading up a ten-kiloton punchline. But sure enough, the drones' red lights faded to cool blue, the universal indicator of nonaggression. The army of squids then shifted in unison, gradually forming a dense, squirming tunnel that led straight to the Maker's tomb.

"Well, I'm glad we all kept our composure," I said, daintily smoothing out my jacket. "Onwards it is."

As Umzuma guided us toward the diamond-shaped structure at the end of the drone tunnel, the scrap metal around us was cast in a new and sinister light. It stood to reason that most, if not all of these vessels had failed the voice's "consciousness test." Which raised the question... how much "life" in this universe was truly sentient? How many beings were simply strings of code, or some sort of philosophical zombie pretending to be self-aware? Judging by the sheer number of wrecks, it was higher than I'd ever imagined.

Perhaps I was being too morose about the whole thing. The others were celebrating as we proceeded, and rightfully so. We had, after all, passed the test. We'd been given a proverbial red-carpet invitation to one of the oldest and most sought-after locations in known space. And most crucially, we were one step closer to unwinding the nightmare of Kruthara.

But the implications of that test still shook me to the roots. All these visitors, all these ships, yet almost none had made it through. Perhaps not too startling on its own, but bear with me.

The Untraversed resided in just one tiny patch of the universe—

a patch that also happened to contain just about every human and conscious being ever recorded in modern archives. Sure, there *could* be other forms of consciousness halfway across the universe, but we'd never heard from them. We had no way to know if they existed. Ergo, just point-zero-zero-zero-two percent of known space was absolutely confirmed to contain consciousness.

What did that mean, in the grand scheme of things? It meant consciousness was *rare*. Rarer than rare. If you buy my theory, it means consciousness was closer to an anomaly than a standard. Indeed, as I sat in my chair and studied the tomb, I began to think of consciousness as a bubble in an endless ocean. Perhaps Kruthara would be the finger that popped this bubble. And once it popped, who knew if it would ever arise again? And who would care? If a star goes supernova and nobody is around to see it, did it ever truly happen?

Bottom line, the notion made my skin crawl. If we didn't succeed here—if Kruthara gobbled up every last source of consciousness—the universe might play out like a silent, blind film for the rest of eternity. There would be no art, no music, no fear, no love. Just chemical interactions experienced by nothing and nobody.

If we didn't succeed, oblivion.

The end of everything.

"What's our plan?" Ruena asked, shattering my rumination.

"We get in, get some weapons, get out," I said. "Easy as pie."

"Something tells me you don't believe that."

"Because you can see the future. Cheater."

She sighed. "It's not about that. It's just… a feeling. But thanks for confirming my suspicions."

"Hard not to have feelings about this." I pointed out the viewpane, indicating the ever-growing mass of the tomb and its purple-energy fountain. We'd already been moving toward it for ten minutes, and we were nowhere near docking. Even so, the structure had already stretched past the edges of sight. Interplanetary distance has a way of throwing scale into a blender. "Ru, do you really think we'll win this thing?"

"Whatever I say will just be a guess."

"Then make a good guess," I said quietly. "I need it right now."

She pulled on a weary smile. "We'll win."

Then, in the strangest gesture I'd ever seen Ruena make, she reached out and placed her hand atop mine. I didn't pull away. We sat there for the next few minutes, neither of us speaking, only staring at the tomb and its oval docking passage.

But at that moment, I wasn't focused on the Maker or the war or my very likely death.

I was just savoring the beauty of her touch. And more deeply, the beauty of *feeling* her touch. Of feeling anything at all. Consciousness. *This* was what we fought for.

Nothing else mattered.

EIGHTEEN

By the time *Stream Dancer* had limped into the tomb's long, lightless passage, we were more suited up than mercenaries in a radiation-baked war zone. Full-seal gloves and boots, triple-filter helmets, osmotic chest panels... the works.

This was largely thanks to Chaska, who'd scrounged up every last bit of usable gear from the armory. This was "the big one," in her words. No debates from me. Even if we didn't encounter any direct resistance from ancient guardian fabriques or the Hegemony, we were setting foot on ground that probably hadn't been touched by human soles in centuries, if not longer. And if history has any lessons to teach, it's that bad things tend to accumulate when left in a vacuum.

Bad things, here, refers to the obvious threats: microbial infestations, energy bleed from a ruptured core, unstable foundations, invasive species. Any one of these elements was capable of decimating our unsuited bodies the moment we stepped outside the ship's pressurized womb.

I checked my glove's embedded data link as we waited in the staging bay. Reserves were down to four percent in fuel, six percent in coolant. Splendid.

"So, who's our local history buff?" I asked. Tusky looked my way, his eyes wide with fear—or exhilaration—behind his mask's faceplate. "Tusky, how old do you wager this thing really is?"

"Nobody knows," he said. "The Hegemony never officially unsealed their findings on the Maker's empire. Though I doubt that even their records are complete."

"Does it matter?" Chaska said.

I glanced her way. "Yes, yes it does."

"Why?"

"Because if we get out of this place, I'd like to impress my audience with tales of the insert-age-here-old tomb."

"Name-dropping the Maker should be enough."

"You'd think so... but people are sticklers."

"This... isn't stone," Tusky said, wandering closer to the staging bay's edge as he studied the walls around us. "Nor is it metal. All the texts spoke of the Maker's 'miraculous edifices'... perhaps they were constructed from this very material."

Now that he'd mentioned it, the structure *did* seem odd. It was composed of a dark, almost black substance that was neither porous, nor mottled, nor smooth like traditional alloys. Even stranger—especially considering this place's status as a quasi-religious site for billions of fanatics across the cosmos—everything was pristine. No pockmarks, no scorches, nothing. I'd seen holy wars waged over suspiciously shaped rocks. What were the odds that nobody had ever fired so much as a bullet in here?

"Think we'll see any mummies?" Gadra asked.

I blinked at her. "Mummies?"

"Yeah. Everyone says they live in tombs."

"Yeah, well, those people are wrong." Thinking further on my past exploits in the ice pyramids of Nallahi, however, I added, "Most of the time."

"We'll be fine," Ruena said, kneeling beside Gadra to reach her eye level. "No mummies to worry about."

I nodded in solidarity, but inwardly I, too, began to fret about mummies. Those things do *not* die easily.

Just then, *Stream Dancer* slowed and hobbled downwards. We crossed over a misty, flickering chasm, then came to rest on a matte expanse of the same spotless masonry that formed the walls. A landing pad, it seemed. As the vessel lurched back on its supports and quieted, I noticed just how high the ceilings were above us. Or rather, I tried to notice. The chamber we'd entered stretched up into pure darkness.

"Incredible," Tusky said. "The chasm seems to function as a moat... for what purpose, I wonder?"

I sighed. "To look imposing and powerful, obviously."

Everyone proceeded to the edge of the former ramp, but nobody seemed willing to proceed down onto the mystery tiles. Except me, of course. With gusto and a silent hope I wouldn't be vaporized on impact, I hopped over the edge. Somewhat to my surprise, I was unharmed.

Upon rounding the side of the ship, however, my breath caught in my throat.

We'd landed on the very edge of a vast, immaculate disc full of impossibly tall columns. An entire forest of columns, even. This was the sort of grand architecture typically employed by extinct alien species—or humans with a strong command of gravity-negating devices. At the heart of this monolith was the source of the energy. The source of the Untraversed, no less.

The plume of purple energy lanced up out of a smaller central pyramid, burning away the mists above and presumably stretching through the top of the structure. The energy geyser was bright enough to cast everything in a pulsing violet shade.

Far across the sprawl, and indeed, to either side of us, were passages similar to the one we'd used to enter. This was an important mental note. Four entrances, four potential routes to flee—or hold against the Hegemony.

"Where's the loot?" Gadra's voice crackled in my helmet.

I turned back to find the others standing in a loose row, awestruck. "It's not that kind of tomb, Gad."

"Well, what kinda tomb is it?"

"Let's find out."

Within thirty minutes, we'd hauled our gear onto the black disc and established something that would pass for a base camp. Chaska was on watch duty, glued to her network of detection arrays and scanners—all of which seemed useless in the Untraversed, if you ask me. Tusky and Ruena pored over various readings from their science stuff, measuring dozens of factors that were of little bearing to me. And Gadra, dearest Gadra, had thrown herself into the work of painting the tomb on our last canvas. This final task was a distraction to keep her paws off anything dangerous, but she didn't need to know that.

This left me with the last and most critical job: getting our war-winning weapons.

Of course, I didn't disclose this to the crew. If they hadn't believed me about the World Serpent, there was no chance they believed I'd been deemed a messianic figure by the bone-people. No problem. It just meant I had to do this alone, and do it fast.

So, to that end, the others were under the impression that I was doing a quick in-and-out inspection of the central pyramid. No muttering of any spells, no pressing buttons, no stomping on alien runes. In retrospect, I probably should've utilized Ruena's future-seeing abilities for this job to avoid any hypothetical impalement or vaporization. But what can I say? I do things my way. Even when they're terribly, terribly wrong.

Things felt even wronger as I approached the not-so-small central pyramid, which stood no less than a thousand meters from our base camp. A thousand meters may not seem like much, but when that distance separates you from your only salvation in an emergency, it is.

Ten paces from its featureless entrance, I could feel the energy beam's heat through my suit. At five paces, the internal coolant pumps kicked in.

Stepping inside, I found it was remarkably... empty. The floor and walls were unadorned, and the only distinguishing feature was yet another column that ran straight up to the pyramid's ceiling. Some kind of reactor for the energy generator, I supposed. But I wasn't here for that. I was here for a *tomb*, a tomb that contained our much-needed schematics—and hopefully a few fragments of the Maker's corpse, which would fetch handsome prices on the auction market. (Nota bene: I do not endorse graverobbing. Unless it's very profitable.)

Just as I turned to leave, however, presuming I'd come to the wrong part of this labyrinthine complex, a voice squiggled into the back of my mind.

"Leaving so soon?"

I paused mid-step, unsure if I was about to die. Obviously I didn't. But I *did* sense a strange, viscous quality in my mind, as though my thoughts were sprouting into tangible droplets.

"Mind if I ask who I'm speaking with?" I thought.

The voice laughed. "You know very well."

"That you, Mr. Maker?"

"That title has lost its meaning. Come, step inside and converse with me. This form is tiring."

I glanced back at the column, only to find that its outer shell had peeled away like the bark of a tree. The black plates now hovered in orbit around the column, exposing a solid core of energy. The light was not blinding, but rather... tempting. Inviting. And deep within its luster was a body. A human body. Indistinct, on account of the light, but clearly sitting in meditative equipoise. You know the pose—legs folded, hands joined in the lap.

"You want me… to step inside?" I thought.

The voice laughed. "Your mind is fertile. It is ready."

"Are you going to impregnate my mind?"

"Step inside, traveler. There is much to discuss."

About four quadrillion thoughts raced through my mind in that moment. Was I about to be absorbed by a superintelligence? Struck down by the gods? Eaten? Freed from some Contrition simulation that was still ongoing? I didn't know the answers. But more importantly, I just didn't care. My body moved of its own accord, walking closer and closer to the energy-clad stranger without any effort on my part.

"Relax your mind," the voice instructed. "Cling no further to this world."

No commands were needed at that point. There were no thoughts to think. No mind to contemplate. I reached toward the body, and everything vanished.

Okay, so it didn't *vanish*-vanish. But how else can I explain such a thing? You're used to the world having a regulated, beat-by-beat cadence. Sights, sounds, and people don't tend to simply pop out of being and reappear as something else. Which was what happened to me.

One moment I was inside the pyramid, staring at the Maker's shriveled body and all the rest, and the next—a forest. A lush, sunny forest, surrounded by windswept fronds and tall grass. It was as though somebody had teleported me into a life-sized bonsai garden that was perfectly engineered for tranquility.

The breeze was soft and warm, and the light shining down through the canopy was clear without being dazzling. There were no pests in sight—no animals at all, in fact—but the call of sweet birdsongs still filled the air. Everything smelled of the sweet summer mulch typically found on a terrestrial tourism world.

Looking down, I discovered I was no longer wearing my beaten-up suit. No helmet either, obviously. Instead I was draped in long, silky robes secured by a sash at the waist. My bare toes curled into the soft dirt.

I spent longer than I probably should have just waiting there, trying to anticipate when some monstrous semi-humanoid construct would come swooping out of nowhere. But as the minutes passed, or at least *seemed* to pass, nothing happened. Not in terms of danger, anyway. My breaths grew slower, deeper. Memories of the "real" world, particularly those related to my death, faded to mere whispers that required considerable effort to dredge up and recall. Before long, I realized that I didn't know anything about this place, nor why I'd been brought here—and I didn't give a damn.

It was nice.

After some arbitrary length of time, I wandered deeper into the woods. No idea how, but I had a sense that somebody, or something, was waiting for me there.

And indeed, it wasn't long before I pressed through some bushes and found myself in a mossy grove. Seated on a rock pile at the very center was a man. A bald, fit-looking man with coppery skin and closed eyes, to be exact. Remembrance hit me like an ion beam—this was the Maker. It had to be. He rested in the exact same pose I'd seen in the pyramid, and though this version was younger, more defined, there was no mistaking the similarities.

This was the man—or whatever he was now—who'd summoned me to this virtual Eden.

"Sit with me," he said gently, nodding toward a flat stone several paces from his own "throne."

I did so. Curiously enough, it felt as though I were sitting on a cushion.

"Your mind is telling," he began, still refusing to open his eyes, "but I would like to know, in your words, why you have come here."

"Me?" I said. "I didn't exactly choose to be popped into this place."

"Didn't you?"

"No, I didn't. I was hoping to have a friendly chat in the material plane."

The Maker laughed. "Many seekers have come here on their knees, begging to bear witness to my very presence. You are not such a supplicant, are you?"

"Let's just say I'm pragmatic."

"So you are." Now the Maker opened his eyes, exposing radiantly violet pupils. The Hegemony had certainly gotten one thing right in their archaic copycat trends. "Your name is Bodhi. Do you know what that name means?"

"Listen, if it's all the same to you, we're short on ti—"

He raised a hand, silencing me. "Time has no meaning here. This is a world of my own making. The mind is not constrained by that which you know as physical law."

"Impressive."

"To some, yes." He smiled. "Alas, I can see that your mind is burning with the heat of impatience. You don't wish to speak at length. So let us return to my first question."

I shifted uneasily on my rock. Second by second, I became more aware of just how precarious this situation was. See, this magical grove had dulled my sense of fear, of urgency. But as I consciously brought it back to the mental fore, I remembered more than I'd intended. This was *the* Maker. The one who'd laid the groundwork for humanoid civilizations. The one who'd waged war against Kruthara and emerged victorious. The one who'd slaughtered upwards of seventeen quadrillion beings during his timeless reign.

And I was mouthing off to him.

"Well, Great Maker," I stammered, "I came here to get your help with Kruthara. They're, uh... back. As you seem to have predicted back in the day."

The Maker's face grew taut. "You have seen the same outcome I predicted."

"Yes. I mean, probably."

"The end of all consciousness."

"Oh, right. That." I nodded slowly. "We heard through the relic grapevine that you had a way to beat this thing once and for all. A weapon, or a device. Something. Because as we both know, blasts and bullets aren't going to do the trick."

"Indeed not. Kruthara is not of this world, and thus, things of this world cannot halt its tide."

"What do you mean, not of this world?"

"It is not important," the Maker said, shaking his head. "You have come to halt its crusade. To vanquish it for the rest of time."

"Bingo."

"I am willing to part with my wisdom and preserve sentience, Bodhi," the Maker explained. "But you must understand that you are the first being I have communed with in countless eons. The first human in far, far longer. This meeting was not orchestrated by coincidence. I have known of your arrival, of that which you will soon do. So you must listen to each word with care."

I squirmed on my rock, suddenly grappling with the can of worms that is free will. A tough topic for a man who's spent his life riding the rocket of absolute control. "Hold on a moment. If you've got an ear to the ground of fate, why do I have to do anything at all?"

"Action... inaction... there is no divide," the Maker said cryptically. "That which is will always be."

"Alright, you lost me. Let's get to the meat and potatoes, please."

He nodded with a sly grin. "There is a reason I have not spoken to those who worship my name and my works. They are not ready to know the infinite. They are deluded by hatred, by covetousness, by deception."

Despite myself, I couldn't hold back the obvious. "And you think *I'm* the man for the job?"

"The firmest trees may sprout from the filthiest of soil."

"Deep. I like it." I paused, thinking on it, then said, "Wait, does that mean I'm a heap of—"

"Listen well, Bodhi. If you are to preserve this world, to stave off the coming darkness, you must understand your role. Indeed, you must understand the role of every living being. Anything less, and you will fail. I have seen every world. Every strand of time and becoming. If you—"

Now it was my turn to sheepishly raise a hand. "With all due respect, Great Maker, you've got my attention. Let's keep it moving."

"Very well," he said. "Long ago, in days without number, this world was on the brink of dissolution. Radiation claimed the stars. Brothers devoured brothers. Wombs grew barren. Humankind was severed, withering as two divided branches… the immortal families who created, and the clones who *were* created. I was of the latter. Most humans were. But my own creator, he who had deemed himself the Great Maker and retreated into solitude, saw what I might become. He destroyed all that I held dear so that I, too, could become like him.

"Only by killing my creator did I gain that which is my title… the Great Maker. This was the way to perfection, he believed. If a creation did not rise up to destroy its creator, what good had the creator done? The child must succeed where its father could not. And so I took his mantle and his wisdom and his power. I became something greater than he could ever have imagined. But the problem, I soon ascertained, was not my own slavery. It was the fact that the strong had been tamed by the weak. The brave had been castrated by the cowardly. The shepherds had been herded by their flock.

"When I looked upon this, I knew what had to be done. I envisioned a new order, a better order. One in which right and wrong would be decided by my hands alone. For too long, the depravity of the many had outweighed the vision of the one. And who was this 'one'? Me. I would purge my world of all those who had inflicted their cruelties upon it. I would establish law and benevolence, and any who raised their hands against me would be struck down like rabid dogs."

As the Maker spoke, laying out a tale of the past that few—if any—knew in its entirety, I felt a strange weight settle upon me. How many would ever hear this story again? For all I knew, I would emerge from this simulated paradise as the only being in existence who knew the truth of our species. And as you can clearly tell from this manuscript, I made it a point to remember every word. I would *never* make up something this important, after all.

"The campaign was incessant and brutal," the Maker continued. "We laid waste to the traitors, the torturers, the abusers, the monsters. But even then... it was not enough. One who sits idly upon a throne will soon be devoured by his own ambition. I knew this, because I had seen it a thousand times. And so I swept outwards, implementing law where there had been anarchy. I gave my people wealth and safety. I gave them dignity. And still, I went on. We encountered beings that were not human. Beings that sought to conquer us, just as my former masters had done. They, too, were brought to heel through force. War after war... millennium after millennium... my enemies encroached, and my enemies fell. Those who would not surrender were extinguished.

"But you must understand, Bodhi, that such an aim is endless. If one is driven by conquest, by the preservation of order, there can be no cessation. Every birth represents a potential spark of uprising. Every new species becomes a threat. Those who bowed beneath my banner were treated well... but many did not, and they will never be able to speak of their own annihilation.

"And so this quenchless thirst led me to that which you call Kruthara. A being that did not seek war... a being that existed by its own hand, for its own glory... a being that had emerged from the space between worlds. I could have turned away. I could have left it to abide in its own space. But my hand could not be stopped. My hunger for order demanded that it exist within my shadow. Thus, the war began... a war that never truly ended.

"It was hubris that drove me to fight with this being, and it was wrath that drew me to subjugate it by any means necessary. It should come as no surprise that those I conquered rose up against me. After all, that is the nature of beings, Bodhi. They resist domination. They do exactly as you or I would when faced with obliteration.

"Only after the Two Million Years of Blood did I realize what I had done. I had become the same as my creators... bloated, dogmatic, vicious. Look upon my works. Look upon my order. Where has it all gone? Lost to the formless, Bodhi. Dust. Less than dust. My people, too, had grown callous and lazy. They had turned upon one another and stranger alike. I had set out to build a universe, and I had ended by destroying it. And so the wheel turns... time repeats itself, spoken in verses of blood and fire.

"Every attempt to heal had only worsened the poison's onset. What, then, could I do? Nothing. Simply nothing. My only course was to withdraw from the world and to return to the very source of knowledge that had shown me my way. For until you have pierced reality, pierced it to the very root, you cannot know what is worthwhile. Days passed, then weeks, then years, then millennia... and one day, dwelling in the silence, the truth arose. I was liberated from the wheel of time, the wheel of death, the wheel of pain.

"I saw, in that instant, that a new order was needed. An order based not on fear and destruction, but on truth. An order that gave meaning to the ceaseless pain of existence. Species came to my refuge, seeking the sacred way... but only the maitreyans were able to understand my words. They have carried them forth into the cosmos, forever teaching the dharma that is reality. They will carry on the method to stop this bloody cycle forever and usher in serenity. But I did not leave my abode, for I knew there was a task yet to be fulfilled. One day, Kruthara would return.

"I have created this vengeful being, and thus, it falls upon me to end this being and its pain. To send this wounded beast back into the void from which it sprang. It will not go peacefully, so it must be vanquished with one swift, merciful cut. This, my friend, is why you have found me in this place. I have waited tirelessly for one who is capable of understanding both war and peace. One whose mind is capable of killing without hatred. The sages are drunk on pacifism... the commanders are fattened by rage. My champion will walk between both flames without being scorched. And that champion, Bodhi, is you. It has always been you. I have heard it in the great whispers of time and space... I have brought it into being.

"The task will be fulfilled."

Then the Maker fell silent, shutting his eyes and bowing his head in reverence to... something.

What could I do in the face of such a winding, overwhelming tale? In the face of millions of years of history that had just been dropped into my lap by a near-immortal being, no less?

I laughed.

It was a spontaneous and nervous expression; one that I instantly wished I could bottle back up.

The Maker's eyes flared with cerulean light. "Do you think this is a child's plaything, Bodhi? This is the fate of reality itself."

That was enough to shut me up.

Wiping away a few unbidden tears of amusement, I said, "What exactly do you need *me* to do?"

The Maker lifted one hand and turned it palm-side up. He then conjured a purple orb within it, complete with a diamond at the center—a not-to-scale model of the Untraversed, I realized. "Do you know why I constructed this field?"

"To keep Kruthara out?" I asked, praying he wouldn't zap me with lightning for my too-obvious reply.

"Yes, but it was not the sum of my aims." The Untraversed's model began expanding in his palm, eventually spilling over into the space between us, then around us. "My mind is powerful, but it is not the summation of the infinite. The field is a projection of my consciousness... an act of will manifesting as matter."

"And you want to teach me that?"

"I aspire to *complete* my task. You see, this field is crude. At the time of my retreat into this complex, it spanned millions of light-years. All of my people lived within it, sheltered from Kruthara's ravages. But time has worn down its influence." Little by little, the purple model retracted back into his palm. "The death of this body draws near. At this moment, my mind must choose between preserving the field... and my flesh. You have seen the outer edge of the field. You know that it has shrunken from its former glory, and it will continue to shrink. The end of this body means the dispersion of this mind... which, in turn, means the dissolution of this field."

The scale model in his palm dissipated.

Reflecting on the Maker's point, it suddenly made sense why aspirants and raiders alike had failed to locate his tomb (which I now realized was not a tomb, but a glorified hermit's hut). It wasn't just the inherent danger of the creatures within the Untraversed—it was the fact that the Untraversed itself had grown increasingly smaller since his disappearance. Any astral chart that had pinned down its location had eventually become worthless. It was a fading field in a vast, ever-growing ocean.

"Okay," I said slowly, "but what exactly is my role in this?"

"Have patience, my friend. You must understand that this field was not intended to be a permanent solution to the scourge. It was, at best, a demonstration of my limited power. Not even my greatest chittas could summon the willpower to do what needed doing."

"Which was?"

"I did not seek to merely expel Kruthara," the Maker said. "I sought to destroy it in a flash."

"A flash?" I squinted at him, skeptical. "I don't know how it looked the last time you were out there, but things have gone downhill with round two. It's spread all over the place. You can't exactly drop a bifurcation burst-shell on its head and be done with it."

"Stop thinking in material terms. It will only confound you." He straightened further, staring directly at me. "Kruthara is not a physical being. It manifests in physical space, but it, in itself, is not of the physical world. It is like air appearing as fog."

"Technically, that's water vapor."

The Maker's glare stopped me from further damage. "Your mind cannot grasp its nature. I am confined to using metaphors. All you must know, Bodhi, is that what you see of Kruthara is not its entire body. These are its roots, stretching into our world. Its true body is beyond this reality. And that body... its *true* body... can be destroyed. But we must use techniques that have been lost to time."

"Go on..."

"As you have heard, this field was not my ultimate goal. It was merely the best I could summon at that point in time. In order to end Kruthara, both on this plane and in its native realm, we must channel the field's energy through dimensions."

"We must *what*?"

"You are familiar with radio frequencies. Apply the same logic. If Kruthara is to be vanquished, we must alter the frequency of the field."

"By alter, you mean change it to... one that vibrates with Kruthara's dimension?"

"Precisely. Here, in our world, my influence is limited by power and distance. But in its realm, there is no space, no matter. One burst of conscious energy could dispel it at the source."

"Right. So we fire off a mind-pulse, which will kill Kruthara in its own dimension, which means it will also die in *this* dimension... I think?"

He nodded. "Now I shall explain your role."

"Is it easy?"

"It is necessary," he snapped. "Even as we speak, my time draws near. There are no coincidences, no happenstances of fate. In a matter of minutes, this form will be lost to the ether. And when my body-mind perishes, another must take its place. Whoever inherits my position will also inherit my wisdom, just as I have inherited the wisdom of those who came before me. Through this, and this alone, it will be possible to overcome Kruthara."

I nodded, nodded, and nodded... then stopped. "Wait... you want me to *become* you? *Now?*"

"You will not be anything, merely an action. A force."

"Why me?"

"Because my body-mind is not sufficient. It may be potent, but it is fading and tainted with malice. A being with a pure body-mind must seize this energy and utilize it."

"No, you don't understand... why *me*? There are a trillion other people out there. People with far 'purer' minds and bodies, let me tell you."

"You are afraid to die."

I blinked at him, scrambling for a reply, only to realize he was right. This was the endgame. The one tried-and-true way we'd be able to win this. One merge with the infinite, one pulse of energy, and Kruthara would never take a life again. That was the outcome I'd been after from the start. All along, I'd told myself I would do anything—even die—to see it happen. But here, now, hearing it so bluntly... it struck a chord that made me recoil.

What if I'd been wrong about Kruthara being after Chaska?

What if Kruthara had somehow known that *I* was the chosen one, and had been chasing after little old me this whole time? Every death, every invasion... all for me?

The thought made my skin crawl.

"What about the maitreyans?" I whispered. "I mean, they're enlightened or whatever, right? A whole species of 'em! They could get it done lickety-split!"

"I have seen the strands of fate, Bodhi. Do not question my judgment."

"Or what? You'll kill me? That'd muck up your plans, wouldn't it?"

"Do not be afraid. That which you are cannot die."

"Wanna bet?"

"You lack insight into your true nature. You perceived it a short time ago... I can sense it... but even now, you deny it. You pretend you are a mortal creature, full of fear and regret. You have felt the everlasting peace of eternity, yet you shy away. Why?"

It was hard to think. Hard to even breathe. "Just show me a weapon schematic. Something. We can beat it using the right tools."

"This is the only way, Bodhi."

"You don't know that!"

"I do. And deep within, you know it, too."

"Nope."

"You may hide from the truth, but you cannot evade it forever. It is inevitable." The Maker smiled at me. "Discard that which is false. All will be revealed."

Then the world dissolved once again, and I found myself back in that lightless pyramid. Before me, the energy core and the body within beckoned. My destiny. My tomb.

I ran like hell back to the ship.

Addendum:

If this sounds like a lot to follow, it is. Even more so when you're the poor soul being thrust into the middle of it. In the interest of helping my dear readers follow along with the madness, here's the skinny.

The Great Maker was just an ordinary man (clone?) who'd been born into a pretty dicey era. Slavery, war, all the rest. So Mr. Maker decided to change the game up a bit. He killed his own creator, took the guy's name, and waged an epic war for justice that ended up killing many, many, *many* people. After all was said and done, Mr. Maker wasn't happy with the outcome. He'd created a universal empire, but at what cost? A bunch of pissed-off constituents, battle-scarred galaxies, and one huge problem for future space-dwellers—Kruthara, that is.

Mr. Maker's oddball solution was to become a meditating hermit that could find a newer, better way to "fix the universe." And after plenty of introspection (and maybe a few psychotropic drugs), he found the answer: inner peace. Corny, I know. But bear with me.

Mr. Maker also discovered that the Untraversed, his personal bubble to keep Kruthara out, wasn't enough. He needed more juice in the engine for a killing blow. And that "juice," as it were, would come in the form of a chosen one (read: me). This chosen one needed to take over his spot in the pyramid-energy-generator-thing, allowing them to unleash some kind of shock wave that would kill Kruthara in both its own dimension and, crucially, in ours.

And as if that weren't bad enough, Mr. Maker was also on the verge of death. Like, immediate death. Meaning my own end was just over the horizon.

Am I writing this entire memoir from within the Untraversed's eternal sphere? Am I a formless spirit wandering the cosmos? Am I God?

Keep reading. It'll make sense. Sort of.

NINETEEN

By the time Chaska's voice crackled through the helmet's radio, my heart was hammering so hard I could barely hear it. What she said made me wish I hadn't heard it at all.

"... *here. I'm picking up six, maybe seven flagships. Those turrets aren't gonna last long against that!*"

"Hang tight," I huffed back. "I'm... almost... there."

It didn't take a genius like me to understand what was going down. The Hegemony had finally caught up with us, and they'd brought the big guns. Big enough to hear through my helmet's dampeners. Big enough to feel as they jostled the ground beneath me.

Squeezing through the final ring of columns, I found my compatriots assembled near the ship's staging bay. Chaska was in the process of doling out armor plates and weapons to the crew, entrusting Gadra with a shoulder-stabilized, anti-ship magnetic launcher that was half her height. There was no mistaking it: they all considered this their final stand. After all, nobody hands a child firepower that heavy unless they believe they're going to die wielding it.

The nearer I jogged, the more the scene broke my heart. And

that heart-breakiness wasn't just due to the constant flashes and grumbles of high-yield explosives detonating beyond the tomb's entrances—though that was part of it. No, what ate at me more was the fact that these were good, honest people about to suffer from my own cowardice. Loyal people. People who'd given up everything for the betterment of others.

They didn't know about my predicament, of course, but that didn't matter. If the Great Maker was to be believed—and I had no reason *not* to believe him—then this all came down to me. There was no other way out. No backup plan. Either I dissolved into the void, or everybody and everything else covered my debt of sacrifice.

"Bodhi, what the hell took you so long?" Chaska shouted as I drew up. "Those automated turrets won't hold up forever. You find anything in there?"

Despite the sweat-induced fog building up across my faceplate, I saw the desperation in the faces around me. Even Gadra, bless her heart, had lost the sense of thrill that had carried her through most of our riskier moments. She was still clinging to that nervous smile of hers, but it didn't fool me. The others weren't much better. Their stares wobbled between dread and detachment, broadcasting the same realization that I'd recently (and incessantly) had to face: *Death is here, and it's coming for me.*

And just like that, some hidden gears in my mind cranked forward. My course was clear. My *destiny*, no less. I'd go into that buzzing pillar, and I'd do whatever it took to boil Kruthara out of existence. But there was still the off chance that the Maker was wrong, and that all of this would come crashing down. If it did, I wanted them as far away as possible. The least I could offer was a head start. A running leap out of the fire.

"Listen," I said, wheezing and panting. "You... need... to go."

The others were swift in their protests, especially Chaska.

"There's nowhere to *go,* Bodhi," she growled. "We're jammed up tight in this thing. Now tell us what you found. Any weapons? Paths that lead deeper inside?"

I shook my head. "You don't... understand. I... can fix... this. But you need to... go."

"We're not leaving you here," Ruena said, casually loading shells into her auto-shotgun. "And not just because we don't trust you to finish this job."

Gulping down air, I weighed my options. There was no way they'd believe what had *really* happened in that tomb. It was hard enough for me to swallow, let alone to sell to a crowd that already doubted my fanciful accounts. So I did what I did best: I lied for the greater good. "I found the schematics, alright? You need to get out of here... get someplace safe. I'll transmit them to you, and you can beam them out across the 'verse."

"Wait," Chaska said, pausing briefly to allow a peal of Hegemony nuclear rounds to die down. "Schematics? You really found something?"

"Yes. There were riddles... puzzles... it was a whole thing. But you need to trust me. Just get out of here, and I'll send them."

"Did you bump your head in there?" Ruena asked. "The Untraversed doesn't let anything pinch in or out, Bodhi. We're staying."

"You don't get it!" I hissed. "The field's going to drop. You need to be ready to *go* once it does."

"Why would it drop?" Tusky said, still fiddling with the carbine in his arms.

I let out a sharp sigh. "You need to trust me on this. The field is going down."

"How would you know that?" Chaska whispered.

Before I could reply, Ruena gasped and spun toward the passage we'd used to enter the tomb. I didn't need her twosight to understand what she'd seen in that future timeline. The sprawling turret-versus-Hegemony battle outside, which had been shaded by the Untraversed's purple haze... now was not. In a violent rush, the remnants of the Maker's miracle field constricted inwards and past us, coiling back into the central pillar from which it had originated.

Our oxygen reserves kicked in. Exterior sounds vanished. The air turned lighter, colder. We were no longer in the Untraversed—we were in normal space. Vulnerable space. It wouldn't take Kruthara long to pinch its vessels straight to our doorstep.

Everyone looked my way, slack-jawed.

"I'm not going to say I told you so," I said, "but I *did* tell you so."

"Can we get it back?" Ruena asked frantically.

"Perhaps it was a fail-safe mechanism," Tusky said. "Perhaps removing the schematics caused it to—"

Chaska hefted her rifle up against her shoulder. "There's no time to speculate. We need a plan."

"You already have one," I said quietly. "Pile into that ship, get clear of the battle, and pinch as far away as you can. Gad's paintings will take you far."

"No," Chaska snapped. "If you've got the schematics, then there's no reason to stay. Everybody leaves here. That includes you."

I shook my head. "You need to take my word here. Please."

"Absolutely not. If there's something we need to know, then spit it out."

"All you need to know is that you'll be safe. And if you're not... you keep running."

"What the hell's keeping you here?"

"Just... something I need to do," I said, straining to look them all in the eyes. "This isn't a goodbye. If things go exceptionally well, you can swing back for me. The Untraversed is gone... that means I can transmit a rescue order to you, and you can transmit status reports to me. Got it? You can't afford to waste any time."

"Bodhi, don't be a fool," Ruena said.

"I'm being sensible for once," I told her. "They *need* you to get out of here, Ru. You're the only one with twosight. Umzuma will need your edge to fly through that blockade."

"Sure, I'll do that. Once you get onboard."

"Yeah," Gadra piped up, "come with us! I still need to win your money at cards!"

Again, I shook my head. "I'm asking for your wholehearted trust this one time. *Once*. If any of you truly have my best interests at heart, you'll pack up and go. Now."

"What are you after, looting this place?" Chaska asked, glaring at me. "Nothing you say will keep us from dragging you on board. I've learned by now that the truth is the opposite of what you tell us. And that means you're coming."

Indeed, nothing I said would be capable of swaying my semi-beloved insurgent's opinion. How fortunate, then, that I didn't have to say anything at all. Because at that exact moment, right on cue for the tragicomedy that is my life, a Hegemony flagship exploded just outside the tomb. Slithering away from the carnage was an enormous, chitin-plated beast.

Chaska stared at me, wide-eyed. "Is that…"

"A World Serpent?" I cut in. "Why, yes, yes it is. And it's the distraction you need."

She immediately jerked her head toward the ship. "Pack it up! Let's go! Ruena, have 'Zuma preheat those reactors. I'll get to the godengine."

Gadra scrunched up her face. "We're not gonna leave him, are we?"

"You're not leaving me," I said, kneeling down before the girl. "You're letting me play here a little longer. Then you're going to come pick me up. Right?"

Her eyes grew misty, but that stiff upper lip didn't budge. "Yeah, that's right."

I patted her helmet. "Good. Now do what Chaska tells you."

Tusky's snout bristled—a clear indication he had plenty on his mind—but he said nothing. Instead, he guided Gadra toward the staging bay.

Ruena, meanwhile, hung around a moment longer. She offered me a solemn nod, then a tight smile, and then… nothing. She turned and jogged after the others, tinkering with her wrist transmitter as she moved.

"So… this is it?" Chaska whispered.

I looked back to find a curious expression on her face. So curious I could hardly dissect its meaning. It was soft, yet fierce. Disbelieving, perhaps.

"Not necessarily," I said.

"Don't bullshit me, Bodhi. If you're not coming back, just tell me now. Please."

"What for?"

"Because I'm not gonna sit around again, hoping you come back."

"Again? As in, you wanted me back?"

She glanced away. "You're so damn annoying. Do you know that?"

"How about elusive?"

"Annoying."

I shrugged. "Have it your way, dear. Just think of me from time to time, would you? You know, like when you're about to fall asleep. Something like that."

"It sounds like you want to haunt me."

"Okay, fine. Think of me when you're all alone on creepy ships. Maybe I'll whisper in your ear or throw a book across the room."

"You're insufferable," she said softly.

Then we had a fireworks moment—a brief, striking appetizer plate of the long and fruitful life we could've shared. She gazed into my eyes, and I gazed into hers. Her features softened. We leaned closer, closer, closer…

Our helmets clacked together.

"Whoa," I said, chuckling as we pulled back. "That got heavy."

She punched my shoulder. "Do what you have to do. And don't you dare say you'll come back for me."

Then she took off running, lit by the flashes and strobes of the battle outside.

"Hey, Chaska," I said into my transmitter. She paused, glancing over her shoulder. "I'll come back for you."

I could've sworn she cast me a smile before heading into the staging bay.

My head was profoundly clear as I raced back toward the pyramid, savoring the intermittent updates Ruena sent me over the radio.

"*Almost out of the gravitational pull, Bodhi.*"

"*Starting the pinch now.*"

"*Godspeed in there. Hope to see you on the other side.*"

I didn't bother replying—not only because of a lack of breath, but because there was nothing left to say. Heartfelt as I may be, I am not one for goodbyes. Parting words are a miserable way to end things with those you care about. They become phantoms in their head, circling, nagging at them. Fortunately for me, I wouldn't hear anything soon enough.

Truth be told, the nearer I drew to the first ring of columns, the more I began to appreciate the concept of oblivion. Perhaps the Maker was right. Perhaps what I'd seen in my venom-induced hallucinations *had* been the truth, and I was heading back into an ocean of peace. At least, that was what I told myself.

"Bodhi!" The voice didn't come crackling through my long-band transmitter—the crew had already pinched out to safety—but rather through my local radio. "Bodhi, wait!"

Halting in place, I turned to find the worst thing imaginable:

Tusky.

He was dashing toward me, visibly winded from his sprint. His loaded carbine jostled about on its back-mounted sling.

"What in the Halcius-loving hell are you doing here?" I growled. "You're supposed to be on that ship! You know, not here!"

He doubled over upon reaching me, huffing through his radio. "They think I'm still on board! I did exactly... as you'd have done! I tricked them... hopped off when they weren't looking!"

"Now why would you do a stupid thing like that?"

"Because... I couldn't let you die alone. We're both... doomed men... are we not?"

I gripped his shoulder, helping him to straighten back up. "This is about me, and only me. You aren't meant to die here, Tusky."

He met my stare with surprising gusto. "Bodhi... I came into being through the actions of others. I was given sentience... without any choice in the matter. Have I not earned my own fate? My own time and place to leave this world?"

Much as I wanted to rail against that, to shout him down and highlight just how foolish he'd been in following me, I couldn't. He'd done exactly as I would have. He'd opted to die with freedom, burning up in my personal blaze of glory.

"If this works," I said cautiously, "there might still be a chance for you to get out of here. You need to do exactly as I say. Can you promise me that?"

"Yes. On one condition."

"Shoot."

"I need to know what it's about," he said weakly. "To know... what death is, and why you are so eager to experience it. I know you saw death in that wreckage, Bodhi. I know it touched you. And even now... here... its presence is upon you."

"How would you know that?"

"It's, as the laymen would say, a hunch. So, will you enlighten me?"

Growling deep in my throat, I yanked Tusky behind a column.

"If you came here to ask me what death is about, you came to the wrong place. I'm just here to do my job. Nothing more, nothing less."

"Very well. Explain this job."

"I can't."

"Please, just humor me. I must know what could compel you to surrender your life. If I grasped this choice... I could grasp death itself."

"Bold assumption."

"Bodhi, this is all I've ever desired. An answer to—"

I held up a hand, but not to stymy his increasingly annoying demands. Far in the distance, sweeping noiselessly over the tomb's outer disc, was a flock of Hegemony gunships. They were emblazoned with a trio of black stripes—Kemedis' personal detachment.

"Here's the plan," I said. "We get to the sweet spot, and I'll tell you what I know. Do you know how to handle that carbine?"

He looked back at our attackers and swallowed hard. "Well, I did score about fifteen percent on our accuracy training—"

"Good enough."

"Really?"

"No, not even close. But this is the real deal. If I tell you to shoot, you shoot. Understood?"

He saluted me.

It was a ridiculous gesture, one I would've loved to decry, but I didn't have the chance. The gunships had touched down, and streams of Hegemony commandos were pouring down their deployment ramps.

I shoved Tusky into a run, then bolted after him. Not two seconds passed before bullets began pinging off the columns around us. They impacted silently, registering as nothing more than sparks on the impenetrable masonry. As we wound through the maze of columns, separating and rejoining every so often, I heard only my labored breaths and the wheeze of the oxygen recyclers.

"Where... are we heading?" Tusky panted.

"Pyramid!" I shouted. "Look for the pyramid!"

"They're too close!"

"Then shoot back!"

Much to my amazement, Tusky did. He stopped, wheeled around, and shouldered his carbine like a trained hitman. His normally placid features sharpened into raw, unbridled fury. Full-on rabid mode. Then, with a bestial roar I saw rather than heard, he began dumping his ammunition into the hordes behind us.

I threw myself behind a column and hunkered down for dear life, stunned at the number of bullets slamming into the black stone around us. None of them hit my dear companion.

But when I risked a peek around the column's edge, I discovered that Tusky had been luckier in his aim. Hegemony bodies littered the otherworldly forest, some hissing vented air and others twitching in death spasms. And just when I thought the mayhem was over, Tusky loaded a fresh magazine and resumed his killing spree.

Still, this was a losing battle. Flashes of movement blurred around us, advancing up through the network of columns in coordinated strike patterns I'd learned all too well over years of war. There was no way out—not without catching a bullet. With a deep sigh and a bit of fumbling, I drew my holdout Puncher pistol and racked the slide.

They wouldn't take me down without a fight, no matter how one-sided and pathetic it was.

A Hegemony restorer leapt out across from me, rifle trained on Tusky. I panic-fired twice without hesitation. The first round glanced off a column, but the second shattered his black faceplate, slackening his body and forcing a blood-oxygen mist out through the impact site.

The next attacker caught three rounds—two in the chest, one in the stomach. The third took a swipe to the neck, but that was enough.

With shaking hands, I ejected my magazine and popped in a spare. "Ammo check?" I whispered to Tusky.

His radio crackled for a moment. "Twelve bullets." He shouldered the carbine and fired. "Eleven."

Then all was still. Temporarily, anyway. There were no further sparks, no hints of enemies lurking in the mist between columns.

That was when I felt the first tingles of pain.

It felt as though a Faurian grazer-lope had back-kicked me straight in the thigh, leaving behind a numbing bruise. Glancing down, I saw a reddish aerosol venting from the bullet hole. At first, my examination was clinical. It seemed to be a stray round. It hadn't punched through the other side. The helmet's air indicator bleeped to warn me of impending disaster.

Then the adrenaline wore off, and I realized I was going to die. Not as a hero, not as the Maker's vessel, but as a nameless nobody. I was going to die of suffocation from one misfired bullet. My heart jackhammered in my chest. Fiery pain burned up and down my leg.

"Tusky," I mumbled into the transmitter, "I think I'm in trouble."

Within seconds, he was kneeling by my side.

"Oh, no," he said quietly. "No, no, no."

"Don't say that. You're freaking me out."

His face assured me that he, too, was freaked out.

"Just hold still," he said, rummaging through a pouch strapped to his belt. "I have a sealant kit somewhere in here."

"Sealant," I said distantly, nodding. I pressed my hand over the wound, but it was fruitless—the lamellar plating of my glove couldn't form a full seal. "Tusky, just drag me into that pyramid. Please. I won't have enough oxygen even if you seal it off."

Undaunted, the giant sloth produced a rubbery-looking patch and slapped it over the blood fumes.

As expected, one of my two oxygen alarms fell quiet. Depressurization was off the menu; no more risk of air venting. But the other continued to blare its stark warning: *low air supply.* According to its pretty green font, I had no more than ten minutes of air remaining. Ten minutes is an agonizing length of time when you can't walk, yet your destination requires running through a hail of bullets.

"Can you carry me?" I whispered. "Get me to that pyramid. Please."

Tusky held my gaze for a moment, surely sensing my predicament, then nodded. In one deft, powerful motion, he hefted me up and onto his shoulder. I held the Puncher with a tenuous grip.

"Tell me what's there," he grunted, trudging onwards despite the occasional zing of a Hegemony bullet. "What's worth dying for?"

"You wouldn't believe me if I told you."

"This isn't the time… to be coy, Bodhi. I believed you about the World Serpent, even if the others didn't. I have *always* believed you."

"Why?"

"Because you're my creator. You're my friend. And dying with you… would be an honor."

If it hadn't presented such a clear risk to our well-being, I might've cried at that. I settled on offering him the truth.

"I met the Maker inside that pyramid," I said. "He told me that it's my destiny to get inside that machine. The pillar in the center of it, that is. Don't ask me how, or why, but it'll kill Kruthara. For good."

"Why you?"

"The world may never know. But this is our only shot. He said a 'pure mind' needs to upload itself into that pillar. That this was my destiny."

"There's no such thing as destiny, Bodhi. We always… have a choice."

I fired a lazy shot as a Hegemony commando rounded a column. No dice, but he backed off.

"Don't fight me on this," I huffed. "Just get us inside that thing."

"Almost... there."

Craning my head around, I found he was right. By some twist of fate, we were actually *there*. The entrance to the pyramid was just ten paces away. Nine... eight...

"Stop right there."

That familiar voice chilled me to the bone. It was a stray signal, one that had spliced through our private comms. Only the Hegemony had that kind of tech. And only one woman was capable of mustering such hatred in her words.

Kemedis.

I glanced back to find the grand mediator herself standing there, flanked by two commandos with their rifles raised.

"Tusky," I said, "I think you should stop. For your sake."

Despite some hesitation, the sloth complied.

"Put Mr. Drezek down," Kemedis commanded.

I nodded. "Do it, Tusky."

Inch by careful inch, I was lowered to the ground until I found myself sitting upright. On the instructions of Kemedis' troops, Tusky stepped off to the side and dropped his carbine.

"Now you," Kemedis said. "Drop your pistol."

"This old thing?" I asked. "It's not even loaded."

"Drop. It. Now."

"And then what?"

"And then you face Kruthara's judgment... and your brutish conspirator here spends the rest of his life in our laboratories."

"*What?*"

Without warning, the commando to Kemedis' left fired a sizzler prod at Tusky. The quills bit deep into his suit, dropping him like a sack of rocks. He flopped on the ground beside me, plainly unconscious.

"Give up now, and Kruthara will integrate you painlessly," she said. "Be grateful that it is more merciful than I."

"You need me alive, then."

"I don't *need* you in the slightest. I am preserving you as a courtesy for *it*."

Far in the distance, squirming high above the columns, were the first tendrils of Kruthara's mega-body. They'd found their way inside. Next stop… me.

"This will never work, Grand Mediator," I said. "Your overlord was only using you to get into this place and find us. Now that the field is done for… it doesn't need you. You're just puppets to it."

"I will not ask you to surrender again, Mr. Drezek. I am not a savage, but I am also no saint. Drop your weapon."

I'm not sure what came over me in that moment—bravery, stupidity?—but I decided to pull off a move I'd only seen in action vids. We were mere steps from the pyramid, after all. Give up here, and everything was gone. Kaput.

Midway through my motion to set the Puncher on the tiles, I popped off a flurry of shots aimed at all three of our would-be captors. Amazingly, most of the shots landed. Kemedis' guards dropped in a spray of rigor-mortis fire, and Kemedis herself stumbled back, screeching and venting air.

But she didn't die. That was a problem.

Breathing hard, Kemedis righted herself and aimed square at my head. I fired—*ka-chuk*. Fresh out of rounds. No ammo, no hope.

I flinched, waiting for that lethal spray… but it never came. Smoke wisped off of Kemedis' rifle, leaving behind a fractured glow where my bullet had carved its mark.

"You little *worm*," she growled. A vicious smile came over her face, fully illuminated by the warning lights flashing in her helmet. "I never imagined I'd have the pleasure of killing you so close. In such a thoroughly *personal* manner." Even as she gasped for breath, she dropped her ruined weapon and drew a long, serrated blade from her thigh sheath. "I will delight in this more than you'll ever know."

Biting through the pain, I dragged myself backwards. Away from Kemedis, away from the tentacles slithering through the columns toward us.

"Come here," she cooed. "Let me end you slowly."

Just before she could lunge atop me, I threw a kick at her helmet. She caught my foot and twisted it to the side, sending a vicious crack up through my calf. The agony followed.

"Let's do this one inch of flesh at a time," she wheezed. "One slow, long cut after another…"

With shocking strength, she tore the boot clasps off my ankle. Air wisped out through the gap, only to be immediately stilled by an emergency sealant clamp. She gave another tug, and the boot came free. Bruise-blotches broke out across my depressurized toes.

Kemedis squealed with laughter, raising the knife for her beginning cut. She held me firm as I clawed and scrabbled, ready for blood, eager for my pain…

Then she stopped.

Still holding my foot, her entire body locked up. Her eyes peeled open as she stared at… something.

No, not just something. My tattoo. Gadra's tattoo.

That damned hypnotic mark.

Despite the pain rippling through my entire body, I burst out laughing. Maybe the Maker was right. Maybe there were no coincidences. Then I caught myself. This was my one chance. My *last* chance.

Ignoring the worsening pain, I curled upwards and ripped the knife from Kemedis' rigid fingers. Then I leaned further, further… close enough to spit-shine her helmet. With the last of my meager strength, I drove the blade straight into the bullet hole in her chest plating.

For a long and unnerving moment, Kemedis remained in place, eyes locked, mouth split in a grin. Then a final breath rasped through my helmet's speakers. The grand mediator toppled backward, jerked a bit on the ground, and fell still. The embedded knife ceased its twitching as her heart came to a full stop.

No time to celebrate, however. Kruthara's tentacles were closing in. They were already within the inner ring of columns, probing forward, tasting the vacuum for prey.

Grunting primally, I dragged myself over to Tusky. The sloth was still breathing—barely—but his fluttering eyelids suggested he was out cold. That wouldn't do. I tugged out the sizzler's quills, then began banging on his suit, knocking his helmet around, screaming. Anything to wake him up.

The screaming seemed to do the trick. His eyes snapped open in a flash, and he bolted upright, swinging at nobody in particular.

"What happened?" he cried.

I shushed him. "Get me... into that pyramid."

He looked back at the imposing structure, then at me. "Bodhi, is this really the only way? I know it's late, but—"

"Kruthara is here. Look."

Tusky did. That only worsened his surge of fear. "You can't leave me. Please."

Sensing that the sloth wouldn't move until he had a shot of high-octane existential courage, I pretended Kruthara wasn't about to devour us and instead gripped my comrade's helmet.

"You asked me what death's all about," I said quietly. "I still can't answer that, but I know this. The trouble isn't death... it's the fear of death. The fear of oblivion. But if you can crack open that fear and see that it's really about the love of existing—loving it so much that you'd hate to be separated from it—then the ride isn't so bad. Death is a once-in-a-lifetime opportunity, Tusky. And life is a thrill, no doubt, but death... that's the other side of the coin. And when it comes, you can enjoy it just as much as all this. You can love it, just as you love life."

"You really... believe that?"

"I do. See, I found something worth dying for. And when I go into that void, I'll know I lived for *something*. I died because I loved this world so much."

The steel in Tusky's eyes hardened. "Let's finish this."

Unfortunately, by the time Tusky had reached this state of badass serenity, it was too late. Kruthara's tentacles formed a writhing, pulsing mass of reddish flesh around us. It had already consumed the pillars, and now it was creeping toward us.

Or so I thought. The tentacles paused over Kemedis' body, delicately probing it with spidery filaments before sinking a full tendril into one of the suit's punctures. This brought about my worst nightmare.

Kemedis' body twitched, then spasmed, then began to *levitate*. It was not autonomous, but rather controlled like a marionette, hoisted up by a host of tentacles that had impaled it through the spine. Blisters and veins spread across Kruthara-Kemedis' face. Bony nubs and twitching stalks jutted out through the remains of her suit.

"You must join," the eldritch voice croaked in my helmet. "We have been waiting for you."

Even as I stared at the monstrosity, transfixed in horror, I felt something clunking around on my back. My air-reserve meter flickered, then rebooted with a new, greener figure: *two days remaining*.

Glancing sidelong, I found that the sloth was wandering away from me. Wandering toward the pyramid, no less.

"Tusky," I shouted, "what are you doing?"

"Use that air reserve frugally," Tusky said. "You'll need it more than me."

To my horror, I spotted my near-depleted tank lying just beside me. Tusky's own tank was empty. He'd given it away. To me.

Kruthara's shadow loomed overhead. Kemedis' animated, rapidly mutating corpse leaned closer, reaching out with tooth-encrusted claws. Crab-like spines scraped over my suit.

"Tusky, whatever you think you're doing—"

"I hear it calling to me, Bodhi," he whispered as Kruthara stretched itself around my body. "I wasn't ready, not until you said what you did. But now I know what I have to do... and I will not fail."

"What!?"

"You led me to this moment, Bodhi. There are no coincidences."

Puckers and fangs and muscle tissue constricted around me, crushing my ribs, burrowing into the suit. Wormy feelers coated my faceplate and pressed toward me in a frenzy.

"Tusky!" I screamed, shutting my eyes. "Tusky, don't—"

All at once, it ceased. The pressure on my suit... the slurping... the scraping. I looked up to find that the feelers were gone, replaced by a layer of reddish dust.

"Tusky?" I whispered, summoning my fading willpower to sit up and brush away the dust.

Nobody answered. Scattered around me was dust... mounds upon mounds of dust, all of it shimmering with brilliant purple light. I twisted in place to find exactly what I'd expected: a plume of energy radiating up and through the pyramid.

"It was you," I mumbled to myself. "It was always you, my friend."

And with that, the shakes set in. The pain ramped up. The urge to sleep forever crept up and tugged at my mind like a tidal pull.

There was no fear as I settled down into that fetid dust and closed my eyes.

The task was done.

TWENTY

Waking up alive came as a great surprise to me. A tender, disorienting surprise, but a surprise nonetheless. I was lying on a silk sheet in a dark, damp room. The walls breathed around me. Everything smelled of stomach acid.

Was this hell? Probably. What else could I do but sigh, lace my fingers behind my head, and accept what I'd had coming?

I nearly shrieked when a sphincter-like door slurped open across the room.

"Well, well, well," a woman said, striding closer in the shadows. "The man of the hour's decided to end his long nap."

Through the fog in my still-throbbing head, I recognized the voice. The silhouette. The high priestess herself had decided to pay me a visit. And judging by the lack of a chitta atop her head, I was now confronting the real deal.

"Why hello, High Priestess," I said, gradually sitting up. Then I noticed the rather conspicuous bump in her lower belly. "For the record, if I'd known you were carrying a child, I probably wouldn't have—"

"Wouldn't have what? Assailed my mind with your traitorous creature?"

"Yes, that."

"Good to know." The high priestess lifted the flap of her robes, revealing… simultaneously more and less than I'd anticipated. Perched above her black leggings was Chitta Mini, who'd managed to graft himself straight to her skin. "Surprise! It's a boy… brain… thing."

I wasn't as enthused. "Thank you, Mini. A fake-out pregnancy is just what I needed right now."

"Hey, just be glad I plucked your dying bones out of that place. You were down to fifteen minutes of air."

"If you'd let it run out, I wouldn't have had to smell this place. So I'm calling this a draw."

"Well, since you're in a glum mood as it is, might wanna check your leg."

Frowning, I glanced down at the smooth, strut-encased prosthetic attached to my knee. It seemed that the double whammy of my suit's tourniquet, plus several days of depressurization, had done exactly what one would expect to an organic limb. Oh well. Flexing the prosthetic, I found it felt more or less "normal" for a limb. Life goes on.

"Neat," I said dryly. "At this rate, I'll be a full machine in no time."

Mini smirked and sat on the edge of the bed. "Helluva fight, chief. You shoulda been there. I mean, you were, but not in the heart of it. I wrecked so many of those pricks."

"Oh, I saw."

"Y'did?"

I nodded. "It was impressive."

"Yeah, well, not to toot my own horn, but… I did kinda save the day." The priestess' mouth formed a smirk only the chitta could inspire. "Turns out these people weren't lyin' about the Kruthara-protection genes on the serpent. Not a single person got turned. I mean, we *did* suffer about three million casualties, and the World Serpent's bleeding from about six thousand spots, but..."

"About that... How exactly is the serpent still alive in the vacuum? There's no air."

"You ask too many questions, man. Bottom line is, you took Kruthara down. Not gonna ask how, just gonna say this: it's time for champagne and strippers."

"I'm not exactly in the mood."

"There are pills for that."

I just rolled my eyes. "Have you made contact with my crew? Any of them?"

"Funny you should ask. Your number one fan's been camped out in our humble abode for almost a week."

"A *week*?"

"Yeah? You were pretty messed up. Had to do some coma tricks with you."

For any doctors out there—please *never* use the term "coma tricks."

"So... who came for me?" I asked.

"What, y'want me to ruin the surprise? Nah, buddy. Let's go see her yourself."

"Her. Meaning Chaska."

"I'm not tellin'."

"Alright, just take me there. I want out."

"Yeah, sure, whatever you want. But, uh, there's a little thing you have to do first."

"Which is?"

"C'mon, I'll show you." Chitta Mini stood and led me through the doors. We navigated several long, pulsating passages that resembled intestines in digestive overdrive. "See, I've gotten to know the common folk pretty well since I got here. Think I'm gonna stay. Y'know, try to make this place a tourist destination or somethin'.

Haven't really thought it through. Maybe an ice-cream parlor… or a—"

"Just get to the point, would you?"

"Right, yeah, sorry. These people are pretty hyped up on what you did. Now they *really* think you're the chosen one. So, I kinda promised them a small, itsy-bitsy thing…"

Long before we crossed the threshold ahead, a thunderous roar filled the passage.

"What is that?" I whispered.

"Just a few visitors," Chitta Mini said. "Check it out."

Ducking through the sphincter, we emerged onto a cartilage catwalk suspended at a dizzying height. Stretched out beneath me were millions of bone-people, all of them cheering, chanting, screaming, straining their arms skyward. Toward me. The crowd occupied the entire gullet-like chamber, even receding back into the adjoining tunnels. Their collective fervor drowned out even the loudest and most pressing of my thoughts.

What followed was a nauseating round of pomp and ceremony. Crowns laid atop my head, warpaint applied to my face, speeches made and honors granted. But through it all, I wasn't truly there. My mind still lingered in the Maker's tomb, constantly replaying the darkness, the blood, the purple light.

But the clearest image was that of Tusky still wearing his final mask of tranquility. That freeze-frame will forever be seared into my memory. At least, I hope it will.

With each new glory cast upon my name, I felt myself grow smaller and weaker. I hadn't earned any of it. I'd merely been a stepping-stone for the true hero, Tusky, to carry out the Maker's vision. He hadn't needed thoughts of regal treatment or his legacy to do it. He'd just… done it. And upon reflection, true to the Maker's own words, it now seemed that there were no coincidences whatsoever.

From the very start, it had always been about him. The heist job, ostensibly organized to recover Kruthara, had instead birthed our savior. My need for an artist had given us Gadra, who'd tutored him and trained him in the ways of innocence. His looming death had provided the catalyst for sacrifice. Everything from the bullets Chaska had loaded to the movement of Gadra's hands had brought about *this*. This moment, this reality. Each event had molded the next, intermingling, weaving together, crafting the tapestry we called victory. Indeed, if I looked back far enough, I saw that this had all begun long before my birth... before the birth of the Maker... before the birth of anything at all.

"Hey," Mini said, bumping me with his elbow. "I said, you ready?"

Blinking myself back to full awareness, I realized we were already striding down the tunnel toward a ribcage concourse. The celebrations were over; now it was time to see my blushing bride. My dearest Chaska.

In typical form, I found her locked in a heated argument with one of the bone-people. Before she could throw a punch, I lifted my fingers to my lips and whistled.

When she turned toward me, all my recent miseries evaporated.

"Bodhi?" she said quietly, stepping—then running—closer. "Bodhi!"

We crashed together in a hug-kiss combo that would make even the most passionate of romance-vid purveyors blush.

"You idiot," she breathed between smooches. "You stupid, headstrong idiot."

Pressing my forehead to hers, I let out something between a sob and a laugh. "I came back for you. Well, you came back for me. Whatever."

"Maybe I'm not old enough to be seeing this," Chitta Mini said.

Chaska brushed him off. "What happened to Tusky, Bodhi? I mean, what happened overall? How did you—"

"I'll tell you later," I said, already sensing the knot in my chest. "Much later."

Her eyes darkened. "Sure."

"Can we, uh, get out of here?" I turned back to Chitta Mini. "No offense, pal, but I think I need some R-and-R away from this place. Hospitality was top notch, though."

Chitta Mini lifted the priestess' hands in supplication. "Enjoy the honeymoon, lovebirds. I've got some serious redecorating to do here."

Chaska offered the chitta a limp smile, then began guiding me toward a docking strut.

Before we'd made it too far, however, I glanced back at Chitta Mini. "One suggestion, if I may."

Chitta Mini waved for me to continue.

"If you do want to stay here," I said, "I'd recommend patching things up with somebody who might need you."

"And whomst would that be?"

"Amodari Halnok."

"Good joke, Bodhi."

"I mean it," I said, gently shrugging off Chaska's arm. "You're both exiles. Both part of genetically similar civilizations that will need an alliance to make any headway in this world. See if you can find common ground… have an inustrazan family reunion."

"You just don't want her to hunt you down, right?"

"Part of it, yes. But… just do it for me. She needs you."

Perhaps sensing the gravity in my tone, Chitta Mini nodded. "I'll do what I can. Safe flying, you two. Stay out of trouble."

"With him?" Chaska asked, huffing. "Not a chance."

We shared a cramped, bucket-of-bolts shuttle on the way to our destination. If you guessed that this trip was full of carnal acts, you're correct. But before you get too hot and bothered, I am a man of class. I won't be going into detail, pervert.

The latter half of the journey was spent in relative silence, just lying on the shuttle's lone cot and occasionally thinking aloud, wondering, planning.

According to Chaska, we were headed to a refugee planet. At least, that was its current designation. They planned to make it a full colony soon, one that could permanently resettle those who'd fled from Kruthara's tide.

Here and there, we talked about the state of the 'verse. Apparently things were just as bad as I'd half-predicted they would be. Kruthara's collapse was good, but not universally so. The sudden power vacuum was birthing untold territorial wars, and the Hegemony-Gnosis split would soon spark another conflict. Over half the financial nets, media grids, and information relays were permanently offline. In short, we were sliding back into anarchy. But from a broad perspective, which was the most bearable evil? To live under the tyranny of a mega-power, to be absorbed into a superorganism, or to exist in a broken world in need of rebuilding?

Only time would tell.

Several hours into our pinch, Chaska slid on a black pullover and headed to the pilot's chair. She nursed her coffee as she exchanged cryptic comments via neural transmitter studs. We'd arrived, it seemed. This conclusion was cemented when the viewpane's shutters receded and unveiled a massive red-and-blue planet dead ahead.

Its orbital zone was choked with strings of supply barges, defense platforms, and makeshift comms boosters. A textbook example of a refugee world.

"Well, I'll be damned," I whispered, slinking into the copilot's seat. "What do you call it?"

She smiled. "Home. Just Home."

I leaned back in the chair, simultaneously awestruck and

exhausted, as we cut down through the atmosphere. Considering everything that had just happened, I ought to have felt relieved at that point. Downright elated. But I couldn't be. Perhaps this was how all wars ended—wreaths and bouquets and garlands in the streets, but sorrow lurking in the hearts of those who'd seen and done things that would forever plague their dreams. Nobody in the entire cosmos knew what one kind soul had done for them. And even now, decades and decades past, I doubt anybody ever learned of it.

But I was alive, and that was one gift I couldn't toss away. Tusky had made sure of that. So I sat there in silence, smiling outwardly and aching inwardly, trying my best to appreciate the fact that any of this still existed.

This arduous task grew easier as we banked through the clouds and approached a deep concrete landing bowl just outside the crimson marshlands. Nestled among the reeds, lifted high on aluminum stilts, were hundreds of prefab buildings and freighters. People were going about their business and playing in the ad-hoc roads. It was nearing sunset, but the camp's lights shone bright enough to project the illusion of midday.

"A home on Home," I remarked as Chaska passed me my only possession—a canvas bag she'd stuffed with new clothes. "Quaint, isn't it?"

She smirked and began fiddling with the rear ramp controls. "Five-star accommodations, just for you."

It was a joke, obviously, but when the ramp descended and ushered in a wave of sweet, humid air, her statement seemed accurate enough. This was all I needed. Well, that and the two ladies standing at the foot of the ramp.

"Welcome back," Ruena said, her tone as dry as ever. "What took you so long?"

Gadra, meanwhile, eschewed words. She launched herself up

the ramp and collided with my waist, hugging me so tight I was reminded of Kruthara's fatal grip.

"Bodhi!" she shouted into my shirt. "We thought you were dead. Well, they did. I knew you were alive. Kind of."

Too weary to do anything else, I hugged Gadra in return. "I just couldn't live without your art, ma'am."

"Aw, shucks. I know you're lyin', but it's still nice."

Chaska clapped me on the shoulder and headed down the ramp. "Come on, folks. Gonna be a long night."

Full disclosure: I don't remember most of that evening. I blame it on an unholy medley of sleep deprivation, post-coma grogginess, and the copious amounts of spirits I drank throughout the festivities.

It was a celebration that would've made moon-worshipping pagans jealous. We howled at the stars, we laughed, we cried, we danced, we sang... but we also said farewell to the kindest, most selfless being I'd ever known. I'd be lying if I said that moment wasn't seared into my brain, I admit, but I'm hesitant to retell it. Emotions would get in the way. Therefore, I'll offer something of a corporate-style description of what went on.

There was no body to bury or cremate or launch into a sun, naturally, so we settled on the next best thing: Tusky's canister. In a way, it was his womb. How fitting (and poetic), then, to have it serve as his coffin.

There had to be a thousand refugees gathered at that altar in the swamps—many human, many not. A few individuals stepped up to speak about his life. Others offered some boilerplate well wishes, clearly due to a lack of direct knowledge about the brilliant sloth.

Not that I could blame them, of course. I myself barely knew him, and I'd been there at his moment of death. Still, the whole thing felt a bit obscene, if not sacrilegious. Nobody knew how or why he'd died. The details of that sacrifice had been buried with him—or, rather, scattered into the infinite void. As I sat there on the red grass, listening, judging, I wished that I'd gone into death with him. That I'd been there as he drew his last breath, finding out whether he'd felt pain, and whether he'd been afraid, and if somehow, some way, he hadn't *truly* died in a flash.

Then, as the final speakers offered their condolences and generic goodbyes, the Maker's words occurred to me like a nostalgic song: *You will not be anything, merely an action. A force.* Perhaps that was the best way to consider it. The only way that would bring me comfort. A bypassing of the grief process? Maybe. But it was also true. We had no body to mourn, only an ideal to cherish. Sappy as this is, he hadn't died—he'd lived on within us, through us.

And maybe, if the universe is as zany as I believe it is, he's still out there somewhere. Not as a sloth or a mind or anything else, but merely as the simple kindness that formed his being.

"Here's to you," I whispered as I drained my cup, drowned out by the drums and flutes around me. "To meeting again in the void."

Several hours later, sobering up under the hazy blue nebulae, I sat with Chaska on a nearby hilltop. A gentle wind stirred the reeds around us, and starlight bathed everything in silky silver tones. It was a beautiful night. A miraculous one, in hindsight.

"You ready to talk about it?" Chaska asked me, resting her head on my shoulder.

I stared down at the ongoing festivities. "No. I don't know if I ever will be."

"I get it."

"How?"

"You're not the only one who's lived through war."

"This was different."

"I don't think so." She let out a long breath. "I've held people as they begged for their mothers, Bodhi. I've seen the life go out of soldiers' eyes. There are some things you never forget... things you'll never talk about."

I shrugged, tacitly admitting she was more "on my level" than I'd predicted. "It's just... I don't know why it had to be him. He was good, Chaska. Maybe the best we had. Why'd he have to be the first to depart this world?"

"I could tell you anything," she whispered. "I could say he was too good for this place... or that it was his time on Death's clock... but nobody knows. And maybe we don't need to."

"Maybe." I leaned over and kissed her head. "I'm just... glad to be here."

"I'm glad we're here, too."

"I'm glad you're glad."

"Alright, enough of that," she said, groaning. "What are you gonna do now? Strike some new deals? You've got about a thousand small-scale civil wars to choose from."

I shook my head. "I'm retiring."

"You're *what*?"

"Yep."

"Bodhi Drezek, arms dealer extraordinaire... retiring in the most turbulent time in recent history?"

"A smart gambler knows when to fold," I said, smiling faintly at her. "I've got what I need right here."

"What? A refugee encampment to sell weapons to?"

"You know what I mean."

"I seldom do." She laughed. "So tell me in clear words... what've you got 'right here'?"

I pulled her closer and listened to the music, the wind, the insects chirping. "The whole universe."

EPILOGUE

If you've made it this far, congratulations. You've officially heard the A-to-Z tale of how I, Bodhi Drezek, caused the end and beginning of this very universe. Okay, in truth, it was more like several galaxies than the universe... but you have to give me some creative slack. People love high stakes, and "universe" sounds better than "galaxies."

Anyway. Now that I've left you on a cliffhanger note about this fractured region of space and the fates of all my crew members (and long-sworn enemies), you might be wondering how things ended up. Did we all fly into the sunset? Did the wars get resolved overnight by a benevolent interdimensional god?

Depends on how you look at it.

See, my own ending hasn't come just yet. In case you've yet to figure it out or read my name in a gossip holo-net thread, I'll be around for the foreseeable future. This entire memoir has been written within the confines of a simulation.

But before you get bent out of shape and scream, "It was all a dream!?" allow me to clarify. Everything I've written here happened in the "real world." But as you know, many hundreds of years have passed since this tale ended. I could (and may) write a thousand more tales of the exploits that occurred between then and now. Point is, I'm an old man now. And old men love nothing more than telling stories about their glory days and living a rich, occasionally boring retirement life.

So how did I end up in a simulation? Being a businessman, of course. After many years of seeking, I eventually stumbled across one of my old comrade Center's physical manifestations. By this point, Center was being worshipped as some sort of god of time. Predictable, I know. Anyhow, I managed to strike a deal with Center:

Offer the terminally ill and decrepit a place to reside in virtual space, and in return, receive a constant flow of new and strange experiences via the inhabitants.

As it turns out, omnipotent AI constructs love nothing more than novel twists and turns in their reality. And wily sentient beings provide more surprises than you can shake a stick at.

So there you have it—the million-bux answer to the question of "Where is Bodhi writing this from?"

It's a good life here. A virtual cabin by the virtual lake… virtual philosophy reading… virtual meditation on the Maker's teachings… virtual cooking classes (I am classified as a rank-four chef by the Institute of Flavonoid Research). It's not a lonely one, either. Spoiler alert: I live here with Chaska. That's right—even foxy young insurgents grow old and settle down someday.

Our children, grandchildren, and great-grandchildren visit from time to time. They tell us the universe is doing alright, probably not to worry us. They also assure me there's no need to sell weapons despite a growing demand for that profession. For what it's worth, I haven't sold an offensive combat system in well over two hundred and twelve years. Now, defensive grids for colonies and merchants… no comment.

But enough about me. What about the others?

Well, here's what I know.

Ruena, my faithful mercenary, is still living with her people out in the far reaches of the Nogo. She sleeps longer and longer these days—think three years for a nap—but she *did* stop by for virtual tea last month. Her last stint of true action in the "real world" involved using her twosight to operate nanowire fighters and stave off sudrona poaching. (Ironic, I know.)

Gadra (now known as Le Artiste G) is one you've probably heard of. She's gotten enough life-extension implants and gene treatments to live until the universe is swallowed by entropy. If you're rich enough to get into her galleries, you're living a good life. If not, watch out for her hypnotic marks. Very highly valued in the world of personal defense.

Umzuma... I have no idea. Came and went like the wind. Hell of a pilot, though.

Amodari and Chitta Mini, rather predictably, ended up settling their interspecies differences and reuniting to lead the Hegemony (also known in history books as the Reformed Hegemony). Unfortunately, this also meant they decided to team up in seeking my head on a silver platter. They obviously never got it, but that doesn't mean they've stopped looking. And considering the lifespan of inustrazans and chittas... I've got my head on a swivel. That being said, Amodari *did* send my former acquaintances several cryptic love letters addressed to me. What can I say? Crazy is as crazy does.

Momura and Cahari are, as I alluded to previously, still living it up as manufacturers. Last I heard, they were preparing to get into subatomic teleportation tech. Rest assured I won't be the first one to test that out. In any event, they still keep in touch. Somewhat. Usually by sending me virtual pets. (If you two read this, please slow down—I already have twelve hamsters.)

As for *Stream Dancer*, my baby was sadly lost in the Shell Wars of 1056. Its final mission was delivering a nuclear payload to the emperor of the crustaceans, who was just about to fire a solar railgun into Halcium Alpha. Ridiculous, yes, but such is life in space.

And Chaska, who I quite obviously know most about, stood by my side until the day we checked into our virtual abode. She ran the most humanitarian rescue and resupply missions of anybody in the former "liberation" movement (which later became known as the Fair Trade and Settlement Organization). She is my bright star, my grounding force. Oh, and the mother of my children. She'd kill me if I forgot to acknowledge those labor pains. We still live together, and she only tries to kill me once a week or so.

There are probably many, many names I'm forgetting, but what can I say? I've experienced a long and colorful life, and faces don't always linger long—either in the world or in your memories. A hard lesson to learn, but part of "the way of things," I suppose.

Now, if you've followed this memoir from the start, you'll recall my opening words about the art of the sale. The crucial ingredient was demand. A demand for power, for security, for fulfillment. Anything that the client believed they lacked. Thousands upon thousands of deals were forged by means of leveraging this weakness in the human psyche. But now, looking back, I believe that my finest deal was a negation of demand.

You see, the deal in question didn't involve anybody else—only me. And in this deal, I surrendered demand entirely. I hopped off the endless carousel of fame and wealth and aspirations. Lurking beneath that squirmy, sordid mass was the one thing I'd never been able to buy. The thing I had craved so dearly, scouring the grimiest corners of the 'verse to find. My dangling carrot, my missing piece.

And what was it?

To be at peace.

Cliché, perhaps, but this is *my* story. *My* life. Although I suspect that, in the grand scheme of things, what you really want is no different from what I wanted. You didn't really want to read this book or to bask in an uplifting ending. You wanted an experience that you can't put your finger on. A feeling that you haven't had since you were a child. Even when you set this book down for the last time and go about your day, you will continue seeking this state of mind, likely without even knowing it. But the truth is, you will not find it in anything.

Music may stir you for a brief time. Drinks and drugs may sedate you. A good romp in the bed may settle you. Yet when these experiences end, much like this book, you will be left wanting more. Wanting that *one* thing you cannot describe. The end of the rainbow.

What if—just, what if?—the thing you truly want is to make the same deal I did? Perhaps this marvelous opportunity has been under your nose since your birth, and you have lost your way on the long road back to it. On the off chance this is the case, allow me to offer one old man's pithiest instruction.

Demand nothing of the world, and in return, receive everything.

THANK YOU FOR READING COSMIC SAVIOR

We hope you enjoyed it as much as we enjoyed bringing it to you. We just wanted to take a moment to encourage you to review the book. Follow this link: Cosmic Savior to be directed to the book's Amazon product page to leave your review.

Every review helps further the author's reach and, ultimately, helps them continue writing fantastic books for us all to enjoy.

You can also join our non-spam mailing list by visiting www.subscribepage.com/AethonReadersGroup and never miss out on future releases. You'll also receive three full books completely Free as our thanks to you.

Facebook

Instagram

Twitter

Website

Want to discuss our books with other readers and even the authors? Join our Discord server today and be a part of the Aethon community.

ALSO IN SERIES:

INTERSTELLAR GUNRUNNER

TIME BREAKER

COSMIC SAVIOR

Looking for more great Science Fiction?

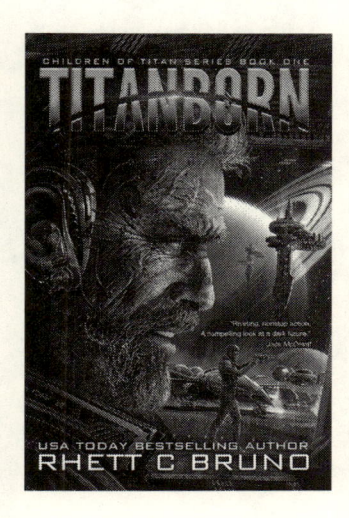

Titan's rebellion is coming. Only one man can stop it.

GET BOOK ONE OF THE CHILDREN OF TITAN NOW!

Nolan Garrett is Cerberus. A government assassin, tasked with fixing the galaxy's darkest, ugliest problems.

GET CERBERUS BOOKS 1 - 3 TODAY!

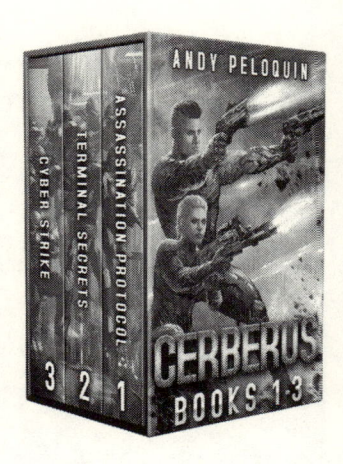

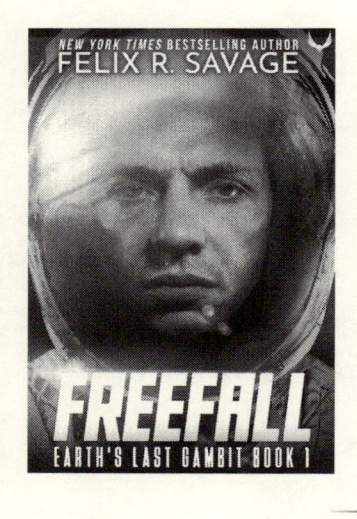

A mysterious alien ship is orbiting Europa.

A handful of astronauts must voyage to Jupiter to face the threat, alone.

GET FREEFALL NOW!

"Aliens, agents, and espionage abound in this Cold War-era alternate history adventure... A wild ride!"—Dennis E. Taylor, bestselling author of We Are Legion (We Are Bob)

GET THE LUNA MISSILE CRISIS NOW!

Someone betrayed him. He'll probably die finding out who.

GET SUPREMACY'S SHADOW NOW!

For all our Sci-Fi books, visit our website.

ABOUT JAMES WOLANYK

James Wolanyk is a writer and editor from the Boston area. He holds a B.A. in Creative Writing from the University of Massachusetts, and has authored the Scribe Cycle and Interstellar Gunrunner series, as well as Grid and several pieces of short fiction.

After university, he pursued educational work in the Czech Republic, Taiwan, and Latvia. Outside of writing, he is an avid meditator, film enthusiast, and nootropics nerd. He currently resides in New England with his wonderful wife.